THE
Royal
HOUSE OF NIROLI

**SEMPRE APPASSIONATO,
SEMPRE FIERO**

Always passionate, always proud

**The richest royal family in the world—
united by blood and passion,
torn apart by deceit and desire**

Complete your collection with all four books!

**The Royal House of Niroli:
Scandalous Seductions**

**The Royal House of Niroli:
Billion Dollar Bargains**

**The Royal House of Niroli:
Innocent Mistresses**

**The Royal House of Niroli:
Secret Heirs**

WELCOME TO NIROLI!

Nestled in the azure blue of the Mediterranean, the majestic island of Niroli has prospered for centuries. The Fierezza men have worn the crown with passion and pride since the Middle Ages. But now, as the King's health declines, and his two sons have been tragically killed, the crown is in jeopardy.

The clock is ticking—a new heir must be found before the King is forced to abdicate. By royal decree the internationally scattered members of the Fierezza family are summoned to claim their destiny. But any person who takes the throne must do so according to 'The Rules of the Royal House of Niroli'. Soon secrets and rivalries emerge as the descendants of this ancient royal line vie for position and power. Only a true Fierezza can become ruler—a person dedicated to their country, their people...and their eternal love!

THE

Royal

HOUSE OF NIROLI

Scandalous Seductions

PENNY JORDAN
MELANIE MILBURNE

MILLS &
BOON

All the characters in this book have no existence outside the imagination
of the author, and have no relation whatsoever to anyone bearing the
same name or names. They are not even distantly inspired by any
individual known or unknown to the author, and all the incidents are
pure invention.

Harlequin Mills & Boon Limited, Eton House,
18-24 Paradise Road, Richmond, Surrey TW9 1SR

THE ROYAL HOUSE OF NIROLI: SCANDALOUS SEDUCTIONS
© by Harlequin Books SA 2011

The Future King's Pregnant Mistress © Harlequin Books S.A. 2007
Surgeon Prince, Ordinary Wife © Harlequin Books S.A. 2007

Special thanks and acknowledgement are given to Penny Jordan and
Melanie Milburne for their contribution to The Royal House of
Niroli series.

ISBN: 978 0 263 88945 1

011-0111

Harlequin Mills & Boon policy is to use papers that are
natural, renewable and recyclable products and made from
wood grown in sustainable forests. The logging and
manufacturing processes conform to the legal environmental
regulations of the country of origin.

Printed and bound in Spain
by Litografia Rosés S.A., Barcelona

The Future King's Pregnant Mistress

PENNY JORDAN

CHAPTER ONE

MARCO opened his eyes, and looked at the bedside clock: three o'clock in the morning. He'd been dreaming about Niroli—and his grandfather, the king. His heart was still drumming insistently inside his chest, its beat driven by the adrenalin surges of challenge and excitement that reliving one of his past youthful arguments with his grandfather had brought him.

It had been in the aftermath of one of those arguments that Marco had made his decision to prove to himself, and to his grandfather, that he was capable of achieving success somewhere other than Niroli and without his grandfather's influence and patronage. He had been twenty-two then. Now he was thirty-six, and he and his grandfather had long since made a peace—of a sort—even if the older man had never really understood his grandson's refusal to change his mind about his vow to make his own way in the world. Marco had been determined that his success would come *not* as the grandson of the King of Niroli but via his own hard work. As simple Marco Fierezza, a young European entrepreneur, he had used his shrewd grasp of finance to become one of the City of London's most lauded financiers and a billionaire.

In the last few years it had caused Marco a certain amount

of wry amusement to note how his grandfather had turned to him for financial advice with regard to his own private wealth, whilst claiming that their blood tie absolved him of paying for Marco's services! The truth was, his grandfather was a wily old fox who wasn't above using whatever means he could to coerce others into doing what he wanted, often claiming that what he did was done for the good of Niroli, rather than himself.

Niroli!

Outside, the icy cold rain of London rattled against the windows of his Eaton Square apartment, and Marco felt a sudden sharp pang of longing for the beautiful Mediterranean island his family had ruled for so many generations: a sun-drenched jewel of green and gold in an aquamarine sea, from where dark volcanic mountains rose up wreathed in silvery clouds.

The same sea that had claimed the lives of his parents, he reminded himself sombrely, and which had not just robbed him of them, but also made him heir to the throne.

He had always known that ultimately he would become Niroli's king, but he had also believed that this event lay many years away in the future, something he could safely ignore in favour of enjoying his self-created, self-ruled present. However, the reality was that what he had thought of as his distant duty was now about to become his life.

Was that knowledge the reason for the dream he'd had? After all, when it came to the relationship he would have with his grandfather if he agreed to do as King Giorgio had requested and return to Niroli to become its ruler, wasn't there going to be an element of the prodigal male lion at the height of his powers returning to spar with the ageing pack leader? Marco knew and understood the older man very well. His grandfather might claim that he was ready to hand over the royal reins, but Marco suspected that Giorgio would still want to control whoever was holding them as much as he could. And yet, despite his awareness of this, Marco knew that the challenge of ruling Niroli and making it the country he wanted to see it become—by sweeping away the outdated and over-authoritarian structures his grandfather had put in place during his long reign—was one that excited him.

There had never been any doubt in Marco's mind that when ultimately he came to the throne he would make changes to the government of the island that would bring it into the twenty-first century. But then he had also envisaged succeeding his gentle, mild-mannered father, rather than having his tyrannical grandfather standing at his shoulder.

Marco gave a small dismissive shrug. Unlike his late father, a scholarly, quiet man who, Marco had recognised early in his life, had been bullied unmercifully and held in contempt by the King, Marco had never allowed himself to be over-whelmed by his grandfather, even as a child. They shared a common streak of almost brutally arrogant self-belief, and it had been this that had led to the conflict between them. Now, as a mature and powerful man, there was no way Marco intended to allow *anyone* to question his right to do things his own way. That said, he knew that taking the throne would ne-cessitate certain changes in his own lifestyle; there were certain royal rules he would have to obey, if only to pay lip-service to them.

One of those rules forbade the King of Niroli to marry a divorcée. Marco was in no hurry to wed, but when he did he knew he would be expected to make a suitable dynastic union with some pre-approved royal princess of unimpeachable virtue. Somehow he didn't think that it would go down well with his subjects, or the paparazzi, if he were to be seen openly enjoying the company of a mistress, instead of duti-fully finding himself a suitable consort.

He looked towards the bed where Emily lay sleeping, oblivious to what lay ahead and the fast-approaching end of their relationship. Her long blonde hair—naturally blonde, as he had good reason to know—was spread against the pillow. To Marco's surprise, he was suddenly tempted to reach out and twine his fingers through its silken strands, knowing that his touch would wake her, and knowing too that his body was hardening with his immediate need for the intimacy of her body. That he should still desire her so fiercely and so constantly after the length of time they had been together—so very much longer than he'd spent with any woman before—astonished him. But the needs and sexual desires of Marco Fierezza could not be compared with the challenge of becoming the King of Niroli, he acknowledged with his customary arrogance.

King of Niroli.

Emily knew nothing about his connection with Niroli, or his past, and consequently she knew nothing either about his future. Why should she? What reason would there have been for him to tell her, when he had deliberately chosen to live anonymously? He had left Niroli swearing to prove to his grandfather that he could stand on his own feet and make a success of his life without using his royal position, and had quickly discovered that his new anonymity had certain personal advantages; as second in line to Niroli's throne he had grown used to a certain type of predatory woman trying to lure him. His grandfather had warned him when he had been a teenager that he would have to be on his guard, and that he must accept he would never know whether the women who strived to share his bed wanted him for himself, or for who he was. Living in London as Marco Fierezza, rather than Prince Marco of Niroli though he was cynically aware that his combination of wealth and good looks drew the opposite sex to him, he did not attract the kind of feeding frenzy he would have done if he'd been using his royal title. Marco had no objection to rewarding his chosen lovers generously with expensive gifts and a luxurious lifestyle whilst he and they were together. He started to frown. It still irked him that Emily had always so steadfastly—and in his opinion foolishly—refused to accept the presents of jewellery he'd regularly tried to give her.

He'd told her dismissively to think of it as a bonus when she had demanded blankly, 'What's this for?' after he had given her a diamond bracelet to celebrate their first month together.

Her face had gone pale and she'd looked down at the leather box containing the bracelet—a unique piece he'd bought from one of the royal jewellers—her voice as stiff as her body. 'You don't need to bribe me, Marco. I'm with you because I want you, not because I want what you can buy me.'

Now Marco's frown deepened, his reaction to the memory of those words exactly as it had been when Emily had first uttered them. He could feel the same fierce, angry clenching of his muscles and surge of astounded disbelief that the woman who was enjoying the pleasure of his lovemaking and his wealth could dare to suggest that he might need to bribe her to share his bed!

He had soon put Emily in her place though, he reminded himself; his response to her had been a men-acingly silky soft, 'No, you've misunderstood. After all, I already know exactly why you are in my bed and just how much you want me. The bribe, if you wish to think of it as that, is not to keep you there, but to ensure that you leave my bed speedily and silently when I've had enough of having you there.'

She hadn't said anything in reply, but he had seen in her expression what she was feeling. Although he'd never been able to get her to admit to it, he was reasonably sure that her subsequent very convenient business trip, which had taken her away from him for the best part of a week, had been something she had conjured up in an attempt to get back at him. And to make him hungry for her? No woman had the power to make herself so important to him that being with her mattered more than his own iron-clad determination never to allow his emotions to control him and so weaken him. He had grown up seeing how easily his strong-willed grandfather had used his own son's deep love for all those who were close to him to coerce, manipulate and, more often than not in Marco's eyes, humiliate him into doing what King Giorgio wanted. Marco had seen too much to have any illusions about the value of male pride, or the strength of will over gentleness and a desire to please others. Not that Marco hadn't loved his father; he had, so much so that as a young boy he had often furiously resented and verbally attacked his grandfather for the way the older man had treated his immediate heir.

That would never happen to him, Marco had decided then. He would allow no one, not even Niroli's king, to dictate to him.

Marco was well aware that, despite the fact that he had often angered his grandfather with his rebellious ways, the older man held a grudging respect for him. Their pride and their tenacity were attributes they had in common, and in many ways they were alike, although Marco knew that once *he* was Niroli's king there were many changes he would make in order to modernise the kingdom. Marco considered that the way his grandfather ruled Niroli was almost feudal; he'd shared his father's belief that it was essential to give people the opportunity to run their own lives, instead of treating them as his grandfather did, like very young, unschooled children who couldn't be trusted to make their own decisions. He had so many plans for Niroli: it was no wonder he was eager to step out of the role he had created for himself here in London to take on the mantle his birth had fated him to wear! The potential sexual frustration of being without a mistress bothered him a little but, after all, he was a mature man whose ambitions went a lot further than having a willing bed-mate with whom he would never risk making an emotional or legal commitment.

No, he wouldn't let himself miss Emily, he assured himself. The only reason he was giving valuable mental time to thinking about the issue was his concern that she might not accept his announcement that their affair was over as calmly as he wished. He had no desire to hurt her—far from it.

He still hadn't decided just how much he needed to tell her. He would be leaving London, of course, but he suspected that the paparazzi were bound to get wind of what was happening on Niroli, since it was ruled by the wealthiest royal family in the world.

For her own sake, Emily needed to have it made clear to her that nothing they had shared could impinge on his future as Niroli's king. He had never really understood her steadfast refusal to accept his expensive gifts, or to allow him to help her either financially or in any other way with her small interior design business. Because he couldn't understand it, despite the fact that they had been lovers for almost three years, Marco, being the man he was, had inwardly wondered what she might be hoping to gain from him that was worth more to her than his money. It was second nature to him not to trust anyone. Plus, he had learned from observing his grandfather and members of his court what happened to those whose natures allowed others to take advantage of them, as his own father had done.

Marco tensed, automatically shying away from the unwanted pain that thinking about his parents and their deaths could still cause him. He didn't want to acknowledge that pain, and he certainly didn't want to acknowledge the confused feelings he had buried so deeply: pain on his father's behalf, guilt because he could see what his grandfather had been doing to his father and yet he hadn't been able to prevent it, anger with his father for having been so weak, anger with his grandfather for having taken advantage of that weakness, and himself for having seen what he hadn't wanted to see.

He and his grandfather had made their peace, his father was gone, he himself was a man and not a boy any more. It was only in his dreams now that he sometimes revisited the pain of his past. When he did, that pain could be quickly extinguished in the raw passion of satisfying his physical desire for Emily.

But what about the time when Emily would no longer be there? Why was he wasting his time asking himself such foolish questions? Ultimately he would find himself another mistress, no doubt via a discreet liaison with the right kind of woman, perhaps a young wife married to an older husband, though not so young that she didn't understand the rules, of course. He might even, if Emily had been sensible enough, have thought about providing her with the respectability of marriage to some willing courtier in order that they carry on their affair, once he became King of Niroli. But, Marco acknowledged, the very passion that made her such a responsive lover also meant she was not the type who would adapt to the traditional role of royal mistress.

Emily would love Niroli, an island so beautiful and fruitful that ancient lore had said Prometheus himself caused it to rise up from the sea bed so that he could bestow it on mankind.

When Marco thought of the place of his birth, his mental image was one of an island bathed in sunlight, an island so richly gifted by the gods that it was little wonder some legends had referred to it as an earthly paradise.

But where there was great beauty there was also terrible cruelty, as was true of so many legends. The gods had often exacted a terrible price from Niroli for their gifts.

He pushed back the duvet, knowing that he wouldn't be able to sleep now. His body was lean and powerful, magnificently drawn, as though etched by one of the great masters, in the charcoal shadows of the moonlight as he left the bed and padded silently toward the window.

The wind had picked up and was lashing rain against the windows, bending the bare branches of the trees on the street outside. Marco was again transported back to Niroli, where violent storms often swept over the island, whipping up its surrounding seas. The people of Niroli knew not to venture out during the high tides that battered the volcanic rock cliffs of a mountain range so high and so inaccessible in parts that even today it still protected and concealed the bandit descendants of Barbary pirates who long ago had invaded the island. In fact, the fierce seas sucking deep beneath the cliffs had honeycombed them into underwater caves and weakened the rock so that whole sections of it had fallen away. The gales that stirred the seas also tore and ripped at the ancient olive trees and the grapevines on the island, as though to punish them because their harvest had already been plucked to safety.

As a boy Marco had loved to watch the wind savage the land far below the high turrets of the royal castle. He would kneel on the soft padded seating beneath an ancient stone window embrasure, excited by the danger of the storm, wanting to go out and accept the challenge it threw at him. But he had never been allowed to go outside and play as other children did. Instead, at his grandfather's insistence, he'd had to remain within the castle walls, learning about his family's past and his own future role as the island's ultimate ruler.

Inside Marco's head, images he couldn't control were starting to form, curling wraithlike from his childhood memories. It had always been his grandfather and not his parents who had dictated the rules of his childhood, and who'd seen that they were imposed on him...

'Marco, come back to bed. It's cold without you.' Emily's voice was soft and slow, warm, full and sweet with promise, like the fruit of Niroli's vines at the time of harvest, when the grapes lay heavily beneath the sun swollen with ripe readiness and with implicit invitation.

He turned round. He had woken her after all. Emily ran her small interior design business from a small shop-cum-office just off London's Sloane Street. Marco had known from the moment he first saw her at a PR cocktail party that he'd wanted her, and that he'd intended to have her. And he'd made sure that she'd known it too. Marco was used to getting his own way, to claiming his right to direct the course of his own life, even if that meant imposing his will on those who would oppose him. This was an imperative for him, one he refused to be swayed from. He had quickly elucidated that Emily was a divorced woman with no children, and that had made her pattern-card perfect for the role of his mistress. If he had known then her real emotional and sexual history, he knew that he would not have pursued her. But, by the time he had discovered the truth, his physical desire for her had been such that it had been impossible for him to reject her.

He looked towards her now, feeling that desire gripping him again and fighting against it as he had fought all his life against anything or anyone who threatened to control him.

'Marco, something's wrong. What is it?'

Where had it come from, this unwanted ability she seemed to possess of sensing what she could not possibly be able to know? The year his parents died, the storms had come early to Niroli. Marco could remember how when he had first received the news, even before he had said anything, she had somehow guessed that something was wrong. However, whilst she might be intuitive where his feelings were concerned, Emily hadn't yet been shrewd or suspicious enough to make the connection between the announcement of his parents' deaths and the news in the media about the demise of the next in line to the Niroli throne. He remembered how hurt she had looked when he'd informed her that he would be attending his mother and father's funeral without her, but she hadn't said a word. Maybe because she hadn't wanted to provoke a row that might have led to him ending their affair, the reason she didn't want it to end being that, for all her apparent lack of interest in his money, she had to be well aware of what she would lose financially if their relationship came to a close. It was, in Marco's opinion, impossible for any woman to be as unconcerned about the financial benefits of being his mistress as Emily affected to be. It was as his grandfather had warned him: the women who thronged around him expected to be lavishly rewarded with expensive gifts and had no compunction about making that plain.

Under cover of the room's darkness, Emily grimaced to hear the note of pleading in her own voice. Why, when she despised herself so much for what she was becoming, couldn't she stop herself? Was she destined always to have relationships that resulted in her feeling insecure?

'Nothing's wrong,' Marco told her. There was a note in his voice that made her body tense and her emotions flinch despite everything she was trying to do not to let that happen. The trouble was that once you started lying to yourself on an almost hourly, never mind daily, basis about the reality of your relationship, once you started pretending not to notice or care about being the 'lesser' partner, about not being valued or respected enough, you entered a place where the strongest incentive was not to seek out the truth but rather to hide from it. But she had no one but herself to blame for her current situation, she reminded herself.

She had known right from the start what kind of man Marco was, and the type of relationship he wanted with her. The problem was that she had obviously known Marco's agenda rather better than she had understood her own. Although she tried not to do so, sometimes when she was feeling at her lowest—times like now—she couldn't stop herself from giving in to the temptation of fantasising about how Marco could be different: he would not be so fabulously wealthy or arrogantly sexy that he could have any woman he wanted, but instead he'd be just an ordinary man with ordinary goals—a happy marriage, a wife… Her heart kicked heavily, turning over in a slow grind of pain. She thought of children—theirs—and it turned over again, the pain growing more intense.

Why, why, *why* had she been such a fool and fallen in love with Marco? He had made it plain from the start what he wanted from her and what he would give her back in return, and love had never been part of the deal. But then, way back when, she had never imagined that she would fall for him. At the beginning, she had wanted Marco so much, she had been happy to go along with a purely sexual relationship, for as long as he wanted her.

No, she had no one but herself to blame for the constant pain she was now having to endure, the deceit she was having to practise and the fear that haunted her: one day soon Marco would sense that deceit and leave her. She loathed herself so much for her own weakness and for not having the guts to acknowledge her love or take the consequences of walking away from him, through the inevitable fiery consuming pain. But, who knew? Maybe walking away from Marco would have a phoenix-like effect on her and allow her to find freedom as a new person. She was such a coward, though, that she couldn't take that step. Hadn't someone once said that a brave man died only once but a coward died a thousand times? So it was for her. She knew that she ought to leave and deal with her feelings, but instead she stayed and suffered a thousand hurtful recognitions every day of Marco's lack of love for her.

But he desired her, and she couldn't bring herself to give up the fragile hope that maybe, just maybe, things would change, and one day he would look at her and know that he loved her, that one day he would allow her to access that part of himself he guarded with such ferocity and tell her that he wanted them to be together for ever…

CHAPTER TWO

THAT was Emily's dream. But the reality was, recently, she'd felt as if they were growing further apart rather than closer. She'd told herself yesterday morning she would face her fear. She took a deep breath.

'Marco, I've always been open and…and honest with you…' It was no good, she couldn't do it. She couldn't make herself ask him that all-important question: 'Do you want to end our relationship?' And, besides, she hadn't always been honest with him, had she? She hadn't told him, for instance, that she had fallen in love with him. Her heart gave another painful lurch.

Marco was watching her, his head inclined towards her. He wore his thick dark hair cut short, but not so short that she couldn't run her fingers through it, shaping the hard bone beneath it as she held him to her when they made love. There was just enough light for her to see the gleam in his eyes, as though he'd guessed the direction her thoughts had taken and knew how much she wanted him. Marco had the most piercingly direct look she'd ever known. He'd focused it on her the night they'd met, when she had tried to cling to reason and rationality, instead of letting herself be blatantly seduced by a pair of tawny-brown predator's eyes…

Emily knew she should make her stand now and demand
an explanation for the change she could sense in Marco, but
her childhood made it difficult for her to talk openly about her
emotions. Instead she hid them away behind locked doors of
calm control and self-possession. Was it because she was
afraid of what might happen if she allowed her real feelings
to get out of control? Because she was afraid of bringing the
truth out into the open? Something *was* wrong. Marco *had*
changed: he had become withdrawn and preoccupied. There
was no way she could pretend otherwise. Had he grown tired
of her? Did he want to end their relationship? Wouldn't it be
better, wiser, more self-respecting, if she challenged him to
tell her the truth? Did she really think that if she ignored her
fears they would simply disappear?

'You say that you've always been open and honest with me,
Emily, but that isn't the truth, is it?'

Emily's heart somersaulted with slow, sickening despair. He
knew? Somehow he had guessed what she was thinking and—
almost as bad—she could see he was spoiling for an argument…
because that would give him an excuse to end things.

'Remember the night I took you to dinner and you told
me about your marriage? Remember how "open" you were
with me then—and what you didn't tell me?' Marco recalled
sarcastically.

Emily couldn't speak. A mixture of relief and anguish
filled her. Her marriage! All this time she had thought—
believed—that Marco had understood the scars her past had
inflicted on her, but now she realised that she had been wrong.
'It wasn't deliberate, you know that,' she told him, fighting
not to let her voice tremble. 'I didn't deliberately hold back
anything.' Why was he bringing that up now? she wondered.
Surely he wasn't planning to use it as an excuse to get rid of
her? He wasn't the kind of man who needed an excuse to do

anything, she told herself. He was too arrogant to feel he needed to soften any blows he had to deliver.

Marco looked away from Emily, irritated with himself for saying what he had. Why had he brought up her marriage now, when the last thing he wanted was the danger involved in the sentimentality of looking back to the beginning of their relationship? But it was too late, he *was* already remembering...

He had taken Emily to dinner, setting the scene for how he had hoped the evening would end by telling her coolly how much he wanted to make love to her and how pleased he was that she was a woman of the world, with a marriage behind her and no children to worry about.

'Just out of interest,' he'd quizzed her, 'what was the reason for your divorce?' If there was anything in her past, he wanted to know about it before things went any further.

For a moment he thought that she was going to refuse to answer him. But then her eyes widened slightly and he knew that she had correctly interpreted his question, without him having to spell it out to her. She clearly knew that if she did refuse, their relationship would be over before it had properly begun.

When she finally began to speak, she surprised him with the halting, almost stammering way in which she hesitated and then fiddled nervously with her cutlery, suddenly looking far less calm and in control than he had previously seen her. Her face was shadowed with anxiety and he assumed that the cause of the breakdown in her marriage must have been related to something she had done—such as being unfaithful to her husband. The last thing he expected to hear was what she actually told him. So much so, in fact, that he was tempted to accuse her of lying, but something he saw in her eyes stopped him...

Now Marco shifted his weight from one foot to the other, remembering how shocked he'd been by the unexpected and unwilling compassion he had felt for her as she'd struggled to overcome her reluctance to talk about what was obviously a painful subject...

'I lost my parents in a car accident when I was seven and I was brought up by my widowed paternal grandfather,' she told him.

'He wasn't unkind to me, but he wasn't a man who was comfortable around young children, especially not emotional young girls. He was a retired Cambridge University academic, very gentle and very unworldly. He read the classics to me as bedtime stories. He knew so much about literature but, although I didn't realise it at the time, very little about life. My upbringing with him was very sheltered and protected, very restricted in some ways, especially when I reached my early teens and his health started to deteriorate.

'Gramps' circle of friends was very small, a handful of elderly fellow academics, and...and Victor.'

'Victor?' Marco probed, hearing the hesitation in her voice.

'Yes. Victor Lewisham, my ex-husband. He had been one of Gramps' students, before becoming a university lecturer himself.'

'He must have been considerably older than you?' Marco guessed.

'Twenty years older,' Emily agreed, nodding her head. 'When it became obvious that my grandfather's health was deteriorating, he told me that Victor had agreed to look after me after...in his place. Gramps died a few weeks after that. I was in my first year at university then, and, even though I'd known how frail he was, somehow I hadn't...I wasn't prepared. Losing him was such a shock. He was all I had, you see, and so when Victor proposed to me and told me that it was what Gramps would have wanted, I...' She ducked her head and looked away from Marco and then said in a low voice, 'I should have refused, but somehow I just couldn't imagine how I would manage on my own. I was so afraid…such a coward.'

'So it was a marriage of necessity?' Marco shrugged dismissively. 'Was he good in bed?'

It continued to irk Marco to have to admit that his direct and unsubtle challenge to Emily had sprung from a sudden surge of physical jealousy that the thought of her with another man had aroused. But then sexual jealousy wasn't an emotion he'd ever previously had to deal with. Sex was sex, a physical appetite satisfied by a physical act. Emotions didn't come into it and he had never seen why they should. He still didn't. And he still had no idea what had made him confront her like that, or what had driven such an out-of-character fury at the thought of her with another man, even though she had had yet to become his. It had caught him totally off guard when he had seen the sudden shimmer of suppressed tears in her eyes. At first he'd wanted to believe they were caused by her grief at the breakdown of her marriage, but to his shock, she had told him quietly:

'Our marriage…our relationship, in fact, was never physically consummated.'

Marco remembered how he had struggled not to show his astonishment, perhaps for the first time in his life recognising that what he had needed to show wasn't the arrogant disbelief so often evinced by his grandfather, but instead restraint and patience, to give her time to explain. Which was exactly what she had done, once she had silently checked that he wasn't going to refuse to believe her.

'I was too naïve to realise at first that Victor making no attempt to approach me sexually might not be a… because of gentlemanly consideration for my inexperience,' she continued. 'And then even after we were married—I didn't want him, you see, so it was easy for me not to question why he didn't want to make love to me. If I hadn't lived such a sheltered life, and I'd spent more time with people my own age, things would probably have been different, and I'd certainly have been more aware that something wasn't right. But as it was, it wasn't until I…I found him in bed with someone else that I realised—'

'He had a mistress,' Marco interrupted her, his normal instinct to question and probe reasserting itself.

There was just the merest pause before she told him quietly, 'He had a lover, yes. A *male* lover,' she emphasised shakily.

'I should have guessed, of course, and I suspect poor Victor thought that I had. He treated me very much as a junior partner in our relationship, like a child whom he expected to revere him and accept his superiority. For me to find him in bed with one of his young students was a terrible blow to his pride. He couldn't forgive me for blundering in on them, and the only way I could forgive myself for being so foolish was to insist that we divorce. At first he was reluctant to agree. He belonged more to my grandfather's generation than to his own, I suspect. He couldn't come to terms with his sexuality, which was why he had tried to conceal it within a fake marriage. He refused to say why he couldn't be open about his sexual nature. He got very angry when I tried to talk to him about it and suggested that, for his own sake, he should accept himself. The truth was, as I quickly learned, that to others his sexuality was not the secret he liked to think. There was no valid reason why he should have hidden it, but he was just that kind of man.

'I'd been left a bit of money by my grandfather, so I came to London and got a job. I'd always been interested in interior design, so I went back to college to get my qualifications and then a couple of years ago, after working for someone else's studio, I set up in business on my own. I wanted a fresh start and to get away from people who had known…about Victor. They must have thought me such a fool for not realising. I felt almost as though I was some kind of freak… Married, but not married.'

'And a virgin?' Marco added.

'Yes,' Emily agreed, before continuing, 'I wanted to be somewhere where no one was going to make assumptions about me because of my marriage.'

Their food arrived before Marco had the chance ask her about the man whom he assumed must have eventually taken her virginity. But he wondered about him. And envied him?

Marco frowned now, not wanting to remember the fierce sense of urgency to make Emily totally his that had filled him then and that had continued to hold him in its grip even when he had ultimately possessed her.

He walked back to the bed whilst Emily watched him, her heart thumping unsteadily into her ribs. They had been lovers for almost three years, but Marco still had the same effect on her as he had done the first time she had seen him; the impact of his male sexuality was such that it both enthralled and overwhelmed her, even now when she could feel the pain of the emotional gulf between them almost as strongly as she felt her own desire. When they had first met, she had immediately craved him, though she hadn't known then that her desire for him would enslave her emotionally as well as physically. And if she had, would she have behaved differently? Would she still have turned on the heels of those expensive Gina shoes she'd been wearing and have tip-tapped away from him as fast as she could?

Emily was glad of the night's shadows to conceal the pain in her eyes—a pain that would betray her if Marco saw it. It had been just before Christmas when she had first noticed that he'd seemed irritated and preoccupied, retreating into himself and excluding her. She had thought at first he must have some big business deal going down, but now she was beginning to fear that the source of his discontent might be her and their relationship. If his withdrawal had begun in the months immediately after the accident in which Marco had lost both his parents, she might have been able to tell herself that it was his grief that was responsible. After all, even a man who prided himself on being as unemotional as Marco did was bound to suffer after such a traumatic event. However, the first thing he had done on his return was take her to bed, without saying a word about either the funeral or his family, making love to her fiercely and almost compulsively.

Marco had rarely talked to her about his childhood, and never about his family. That had suited her perfectly at first. She had looked on her relationship with him initially as a necessary transition for her from *naïveté* to experience, a much-needed bridge across the chasm dividing her past from her future, her passport to a new life and womanhood. Because even then she had hoped that, one day, she would find a true partner: a man with whom she could share her life; a man to whom she could give her love as freely as he would give his to her; a man with whom she could have children.

But how foolish she had been, how recklessly unaware of the danger she had been placing herself in. It had simply never occurred to her then that she might fall in love with Marco! He had been totally open with her about the way he lived his life and what he looked for in his relationships: whilst they were together she could rely on his total fidelity, but once their relationship was over, it would be over, *full stop*. He wanted no emotional commitment from her nor should she expect one from him. And most important of all, she must not get pregnant.

'But what if there's an accident and…?' she asked him uncertainly.

He stopped her immediately

'There will not be any accidents,' he told her bluntly. 'With modern methods of contraception, there is no reason why there should be an accident—if you have any reason to suspect there may have been, then you must ensure that the situation is rectified without any delay.'

She wanted him too much to allow herself to admit how shocked she was by his cold-hearted attitude. Instead, she told herself that it didn't really matter, since she wanted to wait to have her children until she had found the right father for them and the right man for her.

Marco had pursued her so relentlessly and determinedly and she had wanted him so badly that the truth was whatever doubts she might have had had been totally overwhelmed by the sexual excitement they generated between them. For the first time in her life she knew the true meaning of the word 'lust'. Her every waking thought—and most of her dreams too—were of him and what it was going to be like when he took her to bed.

Thanks to the kindness of her first employer, who had passed on to her some of his clients when she had started up on her own, she had established a good and profitable business, which earned her enough to enable her to visit one of London's more exclusive lingerie shops in search of the kind of discreetly provocative underwear her fevered imagination hoped would delight and excite Marco. Within a week of meeting him, she had taken to wearing the seductively skimpy bits of silk and lace to work, just in case Marco appeared and insisted on taking her to his apartment to consummate their relationship. It made her smile now to remember how sensually brave she had felt. And the things she had imagined might happen…

Her fevered imaginings had come nowhere near to matching the reality of her reaction to Marco's skilled lovemaking. He had undressed her slowly and expertly, in her pretty bedroom in her small Chelsea house, almost teasing her by making her quivering body wait for his touch. And then, even when he had finally touched her, his caresses had been tantalisingly—tormentingly—light, the merest brush of fingertips and lips, which had fed her longing for something darker and far more intimate. Just thinking about it now was enough to make her heart turn over inside her chest and make her go weak with longing for him. She remembered how she had tried to show him her impatience, but Marco had refused to be hurried. His lips had teased the tight flesh of her nipples, and his fingers had brushed her belly and then stroked lightly against her thighs whilst she had sighed with arousal. His hand had parted her thighs, his fingers stroking over her sex, his touch making her want to moan out aloud with hunger.

He had just begun to kiss her more passionately when the telephone beside her bed had begun to ring. Idiotically she had answered it, only to discover that the caller was one of her more difficult clients who wanted to discuss her idea for a new makeover. By the time she had got rid of the client, Marco had got dressed, smiling urbanely at her, but making it clear that he was *not* going to take second place to her business.

The incident had shown her that he would always have it his way and she had not made the same mistake again. Or had her mistake been in tailoring her working life around him? That hadn't been just for his benefit though; she had wanted to make room in her life for him. Something deep inside her, which she had only recently begun to recognise, was showing her that she was the kind of woman who secretly longed to be the hub of her family, both as a wife and a mother. She didn't want to be on the other side of the world helping a client to choose the right paint shade for her new décor, leaving her partner to come home from work to an empty house and an empty bed. When she did marry and have children, she wanted to be the one those children ran to with their small everyday triumphs and hurts. She enjoyed her work, and she was proud of the ways in which she had built up her business, but she knew that it was the pleasure of creating a happy environment for those she loved that truly motivated her, rather than the excitement of a large bank balance.

Nonetheless, Marco was the kind of man who enjoyed a challenge, and it had made her feel a bit better when, later, he'd admitted how much he had ached for her that night. It could not have been any more than she had ached for him, she knew. Less than three months after they had first met he had asked her to move in with him. And then they'd had their first quarrel, when she had discovered that he'd expected her to give up her business, saying imperiously that he would give her an allowance that would more than compensate her for any loss of income.

'I want to be with you,' she told him fiercely. 'But I will not give up my financial independence, Marco. I don't want your money.'

'So what do you want?' he demanded, almost suspiciously.

'You,' she told him simply, and their quarrel was forgotten, as he was appeased by her bold request—or so she had thought. It was only later she had learned that, far from respecting her for refusing his money and his expensive gifts, he was both suspicious of her and slightly contemptuous. Perhaps if she had heeded the warning that knowledge had given her, she would not be in the situation she was now.

CHAPTER THREE

THEY had shared such wonderful months. Marco worked hard, but he believed in enjoying the good things in life as well. He had the air of someone who was used to the best of everything. But whilst sometimes she had deplored his inbuilt arrogance, and had teased him gently about it, Emily admitted that she'd enjoyed the new experiences to which he'd introduced her. Marco had taken her out several times a week but, best of all, as a lover he hadn't just fulfilled her fantasies, he had exceeded them and then taken her with him to realms of sexual discovery and delight she had never imagined existed.

Within weeks of them becoming lovers she had been so exquisitely sensually aware of him that just the touch of his hand on her arm, or the look in his eyes when he'd needed her to know that he wanted her, had been enough to have her answering with a look of her own that said, 'Please take me to bed.' Not that they had always made it to a bed. Marco was a demanding and masterful lover who enjoyed leading the way and introducing her to new pleasures, sometimes taking her quickly and erotically in venues so nearly public that she blushed guiltily af-terwards when she remembered, sometimes ensuring their lovemaking lasted all night—or most of the day. And she had been an eager pupil, wanting him more as time went by, rather than less, as her own sexuality and confidence grew under his expert guidance.

The first Christmas they had shared together, Marco had given her a beautiful three-carat diamond, which he had told her she could have set in the ring design of her choice. Emily knew that it had surprised him when she'd asked him instead to make a donation to her favourite children's charity.

Marco hadn't said anything, but on her birthday he had taken her away to a romantic hideaway and made love to her until she had cried with joy. He had then presented her with a pair of two-carat diamond ear-studs, telling her, 'I have sent a cheque of equivalent value to your charity.'

It had been then that she had realised that she had done the unforgivable and fallen in love with him!

Yes, how very foolish she had been to do that. He was back in their bed now, but lying with his back to her. Outside, the gale that had begun to blow earlier last evening hurled itself against the windows as the storm increased in force.

Normally, the knowledge that she was safe and warm inside whilst outside ice-cold rain sleeted down would have given her a feeling of delicious security, especially if she was wrapped up tightly in Marco's arms. But of course she wasn't. *Was* he tiring of her?

Marco could hear Emily breathing softly behind him. His body craved the release physically possessing her would bring, and why shouldn't he have it? he asked himself. He had already decided on the financial amount he was prepared to give Emily in recognition of the time they had spent together—a very generous one. So generous that he felt justified now in thinking that he might as well continue to enjoy her. He couldn't entirely get his head around the fact that he wanted Emily still, when other women who had shared his

bed before her—women who had been so much more experienced and sexually enterprising—had bored him so quickly.
It surprised him even more that he had actually grown to want
her company away from bed, to the extent of talking to her
about his business, and allowing her to persuade him to make
donations to her precious charity. He had scarcely even been
able to believe it at first when he had found out how much of
her modest income she gave to helping a foundation set up to
help London's deprived children and teenagers. Emily would
not approve of his grandfather's refusal to do anything to help
the least wealthy of Niroli's people; King Giorgio did not see
the sense of educating the poor to expect more out of life than
he felt the island could give them.

No, Emily was definitely not suitable material as the King
of Niroli's mistress. But, of course, he was not yet King.
Purposefully Marco moved, swiftly reaching for her, briefly
studying the outline of her figure, the curve of her breast
making him remember how perfectly its softness fitted into
his cupped hand. As always, the strongly sensual core of his
nature reacted to Emily's nearness. He might have already
made love with her a thousand times and more during their
relationship, but that couldn't dim the fierce desire he felt now.
Some-where deep down within himself he registered the potential danger of such a compulsion and then dismissed it. He
intended to end his affair with her before he left for Niroli.
He'd make sure that no vestige of longing for her would cling
to his memory or his senses; he was determined she would be
easily replaced in his bed. If his body recognised something
in her that was particularly enjoyable, that did not mean that
he was in danger of craving her for ever. He relaxed as he dismissed as ludicrous the notion that he was at any kind of risk
from his desire for her.

The moment Marco touched her, Emily could feel her

body becoming softly compliant, outwardly and inwardly, where it tightened and ached, the desire for him that never left her ramping up with a swift familiarity. Marco pushed back the bedclothes; a thin beam of moonlight silvered her breast, plucking sensually at her nipple and tightening it for his visual appreciation and enjoyment. He traced its circle of light, making her shiver with pleasure whilst her back began to arch in an age-old symbolic female gesture of enticement in offering her flesh to her lover.

Marco's hands tightened on Emily's slender form. She looked up at him, her eyes wide with arousal and excitement as she reached up to him. All that mattered to him right now was his possession of her, his pleasure found in witnessing her ecstasy as he took her and filled her, losing himself in her and taking her with him. His need pounded through him, obliterating everything else. He pushed aside her hair and kissed the side of her neck where he knew his touch reduced her to quivering delight, his hands cupping her breasts, kneading them erotically, his erection already stiff against her thigh where he had locked her to him with one out-flung leg.

Emily smiled to herself. Sex to Marco meant physically claiming every bit of her. Even when he kissed her casually, he liked to have her body in full contact with his. Not that she minded. Not one little bit! She loved the possessive sensuality of his desire for her. It was only in his arms, here like this, that she was truly able to let her real feelings have their head, instead of fighting to preserve the protective air of calm control she normally used to conceal them. When he made love to her, Marco never held back from showing her his passion for her, which, in turn, allowed her to set free her equally passionate longing for him. There was sometimes something almost pagan in the way they made love that secretly sometimes half shocked her. Always attuned to Marco's moods, tonight she sensed an urgency about him that added an extra edge to her own growing sexual tension. She gave a soft whimper as his mouth took the silvered ache of her nipple and his hand accepted the invitation of her open legs.

Once in their early days as lovers, sensing her uncertainty and slight awkwardness with her own sexuality, he had relaxed her with an evening of champagne and slow lovemaking, before coaxing her to let him position both of them where she could see the reflection of their naked bodies in a mirror. Then carefully, and with breathtakingly deliberate sensuality, he had revealed to her the mysteries of her own sex, showing her its desire-swollen and flushed outer lips, caressing them so that she could see her body's reaction to his touch, sliding his fingertip the whole length of her wetness before focusing on the tight, excited and oh-so-sexually-sensitive flesh of her clitoris. He had brought her to orgasm there in full view of her own half-shocked, half-excited gaze.

But she'd had her own sweet revenge later, turning the tables on him by exploring him with shamelessly avid hands and lips, spreading apart his heavily muscled male thighs so that she could know the reality of his sex with every one of her senses.

Now, as his fingers probed her wetness, she rose up eager to accept their gift of pleasure. But, for once, he didn't seem inclined to draw out their love-play, instead suddenly groaning and reaching for her, covering her and thrusting powerfully and compulsively into her, as though he couldn't get enough of her, driving them both higher, deeper, closer to the sanctuary that waited for them.

Instinctively Emily clung to him, riding the storm with him, welcoming him and sharing its turbulence.

Marco could feel an unfamiliar urgency possessing him and compelling him, demanding that he thrust harder and deeper. Emily shuddered beneath the intensity of his passion, immediately responsive to it. Her nails raked his back where his flesh lay tightly against his muscles, inciting him to fill her and complete her. The sensation of the tight heat of her wetness as it gripped and caressed him flooded everything but his ability to respond to her sensual urging from his mind. A primitive need surged through him. It had been some time since he'd last used a condom when they had sex; their relationship was of a long enough duration for him to know that there were no health reasons for him to do so, and that Emily was on the pill. Also, he knew how much she herself loved the skin-on-skin contact of their meshing bodies.

Was Marco aware of how deeply he was penetrating her, Emily wondered dizzily, or how intense and primeval a pleasure it was for her, as surges of sensation built, promising her orgasm? Did he know that when he came he would spill so very close to her womb? Did he know how much she wanted him; how much she ached now, right now, for him? She gave a low soft, almost tormented cry as her orgasm began, clutching at Marco, her head thrown back in pagan ecstasy as her pleasure shuddered through her, only to intensify into a second spiral of even greater intensity that shook her in its grip and melted her bones as Marco came hotly inside her.

Emily blinked fiercely. What they had just shared had been incredibly close and physically satisfying. Emotional tears slid down her face. Surely it wasn't possible for Marco to make love to her like this and not be in love with her? Perhaps the change she had sensed in him was because he *was* falling in love with her and he was reluctant to admit it? Tenderness for him, and for the vulnerability she knew he would never admit to, stole through her. She snuggled closer to him, warmed by his body and the intimacy they had shared, and most of all by the glow of the hope growing inside her. She would teach him that their love would make him stronger, not weaker; she would show him, as she'd tried to do all along, that *he* was what mattered to her and not the things he could give her. Marco had never told her why he was so adamant that love wasn't something he believed in or wanted, and she assumed that it must be because as a very young man he had been badly hurt and had vowed never to fall in love again. In a man as proud as Marco, such a wound would go very deep. Although people had been quick to gossip to her about him when she'd first met him, and about the stream of glamorous women who'd graced his arm and his bed before her, no one seemed to know much about his life before he had come to London. Marco was fiercely protective of his past and his privacy, and Emily had learned very early on in their relationship how shuttered he could be when she tried to get him to open up to her. So, it had to mean something that they were still together, Emily told herself sleepily. Why shouldn't that something be that he had fallen in love with her without even realising it?

CHAPTER FOUR

'AND I want the whole place to—y'know—like be totally me. So there'll have to be plenty of pink and loads of open-plan storage for my shoes. All my fans know that I'm a total shoe-freak.'

Emily was finding it a struggle to focus on what her latest client was saying, and not just because the reality-TV star's views on how she wanted her apartment designed and decorated were depressingly banal, she admitted.

The truth was that her normal professionalism and love of her work had in recent weeks become shadowed by her almost constant tiredness and bouts of sickness that had to be the legacy of a virus that she didn't seem to have entirely thrown off.

The reality-TV star was pouting and looking impatiently at her watch.

'Do we have to do this?' she asked the PR executive who was 'minding' her. 'I thought you said that I'd be doing a TV documentary about me designing my new apartment, not doing boring stuff like listening to some decorator.'

Whilst the PR girl attempted to soothe her charge, Emily moved discreetly out of earshot. Marco had left early this morning for his office whilst she had still been asleep, leaving her a scrawled note on the kitchen counter to say that he had some work he needed to catch up on. There was nothing particularly unusual in his early start. As an entrepreneur he often needed to be at his desk while the Far-Eastern financial markets were dealing. But today, for some reason, Emily was conscious of a deep-rooted emotional need to see him, be with him. Why? Surely not just because he had left without waking her to give her a good-morning kiss? A little rueful, she shook her head over her own neediness, determined to dismiss it. But it refused to go away, if anything sharpening so that it became a fierce ache of anxious longing. She looked at her watch. It was almost lunchtime. In the early stages of their relationship before Marco had told her that he wanted her to move in with him, she had, with some trepidation, and with what she had considered to be great daring, taken him up on what she had believed to be a casual invitation to drop in on him if she was ever passing by his office. Emily's heart started to go faster in a sudden flurry of excited little beats, the grating sound of the TV star's voice fading, as she recalled how she had taken him up on his offer...

Marco's initial greeting of her had not been welcoming. 'You were beginning to annoy me with the way you've been deliberately keeping me waiting,' he told her flatly, after his secretary had shown her into his office and then discreetly left them alone together. 'In fact you were beginning to annoy me so much that if you left it another day to visit, you wouldn't have got past my receptionist,' he added arrogantly.

His verbal attack stunned her into a bewildered silence, which had her shaking her head in mute protest.

'If you think that by holding me off, and making me wait, you'll—'

'Why on earth should I do that?' Emily interrupted him, too shocked by his accusations to recognise what she was giving away until she saw the satisfaction gleaming in his eyes and he came towards her saying softly,

'Well, in that case, we've got some catching up to do, haven't we?' When he took hold of her hands and drew her towards him, she was trembling so much with arousal and excitement that he smiled again. Not that he wasn't equally turned on; he told her with sexy intent in between his kisses how much he wanted her and what that wanting was doing to him.

If his telephone hadn't rung, Emily suspected that she would have let him make love to her there and then in his office. She certainly hadn't tried to stop him when he had unfastened her blouse and peeled back the lace of her bra, exposing her breast to his glitteringly erotic gaze and the skilled touch of his hand. His lips had been on its creamy slope when his phone had rung. She had tried to straighten her clothes as he'd answered the call, but he had stopped her, very deliberately tracing the tight excitement of her nipple with one lazy fingertip whilst he'd spoken to his caller. Emily could feel her body tightening now as she remembered the effect the highly charged atmosphere between them had had on her, and the contrast between the calm, businesslike tone of his voice and the deliberately sensual way in which he had been touching her. By the time he had finished his call she had been aching with longing for him to take their intimacy to its natural conclusion, but instead he had released her, fastening her top and then saying calmly,

'Come on, let's go out and have some lunch.'

She hadn't known him well enough then, of course, to realise that his deliberate arousal of her had been his way of punishing her for what he believed had been her attempt to control their relationship, and him.

Those had been such achingly sweet times, when they had first met. Suddenly she yearned to recapture them. Impulsively, she went over to the PR girl and told her firmly, 'I'm afraid I have to go. You've got my e-mail address if you need to contact me.' Emily suspected from the look the TV star was giving her that she wasn't going to get any commission for this project. But then, she told herself, right now being with Marco was more important to her than anything.

Marco stood beside his desk in the sleek modern office suite where he conducted his global financial affairs. When he had left Niroli vowing to make his own mark in the world without his royal status, his grandfather had laughed at him and warned him that he would be back within six months with his tail between his legs. He could have been, Marco admitted: at twenty-two, his belief in his own abilities had been far greater than his financial astuteness; initially he had lost money as he'd played the international stock markets. But, just when he had begun to fear the worst, his mother's great aunt had died in Italy, leaving him a substantial amount of money. A second stroke of luck had led him to come to the attention of one of the City's richest entrepreneurs, who had taken Marco under his wing, teaching him to use his skills and hone his killer financial instincts. Within a year, Marco had doubled his inheritance, and within five years he had become a billionaire in his own right.

Emily had designed Marco's office for him. On the traditional partners' desk she had given him as a birthday gift, there was a silver-framed photograph of the two of them, taken on the anniversary of their first year together, before the death of his parents. Marco now studied it: he saw Emily looking up at him, her expression filled with laughter and desire, whilst his own was shadowed and half hidden. But then, Marco knew, his eyes reflected the physical hunger he had seen in hers, just as the positioning of their bodies mirrored one another. Emily was gazing at him with open happiness in her eyes, because she knew he was a wealthy man and a skilled lover.

'Niroli's kings receive love, Marco,' his grandfather had told him when he was a young adolescent, 'they do not give it. They are above other, weaker men, and they do not try to turn physical desire into mawkish sentiment like other, lesser men. They do not need to. You are maturing fast and you will discover very soon that your royal status will draw to you your pick of the world's most beautiful and predatory women. They will give you their bodies but, in return, they will try to demand that you give them money and status. They will try to scheme, lie and cheat their way into your bed, and if you are foolish enough to let them they will present you with bastard sons who will become permanent remind-ers of your own folly and permanent dangers to Niroli's throne. It is not so many centuries ago that a newly crowned sultan would order the death or the castration of all his many male half-siblings in order to prevent them from trying to take his place. You're welcome to taste the pleasure of the women who offer themselves to you as much as you wish, but remember what I have told you. Ultimately you will make a necessary dynastic marriage with a young woman of royal and unimpeachable moral virtue, and she will give you your legitimate heirs. Your only heirs, if you are wise, Marco.'

Well, he had been wise, hadn't he? Marco told himself grimly. And he intended to continue to be so. He looked down at the letter on the desk in front of him. It had arrived the previous day, its royal crest and the Nirolean stamp immedi-ately marking it out as the reason why he was in the office so early this morning. It was from his grandfather, setting out the final details of his abdication plans. The people of Niroli, King Giorgio had written, were already being encouraged to expect Marco's return and to welcome him as their new ruler. He needed to speak with his grandfather. But protocol meant that, yesterday, Marco had patiently followed an archaic, convoluted procedure, which had ensured that none of the ancient statesmen who surrounded his grandfather would have their pride dented, before finally arranging to speak directly to the king. Marco intended to make a clean sweep of these elderly statesmen once he was on the throne. His plan was to bring a forward-thinking modern mindset to the way Niroli was ruled, via courtiers of his own generation who shared his way of thinking. In fact, this new regime was something he already had in hand after a few discreet one-to-one telephone calls.

He looked at his watch: in another twenty minutes exactly, the telephone on his desk would ring and the Groom of the Chamber would announce in his quavering voice that he was going to connect him to his grandfather. Marco sighed. The elderly courtier was hard of hearing, as indeed was his grandfather, although King Giorgio denied it! Marco had a rueful fondness for his older relative, and he knew that Giorgio had a grudging respect for him, but he also knew that both of them were far too similar to ever be willing to be open about those feelings. Instead they tended to conform to the roles they had adopted in Marco's teenage years, when his grandfather had been the disapproving disciplinarian and he had been the rebellious black sheep. He checked the time again. All this simply so that he could assure his grandfather that he would be returning to Niroli just as soon as he had dealt with his outstanding business in London, something that should have been a simple matter of a quick phone call rather than this long-drawn-out ceremonial.

The part of Marco's outstanding business that concerned Emily was of course something he did not intend to discuss with the old king. He estimated that it would be a few weeks yet before he would be ready to leave, and he had already decided that there would be no sense in telling Emily their relationship had to end until then. One single clean cut, with no possibility of any come-backs, was the best way to deal with the situation. He would tell her they were finished and that he was leaving the country—and that was all. He had taken her to his bed as plain Marco Fierezza and he saw no point in revealing his royal status to her now. She had known him as her lover and a wealthy entrepreneur, not as the future King of Niroli. It was true that she might at some future point come to discover who he was—the paparazzi took a keen interest in the Royal House of Niroli—but by then their lives would be entirely separate. Their relationship had never been intended to end in commitment. He had told her that right from the start. But they had been together for almost three years, when previously he had become bored with his girlfriends within three months. Marco shrugged away the dry inner voice pointing out things to him he didn't want to acknowledge. So, sexually they might have been well suited, or maybe at thirty-six the raw heat of his sex drive was cooling and he demanded less stimulation and variety, which made him content to accept a familiar physical diet? It would do him good to get out of that kind of sexual rut, he told himself coolly.

It would do them both good. Marco started as, out of nowhere, a sharply savage spear of sexual jealousy stabbed through him. What was this? Why on earth should he feel such a gut-wrenching surge of fury at the thought of Emily moving on to another man? His mouth compressed. His concern was for Emily, and not for himself. She was after all the vulnerable one, not him. Emily's sexual past was very different from his own, and because of that—and only that, he assured himself—he was now experiencing a completely natural concern that she was not equipped to deal with a lover who might not treat her as well as he had done.

Marco looked at her picture, reluctantly remembering the first time he had possessed her. He'd planned to surprise her, but in the end she had been the one who had surprised him…

He had seen how excited she'd been when he'd walked into her shop and told her that he was taking her away for a few days, and that she would need her passport. When he'd picked her up later that day, he had seen quite plainly in her expression how much she'd wanted him. As he had wanted her.

He had been totally—almost brutally, some might have said—honest with her about the fact that he had no time for the emotional foolishness of falling in love. He had informed her calmly that he had ended previous relationships for no other reason than that his girlfriends had told him that they were falling in love with him. Emily had greeted his announcement with equal calm. Falling in love with him wasn't something she planned to do, she had assured him firmly. She was as committed to their relationship being based on their sexual need for one another as he was himself, she had smiled, adding that this suited her perfectly, and Marco had felt she was speaking the truth.

He had booked the two of them into a complex on a small private island that catered exclusively for the rich and the childfree. Everything about the location was designed to appeal to lovers and to cocoon them in privacy, whilst providing a discreet service.

The individual villas that housed the guests were set apart from the main hotel block, each with its own private pool. Meals could be taken in the villas or in the Michelin-starred restaurant of the hotel, where there was also an elegant bar and nightclub.

Amongst the facilities included for the guests' entertainment were diving and sailing, and visits to the larger, more built-up neighbouring islands could be arranged by helicopter if guests wished.

They had arrived late in the afternoon, and had walked through the stunningly beautiful gardens. Marco recalled now how Emily had reached out to hold his hand, her eyes shining with awed wonder as they had paused to watch the breathtaking swiftness of the sunset. He remembered, too, how he had been unable to resist taking her in his arms and kissing her, and how that kiss had become so intimate it had left Emily trembling.

They had returned to their villa, undressing one another eagerly and speedily, sharing the shower in the luxuriously equipped bathroom. Emily's physical response to him had been everything Marco had hoped it would be and more. She had held nothing back, matching him touch for touch and in intimacy until he had started to penetrate her. It had caught him off guard to have her tensing as he thrust fully into her, believing she was as eager to feel the driving surge of his body within hers as he was to feel her hot, wet flesh tightening around him.

At first he had assumed she was playing some kind of coy game with him, mistakenly thinking that it would excite him if she assumed a mock-innocent hesitancy. His frustration had made him less perceptive than he might otherwise have been, and more impatient, so he had ignored the warning her body had been giving him and had thrust strongly again. This time it had taken the small muffled sound that had escaped past her rigid throat muscles to make him realise the truth: she was still a virgin.

His first reaction had been one of savage anger, fuelled by the toxic mingling of male frustration and the blow to his own pride that was caused by the fact that he hadn't guessed the truth. Sex with an inexperienced virgin—and the potential burden of responsibility that carried, both physical and emotional—was something he just had not wanted.

'What the hell is this?' he swore. 'Okay, I know about your marriage, but I would have thought that…if only because of that…'

'That *what?* That I'd jump on the first man I could find?' Emily retaliated sharply. But beneath that sharpness he caught the quiver of uncertainty in her voice, and his anger softened into something that caught at his throat, startling him with its intensity.

'Well, it did cross my mind,' she told him. 'But in the end I was too much of a moral coward to go through with it. Blame my grandfather, if you wish, but the thought of having sex with a man I didn't truly want, just to get rid of my virginity, has made it harder rather than easier for me to find a man I did want enough.'

Marco shrugged dismissively, not wanting to have to deal with his own unfamiliar feelings, never mind hers!

'If you're expecting me to be pleased about this, then let me tell you—'

'You don't need to tell me anything, Marco,' she had stopped him determinedly. 'It's rather obvious what you feel.'

'I don't know what you're thinking, or hoping for,' he told her, ignoring her comment, 'but, despite what you may want to believe, the majority of sexually mature men do not fantasise about initiating a virgin! I certainly don't. The reason I brought you here was so that we could indulge our need for one another as two people starting from the same baseline. For me, that means we share matching physical desires for one another and awareness of our own sexual wants and expectations.'

'I'm sorry if you feel that I've let you bring me here under false pretences,' Emily told him, admitting, 'Maybe I should have said something to warn you?'

'Maybe?'

The scorn in his voice made her flinch visibly. 'I didn't want to play the I'm-still-a-virgin card for the reasons you've just mentioned yourself,' she defended. 'I didn't want it to be an issue and, besides, I wasn't even sure that you'd notice.'

Marco remembered how she had coloured up hotly when he had looked at her in disbelief.

'I really am sorry,' she told him apologetically.

'*You're* sorry? I'm so damn frustrated…' he began.

'Me, too,' Emily interrupted him with such candour that he felt his earlier irritation evaporating.

'Frustrated, but virginal and apprehensive?' he felt bound to point out.

'Yes, but not one of those has to remain a permanent state, does it?' she responded.

'You trust me to deal effectively with all three?'

'I trust you to make it possible for *us* to deal with all three,' she corrected him softly. 'I'm a woman who believes that participation in a shared event makes for mutual enjoyment, even if right now in this particular venture I am the junior partner.'

He wasn't used to being teased, or to sharing laughter in an intimate relationship and, as he quickly discovered, shared laughter had its own aphrodisiacal qualities.

He made love to her with a slow intimacy which, he was the first to admit, had its own reward when in the end she showed him such a passionate response. It was she who urged him to move faster and deeper, until he was as lost in the pleasure they were sharing as she was. But not so lost that he couldn't witness the shocked look of delight widening her eyes as her orgasm gripped her…

What the hell was he doing, thinking about that now? It was over; they were over; or rather they soon would be.

Someone was knocking gently on his office door. Marco

frowned. He wasn't expecting anyone and he had expressly told his PA not to disturb him. He was still frowning when the door opened and Emily stepped through, smiling at him. It wasn't often that Marco was caught off guard by anything or anyone, but on this occasion…

'My meeting finished early,' he could hear Emily saying breezily, 'So I thought I'd come over and see if you were free for lunch?'

When he didn't answer her she closed the office door and came towards him, dropping her voice to a playfully soft tone as she told him, 'Or maybe we could forget the going-out and the lunch. Remember, Marco, how we used to…What's wrong?' she asked him uncertainly.

Her smile disappeared and Marco recognised that he had left it several seconds too late to respond appropriately to her arrival.

Normally, the fact that his timing was at fault would have been his main concern. But, for some reason, he found that, not only was he acutely aware that he had hurt and upset Emily, he was also suppressing an immediate desire to go to her and apologise. Apologise? Him? Marco was astounded by his own uncharacteristic impulse. He never apologised to anyone, for anything.

'Nothing's wrong,' he told her flatly, knowing that something was very wrong indeed for him to have felt like that. It couldn't be that he was feeling guilty, could it? a traitorous, critical inner voice suddenly challenged, pointing out: *After all, you've lied to her and you're about to leave her…*

She knew the ground rules, Marco answered it inwardly. That his own conscience should turn on him like this increased his irritation and, man-like, he focused that irritation on Emily, rather than deal with its real cause.

'Yes, there is,' Emily persisted. 'You were looking at me as though I'm the last person you want to see.'

'Don't be ridiculous. I just wasn't expecting to see you.'
He flicked back the sleeve of his suit—handmade, it fitted him
in such a way that its subtle outlining of his superb physique
was a whispered suggestion caught only by those who understood. 'Look, I can't do lunch, I've got an important call
coming through any time now, and after than I've got an appointment.' That wasn't entirely true, but there was no way he
wanted Emily to suggest she wait around for him whilst he
spoke with his grandfather. For one thing, he had no idea just
how long the call would last and, for another... For another,
he wasn't ready yet to tell Emily what she had to be told.

Because he wasn't ready yet to deny himself the pleasure
of making love to her, his inner tormentor piped up, adding
mockingly, *Are you sure that you will ever be ready?* He dismissed that unwanted thought immediately but its existence
increased his ire. 'Mrs Lawson should have told you that I'd
said I didn't want to be disturbed,' he informed Emily curtly.

She heard the impatience in his voice and wished she
hadn't bothered coming. Marco's arrogance made him forget
sometimes how easily he could hurt her, and she certainly had
too much pride to stay here and let him see that pain.

'Mrs Lawson wasn't there when I came in.'

'Not there? She's my PA, for heaven's sake. Where the
hell is she?'

'She'd probably just slipped off to the cloakroom, Marco. It
isn't her fault,' Emily pointed out quietly. 'Look, I'm sorry if
this isn't a good time.' She gave a small resigned sigh. 'I suppose
I should have checked with you first before coming over.'

'Yes, you should have,' Marco agreed grimly. Any
minute now the phone was going to ring and if he picked
it up she was going to hear his grandfather's most senior
aide's voice booming out as he tried to compensate for his
own deafness, 'Is that you, Your Highness?' The Comte

had never really accustomed himself to the effectiveness of modern communication systems and still thought his voice could only travel down the telephone line if he spoke as loudly as he possibly could.

Emily's eyes widened as she registered Marco's rejection and then she stood still staring blankly at him, the colour leaving her face. He was treating her as though she were some casual and not very welcome acquaintance.

'Don't worry about it. I'm sorry I disturbed you,' she managed to say, but she could hear the brittle hurt in her own voice. Right now, she wanted to be as far away from Marco and his damn office as she could get! She was perilously close to tears and the last thing she wanted was the humiliation of Marco seeing how much he'd wounded her. To her relief, she could hear sounds from the outer office suggesting that his PA had returned, enabling her to use the face-saving fib that she didn't want to have Mrs Lawson coming in to shoo her out. Emily opened the door and left, barely pausing to acknowledge the PA's surprise at seeing her, Emily hurried out of the office, her head down and her throat thick with unshed tears.

What was it with her? she asked herself wretchedly, five minutes later as she hailed a taxi. She wasn't a young girl with emotions so new and raw that she overreacted to every sucked-in breath! She was in her twenties and divorced, and she and Marco had been together for nearly three years, the intimacy of their sex life having given her an outward patina of radiant sensuality. It had been so palpable in the first year they'd been together, one of her clients had told her semi-jokingly, 'Now that you're with Marco you're going to start losing clients if you aren't careful.'

'Why?' Emily had asked.

'Jealousy,' had been the client's succinct answer.

Emily remembered how she had smiled with rueful acknowledgement. 'You mean, because I'm with Marco and they'd like to change places with me?' she had guessed.

'They may very well want to do that, but I was thinking more of their concerns that their husbands might be tempted by the creamy glow of sexual completion you're carrying around with you right now, Emily.'

Emily remembered she had blushed and made some confused denial, but the client had shaken her head and told her wisely, 'You can't deny or ignore it. That glow shimmers round you like a force-field and men are going to be drawn to you because of it. There is nothing more likely to make a man want a woman than her confident wearing of another man's sexual interest in her.'

She doubted that she still wore that magnetic sexual aura now, Emily admitted sadly. That was the trouble: when you broke the rules, it didn't only make you ache for what you didn't have, it also damaged what you did.

The taxi driver was waiting for her to tell him where she wanted to go. She leaned forward and gave him the address of Marco's apartment. *Marco's apartment*, she noted—for that was how she thought of it. Not as *their* apartment, even though he had invited her to make it over to suit her own tastes and had given her a lavish budget for its renovation. Material possessions, even for one's home that evoked deep-rooted attachments, were nothing without the right kind of emotions to surround them. Why had it had to happen? Why had she fallen in love with Marco? Why couldn't she have stayed as she was, thrillingly aware of him on the most intimate kind of sexual level, buoyed up by the intensity of their desire for one another, overwhelmed by relief and joy because he had brought her from the dark, wretched nowhere she'd inhabited after her divorce to the brilliant glittering landscape of unimaginable beauty that was the intimacy they shared together?

Why, why, why couldn't that have been enough? Why had she had to go and fall for him?

Emily shivered, sinking deeper into the seat of the taxi. And why, having fallen for him, did she have to torment herself by hoping that one day things would change, that one day he would look at her and in his eyes she would see his love for her? The hope that, one day, it would happen sometimes felt so fragile and so unrealistic that she was afraid for herself, afraid of her vulnerability as a woman who needed one particular man so badly she was prepared to cling to such a fine thread. But what else could she do? She could tell him, honestly, how she felt. Emily bit her lip, guiltily aware that she wasn't being open with him. Because she was afraid in case she lost him…Why was she letting herself be dragged down by these uncomfortable, painful thoughts and questions? Why did they keep on escaping from the place where she tried to incarcerate and conceal them? What kind of woman was she to live a lie with the man she loved? What kind of relationship was it when that man stated openly that there was no place for love in the life he wanted to live?

The taxi stopped abruptly, catching her off guard. She didn't really want to go up to the apartment, not feeling the way she was right now, but another person was already hurrying purposefully towards the taxi, wanting to lay claim to it.

Emily got out and paid her fare to the driver, shivering as she waited for her change. Her stomach had already begun its familiar nauseous churning—this time, it had to be a result of Marco's rejection of her appeal to him, though she had to admit she had also felt too nauseous to want any breakfast this morning. She was definitely beginning to feel slightly dizzy and faint as well as unwell now.

Psychosomatic, she told herself unsympathetically as she headed up to the apartment.

It had started to rain while Emily was getting out of the taxi. Yes, the miserable weather was adding to her feelings of lowness. Why couldn't she talk to Marco? They were lovers, after all, sharing the closest of physical intimacy. Physical intimacy—but they did not share any emotional intimacy. Emily's experiences as a child had made her wary of appearing needy. It was now second nature to her to hide the most vulnerable part of her true self. Only in Marco's arms, at the height of their shared passion, did she feel safe enough to allow her body to show him what was in her heart, knowing that he wasn't likely to be able to recognise it.

She let herself into the apartment, mutely aware of how empty and impersonal it felt, for all her attempts to turn it into a shared home.

'Yes, Grandfather, I do understand, but I cannot work miracles. It is impossible for me to return to Niroli before the end of the month as we had already tentatively agreed.' Marco managed to hold onto his temper as his grandfather's complaints grew louder, before finally interrupting to say dryly, 'Very well, then, I accept that whilst I had talked about the end of the month, you had not agreed to it. But that doesn't alter the fact that I cannot return sooner.'

The sound of his grandfather slamming down the receiver reverberated in Marco's eardrum. Replacing his own handset, he stood up and turned to look out of the window of his office. It was raining. In Niroli, the sun would be shining. Marco's grandfather was obviously furious that he had refused to give in and alter the timing of his return and bring his arrival on Niroli forward. But his grandfather's rage did not worry Marco. He was used to it and unaffected by it, apart from the fact that he too didn't like having his plans challenged. He looked irritably at his watch. He was hungry and very much in need of the gentle calm of Emily's company. That, plus the natural reserve that made her the kind of woman who was never going to court the attention of the paparazzi, or expose their relationship to the avid curiosity of others, were two other major plus-points about her. But not quite as major as the sensuality that spilled from her like sweetness from a honeycomb, even if she didn't realise it.

The direction his thoughts were taking surprised him. It was nonsense for him to be thinking about Emily like this when he was about to end their relationship! Far better that he focused on the things he didn't like about her, such as… Such as the way she insisted on keeping professional commitments even when he had made other plans. *Is that the only criticism you can make of her?* an increasingly voluble and irritating inner voice demanded sardonically. Marco sighed, mentally acknowledging the irony of his own thoughts. Yes, it was true that, in many ways, Emily was the perfect mistress for the man he had been whilst he'd lived in London. But he wasn't going to be that man for much longer.

When the time came for him to take a royal mistress, she would have to have qualities that Emily did not possess. Chief amongst those would be an accepting, possibly older husband. This was an example of the kind of protocol at the royal court of Niroli which, in Marco's opinion, kept it in the Edwardian era. He certainly planned to bring about changes that would benefit the people of Niroli rather than its king. But perhaps there were certain traditions that were better retained. No, Emily could not continue to be his lover, but even so he could have responded better to her arrival in his office earlier, Marco admitted. He could, for instance, have suggested that she go ahead to one of their favourite restaurants and wait there for him. It had, after all, been predictable that his grandfather would lose his temper and end their conversation so abruptly, once he realised that he wasn't going to get everything that he wanted.

Marco toyed with the idea of calling Emily now and suggesting that she meet him for a late lunch, but then decided against it. She wasn't the kind of woman who sulked or played silly games. But honesty compelled him to accept that some measure of compensatory behaviour on his part would be a good invest- ment. Ridiculously in many ways, given the length of time they had been together, just thinking about her triggered that familiar sharp ache of his desire for her. He picked up the phone and rang the number of her shop.

Her assistant answered his call, telling him, 'She isn't here, Marco. She rang a couple of minutes ago to say that she's going to spend the rest of the day working at the apartment. Poor Emily, she still isn't properly over that wretched virus, is she?'

Marco made a noncommittal reply. He himself was never in anything other than the very best of health, but right now his mood was very much in need of the soothing touch that only Emily could give. She had an unexpectedly dry sense of humour, which, allied to her intelligence and acute perception, gave her the ability to make him laugh, sometimes when he least felt like doing so. Not that her sense of humour or his laughter had been very much in evidence these last few weeks, he recognised, frowning a little over this recognition. It surprised him how sharp the need he suddenly felt to be with her was. It was amazing what a bit of guilt could do, he decided as he told his PA that he, too, would be spending the afternoon working at home.

The best way to smooth over any upsets, so far as Marco was concerned, was in bed, where he knew he could quickly make Emily forget about everything other than his desire for her and hers for him…

* * *

Emily scowled as she worried over the message she had just picked up from one of her clients. The lady in question was a good customer, but Emily had still felt slightly wary when she'd been asked a while ago to take on the complete renovation of a property in Chelsea.

'Darling, darling, Emily,' Carla Mainwearing had trilled, 'I am so in love with your perfect sense of style that I want you to choose everything and I am going to put the house totally in your hands.'

Knowing Carla as she did, Emily had taken this with a pinch of salt and had therefore insisted on having her work approved at every single stage. Now Carla had left her a message saying that she hated the colour Emily had chosen for the walls of the property's pretty drawing room, and that she wanted it completely redone—at Emily's expense. Emily recalled that Carla had previously sanctioned the colour of the paint. But discretion was called for in telling her this, so rather than phone Carla back she decided to e-mail instead. Her laptop was in the study she shared with Marco, as were her files, so she made her way there, firmly ignoring the leaden weight of her earlier disappointment at Marco's refusal to join her for lunch.

Five minutes later, she was standing immobile in front of the study's window, her laptop and original purpose of coming to the study forgotten, as she stared in shocked horror at the vellum envelope she was holding. Her hand, actually not just her hand but her whole body, was trembling violently, as she felt unable to move. Waves of heat followed by icy chill surged through her body and somewhere some part of her mind managed to register the fact that what she was suffering was a classic reaction to extreme shock. She could hardly see the address on the envelope now through her blurred vision, but the crest on its left-hand front corner stood out, its *royal* crest, followed by the address: *HRH Prince Marco of Niroli…*

She didn't hear Marco's key in the apartment door, she didn't even hear him calling out her name. Her shock was so great that nothing could penetrate it. It encased her in a kind of bubble, which only concentrated the torment of what she was suffering and branded it on her brain so that it could never be forgotten. It was only finally pierced by the sudden opening of the study door as Marco walked in, but of course there was no way his arrival could ease her pain. Instead she gripped the envelope even tighter, her voice high and tight as she said thinly, 'Welcome home, *Your Highness*. I suppose I ought to curtsey to you.'

She waited, praying that he would laugh and tell her that she had got it all wrong, that the envelope she was holding, addressing him as Prince Marco of Niroli, was some silly mistake.

CHAPTER FIVE

LIKE a tiny candle flame shivering vulnerably in the dark, her hope trembled fearfully. And then the look in Marco's eyes extinguished it as cruelly as a hand placed callously over the face of a dying person to stem their last breath. It was over. Now, in this minute, this breath of time, they were finished. Emily knew that without the need for any words, the pain of that knowledge slamming a crippling body-blow into her. Her stomach felt as though she had plunged down a hundred floors in a high-speed lift.

'Give that to me,' Marco demanded, taking the envelope from her.

'It's too late to destroy the evidence, Marco.' Emily told him brokenly. 'I know the truth now. And I know how you've lied to me all this time, pretending to be something you aren't, letting me think…' She dug her teeth in her lower lip to try to force back her own pain. 'Do you think I haven't read the newspapers? Do you think the people of Niroli know that their prince is a liar? Or doesn't lying matter when you're a member of the Royal House?' she challenged him wildly.

'You had no right to go through my desk,' Marco shot back at her furiously, his male loathing at being caught off guard and forced into a position in which he was in the wrong making him determined to find something he could accuse Emily of. 'I thought we had an understanding that our private papers were our personal property and out of bounds,' he told her savagely. 'I trusted you…'

Emily could hardly believe what she was hearing.

'Did you? Is that why you hid this envelope under everything else?' she challenged him, shaking her head in answer to her own question. 'No, you didn't trust me, Marco, and you didn't trust me because you knew that I couldn't trust you. And you knew that because you are a liar, and liars don't trust people because they know that they themselves cannot be trusted.' She not only felt sick, she also felt as though she could hardly breathe. 'Everything I thought I knew about you is based on lies, everything. You aren't just Marco Fierezza, you are Prince Marco of Niroli. You yourself are a lie, Marco…'

'You are taking this far too personally. The reason I concealed my royal status had nothing whatsoever to do with you. It was a decision I made before I met you. My identity as plain Marco Fierezza is as real to me as though I were not a prince. It has nothing to do with you,' he repeated.

'How can you say that? It has everything to do with me, and if you had any shred of decency or morals you would know that. How could you lie about who you are and still live with me as intimately as we have lived together?' she demanded brokenly. 'How could you live with yourself, knowing that others, not just me, believed you, accepted and gave you their trust, when all the time—'

'Stop being so ridiculously dramatic,' Marco demanded fiercely. 'You are making too much of the situation.'

'Too much?' Emily almost screamed the words at him. 'Too much, when I have discovered that you have deceived me for the whole time we've been together? When did you plan to tell me, Marco? Perhaps you just planned to walk away without telling me anything? After all, what do my feelings matter to you?'

'Of course they matter,' Marco stopped her sharply. 'And it was in part to protect them, and you, that I decided not to inform you of the change in my circumstances when my grandfather first announced that he intended to step down from the throne and hand it on to me.'

'To protect me?' Emily almost choked on her fury. 'Hand on the throne? Don't bother continuing, Marco. No wonder you told me when you first took me to bed that all you wanted was sex. You *knew* that was the only kind of relationship there could ever be between us! You *knew* that one day you would be Niroli's king. No doubt you are expected to marry a princess. Is she picked out for you already, your *royal* bride?'

'No.'

Emily shrugged disdainfully. 'There's no point in replying because, whatever you say, I can't believe you, not now.'

'Emily, listen to me. This has gone far enough. You are being ridiculous. I know you have had a bit of a shock, but…'

'A bit of a shock? *A bit of a shock*?'

When she whirled round and headed for the door, Marco demanded, 'Where are you going?'

'To pack my things,' Emily told him fiercely. 'I'm leaving, Marco, right now. I can't and won't stay here with you. I feel I don't know you any more, and right now I don't really want to.'

'Don't be stupid. Where will you go? This is your home.'

'No, this is *your* apartment, it has never been my home. As to where I will go, I have a home of my own—remember?' she challenged him.

Marco frowned. 'Your house in Chelsea? But your assistant is living there.'

'She was living there, but she moved in with her new partner at the weekend, not that it or anything else in my life is any business of yours, Your Highness. Or should it be Your Majesty?'

'Emily.' He reached for her but she started to pull away from him, a look of angry contempt in her eyes that infuriated him. She had accused him of deceit and duplicity, but what about her actions? What about the fact that she had gone through his private papers behind his back? Her accusations had stung his pride, and now suddenly recognising that control of the situation had been taken from him and that she was about to walk out on him awakened all his most deeply held, atavistic male feelings about her. She was his—his until he chose to end their relationship.

Emily's eyes widened in mute shock as his fingers closed round her wrist, imprisoning her, and she saw the familiar look of arousal darkening his eyes. 'Let go of me,' she snapped. 'You can't really expect…'

'I can't really expect what?'

He wasn't going to let her go, Emily realised. She felt a quiver of sensation run down her spine—and it wasn't fear.

'What is it that I can't expect, Emily?' he repeated silkily. 'Is it that I can't expect to take you to bed any more—is that what you were going to say? That I can't expect to touch you or hold you?'

She had edged towards the study door as he'd advanced, but before she could open it and escape Marco reached past her, kicking it shut. Then, he placed his hands on it either side of her so that she was caught between the door and him. A tell-tale spiral of excitement was sizzling through her, its presence within her reminding her of the early days of their affair, when just to know that Marco wanted her and intended to have her was enough to leave her quivering on the edges of erotic need and surrender. Just as she was doing now. She tried to vocalise her denial, not just of her own arousal but also of Marco's in-

tentions, but the words were locked in her throat. Beneath the
soft wool of her sweater she could feel the growing hardening of her nipples and the desire-heavy weight of her breasts.
How long had it been since she had felt like this? How long
had it been since Marco had shown her this side of himself?
So long that she couldn't remember? So long that, because it
was happening now, she couldn't resist his allure?

Her heart jerked around inside her chest as though it were
suspended on a piece of elastic. The ache in her breasts curled
down through her belly to taunt her sex and tease from it a
throbbing pulse of excitement and longing. She realised that
she should be horrified by the way she was reacting to him,
in view of what she had now discovered, horrified and determined not to let him touch her, sickened by the thought of him
touching her. But she also knew that she wasn't; instead she
wanted him with a physical intensity that held her fast in an
unfamiliar, almost violent grip.

'Is that what you wanted to say to me, Emily—that I can't
make you want me any more, that I can't arouse you, that I
can't do this…?' He lifted his hand and stroked a fingertip
down the side of her neck and along her collar-bone, making
her shudder in violent erotic delight. He had moved closer to
her, so close that she could smell the familiar scent of his
cologne and the aroused heat of his body. Was it *that,* with its
powerful but subtle message of male sexuality, that was
turning her boneless with aching longing for him, even while
her mind was telling her that she should resist him, and that
this was no way for her to behave if she truly wanted him to
believe what she had said?

She should say something, tell him to stop; tell him that
there was no point in this for either of them. But she knew
that she wouldn't, just as she knew that some deep-rooted
female part of her wanted this show of male dominance from

him, wanted her own sense of fierce surging excitement, wanted and needed the pure, fierce searing heat of the mutual lust they had conjured up out of nowhere. She could quite easily have pushed past him, Emily knew, and she knew too that Marco would not try to stop her if she did. But the reality was that she didn't want to... The reality was that her body was possessed by an incendiary mix of anger and desire that took fire from Marco's determination to confront her with her own acceptance of his power to arouse her.

'But that would be a lie, wouldn't it?' Marco challenged her softly as he continued his relentless sensual assault, his lips brushing the bare flesh of her throat in between each word, imprisoning her in her own wild arousal.

'Wouldn't it?' he insisted as he slid his hand beneath her sweater and freed her breasts from the constriction of her bra. A low moan of unappeased longing bubbled in her throat as he fed her craving for his possession.

'You want more?' he demanded, his voice thickening and softening.

'No!' Emily lied. She could feel his hand cupping her breast and his fingertips stroking deliberately against her nipple again. She knew she couldn't hold out much longer against the dammed-up force of her own need. With a low sound of surrender, she reached blindly for him, drawing his head down towards her own, her lips parting for his kiss and the swift, exultant victory of his tongue.

She could feel the thick hardness of his manhood pressing against her body. In her mind's eye she visualised his naked body, familiar now after their years together, seeing behind her closed eyes the thick sheathing of smooth flesh over rigid muscle, where it rose from the dark silky thickness of hair. She could almost feel the smooth warmth of him, so enticingly supple to her touch, and so respon-

sive to the caress of her fingers and her mouth. Fresh
longing seized her. Impetuously she reached down between
their bodies to touch him, spanning his length with the
spread of her fingertips, and then stroking his thickness. A
deep purr of satisfaction gathered in her throat as she felt
him stiffen further and then pulse, becoming a moan of
out-of-control urgency when she felt him tugging at the fastening of her skirt.

Not even in their early days together had she experienced
this degree of intense need, she recognised. It was so much
bolder than anything she remembered feeling before; bolder,
and fiercer and hungrier—the sexual desire of a woman who
must be satisfied.

The demoralising fear that had in recent weeks sucked
from her any delight in their intimacy was as easily sloughed
off by their shared passion as were their clothes, unwanted en-
cumbrances that prevented her from taking all that she could.
Marco was driving both of them to that place where they had
no choice other than to plunge into the turbulent flood of the
maelstrom together.

Emily's fingers trembled over and tugged at his shirt
buttons and trouser fastenings, her endeavours deliberately
interrupted by him when he raked his teeth against the sensitive thrust of her nipple, causing her to gasp and then moan,
unable to do anything other than give in to the intensity of the
sensation he was inflicting on her. When pleasure was this
intense, she thought frantically, it bordered on the almost unendurable. And yet she wouldn't have wanted it any other way,
wouldn't have wanted any other man, wouldn't have been able
to reach this lack of inhibition with anyone else.

'You want me to stop?' Marco demanded. His breath
cooled the aching flesh that had been tormented by his erotic
caress, whilst the subtle touch of his fingertips continued to

play on her nipple, increasing its dark, swollen call for the renewed heat of his mouth.

Emily couldn't speak, she could barely stand up any more. But she knew Marco knew she wanted no such thing. She ran her hands along his sweat-dampened naked torso, deliberately bending her head so that she could graze her tongue-tip along his skin and taste the tangy maleness of his flesh, whilst she breathed in his aphrodisiacal Marco-drenched scent. At times like this, just the smell of him was enough to make her go weak with lust.

The ache deep inside her tightened and burned with a heat that could only be slaked by the possession of Marco's hard flesh filling her and completing her. She could feel the small hungry ripples of sensation caused by her muscles as they tightened with the need to have him fill the empty, wanton place inside her.

'Now, Marco,' she urged him fiercely, 'now!'

When he still waited, she looked up at him. She could see the dangerous look in his eyes, the darkness that said he was on the verge of wanting to punish her and that he was challenging her, needing to force her to acknowledge his supremacy, his ability to control her desire, arouse it and then satisfy it. It was too late for her to try to play him at his own game and deny him his triumph by pretending that she didn't want him. Her own need was too great and too immediate. She would have to punish herself later for her weakness. Right now, no price was too high to pay for the satisfaction her body craved. She had tried to resist…

'Now!' she repeated.

For a second, she thought he was going to refuse, but then he was reaching for her, lifting her up so that she could wrap her legs tightly round him whilst he thrust firmly into her in one long, slow, deliberate movement that made her shudder violently. As he withdrew her muscles tightened, protesting around him, not wanting to let him go, and were then rewarded for their adoration by the almost mind-altering sensation of his second, stronger, deeper thrust. The sensitive nerve-endings in her flesh wept with joy at the intensity. Instinctively Emily drew in her muscles around him, savouring the sensation.

She could feel his hot breath in her ear, the tip of his tongue tracing the curls of flesh. She felt his teeth against the sensitive cord in her neck. Her whole body was being possessed by a pleasure so heightened she thought she might die from it.

'Marco…' She moaned his name as a plea, striking a solitary note of female praise as he thrust deeper, harder and faster now.

'Mmm…more. Marco…more!' she urged him, gasping out aloud in delight as he obeyed her and his movements became fast and rhythmic. Then he drove them to their climaxes, and she was left so boneless and weak that she collapsed helplessly against him, trembling in the aftermath.

The heat of the fury that had driven him was cooling on his sweat-slicked skin. Where he should have felt satisfaction and triumph at making Emily acknowledge that he could still arouse her, Marco could only feel a dark sense of stark awareness that he had crossed over a boundary he should not have breached. In forcing Emily to give in to the desire he had summoned in her, he'd also forced himself to acknowledge his need for her. A fleeting need, brought on by his justifiable anger, he assured himself, that was all! It meant nothing in the broader picture of his life.

'I think we both needed that,' he told her coolly, 'and perhaps it was a fitting end to our relationship, a tribute to the mutual attraction that brought us together.'

Emily couldn't believe what she had done—and what she

might have betrayed. She couldn't bear the thought of Marco thinking now how stupid she had been, maybe guessing she had dreamed that, one day, he might fall in love with her as she had done with him. A wave of irritation surged through her—not against him, but against herself. What a fool she had been, deliberately blinding herself to reality and fixating on something that her common sense could have warned her wouldn't possibly happen. If Marco had really loved her he would have told her so. But he hadn't, and he never would. She had deceived herself just as much as Marco had deceived her, and if anything her crime against herself was even greater than his. The fierce turbulent, almost torrid heat of their love-making had subsided now, and her anger had burned down into stark bleakness and grinding pain. Her dreams had been swept aside, shown to be pitifully worthless. Marco was a stranger to her, but no more so than she felt at this moment she was to herself.

'Mutual attraction then, but perhaps mutual contempt now,' she answered Marco pointedly. 'I'm not the naïve girl that I was when we first became lovers, Marco.'

'Meaning what?' he challenged her, frowning.

'Meaning that I've learned enough about sex from you to know that it isn't always used as an expression of positive emotions. It's common knowledge these days that couples on the verge of splitting up do sometimes use sex as a way of venting their negative feelings. Some couples say that they had the best sex of their relationship when the emotional side of it was dying. Of course, I know that *we* aren't emotionally intimate with one another.' What she meant of course, Emily admitted, was that Marco had never been emotionally close with her, because he didn't want to be, whilst she had had to struggle not to be close when she'd wanted to be. 'But I think both of us would accept that the break-up of any relationship—even one like ours—does bring things to the surface that aren't easy to accept.'

Marco's frown deepened. She was now being far more matter-of-fact about their relationship ending than he had expected—and he didn't like that! But he was being ridiculous. He should feel very relieved that she was being so sensible, especially after her earlier, uncharacteristic outburst…

CHAPTER SIX

FROM his seat on the royal jet, Marco looked down onto his family's private runway at Niroli's airport to where a group of formally dressed courtiers and officials were waiting to greet him. The ostrich-feather plumes of their dress hats fluttered in the breeze as they stood straight-backed, ignoring the heat of the sun. Marco's lips twisted with irony at the thought of the heavily gold-braided, bemedalled uniform that his grandfather had sent him, along with strict instructions that he must wear it when he landed and was greeted by the courtly welcoming committee. In fact, the uniform, appropriate for the rank of Lieutenant Colonel in Niroli's ancient Royal Guard, was lying in its leather dress-trunk in the plane's hold, whilst he wore his own handmade Saville Row suit. His grandfather wouldn't be pleased. But Marco intended to let him, and the court, know right from the word go that he would make his own decisions and judgements and he wouldn't allow them to force theirs on him.

Emily would have appreciated and understood his decision, though she would probably have laughed gently, and teased him as well into wearing that undeniably magnificent, beautifully tailored uniform. Emily…he tried to thrust the thought of her away from him, along with the erotic mental image of her alongside him in his bed that was forming inside his head, but it was too late; she was there, smiling at him, wanting him, as he ached for her. What the hell was this?

He stood up so abruptly that the young Niroli air force aide-de-camp, who'd been sent to escort him home, was caught off guard, and his own attempt to get to his feet before Marco was severely hampered by his ceremonial sword. The red-faced young man saluted as he semi-stuttered, 'Highness, if you wish to have more time in order to prepare, then please allow me—'

'No, I am ready,' Marco told the aide shortly and then relented when he saw his anxious expression. It was not the lad's fault—and he was little more than a boy, a scion of one of Niroli's foremost titled families. Marco had chosen to be the man he was, rather than the grandson his grandfather wanted him to be. Damn Emily for pursuing him like this, insinuating herself into his thoughts where she now had no right to be! Her abrupt departure from his apartment had decided him that he should leave London earlier than he had originally planned—much to his grandfather's delight. Marco suspected the old king would not have been so cock-a-hoop over his 'victory' if he had known that it owed less to his own power than to his grandson's loss of his bed-mate.

The aide-de-camp, who was carrying his own plumed hat as protocol demanded, stood beside his king-to-be as the doors to the royal jet were opened. He bowed as Marco walked past him and stepped out onto the gangway steps and into Niroli's sunshine. Just for a few seconds, Marco stood motionless and ramrod-straight at the top of the steps, not because he was the island's future ruler, but because he was one of its returning sons. He had almost forgotten the unique scent of sunshine and sea, mimosa and lemons, all of which hit him on a surge of hot wind. Not even the strong smell of jet fuel and tarmac could detract from them, and Marco felt emotion sting his eyes: this was his home, his country, and the crowds he could see lining the wide straight road that ran from the airport to the main town were his people. Many of them had not had the benefit of being part of a wider, modern world, but he intended to change that. He would give to Niroli's young the opportunities his grandfather's old-fashioned rule had denied them. Determinedly, Marco stepped forward. The waiting military band broke into Niroli's national anthem and the waiting officials removed their hats and bowed their heads. Their faces were familiar to Marco, although more wrinkled and lined than he remembered—the faces of old men.

As he reached his grandfather's most senior minister the elderly gentleman placed his hands on Marco's arms, greeting him with a traditional continental embrace. His voice shook with emotion and Marco could see that beneath his proud, stern expression and the determinedly upright stance there was a very aged, tired man, who probably would have preferred to spend his last years with his grandchildren than doing his king's bidding. Tactfully, Marco adjusted his own walking pace to that of the courtiers surrounding him as they escorted him unsteadily to the waiting open-topped royal limousine.

At least his grandfather hadn't sent the coronation carriage to collect him, Marco reflected ruefully; its motion was sickeningly rocky and its velvet padded seats unpleasantly hard.

This should be his moment of triumph, the public endorsement of the strength he had gained in becoming his own man. Soon the power of the Royal House of Niroli would become his, and he would step into his grandfather's shoes and fulfil his destiny. So why didn't he feel more excited, and why was there this sense of emptiness within him, this sense of loss, of something missing?

The cavalcade started to move, the waiting crowds began

to cheer, children clutching Niroli flags and leaning dangerously into the road, the better to see him. Marco lifted his hand
and began to wave. The cool air-conditioned luxury of the
limo protected him from the midday heat. *But what about the
people? They must be feeling the heat, Marco.* As clearly as
though she were seated at his side, he could hear Emily's
gently reproachful voice. Angrily he banished it. The limousine travelled a few more yards and then Marco reached
forward, rapping on the glass separating him from the driver
and an armed guard.

'Highness?' the guard queried anxiously.

'Stop the car!' Marco ordered. 'I want to get out and walk.'
As he reached to open his door the guard looked horrified.
'Sire,' he protested, 'the king…it may not be safe.'

Marco's eyebrow rose. 'Knowing my grandfather as I do,
I cannot imagine he has not had ordered that plain-clothes
security men be posted amongst the crowd. Besides, these are
our people, not our enemy.'

As they saw Marco stepping out of the limousine the crowd
fell silent. At no time in living memory had their ruler done
anything so informal as walk amongst them. Marco shook the
gnarled hands of working men, his smile causing pretty girls
to glow with excitement and older women to feel a reawak-
ening frisson of their youths.

One aged woman pushed her way through the people to
reach him. Marco could see from her traditional peasant
costume that she came from the mountains of Niroli. Her back
was bent from long years spent working in the orange groves
and vineyards that covered their lower slopes, her face as brown
and lined as a wrinkled walnut. But there was still a fiery flash
of pride in her dark eyes and as she held out to him the clumsy
leather purse she had obviously made herself Marco felt as
though a giant hand were gripping his heart in a tight vice.

'Highness, please take this humble gift,' she begged him. 'May it always be kept full, just like the coffers and the nurseries of the House of Niroli.' It was plain that the old peasant could ill afford to give him anything. Indeed, Marco felt he should be the one to give something to her, so he was not surprised to see the angry, hostile glower on the face of the shabbily dressed youth at her side.

'This is your grandson?' Marco asked her as he thanked her for her gift.

'Aye, he is, sire, and he shames me with his sullen looks and lack of appreciation for all that we have here on our island.'

'That is because we have nothing!' the youth burst out angrily, his face now seemingly on fire with emotion. 'We have nothing, whilst others have everything! We come to the town, and we see foreigners with their expensive yachts and their fancy clothes. Our king bends over backwards to welcome them, whilst we mountain-dwellers do not even have electricity. They look at us as though we are nothing, and that is because, to our king, we *are* nothing!'

Suddenly, like a cloud passing over the sun, the mood of the crowd gathered around Marco had changed. He could see the anger in the faces of the group of rough-looking, poorly dressed young men who had joined the outspoken youth. The first of his grandfather's security guards rushed to protect Marco, but very firmly he stepped between them, saying clearly, 'It is good to know that the people of Niroli are able to speak their minds freely to me. This issue of getting electricity to the more remote parts of our island is one that has, I know, taxed His Majesty's thoughts for a long time.' Marco put his hand on the angry youth's shoulder, drawing him closer to him, whilst he gave the hovering guards a small dismissive shake of his head. He could see the grateful tears in the old peasant woman's eyes.

'My grandson speaks without thinking,' she told him huskily. 'But, at heart, he is a good boy and as devoted to the king as anyone.'

The youth's friends were hurrying him away and Marco allowed himself to be escorted back to his limo. Once inside, he realised that he was still holding the old woman's carefully made purse. There was anger in his heart now, pressing down on him like an unwanted heavy weight. Niroli's royal family was the richest in the world and yet some of its subjects were living lives of utmost poverty. He could well imagine how upset and shocked Emily would have been if she had witnessed what had just happened. The leather purse felt soft and warm to his touch. He was the one who should be giving to his people, not the other way around. His time away from the island had changed him more than he had realised, Marco acknowledged, and somehow he didn't think his grandfather was going to like what he had in mind…

Huddled into an armchair in the sitting room of her small Chelsea house, a prettily embroidered throw wrapped around her like a comfort blanket, Emily let the full rip-tide of her anguish take her over. What was the point in trying to fight it or escape it? The reality was that Marco, no, *Prince Marco, soon to be King Marco*, she corrected herself miserably, had gone, not just from her life, but from Britain itself, to return to his home, his throne and his people. Ultimately her place in his life would be filled by someone else. She gave a small low cry as more pain seized her, and then reminded herself angrily that the man she loved did not exist; he had been a creation of her own imagination and his deceit. Everything they had shared had been based on lies; every time he had held her or touched her she had been giving the whole of herself to him, whilst he had been withholding virtually everything of his true self. But even knowing this, as the numbing shock of her discovery of the truth rose and retreated, she was left with the agonising reality that she still loved him.

As much as she despised herself for not being able to cease wanting him, because she knew just how much he had deceived her, her self-contempt could not drive out her love.

What was he doing now? Was he thinking at all of her? Missing her? *Stop it, stop it,* all her inner protective instincts demanded in agony. She must not do this to herself! She must accept that he had gone, and that she had to find a way of living without him and the comfort of being able to look back and know that they had shared something very special. It was over, they were over, and her pride was demanding that she accept that and get on with her life. She was as much a fool for letting him into her thoughts now as she had been for letting him into her life. There was one thing for sure: he would not be thinking about her. He would not have given her a single thought since she had walked out of his apartment, following that dreadful discovery and the bitterly corrosive row that had ended their relationship

What a total fool she had been for deluding herself into thinking that he would ever return her love…

CHAPTER SEVEN

'So, Marco, what is this that the Chief of Police tells me about your welcome parade? About your being threatened by some wretched insurrectionist from the mountains? Probably one of the Viallis. Mind you, you have only yourself to blame. Had you not taken it into your head to so rashly get out of the car, it would not have happened. You must remember that you are my heir and Niroli's next king. It is not wise to court danger.'

'There wasn't any real danger. The boy—for he was little more than that—was simply voicing—'

'His hostility to the throne!' King Giorgio interrupted Marco angrily.

His grandfather had aged since he had last seen him, but the old patriarch still had about him an awesome aura of power, Marco admitted ruefully. The problem was that it no longer particularly impressed Marco—he had power of his own now, power that came from living his life in his own way. He knew that his grandfather sensed this in him and that it irked him. That was why he insisted on taking his grandson to task over the incident at his welcoming parade.

'My feeling was that the boy was more frustrated and resentful than hostile.'

Marco watched his grandfather. There was a larger issue at

stake here than the boy's angry words, one which Marco felt was essential, but which he knew wasn't something his grandfather would be happy to discuss.

Nevertheless, Marco had been doing some investigation of his own, and what he had discovered had highlighted potential problems within Niroli that needed addressing before they developed into much more worrying conflicts.

'The boy was complaining about the lack of an electricity supply to his village. He resents the fact that visitors to our country have benefits that some of our own people do not.' Marco held his ground as his grandfather's fist came crashing down on the desk between them.

'I will not listen to this foolish nonsense. Tourists bring money into the country and, naturally, we have to lure them here by providing them with the kind of facilities they are used to.'

'Whilst some amongst our people go without them?' Marco challenged him coolly. 'Angry young men do sometimes behave rashly. But surely it is our duty to equip our subjects with what they need to move into the twenty-first century? Our schoolchildren cannot learn properly without access to computers, and if we deprive them of the ability to do so then we will be maintaining an underclass within the heart of our country.'

'You dare to lecture me on how to rule?' the king bellowed. 'You, who turned your back on Niroli to live a life of your own choosing in London?'

'You're the one who has summoned me back, Nonno,' Marco reminded him, lowering his voice and deliberately using his childhood pet name for his grandfather in an attempt to soften the old man's mood. It was easy sometimes to forget his grandfather was ninety, yet still immoveable about what the right thing was for Niroli and its people. Marco didn't want to upset the king too much.

'Because I had no other choice,' Giorgio growled. 'You are my direct heir, Marco, for all that you choose to behave like a commoner, rather than a member of the ruling House of Niroli. At least you had the sense to leave that…that floozy you were living with behind when you returned home.'

Anger flashed in Marco's eyes. It was typical of his grandfather to have found out as much about his private life in London as he could. It also infuriated him that Giorgio should refer to Emily in that way and dismiss their relationship. Worse, it felt as though, somehow, his grandfather had touched a raw place within him that he didn't want to admit existed, never mind be reminded about. Because, even though he didn't want to own up to it, he was missing Emily. Marco shrugged the thought aside. So what if he was? Wasn't it only natural that his body, deprived of the sexual pleasure it had shared with hers, should ache a little?

'As to what we agreed, it was simply that I should *initially* return to Niroli alone,' Marco pointed out.

Immediately the king's anger returned. 'What do you mean, "initially"?'

When Marco didn't answer him, the old man bellowed, 'You will not bring her here, Marco! I will not allow it. You are my heir, and you have a position to maintain. The people—'

Marco knew that he should reassure his grandfather and tell him he had no intention of bringing Emily to Niroli, but instead he said coolly, 'The people, our people, will, I am sure, have more important things to worry about than the fact that I have a mistress—things like the fact that ten per cent of them do not have electricity.'

'You are trying to meddle in things that are not your concern,' the king told him sharply. 'Take care, Marco, otherwise, you will have people thinking that you are more fitted to be a dissident than a leader. To rule, you must command respect and in order to do that you must show a strong hand. The people are your children and need to look up to you as their father, as someone wiser than them.'

This was an issue on which he and his grandfather would never see eye to eye, Marco knew…

'Emily, why don't you call it a day and go home? No one else will come into the shop now and you don't have any more client appointments. I know you hate me keeping on about this, but you really don't look at all well. I can lock up the premises for you.'

Emily forced herself to give her assistant an I'm-all-right smile. Jemma wasn't wrong, though she didn't like the fact that the girl had noticed how unwell she looked, because she didn't want to have to answer questions about the cause. 'It's kind of you to offer to do that, Jemma,' she answered, 'but…'

'But you're missing Marco desperately, and you don't want to go back to an empty house?' Jemma suggested gently, her words slicing through the barriers Emily had tried so desperately to maintain.

She could feel betraying tears burning the backs of her eyes. She had tried so very hard to pretend that she didn't mind that she and Marco had split up, but it was obvious that her assistant hadn't been deceived.

'It had to end, given Marco's royal status,' she told Jemma, trying to keep her voice light. Initially, she had worried about revealing the truth of Marco's real identity. But, in the end, she'd had no need to do so because her assistant had seen one of many articles appearing in the press about Marco's return to Niroli; most of them had been accompanied by photographs of his cavalcade and the crowd waiting to welcome him. 'I just wish that he had told me the truth about himself, Jemma,' Emily said in a low voice, unable to conceal her hurt.

'I can understand that,' Jemma agreed. 'But according to what I've read, Marco came over here incognito because he wanted to prove himself in his own right. He had already done that by the time he met you, yet I suppose he could hardly tell you his real identity—not only would it have been difficult for him to just turn round and say, "Oh, by the way, perhaps I ought to tell you that I'm a prince," he most probably wanted you to value him for himself, not for his title or position.'

Emily could see the logic of Jemma's argument, and she knew it was one that Marco himself would have used—had they ever got to the stage of discussing the issue.

'Marco didn't tell me because he *didn't want* to tell me,' she retorted, trying to harden her heart against its betraying softening. 'To him, I was just a…a…temporary bed-mate— a diversion he could enjoy, before he left me to get on with the really serious business of his life and return to Niroli.'

'I think I know how you must be feeling,' Jemma allowed, 'but I did read in one article that it wasn't until the death of his parents in an accident that Marco became the next in line to the throne. I'm sure he didn't tell you because he assumed he would continue to live in London with you anonymously.'

'I meant nothing to him.'

'I can't believe that, Emily. You always seemed so happy together, and so well suited.'

'It's pointless talking about it, or him, now. It's over.'

'Is it? I can't help thinking that there's a lot of unfinished business between the two of you,' Jemma told her softly. 'I know from what you told me that you left the apartment virtually as soon as you discovered the truth. You must have still been in shock when that happened, and my guess is that Marco must have been equally shocked, although for differ- ent reasons.'

'Reasons like being found out, you mean, and resenting me being the one to end our relationship, not him?' Emily asked her bitterly.

'So, you wouldn't be interested if he got in touch with you?' Jemma probed quietly.

'That isn't going to happen.' But she knew from the look in her assistant's eyes that Jemma had guessed her weakness and how much a foolish, treacherous part of her still longed for him.

'Be fair to yourself, Emily,' Jemma told her. 'You and Marco have history together, and there are still loose ends for you that need proper closure, questions you need to ask and answers Marco needs to give you. A poisoned wound can't heal,' she pointed out wisely. 'And until you get that poison of your break-up out of your system, you won't heal.'

'I'm fine,' Emily lied defensively.

'No, you aren't,' Jemma responded firmly. 'Just look at yourself. You aren't eating, you're losing weight and you obviously aren't happy.'

'It's just this virus, that's all. I can't seem to throw it off properly,' Emily told her. But she knew that Jemma wasn't deceived.

Emily was still thinking about her conversation with Jemma more than two hours later as she wandered aimlessly round her showroom, pausing to straighten a line of already perfectly straight sample swatches. Jemma had been right about her not wanting to return to her empty house and correct too about how much she was missing Marco.

It had been all very well telling herself that he had lied to her and that she was better off without him. The reality was very different: the empty space he'd left in her life had been taken over by the unending misery of living without him. He had only been gone just a short time, but already she had lost count of the number of times every night she woke up reaching out for him in her bed, only to be filled with anguish when the reality that he wasn't there hit her once more. No matter how hard she worked, she couldn't fill her mind with enough things to block out the knowledge that Marco had left; that she wouldn't be going home to him; that never again would he hold her, or touch her, or kiss her; never ever again. It was over, and somehow she must find a way to rebuild her life, although right now she had no idea how she was going to accomplish that. To make matters worse, as Jemma had already commented, she was losing weight and felt unable to eat properly. Emily had put it down to a flu bug she had picked up earlier in the year. She just couldn't seem to get rid of it.

Allied to which, she had an even nastier heartache bug, Emily recognised. Did Marco think of her at all, now he was living his new life, Emily wondered miserably, or was he far too busy planning his future? A future that was ultimately, and surely, bound to include a wife. Pain seized her, ripping at her all her defences, leaving her exposed to the reality of what loving him really meant. Marco…Marco… How could this have happened to her? How could she have avoided falling in love with him? What was he doing right now? Who was he with? His grandfather? His family? She mustn't do this to herself, Emily warned herself tiredly. It served no purpose, other than to reinforce what she already knew, and that was that she loved a man who did not love her. She reached for her coat. She might as well go home.

'What is this I hear about you returning to London? I will not allow you to leave Niroli to go to London. What possible reason could you have for wanting to be there?'

Marco had to struggle to stop himself from responding in kind to his grandfather's angry interrogation.

'You know why I need to return. I have certain business matters to attend to there,' he answered suavely instead.

'I do not permit it.'

'No? That is your choice, Grandfather, but I still intend to go. You see, I do not need your permission.'

Obstinately they eyed each other, two alpha males who knew that, according to the law of the jungle, only one of them could truly hold the reins of power. Marco had no intention of allowing his grandfather to dominate him. He knew well enough that once he let him have the upper hand, the king would treat him with contempt. Giorgio was the kind of man who would rather die with his sword in his hand, so to speak, than allow a younger rival to take it from him. The truth was that Marco could have dealt with the business that was taking him to the UK from the island, and that, in part, his decision to go to London in spite of his grandfather's objections had been made publicly to underline his own determination and status. It was more than two weeks since he had first arrived on Niroli, and there hadn't been a single day when he and his grandfather hadn't clashed like two Titans. Every attempt he had made to talk to Giorgio about doing something to help the poorer inhabitants of the island had been met with a furious tirade about what a waste of money this would be, and a threat to royal rule.

Marco was determined that electricity should be made available to those living in the more remote villages, and his grandfather was equally adamant that he was not prepared to sanction it.

'Very well, then, I shall pay for it myself,' Marco had told him grimly. But the reality was that things were not as simple as that: the topography of the mountain region meant that they would need to bring in expert outside help, and it was of course Vialli country.

Marco suspected that King Giorgio was being difficult for the sake of being difficult, more than anything else. He could also admit to himself that his years in London running his own life and not having to worry about consulting anyone about his decisions was now making it very difficult for him to conform to the role of king-in-waiting. He was very much the junior partner in this new relationship. He started to walk away.

'Marco, I trust that this visit of yours to London does not have anything to do with that woman you were bedding?'

Marco swung round and looked at his grandfather, his voice flattened by the weight of his fury as he demanded, 'And if it does?'

'Then I forbid you to see her,' his grandfather told him fiercely. 'The future King of Niroli does not bed some commoner—a divorcée, with no pedigree and no money.'

'No one tells me who I can and cannot take to my bed, Grandfather, not even you.' Marco didn't wait to hear what the older man might say in reply. Instead he strode out of the room, fighting to dampen down the heat of the fury burning along his veins. The bright sunshine that had warmed the air earlier that day was turning to vivid dusk as he left the palace. He had refused the offer of a suite of rooms within its walls, preferring instead to stay in the nearby villa he had inherited from his parents. His grandfather hadn't been too pleased about that, but Marco had refused to give in. It was very important to him that he retained his privacy and independence. However, right now, it wasn't the villa he was heading for as he climbed into his personal car. He was bound for the airport, and a flight to London, despite his grandfather's opposition. How dared Giorgio attempt to tell him that he couldn't sleep with Emily? He glanced at the clock on the dashboard of his car. It would be early evening in London, just after six o'clock. Emily would most probably have left her shop and be on her way home.

Emily! It hadn't needed his grandfather's mention of her to bring her into his thoughts. Indeed, it had surprised and disconcerted him to discover just how much she had been there since they had parted. It was only because he was discovering that he wasn't enjoying sleeping alone, he assured himself. The fact that Emily was so constantly in his thoughts was simply his mind playing tricks and had no personal relevance for him.

He turned his thoughts back to his grandfather; despite his frustration with the older man's arrogant and domineering attitude, he was very aware that the king was not in the best of health. He must continue to temper his reaction to him as much as he could. But it wasn't easy.

'Emily, why don't you go and see your doctor?' Jemma suggested, her face shadowed with concern as she studied Emily's wan complexion.

'There's no need for that. It's as I've said before—it's just that virus hanging around,' Emily explained tiredly. 'The doctor will only tell me to take some paracetamol, and that it's bound to wear off soon.'

'You've been sick every morning this week, and now you've left your lunch. You look exhausted.'

'I need a holiday, some sunshine to perk me up a bit, that's all,' Emily replied lightly. She didn't want to continue this discussion, but she didn't want to hurt Jemma's feelings either; she knew her assistant was genuinely concerned about her.

'You certainly need something—or someone,' Jemma agreed forthrightly, leaving Emily regretting that she had ever allowed her guard to slip and admit that she was missing Marco.

'Why don't I pop across the road and bring you back a sandwich and a cup of coffee?' Jemma suggested.

'Coffee?' Emily shuddered with revulsion. The very

thought made her feel nauseous. 'I couldn't face it,' she protested. 'Just thinking about the smell makes me feel sick.'

'I think you're right about you needing a holiday,' Jemma told her firmly.

Emily gave her a forced smile. The truth was, what she needed and wanted more than anything else was Marco—Marco's arms—to hold her close, Marco's body next to hers in bed at night and, most of all, Marco's love, and the knowledge that it would last a lifetime. But she wasn't going to be given any of those. She hadn't realised just how hard it would be for her after their relationship had ended. The emotional pain she was suffering now was almost unendurable; it tore through her emotions like a fever in her blood, burning up her immunity. Every night when she went to bed she told herself that it couldn't get any worse and that soon she would start to feel better. But every morning when she woke up it *was* worse. She hated herself for wanting him like this after the way he had deceived her. However, hating herself couldn't stop her from loving him...

The business that had brought Marco to London had been concluded, and the first consignment of the generators he'd bought at his own expense were already on their way to the airport to be flown out by a cargo plane to Niroli. He had been on his way back to his hotel when, for no logical reason he could find, he had leaned forward and told the cab driver he had changed his mind, then given him the address of Emily's small shop in Chelsea. He didn't owe her anything; she had refused to let him fully explain to her that his decision to conceal his real identity had been one he had made long before he had met her. Sleeping dogs were best left to lie and, anyway, their relationship would have had to end sooner or later.

Marco's purchase of the generators would infuriate his

grandfather, as would the knowledge that he was seeing Emily, he acknowledged as he paid the cab fare and looked along the pretty Chelsea street basking in afternoon sunshine. So was that why he was here? To infuriate his grandfather? Marco's mouth curled in sardonic awareness. The days when he had been immature enough to need to infuriate the man he had seen as an unwanted authority figure were long gone. No, he didn't want to upset his grandfather at all. But he was not quite ready to let go or move on. Therefore a little reinforcement to him of the fact that Marco wasn't going to be dictated to wouldn't do any harm. Plus, he liked the idea of dealing with two separate issues at a single stroke—Emily had walked out on him without giving him the chance to explain his situation to her rationally. She owed him that opportunity and his pride demanded that she retract the contemptuously angry insults she had thrown at him. That was what had brought him here: his own pride. And no one, not his grandfather, and certainly not Emily herself, was going to stop him from seeing her and demanding that his pride was satisfied. And his body, which needed satisfaction so desperately? Any woman could provide him with that! Marco dismissed the throb that was increasing with every step that took him closer to Emily. No way would he ever allow one woman to dominate his senses to that extent.

He could see into the window of her shop-cum-showroom from where he was standing. The simple elegance of the set Emily had created was both immediately refreshing and soothing on his eye. She had a remarkable, indeed an inspired, gift for transforming the dull and utilitarian. His Niroli villa could certainly do with her skills!

Marco began to frown. Whilst he had to admit how poorly the décor of his villa compared with that of the London apartment Emily had decorated for him, he could well imagine his grandfather's reaction if he were to return to the island with her at his side, claiming that he needed an interior designer. His grandfather wouldn't believe him for one moment and he would think that Marco was deliberately flouting his orders. Perhaps he should flout them in this way, Marco reflected ruefully; it would be a sure and certain way of making his grandfather understand that he wasn't going to be pushed around. And Emily's presence on Niroli and in his life wouldn't directly impact on their subjects.

The more he thought about it, the more Marco could see the benefit to himself of Emily's temporary and brief presence on the island as a sharp warning to his grandfather not to trespass into his privacy. Certainly in the unlikely event of Emily being willing to return to Niroli with him, he would want her to share his bed. He would be a fool not to, given the level of his current sexual hunger. Was that really why he was here now? Not solely because of his pride, but because he still wanted her too?

No!

He was already pushing open the shop door, but then he paused, half inclined to turn round and walk away just to prove how unfounded that motivation was. However, it was too late for him to change his mind: Emily had seen him.

She was sitting behind a desk talking with her assistant, Jemma, and the first thing Marco noticed was how much weight she had lost and how pale and fragile she looked. Because of him? It shocked him to discover that a part of him wanted to believe it was because she was missing him. Why? *Why* should he feel like this when, in the past, with other women, he had been only too pleased to see them move on to a new partner after he had broken up with them. But in the past he hadn't continued to want those other women, had he?

He pushed his thoughts to one side, watching Emily's eyes widen as she looked up and saw him, the blood rushing to her face, turning it a deep pink. He saw her lips frame his name. She pushed back her chair to stand up and then he saw her sway and start to crumple, as though her body were no more than one of the swathes of fabric draped over the back of another chair nearby. That deep pink glow had receded from her cheeks, leaving her so pale that she looked almost bloodless.

He reacted immediately and instinctively, pushing his way through the pieces of furniture, reaching her just in time to hear her saying huskily, 'It's all right, I'm not going to faint,' before she did exactly that.

Through the roaring blur of sick dizziness, Emily could hear voices: Jemma's sharp with anxiety, Marco's harsher than she wanted it to be, their words, moving giddily in and out of one another, weaving through the darkness she was trying to free herself from. Then she felt Marco's arms tightening around her, holding her, and she exhaled on a small sigh of relief, knowing she was safe and that she didn't have to battle on alone any more. Gratefully she let the darkness take her as she slid into a faint.

'What the hell's going on?' Marco asked Jemma abruptly. Any idiotic thought he might have entertained that there was something ego-boosting about Emily's reaction to him had disappeared now, banished by his realisation of just how fragile she was. In all the time they had been together he had never once known her faint, or even say that she thought she might be going to, which made it all the more shocking that she had done so now.

'I wish I knew,' Jemma admitted. 'What I do know is that she hasn't been eating properly. She says it's because of that flu bug she had earlier in the year. She just can't seem to throw it off. She isn't the only one, of course. I read in a newspaper the other day that many people are still suffering from its after-effects. The health authorities say that the best cures are rest and sunshine to build up the immune system. Emily's admitted as much herself, although I can't see her taking a holiday. I'm so glad you're here. I've been really worried about her.'

'Will you both please stop talking about me as though I don't exist? I'm all right...' The blackness was receding and with it her nausea. She was sitting on a chair—Marco must have put her there, and no doubt he was the one who had pushed her head down towards her knees as well. She turned her head slightly and saw that he was standing next to her. So close to her, in fact, that she could easily have reached out and touched him. Weak tears stung her eyes, causing her to make a small anguished sound of protest.

'Emily?' She could feel Marco's hand on her shoulder, her flesh responding to its familiar warmth, weirdly both soothed and excited by it. The hardness of his voice lacerated both her pride and her heart. This was not how she would have wanted them to meet for the first time after their split; she must seem so vulnerable and needy, virtually forcing Marco to step in and manage things. Fate wasn't being very kind to her at the moment, she reflected wearily. She held her breath as Marco crouched down beside her, struggling to lift her head and fight off the swimming sensation within it. She would have given a lot for him not to have seen her like this, not to have witnessed her humiliating loss of consciousness.

'There's no need to fuss. I'm fine,' she repeated, sounding as steady as she could.

'Don't listen to her, Marco. She isn't all right at all. She's hardly eating and when she does, she's sick.'

'Jemma!' Emily warned sharply.

'Jemma is hardly breaking the Official Secrets Act,' Marco defended her assistant dryly. 'After all, she hasn't told me anything I can't see for myself. And, besides, there's no reason why I shouldn't know, is there?'

None, except her pride and her aching heart, Emily admitted inwardly. And, of course, those wouldn't matter to Marco. 'I don't know what you are doing here, *Your Highness*,' she addressed him, deliberately underlining his title.

He couldn't just walk away and leave her like this, Marco decided. So what was he going to do? His return flight was already scheduled for later this evening. Emily wasn't his responsibility. She was an adult. There was no good cause for him to involve himself here. But another voice deep inside him told him it was too late for such arguments. He had already made his decision.

'I came to see you because I've got a business proposition to put to you,' he told Emily levelly. He could see her eyes widening with confusion and disbelief. She was lifting her hand to her head, as though she couldn't take in what he was saying. Seeing her look so thin and unwell touched an unfamiliar chord inside him, which he crushed down the instant he felt it.

Emily's head was aching painfully. She was finding it hard enough to grasp that Marco was actually here, never mind anything else. Her thoughts were in complete disarray. She couldn't really comprehend what he was saying. It was difficult enough for her to focus simply on stopping her heart from spinning and shaking her body with the force of its frantic beats, without having to think logically and calmly as well. It had upset her far more than she wanted to admit that the sight of him should have affected her to such an extent that she had collapsed. Worryingly, even now her senses were still clinging possessively to the memory of being held in his arms as he had caught her. Part of her, the sensible part, she told herself firmly, wanted to put as much distance between them as she could, to protect herself from making it even more obvious just how intensely aware of him she was. Whilst the other part longed to be as intimately close to him as it was possible to be: body to body, skin to skin, mouth to mouth— heart to heart.

'A business proposition?' she repeated uncertainly. 'What exactly does that mean, Marco? I'm an interior designer.'

'Exactly,' Marco agreed, 'and a very good one.'

Marco was praising her? *Flattering her?* Why? she wondered suspiciously. It was totally out of character for him to behave like this.

'Since it could be a while before I formally take over from my grandfather, instead of moving into the palace and being cooped up in a suite of rooms there,' Marco told her, 'I've moved into a villa I inherited from my parents. It's in the old part of the town and it's badly in need of modernisation. I want a designer who knows what she's doing and, just as important, one who knows my taste.'

It took several seconds for the full meaning of what he was saying to sink in. But once it had, Emily could hardly conceal her disbelief.

'Are you saying that you want to commission *me* to be that designer?' she asked Marco faintly.

'Yes, why not?' Marco confirmed.

'Why not?' Emily stared at him, as her heart lurched crazily into her ribs. 'Marco, we were lovers, and now our relationship is over. You must see that I can't just let you commission me as your designer as though everything that took place between us never happened.'

'Of course not, Emily. You never let me explain properly to you why I didn't tell you about Niroli or my role there.' Out of the corner of her eye, Emily could see Jemma discreetly edging out of the room to go into the stock room, closing the door after her to give them some privacy.

Emily waited, feeling helpless and weak. She was her own worst enemy, she knew that. She shouldn't even be thinking of listening to him, instead of sitting here desperate for every second she could spend with him.

'As a boy, I had a very difficult relationship with my grandfather. I suppose I was something of a black sheep in his eyes. I resented the way he treated my father, who was too gentle to stand up to him, and I swore that I would never let him control me the way he did my parents. I came to London determined to prove to him and to myself that I could be a success without the power of the Royal House of Niroli. It was for that reason that I came here and stayed incognito, and no other.'

'But when we met, you had achieved that success, Marco,' Emily forced herself to remind him.

'Yes, but I had also grown used to the freedom of living and proving myself as plain Marco Fierezza. It seemed to me then that there was no need for me to live any other way—at least not for many years. My father was still alive and he would have succeeded my grandfather when the time came.' Marco gave a small shrug. 'I had no expectation of becoming king until I was much older.'

'Maybe not. But you would surely have to marry appropriately and produce a son to whom you can pass on the crown,' Emily couldn't help pointing out quietly.

Marco inclined his head.

'Yes, at some stage. One of the archaic rules that surround the Royal House of Niroli is that the king cannot marry a woman who is divorced, or of ill repute. The challenge of finding such a paragon in today's world is such that I was more than happy to remain unmarried until necessity directed otherwise.'

Emily had to blink fast to disperse her threatening tears. Marco obviously had no idea just how hurtful his casual words were. It could never have occurred to him to think of her as someone he might love and want to commit to permanently. She should hate him for showing her how indifferent he was to her, Emily told herself, but somehow she felt too sick at heart to do it.

'Look,' Marco told her crisply, 'I don't have much time, and since you obviously need to eat, why don't we discuss this over an early dinner?'

Emily shuddered and shook her head in instant denial, her reaction making him frown. She'd always had a good appetite, having never needed to worry about what she ate. But now the fact that she had not been eating properly was plain to see in the sharp angles of her cheek-bones and her jaw.

'Jemma's right, Emily, you aren't looking after yourself properly,' Marco announced firmly. 'You need a break. I don't have time to argue with you. I've made up my mind. You're coming back to Niroli with me.'

Was this giddy, soaring feeling inside her really because she was so weak that she was glad that Marco had made up her mind for her? She was an independent woman, for heaven's sake, not some wilting Victorian heroine. She tried to wrench back some control of what was happening.

'I can't do that, Marco. For one thing, there's the business—'

'Of course you can, Em. I can take care of things here,' Jemma piped up from the threshold of the storeroom. With Niroli's back to her, she mouthed to Emily, Go with him, you know you want to… Before announcing to both of them that time was getting on and she had to catch the post with some invoices.

Emily and Marco were alone in the shop now, and she wished violently that she were not so all-consumingly aware of him.

'You can't take me back with you, Marco. It wouldn't work. We were lovers—'

'And still could be, if that's what you want,' Marco interrupted softly.

Emily didn't dare look at him in case he saw the hope and
the longing in her eyes. She struggled between her own
helpless awareness of how much she still wanted him and the
practicalities of the situation, protesting unsteadily, 'Marco,
we can't. Even if I wanted to…to go back, it isn't possible.'

'Why not, if it's what both of us want?'

What *both* of them wanted. Her heart lurched, joyously
intoxicated by the pleasure of hearing the admission his
words contained.

'But what about the rules of the House of Niroli? Surely
your grandfather wouldn't approve, or—'

'My grandfather doesn't rule my personal life,' Marco responded with familiar arrogance.

She had no idea how to handle this. She shook her head. 'I
don't know what to say,' she admitted. 'How long have I got?'

'To share my bed?' Marco cut her off smoothly. 'I doubt
that my grandfather is really ready to step down, for all that
he says he is. We could have the summer together and then
reassess the situation.'

Emily could feel her face burning.

'That wasn't what I meant. When I said how long have I
got, I meant how much time will you give me to think things
through before I make up my mind about your business proposition?' she told him primly. 'Nothing else.'

'No time. Because you aren't going to think about it. You
are coming back with me, Emily—you don't have a choice
about that. What you can choose, though, of course, is in
what capacity. My flight leaves at eight, so we've just got time
to go back to your house and collect your passport, and
anything else you might need. And time for me to show you
exactly what both of us will be missing if you don't,' he told

her, giving her a look that was so explicitly sexual that her whole body burned with longing. And then, as though he had said nothing remotely outrageous to her, he continued smoothly, 'I should warn you, the villa is going to tax even your creative eye, but I'm sure you'll enjoy the challenge.'

He was handing her her handbag and her coat, and somehow or other she was being ushered out of the door, helpless to stop what was happening and not really caring that she couldn't.

'How many bedrooms does the villa have?' she managed to ask Marco slightly breathlessly, once they were outside on the street.

The look he gave her as he turned to her made her heart thud recklessly.

'Five, but you will be sleeping in mine—with me.'

'You're going to be Niroli's next king, Marco!' Emily felt bound to remind him. 'You can't live openly with me there as your mistress.'

'No?' he challenged her softly.

CHAPTER EIGHT

AT SOME stage during the drive from Niroli's airport, into which they had flown by private jet, she must have half fallen asleep, Emily realised as the motion of the car ceased and she heard Marco's voice saying through the darkness of the car's interior, 'We're here.'

But not before she had seen the impressively straight road leading from the airport, with huge placards attached to lamp-posts bearing a photograph of Marco, a royal crown hovering several centimetres above his head and an ermine-edged cape around his shoulders. Underneath were Italian words, which she could just about translate as, 'Welcome home, Your Highness'.

It made her shiver slightly now to think about them and to remember how she had felt at seeing them, how very aware they had made her of the gulf between her and Marco's royal status.

The emotional roller-coaster ride of the last few hours had taken its toll on her, Emily knew. It had drained her and left her feeling so exhausted that she barely had the energy to get out of the car, even though Marco opened the door for her and reached out his hand to support her. Just for a moment she hesitated and looked back into the car. Wishing she had not come? She pushed the thought aside and focused instead on the fact that the night air had that familiar scent of

Mediterranean warmth that she remembered from her many holidays elsewhere in the region with Marco: a mingling of olfactory textures and tints, ripened by the day's sunlight and then distilled by the soft darkness.

Emily breathed it in slowly, trying to steady her own nerves. She was, she realised, standing in the courtyard of what looked like a haphazard jumble of white stone walls, shuttered, arched windows and delicate iron balconies, illuminated by moonlight and lamplight from the surrounding buildings. The courtyard was shielded from the narrow street outside by a pair of heavy wooden doors, and as Emily's senses adjusted themselves to the darkness she could hear from somewhere the sound of water from a fountain falling into a basin.

'It looks almost Moorish,' she told Marco.

'Yes, it does, doesn't it?' Marco agreed with her. 'History does have it that the Moors *were* here at one time, and it's here in the oldest part of the main town that you can see their architectural influence. Although there were also Nirolians who travelled as traders to and from Andalucia in Spain, as well.' He was guiding her towards an impressive doorway as he spoke. Emily hesitated, knowing it was too late now to change her mind about the wisdom of allowing him to bring her here and yet not totally able to overcome her uncertainty.

'You said that you're living here, instead of at the palace?'

'Yes. Are you disappointed? If so, I am sure I can arrange for us to have a suite of rooms there—'

Us? 'No...' Emily stopped him hurriedly. 'Marco...' She stopped, and shivered slightly despite the warmth of the air. She was a fool to have allowed Marco to steamroller her into coming here so that he could have her back in his bed, when she knew there was no real future for her with him. But why think of the future when she could have the present? an inner voice urged her. Every day she could have with Marco, every hour, were things so precious she should reach out and grab them with both hands. Emily squeezed her eyes tightly closed and then opened them again. She wasn't used to this unfamiliar recklessness she seemed to have developed, with its blinkered refusal to acknowledge any-thing other than her determination to be with him. She did love him so much, Emily accepted, but it would be far better for her if she did not.

Fine, the reckless voice told her. *So you spend your time trying to stop loving him, and I'll spend mine enjoying being with him. You can't leave—not now.* What *was* this? She felt as though she were being torn in two. The sensible, protective part of her was telling her that it would be better if she spent her time here learning to recognise the huge differences between them; far better if she made herself focus, not on the fact that Marco was her lover and the man she loved, but on the fact that he was Niroli's future king and as such could never be hers. However, this new reckless part of her was insisting that nothing mattered more than squeezing the intimacy and the sweetness out of every extra minute she had with him, regardless of what the future might bring. How could she bring together two such opposing forces? She couldn't.

'Let's go inside,' she heard Marco telling her, 'then I can introduce you to Maria and Pietro who look after the villa for me.'

Emily still hung back.

'They are bound to talk about my being here.'

'I expect they will, but why should that matter?' Marco knew all too well that they would, and that their talk would very quickly reach his grandfather's ears. There was no need for him to share that knowledge with Emily, though.

'Wouldn't it perhaps be better if…well, you said you wanted me to restyle the villa. Perhaps I should have my own room, for convention's sake, and then you could…'

'I could what? Sneak you into my bed at dead of night?' Marco shook his head, his mouth tightening. 'I am a man, Emily, not a fearful boy.'

'But if we are going to be lovers…'

'"If" we are?' he mocked her softly. 'There is no "if" about it, Emily. You will be sleeping in my bed and I shall be there with you, make no mistake about that. I know you're tired, so I shall not make love to you, but only for tonight. My people will understand that I am a man, as well as their future king, and they will not expect me to live the life of a monk. They will accept that—'

'That what? That I am your mistress, and that you have brought me here to warm your bed?' When Marco talked like this, she felt as though she were listening to a stranger, Emily recognised in sharpening panic. His casual reference to 'his people' and his position as 'their future king' set him on a different plane from her, and a different life path; already he was someone else from the man she had known…a king-in-waiting…

'Are you saying that you don't want to warm it?' Marco asked her, breaking into her thoughts and then adding so seductively, almost like the old Marco that she used to know, 'Did you know there is something about the smell of your skin that right now is filling my head with the most erotic thoughts—and memories?' His voice had dropped to a whisper that was almost mesmeric. 'Can you remem-ber the first time I tasted you?'

Despite the doubts and fears she was experiencing, his words sent a thrill of sensation through her, making her body quiver with arousal at the images he was conjuring up. She wanted to tell him that she wasn't a naïve virgin any more and that she wasn't going to play his game, but instead she heard herself saying thickly,

'Yes.'

'And the first time you tasted me?'

Now she could only nod her head as desire kicked up violently inside her stomach.

Marco's fingers had encircled her wrist and he was stroking her bare skin in a rhythmic, beguiling caress.

'You didn't care then about the staff of the hotel knowing that we were lovers.'

'That was different,' she protested.

'Why?'

'Then we were private lovers. But here, Marco, as you yourself have just said, in the eyes of the people of Niroli you are their future king, and I will be your mistress.'

'So?'

Could he really not understand how she felt? Was he really already so far removed from ordinary life that he couldn't see that she would a thousand times rather be the lover of plain Marco Fierezza, than the mistress of the future King of Niroli?

'I can assure you that you will be treated with courtesy and respect, Emily, if that is what is worrying you,' he continued when she didn't answer him. 'And if it should come to my ears that you aren't, I will make sure that is corrected.'

He sounded shockingly, sickeningly, aloof and regal. The words he had spoken were the kind of statement that previously she would have laughed openly over and expected him to do the same. But she could tell from his expression that he meant them seriously. Marco's always had been a very commanding presence, but now Emily felt there was a new hauteur to his manner, a coldness and a disdain that chilled her through. The hardening of his voice and the arrogance of his stance betrayed his determination to have his own way. And a belief in his royal right to do so? Emily wasn't sure. But she did feel that the subtle change she could sense in him highlighted her own uncertainties. In London, despite the financial gap between them, they had met and lived as equals. Here, on Niroli, she knew instinctively that things would be different. But right now she was too tired to question how much that difference was going to impact on their new relationship. Right now, all she wanted… Marco was still stroking her arm. She closed her eyes and swayed closer to him. Right now, she admitted, all she wanted was this: the scented darkness, the proximity of their bodies and the promise of pleasure to come…

It was the single, sharp, shrill, animal cry of the victim of a night predator who had come down from the mountains to hunt, cut off along with its life, that woke Emily from her deep sleep. At first, her unfamiliar surroundings confused her, but then she remembered where she was. She turned over in the large bed, her body as filled with sharp dread as though the dying creature had passed on its fear to her.

'Marco?' She reached out her hand into the darkness and to the other side of the bed, but encountered only emptiness.

She had been so tired when they had arrived that she had gone straight to bed, in the room to which Marco had taken her, leaving him to explain the situation to the couple who looked after the villa for him. She suspected she must have fallen asleep within seconds of her head reaching the pillow. She had assumed though, after what he had said to her, that he would be joining her in it. She hadn't had the energy to argue, even if she had wanted to.

The door to the room's *en suite* bathroom opened. A mixture of relief and sexual tension filled her as she watched Marco walk towards her. He always slept naked and there was enough light coming in through the window to reveal the outline of his body. Her memory did the rest, filling in the shadow-cloaked detail with such powerfully loving strokes that she trembled.

'So, you're awake,' she heard him murmur as she lifted her head from the pillow to watch his approach.

'Yes.' Her response was little more than a terse, exhaled breath, an indication of her impatience at herself at being unable to tear her gaze from his magnificent physique.

'But still tired?' Marco was standing at the side of the bed now, leaning down towards her.

'A little. But not *too* tired,' she whispered daringly. She had known all along, of course, that this would be the outcome of being with him again. How could it not be when you had a man as sexually irresistible as Marco and a woman as desperately in love as she was?

They looked at one another through the semi-darkness; night sounds rustled through the room, mingling with the accelerated sound of their breathing. The darkness had become a velvet embrace, its softness pressing in on them like an intimate caress, stroking shared sensual memories over their minds.

The sudden fiercely intense surge of his own desire caught Marco off guard, as it threatened his self-control. He knew that he had missed their sex, but he hadn't been prepared for this raw, aching hunger that was now consuming him.

Emily's skin smelled of his own shower gel in a way that made him frown as his senses searched eagerly for the familiar night-warm, intimate scent that was hers and hers alone, and which he was only recognising now how much he had missed... She moved, dislodging the bedclothes, and his chest muscles contracted under the pressure of the pounding thud of his heartbeat. His pulse had started to race and he recognised that the ache of need for her, which had begun here in this bed the first night he had spent in it without her, had turned feral and taken away his control.

'Emily.'

The way he said her name turned Emily's insides to liquid

heat. He and this yearning beating up through her body were impossible to resist. She sat up in the bed, giving in to her love, pressing her lips to his bare shoulder, closing her eyes with delight as she breathed him into her. She ran the tip of her tongue along his collar-bone, feeling the responsive clench of his muscles and the reverberation of his low groan of pleasure. When he arched his neck, she kissed her way along it, caressing the swell of his Adam's apple, whilst his muscles now corded in mute recognition of his arousal. And his desire fed her own, intoxicating her, empowering her, encouraging her to make their intimacy a slow, sweetly erotic dance spiced with sudden moments of breathless intensity.

It felt good to keep their need on a tight knife-edge, refusing to let him touch her until he couldn't be refused any more, and then giving herself over completely to the touch of his hands and his mouth, crying out her need as he finally covered her and moved into her. But it was his own cry of mingled triumph and release that took them both over the edge, to the sweet place that lay beyond it.

Several minutes later, rolling away from Emily, Marco lay on his back, staring up at the ceiling and waiting for his heartbeat to steady, willing himself not to think about what his body had just told him about the intensity of his need for Emily.

If the way in which Marco was rejecting her in the aftermath of the intimacy they had just shared was hurting her, then it served her right for coming here, Emily told herself. She must take her pain and hold onto it, use it to remind herself what the reality of being here with Marco meant. It would do her good to see him in his true role, in his true habitat, because it would show her surely that the man she loved simply did not exist any more, and once she knew that her unwanted love would die. How could it not do so?

CHAPTER NINE

KING GIORGIO wagged a reproving finger. 'Is it not enough that you have deliberately attempted to undermine the authority of the Crown—an authority which is soon to be your own—with these generators you have brought to Niroli, without this added flouting of my command to end your association with this…this floozy? You know perfectly well that there are channels and protocols to be followed when a member of the royal family takes a mistress. It is unthinkable that you should have brought back with you to Niroli a woman who is a common nothing, and who never can and never will be accepted here at court!'

'You mean, I take it, that I could take my pick from the married women amongst the island's nobility? Her husband would of course be instructed to do his duty and give up his wife to royal pleasure and, in due course, both would be appropriately rewarded—the husband with an important government position, the wife with the title of Royal Mistress and a few expensive baubles.' Marco shook his head. 'I have no intention of adorning some poor courtier with a pair of horns so that I can sleep with his wife.'

'You cannot expect me to believe that you, a prince of Niroli, can be content with a woman who is a nothing—'

'Emily is far from being nothing, and the truth is that you insult her by comparing her with the blue-blooded nonentities you seem to think are so superior to her. There is no comparison. Emily is their superior in every way.' The immediate and heated ferocity of his defence of Emily and his anger against his grandfather had taken hold of Marco before he could think logically about what he was saying. His immediate impulse had been to protect her, and that alone was enough to cause him to wonder at his uncharacteristic behaviour. And yet, even though for practical and diplomatic reasons he knew if he could not bring himself to recall his statement, then at least he should temper it a little. But he couldn't do it. Why not? Was it because by bringing Emily here to Niroli he now felt a far greater sense of responsibility towards her than he had done in London?

His grandfather didn't give him time to ponder. Instead the king pushed his chair back from the table and eased himself up, before demanding regally, 'Do you really think that I am deceived by any of this, Marco? Do you think I don't realise that you have brought those generators and this woman here to Niroli expressly to anger and insult me? You may think that you can win the hearts of my people by giving them access to the technological toys you believe they crave, and that they will accept your mistress, but you are wrong. It is true that there are elements of rebellion and disaffection amongst the mountain-dwellers, the Viallis who will give you their allegiance and sell you their loyalty for the price of a handful of silver, but they are nothing. The hearts of the rest of the Nirolian population lie here with me. They, like me, know that on Niroli the old ways are the best ways, and they will show you in no uncertain terms how they feel about your attempts to win round the Viallis.'

'No, Grandfather, it is you who is wrong,' Marco answered

him curtly. 'You may wish to stick with the old ways as you call them, enforcing ignorance and poverty on people, refusing to allow them to make their own choices about the way they want to live, treating them as children. You try to rule them through fear and power, and some of them rightfully resent that, as I would do in their places. I have brought back the generators because your people, our people, need them, and I have brought Emily back because *I* need *her*.' It wasn't what he had planned to say, and it certainly wasn't what he had been thinking when he had walked into this confrontation, but as soon as he had said the words Marco recognised that they contained a truth that had previously been hidden from him. Or had it been deliberately ignored and denied by him? He had known that he wanted Emily; that he desired her and that he could make use of her presence here to underline his independence to his grandfather, but needing her...that was something else again, and it made Marco stiffen warily, ready to defend himself from what he recognised was his own vulnerability.

'The woman is a commoner, and commoners do not understand what it is to be royal. They cause problems that a woman born into the nobility would never cause.'

'You're speaking from experience?' Marco taunted his grandfather, watching as the older man's face turned a dangerously purple hue.

'You dare to suggest that I would so demean myself?'

Marco looked at him.

'Whilst Emily is here on Niroli she will be treated with respect and courtesy, she will be received at court and she will be treated in every way like the most highly born of royal mistresses,' he told his grandfather evenly. 'I have a long memory and those who do otherwise will be pursued and punished.'

He had spoken loudly enough for everyone else in the chamber to hear him, knowing that the courtiers would know as well as he did that he would soon be in a position to re-primand those who defied him now.

Before this he had never had any intention of bringing Emily to court, but he did not intend to tell his grandfather that. How dared the old man suggest that Emily was somehow less worth-while as a person than some Nirolian nobleman's wife? He'd back Emily any day if it came to having to prove herself as a person. She possessed intelligence, compassion, wit and kindness, and her natural sweetness was like manna from heaven after the falseness of the courtiers and their wives. He had seen the pleased looks that some of the flunkies had ex-changed when his grandfather had flown into a rage over the generators. Of course, they couldn't be expected to like the fact that there were going to be changes, but they were going to have to accept them, Marco decided grimly. Just as they were going to have to accept Emily. He was striding out of the audience chamber before he recognised how much more strongly he felt about protecting Emily than he had actually known…

Emily stared at her watch in disbelief. It was closer to lunchtime than breakfast! How could she have slept so late? The sensual after-ache of the night's pleasure gave her a hint of a reason for her prolonged sleep.

Marco! She sat up in bed and then saw the note he had left for her propped up on the bedside table. She picked it up and read it quickly.

He was going to the palace to see his grandfather, he had written, and since he didn't know when he would be back, he had given Maria instructions to provide her with everything she might need, and had also explained to her that Emily was going to be organising the interior renovation of the villa.

'If you feel up to it, by all means feel free to have a good look around,' he had written, 'but don't overdo things.'

There was no mention of last night, but then there was hardly likely to be, was there? What had she been hoping for? A love letter? But Marco didn't love her, did he? The starkness of that reality wasn't something she was ready to think about right now, Emily admitted. It was too soon after the traumatic recent see-sawing of her emotions from the depths of despair to the unsteady fragile happiness of Marco's appearance at the shop and their intimacy last night.

But she would have to think about it at some stage, she warned herself. After all, nothing had changed, except that she now knew what living without him felt like. She mustn't let herself forget that all this was nothing more than a small extra interlude of grace; a chance to store up some extra memories for the future.

It wouldn't do her any good to dwell on such depressing thoughts, Emily told herself. Instead, she would get up and then keep herself occupied with an inspection of the villa.

If Maria was curious about her relationship with Marco, she hid it well, Emily decided, an hour later, when she had finished a late breakfast of fresh fruit and homemade rolls, which Maria had offered her when she had come downstairs. She had eaten her light meal sitting in the warm sunlight of a second inner courtyard, and was now ready to explore the villa, which she managed to convey with halting Italian and hand-gestures to Maria, who beamed in response and nodded her head enthusiastically.

Emily had no idea when the villa had first been built, but it was obviously very old and had been constructed at a time when the needs of a household were very different from the requirements of the twenty-first century. In addition to the dark kitchen Maria showed her, there was a positive warren of passages and small rooms, providing what Emily assumed must have been the domestic service area of the house. To suit the needs of a modern family, these would have to be integrated into a much larger, lighter and more modern kitchen, with a dining area, and possibly a family room, opening out onto the courtyard.

The main doors to the villa opened into a square hallway, flanked by two good sized salons, although the décor was old-fashioned and dark.

The bedrooms either already had their own bathrooms or were large enough to accommodate *en suites*, although only the room Marco was using was equipped with relatively recent sanitary-ware.

On the top floor of the villa, there were more rooms and, by the time she had finished going round the ground and first floors, Emily was beginning to feel tired. But her tiredness wasn't stopping her from feeling excited at the prospect of taking on such a challenging but ultimately worthwhile project. The attic floor alone was large enough to convert into two self-contained units that could provide either semi-separate accommodation for older teenagers, staff quarters, or simply a bolt-hole and working area away from the hubbub of everyday family life. The courtyards to the villa were a real delight, or at least they had the potential to be. There were three of them, and the smaller one could easily be adapted to contain a swimming pool.

It was the second courtyard, which Marco's bedroom overlooked, that was her favourite, though. With giant terracotta pots filled with shrubs, palms and flowers and a loggia that ran along one wall, it was the perfect spot to sit and enjoy the peaceful sound of its central marble fountain.

Standing in it now, Emily couldn't help thinking what a wonderful holiday home the villa would make for a family. It had room to spare for three generations; with no effort at all she could see them enjoying the refurbished villa's luxurious comfort: the grandparents, retired but still very active, enjoying the company of their great-grandchildren, the kids themselves exuberant, and energetic, the sound of their laughter mingling with that of the fountain; the girls olive-skinned, pretty and dainty, the boys strongly built with their father's dark hair and shrewd gaze, the baby laughing and gurgling as Marco held him, whilst the woman who was their mother and Marco's wife—Niroli's queen—stood watching them.

Don't do this to yourself, an inner voice warned Emily. *Don't go there. Don't think about it, or her; don't imagine what it would be like to be that woman.* In reality, the home she had been busily mentally creating was not that of a king and a queen. It was the home of a couple who loved one another and their children, a home for the kind of family she admitted she had yearned for during her teenage years when she had lived with her grandfather. The kind of home that represented the life, the future, she wished desperately she would be sharing with Marco, right down to the five children. The warmth of the sun spilling into the courtyard filled it with the scent of the lavender that grew there, and Emily knew that, for the rest of her life, she would equate its scent with the pain seeping slowly through her as she acknowledged the impossibility of her dreams. If this were a fantasy, then she could magic away all those things that stood between her and Marco, and imagine a happy ending, a scenario in which he discovered that she loved him and immediately declared his own love for her. But this was real life and there was no way that was going to happen.

One day—maybe—there would be a man with whom she could find some sense of peace, a man who would give her children they could love together and cherish. But that man could not and would not be Marco, and those dark-haired girls and boys she had seen so clearly with her mind's eye, that gorgeous baby, were the children that another woman would bear for him.

And, poor things, their lives would be burdened by the weight of their royal inheritance, just as Marco's was, and that was something Emily knew she could not endure to inflict on her own babies. For them she wanted love and security and the freedom to grow into individuals, instead of being forced into the mould of royal heirs.

It was just as well that Marco had no intentions of wanting to make her his wife, on two counts, Emily told herself determinedly as she battled with her sadness, because the revealing nature of her recent thoughts had shown her what her true feelings were about Marco's royal blood. Plus, of course, as he had already told her, it was not permissible for him to marry a divorced woman.

The sound of crockery rattling on a tray and the smell of coffee brought her back to the present as Maria came into the courtyard carrying a tray of coffee for her, which she put on a table shaded from the heat of the sun by an elegant parchment-coloured sun umbrella.

Thanking her with a smile, Emily decided that she might as well start work.

Within half an hour, she was deeply engrossed in the notes she was making, having moved the coffee-pot out of the way. Although she hadn't felt nauseous this morning, the smell of the coffee had reminded her that her stomach was still queasy and not truly back to normal.

An hour later, when Marco drove into the outer courtyard, Emily was still hard at work. After leaving the palace he had been to the airport where the generators had already been unloaded. He had already made a list of those villages up in the mountains most in need of their own source of power and whilst in London he had spoken with the island's police chief and the biggest road haulier to arrange for the transport of the generators. However, whilst he had been at the airport, he had received a message from the police chief to say he had received instructions from the palace that the generators were not to be moved.

It had taken all of Marco's considerable negotiating skills, and the cool reminder that he was Niroli's future king, to persuade the police chief to change his mind and go against what he described to Marco almost fearfully as 'orders from the palace'.

Because of this Marco had decided to drive into the mountains himself to make sure that the generators were delivered safely. If his grandfather thought he could outmanoeuvre him, then he was going to have to learn the hard way that it was just not going to happen.

Marco's mouth compressed. As a successful entrepreneur whose views were respected he wasn't used to having his decisions questioned and countermanded. Had his grandfather really no idea of the potential damage he was inflicting on the island by his stubborn refusal to recognise that the world had changed and its people with it, and that it was no longer viable for a king as hugely wealthy as Niroli's to allow some of his subjects to live in conditions of severe poverty? Apart from anything else, there was the threat of civil unrest amongst the mountain-dwellers, which would be seized upon and further orchestrated by the Vialli gang that lived amongst them.

His step-grandmother had in part to be behind this, Marco decided grimly. Queen Eva was his grandfather's second wife, and it was Marco's personal opinion that she was and always had been hostile towards her predecessor's side of the family. That naturally included Marco and his two sisters. Given their step-grandmother's attitude, it was no wonder that Isabella rarely visited the palace, and that Rosa preferred not to live on the island, just as he hadn't, until recently…

* * *

Emily had been deeply engrossed in the notes she was making, but some sixth sense alerted her to Marco's presence, causing her to put down her pen and turn to look towards the entrance to the courtyard. Despite the sombreness of her earlier thoughts, the minute she saw Marco standing watching her all the feelings she had promised herself she would learn to control rushed through her. Pushing back her chair, she got up and hurried over to him.

As he watched her coming towards him Marco could feel the anger his morning had caused being eased from his body by the warmth of her welcome. He wanted to go to her and take hold of her, he wanted to take her to bed and lose himself and his problems within her. His need for her was so intense... He tensed once more. There it was again, that word need, that feeling he didn't want to have.

'What is it? What's wrong?' Emily asked him uncertainly when she saw his sudden tension.

'Nothing for you to worry about. An administrative problem I need to sort out,' he told her dismissively. 'I'll be gone for most of the afternoon.'

Emily did her best to hide her disappointment, but she knew she hadn't succeeded when she heard him exhaling irritably.

'Emily—' he began warningly.

'It's all right, I know. You're a king-in-waiting and you have far more important things to do than be with me,' she interrupted him briskly.

Marco looked at her downbent head.

'You can come with me if you wish, but it will mean a long, hot drive along dusty roads, followed by some boring delays whilst I speak with people. And since you haven't been feeling well...'

Emily wanted to tell him that being with him could never bore her, but she managed to stop herself just in time. Instead she assured him quickly, 'I'm feeling much better now. I've had a look round the villa and I could run some options by you in the car, unless…' She paused uncertainly, suddenly realising how very little she knew about what was expected of him in his new role. 'That is, will you be driving yourself, or…?'

'We aren't going on some kind of royal progress in a formal cavalcade, if that's what you mean, and, yes, I shall be driving myself,' Marco answered her. 'You'll need a hat to protect your head from the sun and a pair of sensible shoes for if you do get out of the car. Some of the villages we shall be going to are pretty remote and along single-track mountain roads. I don't want to delay too long though.' He didn't want the police chief getting cold feet and instructing the haulier to stop his fleet of lorries, or, worse, turn back.

Emily's eyes were shining as though he had offered her some kind of priceless gift, he reflected. He had a sudden impulse to take hold of her and draw her close to him, to kiss her slowly and tenderly. He shook the impulse away, not sure where it had come from or why, but knowing that it was dangerous…

CHAPTER TEN

'AM I allowed to ask any questions?' Emily said lightly. It was nearly an hour since they had left the villa. Marco had driven them through the main town and then out and up into the hills. 'Or is this trip a state secret?'

'No secret, but it is certainly a contentious issue so far as my grandfather is concerned,' Marco told her.

'If it's private family business,' she began, but Marco stopped her, shaking his head.

'No. It's very much a public business, since it involves some of the poorest communities on the island. But instead of acknowledging their need and doing something about it, my grandfather prefers to ignore it, which is why I have decided to take matters into my own hands. The more remote parts of the island do not have the benefit of electricity,' he explained. 'Because of that, these people are denied modern comforts and communication, and their children are denied access to technology and education. My grandfather believes in his divine and royal right to impose his will and keep them living as peasants. He also believes he knows what is best for them and for Niroli. Because there has been a history of insurrection amongst our mountain population, led by the Viallis, in the past, he also fears that by encouraging them to become part of today's world he will be encouraging them to challenge the Crown's supremacy.'

'And you don't agree,' Emily guessed sympathetically.

'I believe that every child has the right to a good education, and that every parent has the right to want to provide their child with the best opportunities available. My grandfather feels that by educating our poorest citizens, we will encourage them to want much more than the simple lives they presently have, he fears that some will rise up, others will desert the land and maybe even the island. But I say it's wrong to imprison them in poverty and lack of opportunity. We have a duty to them, and for me that means giving them freedom of choice. You and I know what happens when young people are disenfranchised, Emily. We have already seen it in the urban ghettos of Europe: angry young men ganging up together and becoming feral, respecting only violence and greed, because that is all they have ever known. I don't want to see that happening here.

'I have tried to persuade my grandfather to invest some of the Crown's vast financial reserves in paying to install electricity in these remote areas, but he refuses to do so. Just as he refuses to see the potential trouble he is storing up for the island.'

Emily could hear the frustration in his voice. It had touched her immensely that Marco had connected the two of them together in their shared awareness of the downsides of keeping people impoverished and powerless.

'Perhaps, once you are King...' she suggested, but Marco shook his head again.

'My grandfather is very good at imposing conditions and I don't want to trap myself in a situation where my hands are tied. Plus, it seems to me that some of Niroli's youth are already beginning to resent my grandfather's rule, just as previous generations resisted the monarchy. I do not want to inherit that resentment along with the throne, so I have decided to act now to take the heat out of the situation.'

'But what can you do?' Emily asked him uncertainly 'If your grandfather has refused to allow electricity to be supplied…'

'I can't insist that it is, no,' Marco agreed. 'But I can provide it by other means. Whilst I was in London, I bought what I hope will be enough generators to at least provide some electricity for the villages. My grandfather is furious, of course, but I am hoping that he will back down and accept what I have done as a way of allowing him to change his mind without losing face. He is an old man who has ruled autocratically all his life. It is hard for him, I know that, but the Crown has to change or risk having change forced upon it.'

'You think there will be some kind of uprising?' Emily was horrified, instantly thinking of the danger that would bring to Marco.

'Not immediately. But the seeds are there. And still my grandfather is so determined to hold absolute power.'

'You pretend not to do so, but in reality you understand him very well, and I think you feel a great deal of compassion for him, Marco,' Emily said gently.

'On the contrary, what I feel is a great deal of irritation and anger because he refuses to see the danger he is courting,' Marco corrected her. Her perceptiveness had startled him, making him feel that she knew him rather better than he had realised. 'There are so many changes I want to make, Emily, so much here for me to do, but my grandfather blocks me at every turn.'

'You've lived away from the island for a long time and you've grown used to making your own decisions without the need to consult others. Perhaps your grandfather is being difficult because he sees this and in some ways he fears it—and you. You said yourself that he's an old man—he obviously knows that he can't continue to be King, but my guess is that he doesn't want to acknowledge that publicly, and that a part of him wants to continue to rule Niroli through you. When you come up with your own plans and they are opposed to his, he tries to block you because he's afraid of losing his power to you.'

'I doubt you would ever get him to admit any of that.'

Emily could hear the frustration in Marco's voice and, with it, his hunger to right what he saw as wrongs. He would be a strong king morally, socially, politically and in all the other important ways, she recognised. Listening to him had brought home to her the reality of her own situation. Even if by some miracle he should return her love, there was no future for them. She could not be his queen, and she could never do anything that would prevent him from being Niroli's king. Not now, after hearing him speak so passionately about his country and his people. If Marco had a duty to his people, then she too had duties to him and her love for him; loving someone meant putting them first and their needs before one's own. Marco's great need was to fulfil his duty and he could not do that with her in his life. A small, sad shadow darkened her eyes—the ghost of her dreams. Seeing it, Marco frowned.

'I'm boring you,' he announced curtly.

'No,' Emily told him. 'No! I like listening to you talking about your plans. I just wish that you had told me who you were when we first met.' Had he done so, she would have been so much better armoured against her vulnerability to him, and she would certainly never have started dreaming they could have a permanent future together.

'It wasn't a deliberate deceit on my part,' Marco defended himself coolly.

'Maybe not, but you could have said something… warned me. Then, at least…' She stopped, shaking her head, not wanting to admit her own folly where he was concerned.

'In order to live the kind of life I wanted, to prove myself on my own terms, it was necessary for me to do it with anonymity and without the trappings of royalty.

'I grew up here as a renegade in my grandfather's eyes. I was his heir, but I refused to conform or let him turn on me and bully me the way he did my father.' Marco's expression changed, and Emily ached to reach out and comfort him when she saw that look in his eyes.

'My father was too gentle to stand up to my grandfather. As a child, I hated knowing that. As a form of compensation, I suppose, I rebelled against my grandfather's authority and I swore that I would prove to him, and to the world, that I had the capability to succeed as myself.'

'But while you were proving yourself, you missed the island and your family, your father?' Emily guessed tenderly.

Marco opened his mouth to reject her words and then admitted huskily,

'Yes. It was such a shock when he was killed in a freak accident off the island's coast. Something I'd never imagined happening…never considered.'

And along with his natural grief at the loss of his father, Marco had had to deal with the irreversible changes in his own circumstances that had followed, Emily acknowledged silently. It must have been so hard for him—a man used to taking control of every aspect of his personal life, to have to come to terms with the fact that, as King, a huge part of his life would now be beyond his control. Just listening to him was causing a change within her own thoughts, turning her angry bitterness and pain into compassionate understanding and acceptance. It altered everything for her. Did he recognise how very alone he was emotionally? Was that a deliberate choice, or an accidental one? If he knew about it, did he care, or did he simply accept it as part of the price he paid for his royal status?

'I would hate to be in your shoes.' The words had slipped out before she could stop them.

Marco looked searchingly at her.

'What do you mean?' he demanded.

'I can hear how important your people are to you, Marco, and how strongly you feel about helping them, but...' She paused and shook her head. 'I couldn't pay the price you're about to pay for being Niroli's king. On the one hand, yes, you will have enormous wealth and power, but on the other you won't have any personal freedom, any right to do what you want to do. Every-thing will have to be weighed against how it affects your people. That is such a tremendously heavy responsibility.' She gave a small sigh. 'I suppose it's different if you're born to it. I'm beginning to see why princes marry princesses,' she added ruefully. 'You really do have to be born royal to understand.'

'Not necessarily. You're doing a pretty good job of showing you have a strong grasp of what's involved,' Marco told her dryly. They had rarely spoken so openly to one another and it surprised him how much he valued what she had said to him. Impulsively, he slowed the car and reached for her hand, giving it a small squeeze that caused her to look at him in surprise. Such a small, tender gesture was so very unlike him.

'I'm glad you're here with me, Emily.'

Her heart was thumping and thudding with the sweetness of the emotions pouring through her. Marco brought the car briefly to a halt and leaned across and kissed her—a hard, swift kiss that contained a message she couldn't manage to decipher, but which sent a physical craving for him soaring through her body. She had never, ever known him exhibit such extraordinarily un-Marco behaviour before. Her heart felt as though it had wings, her own happiness dizzying her.

She mustn't let a casual moment out of time lead her into

forgetting what she had just recognised, she warned herself. But, then, should she let what she knew to be their separate futures prevent her from enjoying their shared here and now? a different voice coaxed.

'At this stage of the game, when you've got so much to deal with, it's only natural that you need someone to bounce ideas off and confide in,' she told him, 'and…' She paused, unsure of just how much she dared say without giving herself away completely.

'And?' Marco probed as they bounced along the narrow track past a cluster of small houses.

'And I wouldn't want that someone to be anyone else but me,' Emily told him simply.

A young man, tall and gangly and outgrowing his clothes, was standing in the middle of the road in front of Marco's car waving his hands, his face alight with excitement.

Emily looked questioningly at Marco.

'Tomasso,' he informed her as he brought the car to a halt. 'He is the leader of a gang of young Vialli hotheads, and he is also the person I have chosen to be my representative in taking care of the generator and introducing his village to its benefits.'

The moment Marco opened the car door and got out, Tomasso bounded up to him exclaiming, 'Highness, Highness, it is here! The generator, just as you promised. We have built a special place for it. Let me show you…'

An elderly woman appeared from the nearest house, tutting and looking very disapproving as she came over to join them.

'What is this—where is your respect for our Crown?' she demanded. 'Highness, forgive my thought-less grandson,' Emily could hear her saying as she curtseyed to Marco.

This was a side of him she had never seen, Emily thought to herself as Marco leaned forward and assisted the elderly woman to her feet, accepting her homage with easy grace, whilst maintaining a very specific formal dignity that Emily could see the elderly woman liked. As more villagers surrounded him, he was very much the future king, so much so that Emily's emotions blocked her throat. She felt so proud sitting in the car watching him and yet, at the same time, so painfully distanced from him. What she was witnessing was making her even more aware of how impossible it would be for them to sustain a long-term relationship. Already she could see the curious and even hostile glances being directed towards her, and she guessed when Marco turned to look at the car that he was being asked who she was.

She looked away, her gaze caught by an array of brightly painted and beaded leather purses spilling out of a basket, just outside the door to one of the houses. Her artist's eye could immediately see how, with some discreet direction, highly desirable objects could be made by adapting the leather and bead-work to cover boxes. She was constantly on the lookout for such accessories to dress her decorating schemes; they walked out of her shop faster than she could buy them. She made a mental note to ask Marco a bit more about the leather-work and those who produced it.

It was nearly half an hour before he returned to the car, having been pressed into going and viewing the generator in its new home. When he returned he was accompanied by a group of laughing young men, whilst Emily noticed the older people of the village held back a little, still eyeing her warily. One of them, a bearded and obviously very old man, went up to Marco and said something to him, shaking his head and pointing to the car. Emily saw the way Marco's expression hardened as he listened.

'What was that old man saying to you?' she asked him, once he was back in the car and they had driven out of the village.

'Nothing much.'

'Yes, he was. He was saying something about me, wasn't he?' Emily pressed him. 'He didn't like you tak-ing me there.'

Marco looked at her. Rafael, the elder of the village, was very much his grandfather's man. He did not approve of the generator and had said so, and then, when he had seen Emily in the car, he had berated Marco for—as he had put it— 'bringing such a woman to Niroli'. 'Where is her shame?' Rafael had demanded. 'She shows her face here as boldly as though she has none. In my day, such a woman would have known her place. It is an insult to us, the people of Niroli, that you have brought her here,' he had told Marco fiercely.

'Rafael has a reputation as someone with very strong views. He is even older than my grandfather and tends to think of himself as the guardian of the island's morals...'

'You mean he disapproves of me being here with you,' Emily guessed.

Marco was negotiating a tight bend, and Emily had to wait for him to answer her.

'What he thinks or feels is his business. What I choose to do is my own,' he told her grimly.

But the reality was that it wasn't, and that whatever Marco chose to do *was* the business of the people of Niroli.

In an attempt to change the subject, she asked him brightly, 'I saw a basket of leather purses...'

'Yes, the women of the villages make them. They sell them to tourists, if they can, although these days the visitors who come to Niroli would far rather have a designer piece than something fashioned out of home-made leather.'

'Mmm...I was thinking that, with a bit of time and effort, the leather could be used to cover trinket boxes, the bead or-namentation was so pretty, and I know from my own experi-ence there is a huge market for that kind of thing. If, as you say, the villagers are short of money, then...'

'It's worth thinking about, but there's no way I want my people involved in any kind of exploitation.'

'It was only a thought.'

'And a good one. Leave it with me.'

When the time came for him to marry, Marco reflected, he would need a wife who would take on the role of helping him to help his people. Emily could easily fulfil that role. Somehow, that thought had slipped under his guard and into his head where it had no right to be. Just as he had no right to allow Emily into his heart. *Into his heart?* Now, *what* was he thinking? Just because Rafael's objection to her presence had made him feel so angry and protective of her, that didn't mean that she had found her way into his heart. Did it?

CHAPTER ELEVEN

EMILY sighed to herself as she parked the car Marco had hired for her to use whilst she was staying on Niroli outside the island's elegant spa. Although he had made love to her last night and it was at his suggestion that she was visiting the spa today, she knew that she would far rather have had his company. Marco, though, was too busy with royal affairs to spend time with her. His purchase and distribution of the generators had led to yet another row with his grandfather, which had resulted in Emily asking Marco if there wasn't someone within his family who could mediate between the two of them.

'Someone, you mean, like my sister Isabella?' he had replied. 'She claims that my grandfather doesn't value her because she is female. No, Emily.' He had shaken his head. 'This is something I have to deal with myself.'

To Emily's relief, she had now gone three whole days without being sick, although she had noticed that, despite the fact that she wasn't eating very much, the waistline of one of her favourite skirts was now uncomfortably tight, and even more uncomfortable were her breasts, which felt swollen and tender. It must be due to too-rapid a change of climate, she had told herself this morning as she'd dressed.

Marco had told her that the spa was owned and run by

Natalia Carini, daughter of Giovanni, the Royal Vine-keeper. Emily had been a bit hesitant about coming here and putting herself forward for 'inspection' when she was at her most vulnerable. But as she walked into the spa foyer she heard the pretty girl behind the reception desk saying to another client, 'I'm sorry, but Miss Carini isn't here today.'

Emily hadn't really been sure how she felt about meeting someone who might have known Marco when he was younger. Like any woman in love, she longed to know everything there was to know about him and yet, at the same time, the reality of her position in his life made her feel that she wanted to remain anonymous. In London, it might be acceptable for a couple to live together as lovers without any intention of making their relationship permanent, but she suspected that things were different here on Niroli—even if Marco weren't who he was and destined to be King and, no doubt, to make a dynastic marriage.

'May I help you?'

Emily returned the receptionist's smile. 'I don't have an appointment, but I was wondering if it was possible to have a treatment?'

'Since it isn't the height of the tourist season yet, we should be able to fit you in. What kind of treatment would you like? We specialise here in using natural substances, especially the island's own volcanic mud. It's very therapeutic, especially when we use it in conjunction with our specially designed massage treatments.

'Here's a list of the treatments we offer, and a medical questionnaire.' The girl smiled again. 'The owner of the spa takes her responsibility to our clients very seriously, and I should point out to you that some of the more vigorous massages are not suitable for women who are pregnant.'

Pregnant! Emily almost laughed. Well, she certainly

wasn't. And then suddenly it hit her, her brain mentally registering the facts and assembling them: her sickness, her aching breasts, her growing waist… A wave of sickening shock and disbelief thundered through her, and she could hear the receptionist asking her anxiously if she was all right.

'I'm…fine…' she lied.

But of course she wasn't. She was anything but. How could she be 'fine', when the reason for the sickness she'd been suffering these last few weeks, and the fact that, oddly, her waist seemed to have expanded making her clothes feel tight, had suddenly been made blindingly obvious to her?

Was she right? Was she pregnant? She did some hasty mental calculations, whilst her heart banged anxiously against her ribs.

She needed very badly to sit down, but not here. Not anywhere where the truth might out and there could be any hint of a threat to her unborn child. It had only been seconds, minutes at the most, since she had realised the reality, but already she knew that there was nothing she would not do to protect the new life growing inside her. She would allow nothing or no one to imperil her child's safety and right to life!

Emily stared at her own reflection in the bedroom mirror and tried not to panic. There was little to show that she was pregnant as yet, apart from that slight thickening of her waist, but how much longer would she have before Marco became suspicious? She couldn't afford to be still here on Niroli by then. Her throat went dry. Inside her head she could hear Marco's voice telling her, at the very beginning of their relationship, that there would be no accidents, and what he expected her to do if one occurred.

Of course, what he had meant and not said was that he didn't want any royal bastards.

But there was no way she could destroy her child. She would rather destroy herself.

However, logically, Emily knew that, even if Marco had not made it plain he did not want her to have his child, there would be no place here on Niroli for the future king's pregnant mistress, or his illegitimate baby! What on earth was she going to do? She had never felt more alone.

'And now the village elder says that his orders have been ignored, and that the generator-shed has been broken into and the generator itself stolen. You see what you have done, what trouble you have caused by your interference?'

Marco forced himself to count slowly to ten before responding to his grandfather's angry but also triumphant accusations.

'You say that Rafael gave orders that the shed housing the generator was to be boarded up for the safety of the villagers. What is that supposed to mean?'

One of his grandfather's aides bent his head close to the Royal Ear and murmured something in it.

'The peace of the village was being destroyed—by the noise of the generator and various electrical appliances. Several villagers had complained to him that it had put their hens off laying and stopped their cows producing milk.'

Marco didn't know whether to laugh or cry. 'And because of *that* he stopped the villagers using the generator?' he demanded incredulously. 'No wonder they decided to ignore him!'

'Rafael says that he has long had concerns about the rebellious Vialli tendencies amongst this group of young men. Now that they have stolen the generator and are refusing to say where it is, he has had no other option but to order that they are punished.'

'*What?*'

'Furthermore, Rafael has told me his village is on the verge of anarchy, and that it will spread to other villages in the mountains.'

'This is crazy,' Marco told his grandfather. 'If anyone should be locked up, it's Rafael with his prehistoric views. Grandfather, you must see how foolish it was for him to have done this,' Marco implored. His grandfather was after all an educated, astute and wily man, whilst Rafael was a simple peasant.

'What I see is that you are the cause of this trouble with your reckless refusal to obey my commands.'

Marco didn't trust himself to stay and listen to any more, in case it provoked him into open warfare with his grandfather and his outdated ideas. Giving King Giorgio a small, formal half-bow, he then turned on his heel and strode out of the room.

In the corridors dust motes danced on the warm afternoon air. Emily would be back at the villa by now. An image of her slid into his head: she would be sitting in the shade, and when she saw him walking towards her she would look up at him and give him that welcoming smile. She would also look cool and calm, and just seeing her would take the edge off his own frustration. Right now, he admitted, he would give anything to share his experiences of the morning with her. Emily, with her understanding and her sympathetic ear—he needed both of those very badly.

He paused. There it was again, that word, 'need'. It suddenly struck him how very alone he would be feeling right now if Emily hadn't been here on Niroli with him. It was only since bringing her to the island that he had recognised how good she was with people, and at problem-solving, and how much it meant to him to have the safety valve of being able to talk openly to her about the situation with his grandfather. Increasingly he was beginning to feel that he didn't want her to leave either the island or his bed. But whilst he might flout the royal rules for the benefit of his people, where his personal life was concerned he couldn't do the same and succeed. The only way he could keep Emily on the island was by elevating her to the position of Royal Mistress, and to do that he would have to procure a suitably noble husband for her, one who understood the way in which these things were done. Whilst he knew he would be able to find such a husband, he also knew that Emily would refuse point-blank to enter that kind of marriage and, besides… Besides what? He didn't *want* her to have a husband…

He had no time to delve into the inner workings of his mind at the moment, he reminded himself; nor could he go back to the villa—and Emily—no matter how much he wanted to do so. First he must go up to Rafael's village and deal with the situation there before it got any worse. And what about his growing dependence on Emily? When was he going to deal with that—before it got worse?

'Emily.'

She tensed as she heard Marco call out her name as he came out into the sheltered inner courtyard, where she was seated in the shade, one hand lying protectively against her stomach as she tried to come to terms with everything.

It was early evening and she could hear the sharp edge of something unfamiliar in his voice. What was it? Not tiredness or irritation, and certainly not anxiety, but somehow a *something* that made her heart ache for him, above and beyond her own pain and fear for herself and their child. Was it always going to be like this? Was she always going to have this instinctive need to give him the best of her love? How could she do so now?

'I would have been back earlier,' Marco told her, 'but I had to go up to Rafael's village to put an end to some trouble brewing there, as my grandfather informed me with great delight earlier.'

'What kind of trouble?' Emily asked anxiously.

Marco sat down next to her. She could smell the dusty heat

of the day on him, but under it she was, as always, acutely conscious of the scent that was so sensually him. However, this evening, instead of filling her with desire, it filled her with a complex mix of emotions so intense that they clogged her throat with tears—tears for their baby, who would never know and recognise his father's scent, tears for herself because she would have to live without Marco. But, most of all, tears for Marco himself, because he could never share with her the unique feeling that came from knowing they had created a life together. Her child, their child, his first-born child. The huge tremor of emotion that seized her shook her whole body, overwhelming her with a flood of love and pain in equal proportions. She wanted this baby—his child—so very much. Its conception might have been wholly unplanned, but if she could go back and change things she knew that she would not do so. She was a modern woman, financially independent, with her own home and her own business, and more than enough love to give to her baby. A baby that would never know its father's love, she reminded herself as Marco answered her question, forcing her to focus on what he was saying and to put her own thoughts to one side.

'Rafael had tried to stop the villagers using the generator,' he explained. 'So Tomasso and some of his friends rebelled and hijacked it. Then Rafael—with my grandfather's approval—had the young fools punished. They were already antagonistic towards a way of life that traps them in the past and my grandfather's old-fashioned determination to enforce a way of life on them to their detriment.'

'It can't be good that they feel so disenfranchised,' Emily felt bound to comment.

'I know,' Marco acknowledged. 'If my grandfather was more reasonable, I could discuss with him my concern that these youngsters could, if handled the wrong way, become so disaffected that ultimately it could result in civil unrest and even violence. But the minute I tell him that, his reaction will be to have them imprisoned.'

'You need to find a way of getting them onside and opening a dialogue with them that allows them to feel their concerns are being addressed,' Emily offered.

'My views exactly,' Marco agreed. 'I've told them that it's an issue I intend to take on board once I take over from my grandfather and I've asked them to be patient until then. But I also know that the moment I start instituting any reforms, the old guard is going to react against them, because my grandfather has drip-fed them the fear that change means that they will lose out in some way.'

Emily listened sympathetically. She could see how passionately Marco felt about the situation. But she also sensed that the more angry and opposed to his grandfather Marco became, the less chance there was of them reaching a mutually acceptable solution.

'I don't have to tell you that your grandfather is an old man,' she replied. 'It may be that his pride won't allow him to admit that he has got things wrong and they've gone too far, or that the way the island is ruled needs to change. You might have to backtrack a little, Marco, and find a way to offer him a face-saving way of accepting your changes. Maybe you could handle them in such a way that he could feel they were his ideas—in public at least.' She could see from Marco's expression that he wasn't willing to take on board what she was saying. It seemed to her that he and his grandfather were two very proud and stubborn men and that neither was prepared to give in to the other.

'You haven't seen anything of the island yet,' he told her abruptly. 'We'll remedy that tomorrow.' For Emily's benefit, or for his own, because he needed to put some distance between himself and his grandfather?

CHAPTER TWELVE

'ARE you sure you've got time to do this?' Emily queried as Marco held open the door of the car for her before they set off to see something of the island. The morning sunshine cast sharp patterns on the worn flagstones of the courtyard and Emily was glad of the welcome coolness of the air-conditioned car. Hadn't she read somewhere that pregnancy increased the blood flow and made one feel warmer? Pregnancy. She ached to be able to share her joy with Marco and yet, at the same time, she was also afraid of his reaction. If he should try to pressure her into having a termination it would break her heart, but, logically, what else could he do? Even if he was prepared to understand and accept that she wanted to have this baby and bring it up alone, she suspected that his grandfather would be totally opposed to the idea. The old king would surely put pressure on Marco to deal with her. She didn't want to put Marco in that position and she wanted to keep her child as far away as possible from what increasingly she felt was a very negative kind of environment. The Nirolian royal family might be the richest in the world, but so far as Emily was concerned they seemed to be as dysfunctional as they were wealthy. Money wasn't important to her, so long as she had enough for her needs. She wanted her child to grow up confident that he or she was rich in love rather than money. What she wanted, she admitted, was for her child to be raised somewhere very far away from Niroli and without the burden of being a royal bastard. So what was she going to do? Return to London without telling Marco she was having his child?

That was certainly her easiest option, Emily felt. But did she have the strength to do it? Could she walk away from Marco without telling him? She loved her child enough already to do whatever she had to do to protect him or her, including leaving the man she adored; she knew that, almost without having to think about it. However, did she also love Marco enough to spare him the necessity of having to take on board prospective fatherhood and the problems that would cause for him? Was she strong enough to deny her instinctive longing to share her news with him, even though she knew he couldn't, and wouldn't, share her growing joy at the prospect of having his baby?

It was an extraordinarily wonderful gift that fate was giving her: a child, and not just any child, but the seed of the man she loved. She could picture him now; somehow Emily already knew that her baby would be a boy. He would have Marco's features and perhaps a little of his arrogance. He would look at her with Marco's eyes and she would melt with love for him and the man who had fathered him. And, later, when he was old enough to demand his father's name? She would deal with that when it happened. For now, what concerned her most was her baby's health and whether she could leave Niroli without Marco suspecting anything. So how was she going to do that? She couldn't just tell him she didn't want him any more. He would never believe her.

Perhaps he would believe her if she told him she wasn't comfortable with her role in his life. She wasn't even his formally recognised mistress, and she felt it could reflect on her business reputation. Marco's own pride meant that he would be able to identify with that. Last night, when they had made love, he hadn't questioned the way she had encouraged him to gentle his possession of her, holding her breath a little, caught as she was between her maternal anxiety for her baby and the intense physical desire he always aroused in her. But Marco was a skilled and a sensual lover, who knew every single one of her body's responses and how to invoke them. There was no way he wouldn't soon notice a new desire on her part to make his penetration of her less intense.

A small, sad semi-smile touched her lips. Marco didn't know it yet, but the sightseeing journey they were taking together today could well be the last they would make together. Now she was destined to set out on a new path, which she would share with this gift he had given her.

'Seat belt,' Marco reminded her. He reached across to secure the belt for her, before she could stop him. Immediately Emily breathed in, protectively. There was no bump of any kind to betray her, but still she felt a sharp clutch of anxiety for the vulnerability of her child. It would be like this for the rest of her life, she recognised. No matter that one day this baby she had conceived so unintentionally would be an adult; as a mother she would always be fiercely protective. Though, of course, there would be many things she could not protect her child from, foremost amongst which would be the pain of knowing his father hadn't wanted him.

'Emily?'

To her shock, Marco had placed his hand flat against her belly. Fearfully she turned to look at him. Had he, by some intuitive means, actually guessed?

'You're looking so much better than you did when you first arrived here,' she heard him tell her. 'Niroli's sunshine has done you good.'

Shakily, Emily released her pent-up breath. He hadn't guessed; it was just her own anxiety that was making her think that he must have done.

'I don't think anyone wouldn't enjoy it. I know I haven't seen much of the island…'

'Today, we're going to see as much of it as we can,' Marco told her as he started the car, 'and my royal duties will just have to wait.'

Whatever else the future held for Marco's child, she was glad that it wouldn't be the dark shadow of duty that fell across Marco's life, Emily decided emotionally. The little boy might have to grow up not knowing his father, but he would be free of the burden Marco carried, and she was passionately grateful for that. Though, at the same time, almost overwhelmed by the intensity of her love for Marco, she reflected as he turned the car off the main road into a much narrower lane that ran close to the high, rocky coastline where cliffs plunged down into the sea.

'This was one of my favourite places when I was a boy,' Marco confided as he stopped the car.

Emily could understand why. There was an elemental wildness about it; in some ways, the landscape matched the man.

'Come on, let's get out of the car.'

Emily wasn't sure she wanted to. The height of the cliffs gave her an uncomfortable feeling of vertigo. But she could see that Marco was determined and she didn't want to have to explain to him how she felt.

'I used to come here and gaze out to sea, and promise myself that one day I'd get away from here and from my grandfather. But, of course, even then I knew that ultimately I would have to come back,' Marco confessed, once they were standing a few feet back from the edge of the cliff-top. He bent down and picked up a handful of the thin, stony soil that lay at the roots of the weather-beaten gorse bushes that grew in such abundance along this part of the coast, and flung it as far out to sea as he could.

Watching him, Emily knew that this was a re-enactment of something he had done many times as a boy—as a way of releasing the anger inside him? It was an emotion he had partially dissipated by leaving the island and making a life for himself. But it would never really leave him so long as he and his grandfather struggled for supremacy one over the other. And whilst they were embroiled in that struggle, others would suffer. She could not allow her child to be one of them…

All of a sudden it hit her: she *had* to tell Marco that she intended to leave. She couldn't stop herself from reaching out to touch him and placed her hand on his bare forearm. Immediately he turned towards her.

'Marco,' she began tentatively, and then stopped. Unexpectedly he reached for her and took her in his arms, kissing her with such fiercely sweet passion that it made her eyes sting with tears.

Why was he doing this? Marco asked himself. He knew that it couldn't go on. Already, deep down inside, he knew he was becoming too dependent on her, and she was becoming too important to him. That couldn't be allowed to happen. There was no room in his life for that kind of relationship with her. He was Niroli's future king and he intended to devote every ounce of his mental and physical energy to his country and its people. He would break down the restrictions that centuries of royal rule had placed, he would open the door for Niroli's population to walk freely into the new century. There was no legitimate place in his life for the kind of relationship he had with Emily. He was reeling at the way he felt about her now, the intensity that was being demanded of him. It was only recently he had started to feel like this, to recognise there was within him this dangerous need to have her close, a need that went far beyond any kind of sexual desire. But such emotion could not be allowed to exist, it could not be given a name, or a place in his life.

He started to pull away from her and then stopped, smothering a savage groan before he tightened his hold on her and kissed her again.

Emily's mouth felt soft and giving beneath his own, her body warm, and he longed to possess her and fill her and lose himself in her and know the passion of loving her.

'Marco!' Emily objected, somehow managing to stem her own longing and drag her mouth from beneath his. She was trembling from head to foot, afraid not of him but of herself and the intensity of her feelings, and stumbling over the words in her desperation.

'There's no easy way to say this, but the truth is that I should never have come here. Niroli is different from London, and my role in your life has changed. I can't live like this, Marco, a semi-secret mistress, despised and ignored by the court, and forced to live in the shadows. I'm going back to the UK just as soon as it can be arranged. It will be best for both of us.'

She was only saying what he already knew to be true, and yet he felt as shocked as though his guts had been splintered with ice picks. She couldn't do this! He wasn't ready to let her go. He needed her here with him. He should, he knew, be feeling relieved, but instead he felt more as though he had suffered a mortal blow. Pain rolled over him in mind-numbing waves, crashing through him and drowning out reason, spreading its unbearable agony to every part of him. He could hardly think for it, do anything other than try somehow to survive its rapacious teeth as it savaged him and tormented him. How could this have happened? How could he be experiencing this? The thoughts and feelings that filled him were so new and unfamiliar that they made him feel as though he was suddenly a stranger to him-self. He felt like a man possessed by…by what? He shook his head, unable to allow the word pulsing in his heart to form. He had wanted it to happen, he had wanted her to leave. But not like this… He'd wanted to be the one to tell her to go… But how? That he didn't want her here because he was afraid that she would come between him and his duty? His whole body shuddered as the pain savaged it once more.

Why didn't Marco say something, anything? Emily worried anxiously.

What could she say without risking betraying the truth?

'I loved the life we shared together in London, Marco. But things are different here. The time we're sharing together is borrowed time, stolen time, perhaps,' she told him sadly. 'It's better that I go now.'

Marco could feel the heavy drum of his heartbeat thudding out a requiem for their relationship as he heard the finality in her voice.

'There'll never be anyone else in my life like you, Marco, nor a relationship to match the one we've shared.'

The words felt as though they were being ripped from her like a layer of her skin, but she couldn't hold them back; they were after all the truth, even though she knew she was a fool for having said them.

But it didn't matter now that she was compounding that error by lifting her hand to his face, tears burning at the backs of her eyes as she felt the familiar texture that was hard with the beginnings of his beard against the softness of her palm.

'Emily.'

He had caught hold of her hand before she could stop him, lifting it to his lips and then dropping it when he felt her tremble, to pull her bodily into his arms and then plunder her mouth with his own. Not that she made any attempt to resist him. Instead, she gave him the sweetness he was demanding whilst she clung helplessly to him.

Few people visited this part of the island, and Marco realised that an irresistible need was flooding through him to know the intimacy of sex on this wild headland. He couldn't let her go without this one last time, a final memory he would have to make last a lifetime of days and nights once he was without her. There had been many many times when their pleasure had been more sensual and more sustained, when he had deliberately set himself the task of pleasing her. But no time had ever been more intense than this, or more emotional. Because this was the last time that finally he could give to himself what he had previously so rigidly denied, and that was the right to feel with his emotions what he was feeling with his flesh.

This was too much, Emily told herself. She just wasn't strong enough to endure this kind of passion. It was as though Marco had wrenched away, with his clothes, the barrier she had always sensed he kept raised against her.

As they lay together on the lavender-scented turf, the sun warming their naked bodies, the kisses he lavished on her body were hot and fierce with a desire that went beyond the merely physical. As though by shared consent, neither of them spoke. What words were there to say, after all? Emily wondered, with dry-eyed hurt. Words would only be lies, or, worse, create wounds. It was better this way, that their last memory of one another was one filled with a shared but unspoken awareness of what they'd shared and what they would never have again. It seemed to Emily as she touched him that she had never loved him more. Something within her, that was maybe both lover and prospective mother, swelled her heart with bitter-sweet emotion.

They kissed and touched, their lips clinging, their bodies urgent, trying desperately to hold onto every second of their pleasure. But, like sand, it could not be held, running swiftly through their fingers instead as Emily's cries of pleasure became soft sighs of contentment.

She would treasure her memories of this day for the rest of her life.

She smiled lazily up at Marco as he leaned over her.

'I don't want you to leave.'

Marco had no idea where the words had come from. No! That was lie. He knew exactly where they had come from and why. And even if he hadn't, the heavy pounding of his heart would have told him. What on earth was he doing, when he had already decided that she must go? What had happened to him to make him want to change his mind on the strength of a few minutes of good sex? he derided himself. But it wasn't the good sex he didn't want to lose—it was Emily herself.

Emily wondered if anything else in her life could ever be as poignant as this. Marco had never, ever asked her for anything, never mind pleaded with her so emotionally! She so wanted to fling herself into his arms and cover his face with passionately joyful kisses as she told him there was nothing she wanted more than to be with him. But how could she?

'Marco, I'm sorry. I can't.' Her voice was little more than an anguished whisper, but Marco heard it, releasing her abruptly and turning away from her. She knew how much it must have cost him to ask her to stay. Given his inbuilt sense of male arrogance and his pride, along with his background and upbringing, she could only marvel that he had.

She got to her feet and said his name unsteadily, but he was already heading back to the car.

'Marco!' she protested. 'Please listen to me…'

He stopped walking and turned around. She saw his chest

lift as he breathed in sharply and the sadness that filled her was not just for herself, but for both of them. She knew what she had to do, where her responsibility now lay, but how could she walk away letting him think that she hadn't wanted to stay with him? She couldn't, she decided frantically. Yes, she had her baby to think of and, yes, she was afraid of Marco's reaction to the news that she was pregnant. But she loved Marco, too, and the knowledge that he wanted her enough to actually ask her to stay was too sweetly precious that she couldn't deny its tremendous effect on her.

She still had to leave, nothing could change that, but she knew she couldn't go away from him without telling him why it was so important that she went.

She took a deep breath; this was the most difficult thing she had ever had to do. 'I don't *want* to leave you, Marco. But I *have* to. You see, I'm having your child. I'm pregnant.'

What? Marco could feel her words exploding inside his skull as he battled with his own disbelief.

'I know you told me at the beginning of our relationship that there must not be any accidents,' Emily continued, carefully cutting into the tension of his complete silence, 'and…and of course I understand now why you said that. The future King of Niroli's bastard isn't the title I want for our baby.' She gave a small shrug. 'The truth is, I don't want him to have any title at all, and if there is one thing in all of this that I am grateful for, it's that our son won't ever have to live the kind of controlled and confined life you will have to live. What I want for him more than anything else is the kind of personal freedom that you don't have and that you can't give to your legitimate children. I want him to grow up in a home filled with love, where what matters most is that he finds his own sense of where his life lies and how his talents should be used. I don't want his future to be corrupted by wealth and position. I don't want him to have to carry the burdens I can see you carrying, Marco. I can't give him his father, but I can give him the right to define his own life, and to me that heritage is of far more value than anything your legitimate children will inherit.'

For a few seconds, Marco was too taken aback by what she had said to speak. From the moment of his birth he had been brought up to be aware of the tremendous importance of his role and his family. The thought that someone was not awed and impressed by it was something he found hard to take in. But he could see that Emily meant what she'd said. Senses of isolation and aloneness, of having lost something he could never regain, an awareness that somehow, somewhere, he had turned his back on something precious stabbed through him. With it came the drift of painful memories: of himself as a young boy longing passionately for the freedom to be himself. He could see his father's struggles and his mother's anguish and, of course, his grandfather's anger. He could also hear the echo of his own childishly piping voice stating defiantly, 'When I am grown up and I can do what I want, I won't be a prince!' But with a kick like an iron-tipped boot, slowly but surely his position and its claims on him had reshaped him. He pictured two small boys, both dark-haired and sturdy, one of them grubby and laughing as he played happily with his friends. The other was sad-eyed and alone, held at a respectful distance by his peers, protected by privilege, or was he imprisoned by it?

What folly was this? Marco forced back the memories, refusing to acknowledge them any more, letting his pride take over instead. 'You are being naïve. No one else will share your views, Emily. In fact, they will think you a fool. And, besides, being King of Niroli is about more than any of those things,' he retaliated sharply. 'It's about making a difference to my people, it's about leading them to a better future. Do you really think our son, my son, will thank you for denying him his birthright?'

'He has no birthright here on Niroli. I am your mistress, and he will be illegitimate.'

'He has the birthright I choose to give him.'

'By recognising him and making him face the world as less than your children born within royal wedlock? By making him grow up in an environment where he will always be beneath them—in their eyes and, ultimately, in his own?'

'He will be a member of the Niroli royal family, how can you think of denying him that? Do you really think he will thank you when he is old enough to know what he has lost?'

In the space of a few heated sentences, they had become opponents, Emily recognised.

'It doesn't matter how much we argue about our own feelings,' she told him. 'You are not yet King Marco, and I doubt that your grandfather would welcome the birth of an illegitimate child to a woman of such lowly status as me.'

There was just enough edge to her voice to warn Marco that, at some stage, she had learned of his grandfather's opinion of her.

'The fact that I am his father automatically gives him his own status,' Marco retaliated, and then realised his words had added to Emily's fury rather than soft-ened it.

'Yes, as your bastard—a royal bastard, I know. But he will still be your bastard. I won't let him suffer that, Marco. I'm going home.'

'Niroli is my child's home, and this is where you and he are staying. When did you find out—about the child?' he demanded abruptly.

'Very recently. I had no idea…' Emily looked away from

Marco, remembering how shocked she had been. 'I would never have agreed to come here with you, if I'd known.'

'So how would you have informed me that I'd become a father? Via a birth notice in *The Times?*'

Emily flinched as she heard the savagery in his voice. 'That wouldn't happen,' she told him quietly. It had been foolish of her to give in to her urge to comfort him, because now she had created a new set of problems. Why had she told him? Because secretly she had been hoping—what? That he would sweep her up into his arms and say that he was thrilled she was expecting their child?

'I'm sorry if I've given you a shock. I was stunned myself when I realised. But I didn't want you to think I was leaving because…' The words 'because I don't love you' formed a tight knot that blocked her throat. How could she say them when she knew he didn't want her love? 'I wanted you to know that I have a valid reason for leaving the island,' she amended, her voice growing firmer as she underlined, 'a reason that matters to both of us. We already knew that one day we would have to part. The fact that I have accidentally conceived your child only makes that parting all the more essential. We both know that. I will not be your pregnant mistress, Marco.'

Emily was having his child, their child! A complex mixture of unfamiliar emotions were curling their fingers into his heart and tugging hard on it.

'How far advanced is this pregnancy?' he asked her brusquely.

Emily felt as though her whole body had been plunged into ice-cold water. This was what she had dreaded. An argument with him, in which he would try to demand that she terminate her pregnancy—something she had absolutely no intention of doing.

'I'm not sure,' she admitted honestly. 'I think that possibly it could have happened when I had that stomach bug. I remember reading somewhere that that kind of thing can neutralise the effect of the contraceptive pill. I should have thought about that at the time, but I didn't.' She lifted her head and told him firmly, '*You* needn't worry about the consequences, though, Marco. I am fully prepared to take sole responsibility for my child.'

'My child.' Marco stopped her ruthlessly. 'The child is my child, Emily.'

She looked at him uncertainly. It hadn't occurred to her that he would react like this. He sounded almost as though he felt as possessive about the baby as she did herself.

'I don't want to discuss it any more, Marco. There's no point. I can't stay here now.'

The morning sun was slanting across the courtyard. The coffee Maria had brought him half an hour earlier had grown cold as Marco sat deep in thought. He was not going to let Emily leave. And he was not going to allow his child to grow up anywhere other than here on Niroli. Both were unassailable and unchangeable tenets of what he felt about his role as king-in-waiting and as the father of Emily's expected baby. It wasn't any longer a matter of what he did or didn't want; it was a matter of his royal duty, to his pride, to his name and to his first-born.

It was ridiculous of Emily to suggest that their child would have benefits that his so-called legitimate children would not, folly for her to claim that he would one day thank her for denying him his royal status. Marco might have enjoyed the freedom of his time in London, but he had also never forgotten who and what he was. Having royal blood and being able to lay claim to it, even if one was born on the wrong side of the blanket, was a life-enhancing benefit that couldn't be

ignored. His son, growing up here on Niroli as his accepted
child, could look forward to the best of everything and, when
grown, a position of authority at his father's court. He would
be revered and respected, he would wield power and he would
be on hand to support his legitimate half-sibling when finally
he became King. Would he be imprisoned by his royal status,
as Marco had sometimes felt he had been? No!

All of that and more could be made possible for this child,
provided that Emily was prepared to see sense. She didn't have
the status of a proper royal mistress, that was true. But his
grandfather, for all his faults and stubbornness, also had a
strong sense of duty and family. He, too, would want his great-
grandchild to remain on Niroli. There was a way in which it
could be made possible for her to stay and be elevated to a
position in which she and their baby would have the respect
of the people.

He swung round as he heard Emily come out into the courtyard. The sun had brushed her skin a warm gold, driving
away its London pallor. She wasn't showing any visible sign
of her pregnancy yet, but there was a rich glow about her,
somehow, a sense of ripeness to come. Watching her, Marco
experienced a swift surge of possessive determination not to
let her go. She was having his child; whether by accident and
not by design, that did not alter his paternal responsibilities
or that a baby of royal blood was to be born. Who other than
he could tell that child about his heritage and where better a
place to do that than here on Niroli?

'I've just seen Maria and she's going to bring out some
fresh coffee for you.' How domestic and comfortable that
sounded, Emily thought tiredly as she sat down on the chair
Marco had pulled out for her. She had hardly slept, her
thoughts circling helplessly and tumultuously.

'I'm not prepared to let you leave the island, Emily. You,

and my child, are going to stay here where both of you belong. It seems to me that marriage is the best way to secure our son's future and your position at court.'

Marriage! Emily almost dropped the glass of water she had been drinking. Marco wanted to marry her? She was shaking from head to foot with the intensity of her joy. Emotional tears filled her eyes. She put down the glass, and protested shakily, 'Marco! You can't mean that. How can you marry me?'

She realised immediately from his expression that something was wrong.

'I can't marry you,' he told her flatly. 'You know that. What on earth made you think that I could?' Why did he feel this dragging weight wrapping itself around him? He couldn't marry Emily, and he was surprised that she had thought he might. And, yet, just for a moment, seeing the joy in her eyes, he had felt... He had felt *what?* A reciprocal surge of joy within himself? That was ridiculous.

'You need a husband, Emily, and a position at court. There is within European royal families a tradition whereby noblemen close to the throne marry royal mistresses. This kind of marriage is rather like a business arrangement, in that it benefits all parties and, in the eyes of the world, bestows respectability on the mistress and any children she may bear. The nobleman in question is of course rewarded for his role and—'

'Stop it. Stop it. I have heard enough!' Emily had pushed back her chair and got to her feet. She could hardly breathe but she struggled to speak. 'I thought I knew you, Marco. I even felt sorry for you, because of the heavy responsibility your duty to the Crown lays upon you! But now I realise that I never really knew you. The man I thought I knew would never in a thousand years have allowed himself to become so corrupted by power and pride that he would suggest what you have just suggested to me!'

'What I propose is a traditional solution to a uniquely royal problem,' Marco persisted curtly. 'You are overreacting.' Her outburst had made him feel as though he were doing something wrong, instead of recommending a logical solution to their problem. A logical solution of the kind his grandfather would have suggested? Was the pressure of becoming King turning him into a man like his grandfathe, the kind of man he had once sworn he would never allow himself to be? His critical inner voice would not be silenced, and its contempt echoed uncomfortably inside him.

'Am I? Take a look at yourself, Marco, and try seeing yourself through my eyes, and then repeat what you have just offered as a solution. You want to bribe another man to marry me so that—so that *what?* You can have your child here, conveniently legitimised by a convenient marriage between two strangers, though I'm sure that won't stop the gossip. But what about me? Am I expected to be a dutiful bride to this noble husband you're going to find for me? Am I supposed to submit willingly to having sex with him, bear his children, be his wife in all senses of the word?'

'No, there will be no question of that.' The harshness of his own immediate denial caught Marco off guard. But he couldn't retract his words, nor deny the feeling of fierce possessiveness that had gripped him at the thought of Emily in another man's bed.

'What kind of man are you, Marco, if you think that I would be willing to sell myself into such an arrangement? But then I was forgetting: you aren't a mere man, are you? You are a king! I'm not staying on the island a minute longer than I have to. Everything you've just said underlines all the reasons why I don't want my son growing up here. Your proximity to the throne has corrupted you, but I don't intend to let it corrupt my child.'

'And I don't intend to let you leave Niroli.'

They had been the closest of lovers, but now they were enemies locked in a battle to the bitter end for the right to decide the future of their child.

CHAPTER THIRTEEN

THE plane had taken off, but Emily was holding her breath, half expecting that, somehow, Marco still could prevent her from leaving Niroli.

She'd hated having to appeal to Marco's grandfather for help behind his back. At first, the king had refused to see her when she'd made her secret visit to the palace. She had been expecting his rejection, though, and so had lifted her chin and told the stiff-faced, uniformed equerry who had told her that the king would not receive her, 'Please tell His Majesty that the favour I want to ask him will benefit both of us and the throne of Niroli.'

She had been made to wait over an hour before she had finally been shown into the royal presence. It had shocked her to see how very like the king Marco was, traces of Marco's stunning good looks still visible in the older man's profile.

She had chosen her moment with care, waiting until she knew that Marco had gone up to the mountains to see Rafael before she visited the palace.

'I want to leave Niroli,' she told King Giorgio. 'But Marco does not wish me to leave. He has said he will do everything in his power to stop me and to keep me here.' She didn't tell the king about her pregnancy, just in case he echoed Marco's insistence that her child be brought up under the cover of an arranged marriage between herself and a nobleman.

'Only you have the authority to enable me to leave without Marco knowing.'

'Why should I do that?' the king challenged her.

Emily was ready for that. 'Because you do not want me here,' she replied. 'You do not consider me good enough to be Marco's mistress.'

'He is not the man I thought if he cannot provide sufficient inducement to keep you in his bed, if that is where he wants you.'

'Marco is more than man enough for any woman,' Emily defended. 'But I am too much of a woman to be prepared to share him with the throne and everything else that entails.'

She thought she saw a glimmer of grudging respect in the king's eyes before he gave a stiff nod of his head. 'Very well. I will help you. A royal flight will be made ready for you, and I shall ensure that Marco is kept out of the way until it has taken off.'

The king had kept his promise to her, and now she was on her way home. She closed her eyes against the acid burn of her tears and pressed her hand against her body as though in mute apology to her baby for what she was doing. 'You may not understand it now, but I'm doing this for you and for your future,' she whispered to him.

'How dare you do this?' White-faced with rage, Marco towered over his grandfather, royal protocol forgotten in his fury. Now he knew why Rafael had kept him at the village for so long with his endless complaints against young Tomasso and his friends.

When he had returned to the villa to find Emily missing, he had summoned Maria, and she had been the one who had told him that a car bearing the royal crest had arrived for her.

He had gone straight to the palace, demanding to see his grandfather.

'Emily applied to me for aid, because she feared you would force her to remain here on Niroli against her will. Naturally, I helped her.'

'Naturally,' Marco agreed grimly, registering even more grimly that her departure had elevated Emily from being a floozy to someone his grandfather was prepared to speak of with far more intimacy. 'After all, you never wanted her here.'

'Whatever role she might have played in your life in London, there is no place for her here on Niroli. She herself accepts this and, in doing so, she shows far more sense and awareness of the importance of your future role than you do, Marco. I confess that she impressed me with her grasp of your responsibility. She fully understands what will entail when you become Niroli's king.'

'She also fully understands that she is to be the mother of my child,' Marco told his grandfather sharply. 'That is why she has left—but I don't expect she told you that, did she?'

'She is having your child?'

'Yes,' Marco confirmed unashamedly.

The king was frowning imperiously. 'But that alters everything. Why did you not say something to me about this? She must be brought back, and at once! What if this child she is carrying should be a son? It is unthinkable that he should be brought up anywhere but here. Sons are a precious commodity, Marco, even if they are illegitimate. It is important that this child grows up on Niroli knowing his duty and his responsibility to the Crown. That knowledge cannot be instilled in him too early. When is the birth expected? There is much to do—the royal nursery will have to be prepared, and a suitable household established to take charge of him. The mother can stay in London if she wishes, in fact it would be better if she did,' the king continued dismissively.

His grandfather was only painting a picture that was similar to the one he himself had put before Emily. But instead of feeling vindicated, Marco could feel a cold heaviness seeping through him, as though leaden weights had been tied to his hands so that he was effectively imprisoned.

'You will order the woman to return, and when you do you will inform her that it is against the law of Niroli for anyone to remove a child of royal blood from the island, on penalty of death.'

Marco shook his head.

'Don't be ridiculous, Grandfather. Once in some mediaeval age it might have been possible to make such a threat, but I can tell you now that the British courts will take a dim view of it, and that Emily is totally within her rights to want to keep her child with her. I would certainly support her in that. I want my child to grow up here, yes, but I also want his mother to be here for him, as well.'

'Ridiculous sentimentality. I blame your mother for it. And your father. He should have insisted that she followed tradition and handed you over to those appointed to be responsible for your care as a future king, instead of meddling in matters that did not concern her. It is thanks to her that you developed this stubborn streak that puts you at odds with your duty.'

Marco forced himself not to say anything. Instead he focused on his childhood. He could see himself playing, running and his mother chasing him, and he could see too the disapproving looks of the elderly courtiers his grandfather had insisted were to be responsible for his upbringing and formation. His mother, had she still been alive, would have supported Emily and helped her. They would have got on well. His father had struggled to oppose the king's insistence that Marco was brought up to be a prince, rather than as a member of a warm and loving family. His grandfather would try to impose his will on his great-grandchild, Marco knew. He frowned, suddenly sharply aware of his own desire to protect his child from the cold discipline and royal training he had known in his own childhood. He was not his father, he reminded himself. He was more than strong enough to ensure that his son was not subjected to the misery of his boyhood.

'Whilst you are here,' his grandfather was continuing imperiously, 'I have decided that the generators will have to be removed from the island completely. They are causing too much conflict between our peoples. It is just as I had thought, these young dissidents in the mountains have been encouraged by the Viallis to band together and challenge the authority of their village elders. And the blame for that can be laid at our door, Marco. By publicly going against my wishes, you have turned yourself into a figurehead for their rebellion. Various informants have told me of their concern that they are only waiting until you are on the throne to force your hand and make demands that can never be granted. If there is any more trouble, I shall impose a curfew—that will teach them to respect the law and the Crown.'

'If these youngsters are angry and filled with resentment, who can blame them?' Marco demanded. 'They need the controls on their lives relaxing, not tightening to the point where there is bound to be increased conflict. By imposing a curfew, all you will be doing is driving their feelings underground and alienating them further. What we need is to establish a forum in which they feel they can be heard and their views properly addressed.'

'What, reward them for their rebelliousness and their disrespect? They need teaching a lesson, not to be indulged.'

'Have a care, Grandfather,' Marco warned. 'Feed their sense of injustice by imposing your royal will, and in the end we will all pay a heavy price.'

'Bah…! You are too soft, too much the modern liberal. You cannot rule Niroli like that, Marco. You rule it like this!' The old king closed his fist and banged it down hard on the table in front of him. 'By letting them know what it is to fear your anger.'

As he had learned to fear his grandfather's anger as a child? As his son would be forced to learn to fear it? Marco was filled with a sense of revulsion. He had returned to Niroli committed to working to improve things for its people, but now he was beginning to question his ability to do that. With his grandfather so opposed to the changes he wanted to make, and his own views so diametrically opposed to the king's, weren't they more likely to tear Niroli apart between them than anything else? Perhaps Emily was right to refuse to allow their child to be brought up here?

Marco closed his eyes, deep in thought. No, his son should be here because he, his father, was here. Emily would have to accept his determination to play his royal role, whether she liked it or not…

CHAPTER FOURTEEN

EMILY sat huddled in the squashy, cream-ticking-covered chair in the pretty sitting room of her Chelsea home, staring numbly at the letter she was holding. Not that she needed to read it again. She knew its every word off by heart, she had read it so many times since it had arrived two days ago: the consultant at the hospital where she had been for her twenty-week pregnancy scan wanted her to return, so that they could do a further test.

She had of course rung the hospital the moment she had received the summons, and the nurse she had spoken to had assured her that there was no need for her to worry. But Emily was very worried. In fact, she was worried sick, reliving over and over again that tell-tale moment during the ultrasound when the young operative had suddenly hesitated and then looked uncertainly at Emily before carrying on. Nothing had been said; she knew the scan had shown that her baby had all the right number of fingers and toes, and had even confirmed her belief that she was carrying Marco's son. If she hadn't received the letter requesting her to go back, she suspected she would never have given the girl's hesitation another thought. Why had she hesitated? Was there something wrong with her baby? Oh, please, God, don't let there be! Was she being punished because of what she had done? Because she had left Niroli? Because she was deliberately planning to lock Marco out of their son's life?

But that was to protect the baby, not punish Marco, she protested to herself.

The sound of someone ringing her doorbell brought her out of her painful thoughts: it would be Jemma. The shock of being requested to return for a second scan had brought home to her how alone in the world she was, and upset her so much that she had unburdened herself to her friend and assistant. As a result, Jemma had started to adopt an almost maternal attitude towards her and had insisted she would accompany her to her repeat scan. Smoothing down the skirt of the loose linen dress she was wearing, Emily got up to answer the door. Whilst she had been on Niroli a heatwave had come to the city and, at first, when she opened the door the light pouring in from the fashionable London street outside dazzled her so much that she thought she must be imagining things: it couldn't possibly be Marco who was standing on her immaculate doorstep, the formality of his dark business suit a perfect foil for the bright red of the geraniums that filled the elegant containers that flanked the entrance.

But it *was* Marco, and he was stepping into her hallway and closing the door behind him, looking just as impressive against the interior's old-English-white walls as he had done outside.

For a while after her return from Niroli, she had barely slept for fear that he would come after her and demand she go back. But there had been no sign of him. Then, the arrival of the letter had given her something much more worrying to keep her awake at night. Her heart was thumping in jerky uncoordinated beats; he had brought with him in the hallway, not just his presence, but also his scent. Helpless tears of longing pricked in her eyes, blurring her vision.

'Is this what you're planning to take to the hospital?'
Without waiting for her response, Marco leaned down to pick
up the pale straw basket into which she had packed everything
she thought she might need.

'The hospital?' Her voice faltered she was shocked by
those words, her face nearly as pale as her hall walls.

'I've just been round to the shop. Jemma told me about the
scan. I've got a cab waiting. Where are your keys?'

'Marco, there's no need for this. Jemma's coming with me.'

'No, she's not. *I* am going with you—there is every need
for me to do so. This is my child you are carrying, Emily. Are
you ready?'

She shouldn't be letting him take charge like this, Emily
told herself, but the stress of the last few days was telling on
her and she simply felt too weak and drained to argue with
him. And, besides…if she was honest, wasn't there something
comfortingly bitter-sweet about having him here with
her…with them… Her hand went to her tummy as inwardly
she whispered comforting words to her baby, promising it
that, no matter what the scan showed, no matter what anyone
said, he would have life and she would love him.

The stress of worrying about the baby had stolen from
Emily the bloom she had gained whilst she'd been on Niroli,
Marco recognised as he took hold of her arm and guided her
to the waiting taxi.

Marco gave the driver the name of a private hospital,
ignoring Emily's small start of surprise. It hadn't been difficult getting Jemma to tell him what had happened. In fact she
had been so relieved to see him that she had told him everything he needed to know without him having to probe. He had
come to London with the sole intention of taking Emily back
to Niroli with him, and of telling her that their child would be
born on the island and would remain there; whether or not she

chose to do the same was up to her. Since he had last seen her, his feelings towards Emily had turned both angry and hostile. She had gone behind his back to his grandfather; she had walked out on him, she had insulted him. She'd given him, for no good reason whatsoever, sleepless nights analysing what she'd said and what she hadn't, trying to find ways he could fit together the pieces of the jigsaw his life now was, working out what would make it possible for him to have her living on Niroli with him—and willingly. And then going over everything he had already analysed once more, to double-check that the reason he wanted her there was only because of his child. Because, somehow, though he found it hard to admit, deep down inside, a suspicion still lurked that he wanted *Emily*.

But the news Jemma had given him about Emily being called back for a second scan had caused a seismic emotional shift within him, so that all he could think about now, all that concerned him and occupied his thoughts, was Emily and their baby.

The hospital was one of London's most exclusive and private and Emily's obstetrician had been likely recommended to her. He was a charming middle-aged man, with a reassuring smile and a taste for bow ties. In his letter, he had stated that he would be on hand once Emily had had her repeat scan to discuss the results. It made her feel sickly cold inside every time she thought about the underlying hint that there might be some kind of problem.

'Has anyone said why you are having to have a second scan?' Marco asked her as the taxi pulled up outside the hospital.

Emily shook her head.

'But you have asked?'

'I rang Mr Bryant-Jones, my obstetrician, and he said that sometimes a repeat scan was needed.'

'But he didn't explain why?'

'No,' Emily admitted shakily. Marco's terse words, along with his grim expression, were increasing her fear.

Marco paid the taxi driver and, still carrying her basket, put his free hand under her elbow, for all the world as protective as though he were a committed husband. But he wasn't, and Emily knew she must not give in to her longing to turn to him and get him to reassure her that she had no need to worry, and that everything was going to be all right.

The hospital's reception area could well have been that of an expensive hotel, Emily recognised, looking at the two receptionists who were stunningly attractive and very smartly dressed.

It was Marco, and not she, who stepped forward and gave her name. But any thought she had of objecting to his high-handed manner or to his taking charge disappeared when she heard him telling the receptionist very firmly, 'Please inform Emily's obstetrician, Mr Bryant-Jones, that we are here.'

'My appointment with him isn't until after I've had my scan,' Emily reminded Marco. She could see that he was about to say something, but before he could do so a smiling nurse came up to them, asking, 'Emily? We're ready for you now, if you'd like to come this way.'

'I shall be coming with her,' Marco informed the nurse imperiously.

'Yes, of course. It's this way,' the nurse replied pleasantly.

'This isn't where I had my last scan,' Emily commented anxiously.

'No. Mr Bryant-Jones has requested a three-D scan this time.'

'A three-D scan—what's that?' Emily asked apprehensively.

'Nothing to worry about,' the nurse reassured her cheerfully. 'It's just a special imaging process that gives us a clearer, more in-depth picture of the baby, that's all.'

'But why…I mean, why do you need that?'

Emily wasn't aware that she had stopped walking until she felt Marco reach out and take hold of her hand. Anxiously she looked up at him, mutely telling him that she didn't feel able to go any further.

'Here we are,' the nurse announced, opening a door several yards up the corridor and holding it open, waiting for Marco and Emily to catch up with her. 'I'll hand you over to Merle, now,' she told Emily as another nurse came forward to direct her over to the waiting bed.

'Once you've put on your gown, the ultrasonographer will start the scan. I'll be putting some gel on your tummy, like the last time,' she told Emily kindly.

'You don't need to be here for this, Marco,' Emily told Marco firmly as she pulled the curtains round the bed and got undressed. For once, the thought of the potential indignity of wearing the universal hospital gown, with its open back fastening, didn't bother her. All she could think about was her baby. Why wouldn't anyone tell her anything? Part of her was relieved that Marco was ignoring her request and not making any move to leave, but another part of her felt even more anxious. If there was something wrong with their baby, Marco's pride... It didn't matter what Marco thought. She would have her baby, no matter what.

When Emily had changed into her gown and she drew back the curtains, she looked both vulnerable and afraid. Just looking at her caused a sensation in Marco that felt like a giant fist squeezing his heart and wringing from it an emotion so concentrated that it burned his soul.

The nurse helped Emily lie down on the bed next to the scanner and covered her legs with a blanket, then she started applying the necessary gel.

Given she was around twenty weeks pregnant, her stomach was only gently rounded. Emily held her breath anxiously as the ultrasonographer, a very professional-looking young woman passed, the probe over her bump, whilst studying the resulting images on the screen in front on her.

'Why am I having to have this kind of scan?' Emily asked her.

'See—look, your baby is yawning.' The ultrasonographer smiled, ignoring her questions. Emily stared at the screen, her heart giving a fierce kick of awed joy as she stared avidly at the small but perfect form.

'Maybe he's not a he, but a she.'

Emily had been so engrossed in watching the screen that she hadn't realised that Marco had come to stand behind her and was looking over her head at the image of their baby.

'Oh, I think we can safely say that he is a he,' the girl told him with a broad smile and pointing, before suddenly going silent as she moved the scanner further up the baby's body. Then her smile gave way to a frown of concentration.

Why wasn't she saying anything? Emily worried. Why was she staring at the screen so intently? Her heart thumped with fear.

'What is it?' Emily asked anxiously. 'Is something wrong?'

'I'm almost finished and then you'll be able to go and get dressed,' the girl told her smoothly. 'You've got an appointment to see Mr Bryant-Jones, I think?'

'Yes,' Emily confirmed. 'Look, if there's something wrong with my baby…'

'Mr Bryant-Jones will discuss the scan with you.' The girl was using her professional mask to hold her at a distance, Emily recognised shakily. She looked at Marco. She could see in his eyes that he too was aware of the heavy weight of what the girl had not said hanging in the room. What was it? What was wrong? The tiny being she'd seen on the scan had been yawning and stretching—to her eye, he looked completely perfect. Maybe she was worrying unnecessarily. Maybe this *was* just a routine check.

Her fingers trembled as she re-dressed herself. On the other side of the curtain, she could hear Merle, the nurse, telling Marco that as soon as Emily was ready she would escort them down to see the obstetrician…

CHAPTER FIFTEEN

EMILY could feel her anxiety bathing her skin in perspiration as they were shown into the obstetrician's office. Mr Bryant-Jones was smiling, but not as widely as he had done the first time she had seen him.

'Ah, Emily, good. Good.' He was looking past her towards Marco, but before Emily could introduce him Marco stepped forward, extending his hand and saying curtly, 'Prince Marco of Niroli. I am the baby's father.'

'Ah. Yes…. Excellent.'

'Mr Bryant-Jones, why have I had to have another scan?' Emily demanded, unable to wait any longer. 'And this three-D scan, what is that—? Why…?'

'Please sit down, both of you.' The obstetrician wasn't smiling any more. He was looking at the scanned images he had on his desk, moving them around. 'I'm sorry to have to tell you this, but it looks as though your baby may have a heart defect.'

'A heart defect? What exactly does that mean? Will my baby—?' Emily couldn't get any further; her pent-up emotions were bursting out and making it impossible for her to speak.

'The baby will have to be between twenty-two to twenty-four weeks before we can make a full diagnosis. At this stage, all we can tell from the scans is that there is a likelihood that your baby could have a foetal heart abnormality.'

'You said there *could* be a heart abnormality.'

Marco's voice seemed to be reaching Emily from over a great distance, as though she weren't really here and taking part in this dreadful, dreadful scene, as though she and her baby had gone away somewhere private and safe where nothing bad could touch them.

'What exactly does that mean?' Marco questioned the obstetrician.

'It means that the baby's heart does not seem to be forming as it should. Now, this can be a small problem, or it can be a far more serious one. We cannot tell which, as yet. That is why you will need to see a cardiac specialist. There is a very good one here in this hospital, who collaborates with our specialist neo-natal unit. My recommendation would be that we arrange for you to visit him as soon as it can be arranged.'

'Is…is my baby going to die?' Emily's voice shook with fear.

'No,' the obstetrician assured her. 'But depending on how severe the abnormality is, there could be a series of operations throughout his childhood and teenage years and, maybe, if things are extreme, there will be the necessity for a heart transplant at some stage. Severe heart malfunctions do limit the kind of life the sufferer can live. If this is the case, your son will need dedicated care; boys like to run and play vigorous games, but it might be a possibility that he'll not be able to do that.'

Her child could be a boy who might not be able to run and play like other children, a boy who could be subjected to operation after operation to keep him alive! But he would have a life, and she would give every hour, every second, of her life to him and his needs, Emily vowed fiercely.

Marco looked across at Emily; he could see the devasta-

tion in her eyes. He wanted, he realised, to take her in his arms
and hold her there. He wanted to tell her that there was nothing
to fear and that he would keep both of them safe, her and their
child. He wanted to tell her that he was there for them whatever
happened and he always would be, and that they were the
most, the only, important things in his life. The news they had
just received had at a stroke filled him with an emotion so
complex and yet so simple that it could not be denied.

Love…

What he was feeling for Emily right now was love: a man's
love for his woman, the mother of his child, for his companion
and soul mate, without whom his life would never be complete.

Earlier, while watching the scan take place, he had experienced the most extraordinary sense of enlightenment, of
knowing that he had to be part of his son's life. Now had come
the knowledge that nothing could ever be more important to
him than guarding this precious, growing life and the woman
who was carrying it.

Not power, not wealth, nothing; not even the throne of Niroli.

Marco knew that others would not understand; he barely
understood what he was experiencing himself. But,
somehow, it wasn't necessary for him to understand, or to
be able to analyse; it was simply enough for him to know.
Maybe he had been travelling towards this place, this crossroads in his life, for longer than he realised; maybe there
had been many signposts along the journey that he had not
seen. However, now, not only had the crossroads been
reached, they had been traversed simply and easily, without
any kind of hesitation or doubt. He could not be Niroli's
king *and* his child's father—certainly not this child's father,
whose young life might always hang precariously on a
thread, and who should never be subjected to the rigours
of kingship. This boy would need his father's loving

presence. And he would have it. Singularly, neither he nor Emily was strong enough for their child, but together they would be.

'I have to return to Niroli.'

They were back home in Emily's kitchen. The necessary appointment had been made with the cardiac specialist, and now Emily inclined her head slightly as she listened to Marco.

'Yes, of course,' she agreed. She had been expecting him to say this, and she knew, too, that there would be no demands from him now that she should return with him so that his son could grow up on the island. The royal family of Niroli were arrogant and proud, too arrogant and proud to want to accept that one of their bloodline could be anything less than perfect. No, Marco would not want a sickly, ailing child around to remind him of that. She could feel the pain of the rejection on behalf of her baby, but she stifled it. It was Marco who was not worthy of their child, not the other way around. Not worthy of her child and not worthy of her love.

Marco desperately wanted to tell Emily how he felt—but this was not the right time. Unfortunately, he had a duty to inform his grandfather first of his intentions. Once he had done that, then he could tell Emily how much he loved her. Did she love him? His heart felt as though there were a knife twisting inside it. But even if she didn't love him, he still intended to be a full-time father to his son.

'I'll be back in time for the appointment with the cardiac specialist.'

Emily bowed her head. She mustn't let her own feelings swamp her. She had to be strong—for her son. Was it something she had done, or not done, that had caused his heart defect? she had asked the obstetrician.

No, Mr Bryant-Jones had told her, sometimes the condition ran in families, but sometimes it 'just happened', without there being any reason.

'What do you mean you no longer wish to succeed to the throne?'

'I mean, Grandfather, that I am abdicating my claim to the Crown. I intend to make a formal speech to that effect, but I wanted you to be the first to know,' Marco told his grandfather calmly.

'You are giving up the throne of Niroli for the sake of a woman and her child.'

Marco could hear the disbelief in his grandfather's voice.

'*My* woman and *my* child. And, yes, I am giving up the throne for them. For them, and for our people.'

'What do you mean by that?'

'It would never have worked, Grandfather. I could never step into your shoes.' Marco saw that the old man was looking slightly gratified.

'For me, they would be constraining, too limiting,' he finished firmly. 'We have done nothing but argue since I first arrived. You block every attempt I make to make reforms—'

'Because they are not right for our people.'

'No, because they are not right for you.'

'What you want to do would cause a schism that would split the island.'

'If you continued to oppose me, then, yes, there is that possibility. Niroli needs a king who will bring it into the twenty-first century—I firmly believe that. But I also believe now that Niroli's king can never be me. That does not mean that I don't care about my homeland and my people, I do—passionately—but I now know that I can do more for it and for them by working from outside its hierarchy.'

'By spreading anarchy, you mean?'

'By setting up a charitable trust to help those who most need it,' Marco corrected him evenly.

There was a certain irony in the fact that, whilst he had refused to wear the heavily decorated formal uniform his grandfather had had made for him on his arrival in Niroli, he was wearing it now to take his formal leave, Marco admitted as he waited for the king's equally elderly valet to finish fastening him into the jacket with its heavy gold braid. But somehow it seemed fitting that, on this one occasion, he should defer to tradition.

The world's media had been alerted to the fact that he intended to make a public speech; TV and radio crews had already arrived and the square below the palace balcony, from which he had chosen to address the people, was already full.

How different he felt now, compared with the way he had felt when he had first returned. Then, he had been filled with a fierce determination to fulfil his destiny; it had ridden him and possessed him.

This morning he had woken up with a sense of release, a sense of having gained back a part of himself he was only just becoming aware he had been denying.

The valet handed him his plumed hat. He could hear the shrill sound of trumpets. Walking slowly and majestically, he headed for the balcony, timing his entrance to when the military band broke into the Nirolian national anthem. Then he stepped forward...

CHAPTER SIXTEEN

EMILY stopped outside A shop window to look at her reflection and push her hair off her face. It was a sullenly hot day and her back was aching. She had been to see a client, but had hardly been able to focus on what the man had been saying to her because of her dread of what the cardiac specialist might say. Part of her wanted to rush the appointment and the specialist's opinion of her baby's future forward, whilst another part of her wanted to push it away. She was standing outside an electrical store that sold televisions. Its windows were filled with a variety of large screens. She glanced absently at them and then froze in disbelief when she realised she was looking at Marco. A camera homed in on his face, and then panned to the crowd in the square beneath him.

What was happening? Emily could think of only one thing: Marco must already be formally taking his position as the new King of Niroli. She wanted to ignore the screens and walk on past the shop, but instead she found that she was going inside.

'This is a most extraordinary event,' she could hear a TV news commentator saying excitedly. 'The royal family of Niroli is one of the richest in the world. They live according to their own set of rules. Of course the current King of Niroli is Giorgio. However, there have been rumours for some time that he is about to step down in favour of his grandson, Prince Marco. Now we have learned that Prince Marco has said that there is something he wants to tell his people. It can only mean one thing. What a change this will be for the island. There are already mutterings that Prince Marco wants to make too many changes too quickly, and that these could stir up unrest…'

Whilst the commentator talked over the last notes of the Nirolian national anthem, Emily focused feverishly on Marco's face. This could be the last time she would ever see him.

'People of Niroli…' he said in Italian. Tears stung Emily's eyes as she read the English subtitles at the bottom of the screen. She could hear the strength of purpose in Marco's voice as he went on, 'What I have to tell you today causes me great joy and also great sadness. Great joy, because when I leave you I shall be making the most important commitment a man ever can make, a commitment to the future through the next generation. Great sadness, because, in order to do that, I must abdicate my responsibility to you, the people of Niroli—'

Emily could almost feel the ripple of shock surging through the listening crowd. Her own thoughts were in turmoil. What was Marco doing? What was he saying? He was Niroli's future king and nothing could or should change that… She had listened to his passionate diatribes against his grandfather and she had known his fierce longing to do something to help his people. And yet now he was saying…

Marco was still speaking, so she moved closer to the screen.

'It is my belief that Niroli and its people need a ruler with a different mindset from my own, a ruler who can combine the best of the old ways with a new path into the twenty-first century. I am not that man, as both my grandfather and I have agreed. King Giorgio needs an heir to step into his shoes whom he can trust to preserve all that is good in our traditions.

Niroli also needs a new king who can take it forward into the future. With the best will in the world, I cannot be that king.'

A low murmur of objection filled the air accompanied by younger male voices shouting angrily and declaring, according to the TV commentator, that Marco was the king they wanted. Tomasso and his friends, Emily guessed.

'Do not think, though, my people, that I am deserting you, for I am not. I am soon to be the father of a child, and that knowledge has taught me how important the bond is between parent and child, between generation and generation, between a ruler and his people. My love for my child fills me and humbles me, and reinforces in me my love for the people of Niroli. It is out of this love—both for my child and for you, my people—that I am stepping down from the succession line to the throne, but never think that I am deserting you. I intend to set up a charity which will make available funds to help those citizens of Niroli who are most in need. It will provide the opportunity for our young people to be educated and to travel abroad, to broaden their horizons and then bring back to Niroli the gift of what they have learned so that they may share it. It is my passionate belief that this island needs a better system for encouraging its young to reach their full potential. I can do this best from outside the hierarchy of kingship and all that goes with it. At the same time, I shall remain at all times supportive of my grandfather and whoever he chooses to take the throne after him.

'I ask for your blessing, people of Niroli, and your understanding that sometimes it is more important for a man to be just that, than for him to be a king…'

'Excuse me, love, only we're about to close the store.' Her gaze blurred with her tears, Emily looked at the young man who was addressing her. Marco had left the balcony. The young man was looking impatient. Reluc-tantly, she nodded her head and headed for the exit.

It wasn't a long walk from the shops back to her house, but it was long enough for Emily to mentally question what Marco had done. He had told his people that he was giving up the throne because of his child—her child. Why? Marco was arrogant and proud, a perfectionist; did he—or his grandfather—fear the exis- tence of a child who was not perfect might somehow damage the power of the Nirolian royal family? Had his grandfather pressured Marco into stepping down, or had his own resolve spurred his abdication? Either way, she had no wish to be a party to depriving Niroli of its future king, and nor did she want her son growing up carrying the burden and the blame for his father's decision to deny himself a role Emily knew he had been eager to take on.

She turned the corner into her street and then stopped, her heart hammering against her ribs as she saw Marco standing outside the front door of her house. Ridiculously, her first impulse was to turn and walk away, but he had already seen her and he was walking towards her.

'What are you doing here?' she demanded when he reached her. 'I've only just seen you on television! Marco, you can't give up the Crown. Why have you? It isn't—'

'It isn't your decision,' Marco told her calmly. 'It was mine, and as for you seeing me on TV, well, it must have been on a rolling news programme rounding up the day's events. I made my resignation speech at eleven a.m. this morning, Nirolian time. I had a private jet standing by, another personal decision, before you ask,' he added dryly.

'It isn't fair of you to do this and to say publicly that it's because of my baby,' she told him passionately. 'Isn't he going to have enough to cope with, without the added blame of being responsible for—'

'We can't discuss this out here,' Marco interrupted her. 'Where are your keys?'

Helplessly, Emily handed them over and let him open the door for her.

The small house smelled of Emily's delicate scent, Marco recognised, also realising how much he had missed her. Soon, no doubt, the air around her would be filled with the scent of baby powder. With every mile that had brought him closer to her, his conviction that he had made the right decision had grown and, now, recognising how much he was looking forward to being part of the family unit they would form with their child was like one door closing behind him on an old habitat that no longer had any relevance to his life and another opening that had everything to do with it.

'There was no need for you to abdicate, Marco,' Emily burst out as soon as they were inside. 'I know how much you wanted to be King, so why?'

'If you had heard my speech in its entirety, then you would have known why I decided to step down, and why it was necessary for me to abdicate.'

'Because of our baby? Because he might not be perfect? Because you're ashamed of him, and you and your grandfather don't want him associated with Niroli?'

'What? Ashamed of him? You wouldn't be more wrong. If there's anyone I'm ashamed of, it's myself for taking so long to recognise what really matters to me. Or perhaps I did recognise it, but tried to pretend that I didn't. Emily, when you were having your scan and I saw our baby, I knew beyond any kind of doubt that you and he are the most important things in the world to me, and that nothing could ever or would ever matter more. Actually, I think I knew a little of that when I first came to Niroli and I missed you so much I had to come back for you. I certainly knew it when you told me you were pregnant and all I could think of was finding a way to keep you with me. I couldn't and wouldn't accept that it wasn't possible for me to be King and to have you and our child. And then you told me why you were pleased that our child would never be King, and it was as though you had unlocked a door inside me. Behind it lay the memories of my own childhood, my parents' constant battles with my grandfather to provide me with a normal childhood, my own sense of aloneness because of what I was, and I knew unequivocally that you were right not to want that for our child.'

'But you wanted to be King! You had so many plans, there was so much you wanted to do—you can't give that up.'

'I don't intend to. I can still do all those things without being King. In fact I can do them more easily. My grandfather would never really release the reins of government to me, and the hostility between us and the constant fight for supremacy would not aid our people. I can do far more outside the constraints of kingship, and I can do those things with you at my side. I love you, Emily.'

There was so much she wanted to say, so many questions, so many reminders to him of times when he had not seemed to love her at all. But, somehow, she was in his arms and he was kissing her with a fierce, demanding passion that said more clearly than any amount of words what he truly felt.

'I still can't believe this is happening,' Emily whispered to Marco half an hour later. She was still in his arms, only now they were upstairs in her bedroom, lying side by side in her bed. The way Marco had controlled his need to possess her, been gentle to protect their child, had brought emotional tears to her eyes and flooded her heart with the love for him she had dammed up for so long.

'You want me to convince you?' Marco teased her suggestively, his hand cupping her breast.

'Maybe,' she agreed mock-demurely.

His, 'Right, come on then, let's get dressed,' wasn't the response she had been expecting and her chagrin showed, making him laugh.

'We're going shopping,' he told her. 'For a wedding ring and a marriage licence.'

When her eyes rounded, he pointed out, 'You said you wanted me to convince you. I can't think of a better way to do that than marrying you, just as soon as we can arrange it.'

'Oh, Marco... Shouldn't we wait to make plans until after the scan?'

'Why? The potential severity of our baby's heart defect doesn't make any difference to my feelings for you or for him. You suggested earlier that I might be ashamed of our baby for not being perfect. That could never happen. He will be perfect to me, Emily, because he is ours, perfect in every way, no matter what.'

'Oh, don't,' Emily protested. 'You'll make me cry all over again.'

'And then I'll have to kiss you all over again,' Marco said, pretending to give a weary sigh, but smiling whilst he did so.

'Well, then, let's have a look. It's been a few weeks since we did your last scan, and that will have given your baby a chance to grow and us the chance to get a better idea of what's going on. As I told you at your first consultation with me, these days, in-utero surgery means that we can do so very much more than we once could. Even with the most severe cases.'

Emily felt Marco squeezing her hand, but she dared not look at him just in case she broke down.

These last weeks since their initial appointment with the neo-natal heart consultant had seemed so long, despite the fact that they had managed to squeeze getting married into them, along with a flying visit to Niroli, where Marco's grandfather had very graciously welcomed her formally into the family. Marco had also brought his grandfather up to date with his plans to establish the charity he had promised during his abdication speech.

New scans had been done, and now they were waiting anxiously for the specialist's opinion.

'However, in the case of your baby, I don't consider that an operation would be appropriate.'

Emily gave a small moan of despair. Was he saying there was no hope? 'What exactly is our baby's prognosis?' Marco's voice wasn't quite as level as normal, and Emily could hear the uncertainty in it.

'Very good. Excellent, in fact,' the specialist told them, smiling. 'There is a small area that we shall need to keep an eye on, but if anything it seems to be healing itself—something we do see with this condition. Sometimes babies will grow in stops and starts, and this leads us to make diagnoses we later have to amend. That is what has happened here. Initially, it did look as though your baby's heart might not be developing properly, but these latest scans show that everything is just as it should be.'

'Are you sure?' Emily asked anxiously. 'I mean, should I have another scan in a week or two? What if—?'

'I am perfectly sure. In fact, I was pretty sure when you first came to see me, but I wanted to wait and see how things went before I said anything, which is why I wanted to do this last scan. Of course, I am going to recommend that we continue to monitor the situation, just to be on the safe side, but my view is that there is nothing for you to worry about. Your baby is perfectly healthy and developing normally.'

Outside on the street, oblivious to the amused looks of passers-by, Marco held Emily close and tenderly kissed the tears from her face.

'I can't believe it,' she whispered to him. 'Oh, Marco... It's like a miracle.'

'You are my miracle, Emily,' Marco told her softly. 'You and our child, and the future we are going to share.'

'How has the king taken things?'

'Not as badly as we might have feared.' The senior courtier was well versed in tact and diplomacy, and he had no intention of telling the junior aide anything about the extraordinary scene he had just witnessed in the Royal Chamber, when the king had stopped in mid-rant about the stupidity of his grandson and heir to stare at the report he had just been handed, about an Australian surgeon who was pioneering a new treatment for the heart condition from which the king himself suffered.

On the face of it, there had been nothing in the grainy photograph and short biography of the young Australian to cause such a reaction. But the senior courtier had been in service at the palace for a very long time and when the king had handed the report to him in an expectant silence he, too, had seen the same thing that the king had seen.

'I want that young man brought here, and I want him brought here now,' the king had instructed....

Surgeon Prince,
Ordinary Wife

MELANIE MILBURNE

To Bev and Darrell Crocker,
thank you for being right there from the start
of this dream. Your continued belief in me
has carried me through some of life's
toughest times. Love you both.

CHAPTER ONE

IF SHE hadn't been running so horrendously late, she would never have taken the short cut in the first place.

Amelia let out a stiff curse as she tried to free herself from the rambling briar that had caught her as she'd climbed over the back fence adjoining the property of her last community health home visit of the day.

'Well, what do you know?' a deep male voice drawled from just behind her. 'The legend is true after all—there *are* fairies at the bottom of the garden.'

She swivelled her head around to see a tall man looking up at her where she was perched so precariously, his black-brown gaze twinkling with amusement.

It was very disconcerting as he looked so very Italian with his deeply tanned olive skin and his thick, short hair so dark, and yet she couldn't decide from his accent if he was American or British. He was even wearing what looked like an Italian designer shirt and trousers, the top four buttons of the shirt undone casually, leaving a great expanse of tanned, muscular chest on show.

'Is this *your* house and garden?' she asked, tugging at her lightweight cotton skirt to free it, with little success.

'No,' he said with a lazy smile. 'I'm just renting for a few weeks, but the landlord didn't tell me about the little bonus in the back garden. He should have charged me more rent. I would have gladly paid it.'

Amelia felt the colour begin to flare in her cheeks and, frowning at him, gave her skirt another little tug but it wouldn't budge.

His smile widened, showing very white teeth as his dark gaze ran over her appraisingly, taking in her petite shape and elfin features. 'Actually, I've changed my mind,' he said. 'You're not a fairy. You look more like a pixie to me.'

Amelia had to force herself not to roll her eyes at him in disdain. '*Actually*, I am a community nurse who is now more than half an hour late to visit an elderly patient,' she said through tight lips. 'And if you or your landlord took better care of your garden I would not be stuck up here like this!'

He folded his arms across his chest, rocking back on his heels as his eyes glinted at her playfully. 'And if you were not trespassing on private property you wouldn't have been ensnared by that bramble in the first place.' He unfolded one of his arms and waggled one long, tanned finger at her re-provingly.

She sent him an arctic glare and gave her skirt another vicious tug, but all she succeeded in doing was giving him a rather generous view of her thigh.

'If you tug any harder on that dress, you'll have me blushing to the roots of my hair,' he warned.

Amelia knew *she* was the one blushing to her backbone. She had never felt so embarrassed nor so annoyed in her life. 'Will you please leave me alone to extricate myself?' she clipped out. 'I would prefer not to have an audience right now.'

He put his hands up to his eyes. 'I promise not to peek.'

She let out a tight little breath and began to attend to her skirt, but she could feel those dark, laughing eyes watching everything from between his deliberately splayed fingers.

She finally tugged one part free of the bramble and shifted

position to attend to where her skirt had snagged on a nail on the fence.

'Can I look now?' the man called out.

'No,' she said, giving another forceful tug. There was a ripping sound and, before she could do anything to counteract it, she toppled down from the fence into the man's hastily outstretched arms below.

'*Oh!*' she gasped as he deftly caught her.

'Wow!' he said with a devilish grin. 'I haven't lost my touch after all. And here I was thinking that no woman was ever going to fall for me again.'

Amelia hastily pushed what was left of her skirt over her bare thighs, her face aflame. 'Please put me down,' she said as stiffly as she could, considering the sudden escalation of her pulse rate and breathing.

His face was so close she could see the black pupils of his eyes which were almost as dark as his irises. It looked as if his leanly chiselled jaw hadn't been anywhere near a razor for at least a day or two, but in spite of his lack of grooming she could smell the citrus fragrance of his aftershave mingled intoxicatingly with the muskiness of a man's body warmed by the hot spring sunshine.

He placed her on the ground in front of him, taking his time about it, she noted crossly.

'There, now turn around and let's see the damage,' he said.

Amelia stood completely frozen; she could feel air where she shouldn't be feeling air, and to make matters even worse—she was certain she was wearing her oldest pair of knickers.

'What's wrong?' he asked, but then, noticing the worried flick of her hazel gaze towards the fence, he whistled through his teeth and said, 'Uh oh.'

Amelia inwardly groaned as he walked up to the fence and removed what appeared to be the back half of her skirt from the nail. He came back and handed it to her, his mouth twitching at the corners. 'It might need a stitch or two, I'm afraid.'

'It's fine,' she said, backing away, doing her best to tuck the hapless bit of fabric into the elastic of the waistband of her skirt.

'Would you like me to give you a leg up over the fence?' he offered.

'No, thank you. I'll take the long way around.' She took a deep breath and picked up her bag with her free hand, the other one holding her skirt in place as she stalked back the way she had come with the precious little dignity she had left.

'Hey, you didn't tell me your name,' he called out after her, his mouth still tilted in a smile. 'Let me guess—is it Tinkerbell?'

She turned around and gave him one last cutting look. 'You do not need to know my name as I will not be coming this way again.'

'Pity,' he said, his eyes twinkling again. 'I kind of like the idea of having my very own pixie to play with.'

She stomped off muttering under her breath but the sound of his deep chuckle of laughter followed her all the way to Signora Gravano's house.

'You look like you have been through a hedge backwards,' the elderly woman said as she ushered Amelia into her neat little cottage.

'I have,' Amelia said, grimacing as she looked down at her tattered skirt, although she was relieved to find it had so far stayed in place.

'Did you take the short cut again?'

'Yes, unfortunately.' She gave the old woman a speaking glance and added, 'I met the new tenant.'

'Ah, yes, the associate professor. He just moved in this morning.'

Amelia's head jerked up. 'The associate *what?*'

'The Australian doctor,' Signora Gravano explained. 'I thought you knew about it. Dr Alex Hunter was summoned to Niroli to see the king about his heart. He very generously decided to use his sabbatical period to work with the Free Hospital staff to set up some sort of new heart procedure.'

'But he's not due until the end of next week,' Amelia said, her own heart suddenly feeling as if it needed an ECG. She turned to wash her hands to disguise her shock, taking her time with the soap and towel before she turned back round.

'I expect he has come early to enjoy the spring sunshine before he starts work,' the old woman said as she put her leg up on a foot stool for Amelia to inspect. 'It is quite a coincidence, don't you think?'

'Coincidence?' Amelia frowned in puzzlement. 'What do you mean?'

'He looks so Italian you could almost swear he was born and bred on the island.'

She frowned again as she turned back to her bag. 'I couldn't quite work out the accent,' she said as she opened her bag to retrieve the dressings she'd brought with her. 'I thought he sounded more British than anything.'

'He is very highly educated, of course. I believe he has spoken at conferences all over the world on this new technique. Perhaps his accent has become a little diluted by now.'

'So why is he renting that run-down cottage behind yours?' Amelia asked. 'If he's such a hot-shot doctor surely he would want to stay at Santa Fiera where the casino and all the resort hotels and restaurants are.'

'I suppose he wants to be close to the hospital and the older part of the island. Besides, he is only here for a month so a rustic working holiday might hold more appeal. The cottage is not that bad—it just needs a bit of a clean-up in the garden.'

There was no arguing with *that*, Amelia thought wryly, but

somehow she couldn't see the highly regarded cardiac surgeon getting down and dirty with a fork, spade and wheelbarrow.

'So what did you think of him?' Signora Gravano asked.

Amelia pursed her mouth as she unwrapped the old dressing on the old woman's leg. 'I thought he was…er…'

The old woman chuckled at her hesitation. 'He is very handsome, enough to make a woman's heart race, eh, Amelia? Good thing he is a cardiac specialist. He probably leaves a trail of broken hearts wherever he goes.'

'Yes, well, I am sure I will not be affected in such a way,' Amelia said firmly, doing her level best to block the memory of his strong arms around her.

'You have spent too long with the nuns,' Signora Gravano said. 'I always thought it would do more harm than good when you went to that convent after your mother passed away. You are too young to devote yourself to the sick without having a life of your own.'

'I do have a life of my own.'

The old woman grunted. 'You call that a life, living so far away in the foothills of the mountains like a peasant, cleaning up after your father and your brothers? You should be out dancing and enjoying yourself like other people your age. You work too hard, Amelia, far too hard.'

'I won't have to work so hard for ever. I've got a new job. I'm starting tomorrow.' Amelia straightened and added, 'The king needs a private nurse two days a week and I've landed the job. It fits in beautifully with my community work and my shifts at the Free Hospital.'

The old woman's grey brows rose over her black button eyes. 'What does your father think of you working for King Giorgio?'

'I haven't told him…yet.'

'Wise of you. Staunch Republican that he is, I do not think he would approve of you slaving at the Niroli palace.'

'I am thirty years old, Signora Gravano,' Amelia said. 'I

think I am old enough to work wherever I choose without the approval of my father or brothers.' She closed the bag with a little snap and added, 'Besides, my father is not likely to live much longer.'

'How is he?'

She let out a tiny sigh. 'Going downhill every day but he refuses to admit it. He won't go to the hospital and will not allow anyone to visit. Anyway, what doctor would travel all that way to see him only to be turned away? I do what I can but I fear it will not be long before he is beyond help.'

'Can you not convince your brothers to help you?'

'They help me when they can but they have struggles of their own. It is not exactly easy being a Vialli on the island of Niroli. Everyone has such long memories.'

'It was a terrible time on the island back then,' Signora Gravano said, her expression clouding. 'You are lucky you were not yet born. There was such hatred and violence, so much bloodshed.'

'I know…' Amelia released another sigh. 'My father's never really got over it.'

'There are many who believe he deserved to die as well,' Signora Gravano said with gravitas.

Amelia didn't respond, but she felt her blood chill just as it did every time she thought about the incident that had changed her family for ever.

'I must not keep you,' Signora Gravano said with a fond smile. 'You are a good girl, Amelia. Your mother would be very proud of you.'

Amelia bent down and gave the old woman a gentle hug. 'Thank you.'

'Why don't you leave your skirt with me to mend,' Signora Gravano offered as Amelia straightened once more. 'You can borrow something of my daughter's. She still has things in the wardrobe for when she visits.'

'I don't want to put you to any bother…'

'It is no bother,' she insisted. 'You are much smaller than her but it will see you home without embarrassment. You never know who you might meet and what would they think of you looking like a gypsy?'

A few minutes later Amelia looked down at the huge sack of a dress she had borrowed and wondered how she was going to walk the distance back to the Free Hospital in the stifling heat. Her brother Rico had yet again borrowed her car and had agreed to meet her back at the hospital once she had seen the last of the community patients.

She kept her head well down as she hurried past the visiting doctor's cottage, sure she could feel that dark, mocking gaze following her even though there was no sign of anyone about.

A flashy-looking sports car turned the corner and she stepped onto the grass verge to avoid its dust, but instead of going past it came to a halt beside her.

'Hey there, little pixie.' The man she had met earlier grinned at her through the open window. 'I see you've changed into something a little more comfortable.'

Amelia tightened her spine, her eyes flashing with sparks of ire. 'I believe you are the Australian doctor we have been expecting,' she said. 'What a pity you didn't think to introduce yourself properly when you had the chance.'

He turned off the engine and unfolded his long length from the car to come to stand in front of her. 'You didn't tell me your name so I didn't see why I should reveal mine,' he said with a teasing glint in his eyes. 'Fair's fair. It's my very first day on the island. A guy can never be too careful these days. For all I know you could be a dangerous criminal.'

She stared at him for a moment, wondering if he had heard the rumours about her family, her heart starting to clang like a heavy bell in her chest.

'You're not…' he bent slightly to peer deeply into her eyes '…are you?'

She took a little step backwards, almost tripping over the hem of the borrowed dress. 'W-what?'

'A dangerous criminal.'

'I—I told you before—I'm a…a nurse.'

His eyes flicked to her outfit before returning to her face. 'A plain-clothes nurse it seems. Are you on some sort of undercover operation?'

'I don't wear a uniform when I do my home visits,' she said. 'The patients feel less threatened that way.'

'Do you work at the Free Hospital as well?' he asked.

'Yes.'

'Which ward?'

She looked as if she had just bitten into a lemon as she answered, 'The cardiac ward.'

'Well, so we'll be work buddies, eh?' His dark eyes danced with merriment.

'It looks like it,' she said coldly.

He smiled down at her. 'So are you going to tell me your name or am I going to have to address you as Nurse Pixie for the rest of my stay?'

'Amelia Vialli,' she mumbled, but didn't offer him her hand.

'Alex Hunter,' he said and, reaching for her hand, held it in the huge warmth of his. 'How do you do?'

Amelia tugged at her hand but he didn't release it. She gave him a pointed glare but he just laughed. 'You can hardly rip half your arm off, now can you?'

'Are all Australians this rude or have you taken a special course in offending people?' she asked, wrenching her hand from his and rubbing at it with exaggeration. 'No doubt you passed it with flying colours.'

'And are all Niroli natives so unfriendly or is it just you?' he returned.

She scowled at him darkly. 'I am not being unfriendly.'

He grinned again. 'I'd hate to see you being hostile.'

'Excuse me,' she said and made to brush past. 'I have someone waiting for me.'

He stalled her with a hand on her arm. 'Would you like a lift?'

She sent him a haughty look as she brushed off his arm as if it were a particularly nasty insect. 'I don't think so.'

He raised his dark brows. 'You're going to walk all that way in that dress?'

She gave her head a defiant little toss. 'Yes.'

'What are you doing—moonlighting as a street sweeper or something?'

She rolled her eyes and swung away, and, picking up the voluminous skirt of her borrowed outfit, began to walk purposefully towards town, the fabric swishing around her ankles making her look like a small, angry black cloud.

Alex stood watching her, a little smile playing about his mouth. 'How cute is that?' he said out loud.

A light breeze carried the sweet fragrance of orange blossom and he closed his eyes and drew in a deep breath, relishing the fresh spring air after the long-haul flight from Sydney.

A whole month on the beautiful Mediterranean island of Niroli, by royal invitation no less.

Sure, there was a lot of work to do in a short time, but he would hopefully have enough free time available to explore the beaches and the nightlife, perhaps even do a hike up to the volcanoes.

Thinking of the volcanoes made him open his eyes to look back at the stiff little figure who was now almost at the end of the street.

He watched as a beaten-up car pulled up at the T-junction, a swarthy and scruffy-looking man in his early thirties opening the door from the inside so she could get in.

Alex blew out a long breath as the car rumbled on its way,

finally disappearing out of sight, although he could still hear it rattling and spluttering in the distance.

'Look's like she's already taken, mate,' he said as he turned back to his own vehicle and got back behind the wheel. He fired up the engine, giving it a few extra revs, and put it into gear. 'Now isn't that just the story of your sorry life?'

CHAPTER TWO

'How was your time at the palace with the king?' Lucia Salvati, the nurse on Amelia's afternoon roster, asked three days later.

'It was better than I feared,' she answered as she glanced at the patient list in the nurses' station.

'Why? Did he give you a hard time being a Vialli and all?'

Amelia shook her head. 'No. I don't think his bodyguards even mentioned my name to him. I just had to help him into bed and be on call in case he needed anything during the night. He barely addressed a single word to me the whole time I was there.'

'No wonder you look so tired,' Lucia said. 'Do you really have to take on this extra job? You already have enough on your plate with this place, not to mention the community work you insist on doing.'

'I've got nothing better to do. Besides, I need the money.'

'Don't we all?' Lucia groaned in agreement. 'Just wait until you're married with a couple of kids—that's when you'll be needing money and lots of it.'

'Yes, well, I'm not planning on getting married,' Amelia said with determination.

'Why? You're not still thinking of going back to the convent, are you? I thought you gave up on that idea—what was it…five or six years ago?'

'No, I'm not planning on going back. I just don't want the complication of a relationship,' Amelia said. 'I saw what it did to my mother—loving a man too much, losing her sense of self, her self-respect. I've decided I'd much rather be alone.'

'Your parents' situation *was* a little unusual,' Lucia pointed out. 'Besides, your mother wasn't to know what was going on in the background—hardly anyone did until it was over.'

Amelia released a heavy sigh. 'I know, but sometimes it seems as if the whole island would be happier if every one of us Viallis were dead and buried.'

Lucia gave her an empathetic look. 'Have your brothers been in trouble again?'

Amelia lifted her gaze to meet her colleague's. 'Rico lost his job at the vineyard. He got into a fight with one of the other workers. He wouldn't tell me what it was about but I can guess. It's always the same.'

'What about Silvio? Is he still employed down at the port?'

'I haven't heard from him for two weeks,' Amelia said. 'It might be because he has a new girlfriend or it might be because he's doing some underhand deal like the last time, which will no doubt bring even more disgrace to our family.'

'So you are working three jobs to keep food on the table,' Lucia said.

'What else can I do?'

Lucia gave her arm a little squeeze. 'You're right, there's nothing else you can do. I would do the very same but it seems a shame you are the one paying the biggest price.'

'My mother paid the biggest price, Lucia,' Amelia said as she got to her feet. 'She died because she fell in love with the wrong man at the wrong time.'

'How is your father?'

'As difficult as ever.'

'You still can't convince him to have treatment?' Lucia asked.

'He hates doctors. Ever since he was diagnosed with cancer

he won't have anything to do with anyone medical, apart from me, of course, but even with me he's becoming increasingly uncooperative.'

'Speaking of doctors, have you run into the Australian yet? Word has it he's come a few days early to get a feel for the island before he meets the king. Apparently this new technique could be the answer to the king's heart problem. At ninety years of age a triple bypass is terribly risky, but Dr Hunter has pioneered this off-pump bypass procedure. It's apparently much less traumatic than being cooled on bypass and having your heart stopped, especially for older patients.'

'I can't see it ever happening at this hospital,' Amelia said, carefully avoiding answering Lucia's original question. 'We haven't got the beds for one thing, and we're constantly short-staffed.'

'The king will no doubt insist on having it done at the private hospital, but Dr Hunter has come to train the cardiac team here. I think it's very good of him to give up his time. He could just as easily have refused and gone off to sun himself before returning to Sydney. We should do all we can to support him while he's here.'

Amelia shifted her gaze and began to shuffle some papers on the desk in front of her. 'I'm thinking about a transfer to another ward.'

'*What?*' Lucia's tone was incredulous. 'You can't be serious! But you are cardiac trained.'

'I know, but I feel like a change.'

'But that's crazy, Amelia. You'll be needed more than ever with Dr Hunter here. It would be embarrassing if we were short of cardiac nurses to help with the recovery of the patients he's operated on.'

'There are other nurses who could do the job.'

'That's not true. We're chronically under-staffed, and, besides, you know you are the most experienced nurse amongst us. You can't possibly consider leaving us in the lurch like that.'

Amelia chewed at her bottom lip. She knew Lucia was right, but the thought of seeing that seductive smile across a patient's bed was unthinkable. It was cowardly, but she didn't have the aplomb to follow through from such a mortifying first encounter.

'Don't tell me you have something against Australians,' Lucia filled the tiny silence. 'Practically half of us on Niroli have relatives living over there. Besides, from what one of the other nurses said Dr Hunter looks more Italian than anything else.'

'Yes, I know,' Amelia said with a little frown. 'I thought so too when I met—'

'You've met him?' Lucia's eyes bulged.

'Er…yes…'

'So what's he like? Does he say "G'day, moite" and "crikey" and stuff like that?'

Amelia couldn't help laughing at her friend's attempt at an Australian accent. 'No, he sounds…' she suppressed a tiny shiver as she recalled that deep velvet voice '…well educated and…'

'And?' Lucia prompted eagerly.

'He's…very strong.'

'Strong?'

'As in big muscles,' she explained with heightened colour.

Lucia's brows rose slightly. 'So how did you get to see the size of his muscles?'

Amelia gave her a wry look. 'Believe me, you don't want to know.'

'Oh, but I *do!*' Lucia called after her as Amelia left the nurses' station. 'You'll have to fill me in sooner or later!'

Amelia opened her mouth to politely tell her to mind her own business when she caught sight of a tall figure striding down the corridor towards them with Vincenzo Morani, the senior cardiac surgeon, by his side.

'Ah, this is the nurse I was speaking to you about,' Dr Morani said as they drew closer. 'Amelia, this is Dr Alex Hunter from Australia. I have been telling him you are our most experienced cardiac nurse, one of our most valuable assets in post-operative care.'

Amelia stretched her mouth into what could loosely be described as a smile. '*Buongiorno*, Dr Hunter.'

'We've already met, haven't we?' Alex said with a cheeky grin that crinkled the corners of his dark-as-night eyes.

'Oh?' Dr Morani looked faintly relieved. 'Well, then…I'll leave you two to have a chat while I get organised for Theatre.' He turned back to Amelia. 'You don't mind showing Dr Hunter around the rest of the department, do you? I have an urgent matter to see to in ICU.'

'But I—' She stopped when she saw the look Alex Hunter gave her.

'Don't tell me you're embarrassed about our meeting the other day?' he asked in a gravelly undertone once the other surgeon had left.

'Of course not,' she lied. 'It could have happened to anyone.'

'Anyone wearing a dress that is.'

She turned from his teasing look and began quickly striding up the corridor reciting mechanically, 'This is the nurses' station and over there is the tea room and over there is the storeroom for the—'

'What are you doing tonight?' he asked.

Amelia stopped in her tracks and gaped up at him. 'I beg your pardon?'

'I've seen so many hospitals in my time I'm sure I'll be able to find my way around this one without a guided tour. What I would prefer is if you would show me around the island.' He gave her a little wink. 'How about it?'

She struggled to get her voice into gear. 'I—I don't think that is such a good idea.'

'I'm sure your boyfriend won't mind if you tell him it's work-related,' he said.

'I do *not* have a boyfriend.'

His eyes lit up. 'Great, then it's a date. I'll pick you up. Where do you live?'

She glanced up at him in alarm. 'I am not going anywhere with you.'

He gave her a mock-forlorn look. 'Hey, just because I saw your knickers the other day doesn't mean I want my wicked way with you. I just want you to show me around.'

'Find someone else,' she bit out frostily, her colour at an all-time high as she resumed stalking down the corridor. 'I'm not interested.'

Alex smiled to himself as she disappeared around the corner.

He had a month to change her mind.

Amelia had arranged for Rico to pick her up after her shift was finished, and he was in another of his foul moods.

'Hurry up. I've been waiting for twenty minutes,' he growled as she got in the car.

'Sorry, I had to spend some time with the relatives of a patient,' she said. 'Is *Papà* all right?'

His mouth twisted as he put the car into gear. 'You're not going to believe this but he wants to see a doctor.'

She swivelled in her seat to gape at him. 'Really?'

He flicked a quick glance her way. 'I couldn't believe it myself but he insists he wants to see the new doctor.'

Amelia felt her stomach drop. 'The Australian one?'

'Yes. He thinks he of all people will not be biased against him.'

She let out a prickly breath. 'Dr Hunter is a cardiac surgeon, Rico, not an oncologist. There's no cure for lung cancer, or at least certainly not for the stage *Papà* is at. He's coughing blood every day and the original cat-scan showed the rapid expansion of the tumours and—'

'He wants to see him and he wants you to arrange it as soon as you can.'

She sat back in her seat, a hollow feeling settling in her stomach. Her father needed palliative care, not a social call from a visiting heart specialist who was the biggest flirt she had ever met. Well, maybe not quite the biggest flirt, she thought bitterly. Even now, eleven years on, she still couldn't help that empty sinking feeling whenever she brought Benito Rossini's features to mind. She had been a fool to fall for his easygoing charm, not for a moment stopping to think if the handsome businessman visiting Niroli from Milan was already taken. It had devastated her to find he had a wife and two children at home. She had given him her innocence and he had betrayed her in the worst possible way.

'Have you heard from Silvio?' Rico disturbed her painful reverie.

'No… I just hope he's not doing anything illegal,' she said, looking out at the grey-green of the olive groves they were passing. 'I couldn't bear it if we had something else to live down.'

Her brother gave a rough grunt. 'As soon as I get some money together I'm going to leave the island. I am tired of living with the shame of the past.'

Amelia turned to look at him. 'But what about *Papà*? Surely you're not thinking of leaving before he…' she hesitated over the word '…goes.'

He lifted one shoulder dismissively. 'It's his fault we have been forced to live this way.'

'That's not true!'

Rico sent her a cynical glance. 'You are just like *Mamma* was, too innocent to see the truth until it was too late.'

She frowned at his tone. 'What do you mean?'

'There are things about *Papà* you should know.'

Amelia felt her throat tighten. 'W-what sort of things?'

'Things about his role with the bandits thirty-four years ago.'

'He wasn't a key person. *Mamma* told me he got caught up in it but had never intended to play a major role. He's told me that himself, and I believe him. Think about it, Rico. Our father is a bit rough and unpolished around the edges, but he's not a violent man. He has never raised a hand to any of us—how can you possibly think him capable of condoning the activities of such a despicable movement?'

'There are rumours circulating on the island that he had something to do with the kidnapping of the infant prince,' he said.

Amelia felt her heart begin to pick up its pace at the grim expression on her older brother's face. 'There have always been stupid rumours. It doesn't mean you have to believe them.'

'But what if someone has irrefutable proof of his involvement?'

She stared at him, shock rendering her speechless.

He met her eyes briefly. 'You have heard that Prince Marco has renounced his right to the throne once King Giorgio abdicates?'

'Yes…I have heard about it,' she answered.

Marco Fierezza's parents and his uncle had been tragically killed two years ago in a yachting accident, which had left him as the next in line after his grandfather, King Giorgio. There had been some speculation about the nature of the accident, some people suggesting it had been yet another attempt to bring the monarchy down, but so far no evidence had been brought forward to convict anyone of anything untoward. The coroner had made his decision that the yacht had come to grief as a result of the wild storms that had ravaged the coast of Niroli that year and which had been fiercer than ever before.

The island had lately been buzzing with the news that Marco had decided to marry his mistress, Emily Woodford, a young Englishwoman, who—because she had been previously divorced—made it impossible for Marco to claim his right to the throne.

Amelia had thought it incredibly romantic that a man would give up his birthright for the love of a woman. Renouncing the throne of Niroli, with its long and ancient history, must have been a huge decision for Prince Marco. And a sacrifice she was sure few modern men would be prepared to make.

The Fierezza family had ruled the island since the Middle Ages, and with its rich volcanic soil and temperate climate the island had prospered as a key port on a major wine, spice and perfume trading route. But while the island of Niroli was ruled by the monarchy headed by the ageing and increasingly unwell King Giorgio, the neighbouring island of Mont Avellana was now a republic partly due to the resistance movement that had occurred in the nineteen seventies.

Amelia was well aware of the ongoing resentment and rivalry between the two islands and often wondered if her younger, somewhat wayward, brother Silvio was in some way involved in a resurgence of the movement that had cost both the monarchy and her family so dearly.

'King Giorgio is becoming impatient to find a contender for the throne,' Rico said. 'His fading health makes it imperative he does so soon, otherwise the continuation of the monarchy could be under threat.'

'I suppose that's why he invited the Australian specialist all this way to see him,' Amelia said with a cynical twist to her mouth. 'I wonder how much he paid him.'

Rico gave her a quick sideways glance. 'The doctor would not accept payment of any kind.'

She stared at him again. 'How do you know?'

'I have it on good authority that Dr Hunter refused all

offers of money from the king. He came to the island because he is keen to bring this new technique to less affluent hospitals around the globe. He agreed to meet the king and give his professional opinion on his condition and whether he would be a suitable candidate for the surgery, but apart from that he insisted he spend the majority of his time at the Free Hospital and that any donations made go towards its upkeep.'

Amelia sat back in her seat with a little frown pulling at her forehead. She felt a little ashamed of her too hasty assessment of Alex Hunter as an opportunistic playboy on a royally funded visit. If what her brother had said was true, the visiting specialist had similar goals to her own—bringing a much better standard of care to the patients who couldn't afford the expense of private health care.

But he was still an outrageous flirt, she reminded herself in case she was tempted to recall again the feel of those strong, muscular arms around her. The last thing she needed in her life was a man with a smile that could melt a glacier.

'You said someone has proof about *Papà*'s involvement with the rebellion,' she said. 'What sort of proof?'

'There is talk that the infant prince who was kidnapped wasn't actually killed.'

Amelia gave him an incredulous look. 'But that's crazy, Rico. I walked past the little boy's grave the other day at the palace.'

He sent her a quick unreadable glance. 'A child was certainly killed during the rescue operation, but what if it isn't Prince Alessandro Fierezza that is buried at the castle?'

Amelia felt a shiver run from the base of her spine to disturb the tiny hairs on the back of her neck. 'What are you saying? That *Papà* was somehow involved in this?'

'You said it yourself. *Papà* is not a violent man. What if he couldn't go through with the orders he was given by the leader of the bandits and spirited the prince away instead of killing him?'

She frowned as she considered the possibility. 'But a child *was* killed.'

'Yes, that's true.'

'But not necessarily by *Papà*…'

'You still want him to be innocent, don't you?' he asked.

'I can't bear the thought of our father killing an innocent child, prince or not,' she said. 'He just couldn't possibly have done such a thing.'

'The rumours are not going to die down. It will make life even more difficult for us on the island.'

'Is that why you lost your job at the vineyard?' she hazarded a guess.

'I was going to leave anyway. I am sick of being treated like a peasant.'

'You should have stayed at school like *Mamma* wanted. You would have had more choices in terms of a career.'

'Like you, you mean?' he said with a cynical movement of his lips. 'At least I have some sort of life.'

'I wish people would not keep criticising me for choosing to care for others instead of myself,' she grumbled. 'I love my work. It fulfils me.'

'You don't have to give your life away in order to serve others.' He threw another quick glance her way. 'Once *Papà* dies you will be free to do what you want with your future. You could even leave the island, go and work in some other place for a while. It would make you realise there is a whole world outside of Niroli.'

Amelia knew there was an element of truth in what he said. She had cloistered herself away for too long, but the alternatives were just too threatening. She was frightened of making another dreadful mistake. She didn't have the experience that other women her age took for granted. She had only had one lover and it had turned her world upside down. The lingering shame of it still clung to her like a scratchy fabric against her tender skin. How had she been so blind, so gullible and so trusting? She just didn't know how to relate to men other than as patients or relatives, and as for her medical colleagues—she kept them at a professional distance at all times.

It was safer that way.

'I will need the car again tomorrow,' Rico said as he took the turn to their run-down cottage in the foothills. 'I have some business to attend to. I can give you a lift to the hospital but I think I should warn you I am leaving before sunrise and I might not be back until midnight.'

'I'll take the pushbike,' she said, her heart sinking at the thought of the long ride into town. At least most of the journey was downhill, but the return trip after a day on the ward was no picnic.

'Maybe you could ask Dr Hunter to give you a lift home tomorrow,' Rico suggested. 'That way you can kill two birds with one stone.'

'I hardly think Dr Hunter is going to make a house call way up here,' she said. 'I'll try and convince *Papà* to see him at the hospital or even the community clinic.'

'He won't go. You'll have to get the doctor to come here. I am sure he won't mind. Perhaps you could offer to show him around the island as a return favour—he probably won't expect payment.'

Oh, yes, he will, Amelia thought as she brought that sensual smiling mouth to mind. 'I'll see what I can do, but I'm not making any promises,' she said.

Rico sent her one of his rare smiles. 'You're a good sister, Ammie. I don't know what we would do without you.'

She smiled back at him shyly. It was indeed a rarity to receive a compliment from either of her brothers and certainly never from her father. 'Thank you, Rico. I just want us all to be happy and free of the past.'

The smile instantly faded from her brother's face. 'We can

never be free of the past. It has cast a shadow over us that will not go away.'

Amelia followed him into the cottage with a despondent sigh. She hated to admit it but her brother was right.

What the nuns had taught her was true: the sins of the fathers were revisited on the next generation.

All her life she had lived with the burden of being a Vialli, the most scorned and hated family on the island of Niroli for what they had done to the king's little grandson.

She suppressed a little shudder at the thought of that tiny broken body buried in the palace grounds, the Fierezza coat of arms emblazoned on his headstone, the family motto inscribed below.

Sempre Appassionato, Sempre Fiero.

Always passionate, always proud.

She had stood in respectful silence that day, comforting herself that at least the little prince was now at rest with his parents in heaven.

But what if he was still alive as her brother had suggested, but totally unaware of his royal heritage?

And if he was indeed alive, then who was the little boy who now lay in the Fierezza family vault…and why hadn't his real parents come forward to claim him?

CHAPTER THREE

'THERE'S a parcel for you in the third drawer of the filing cabinet,' Lucia said on Amelia's arrival at the hospital the next morning.

'A parcel?' Amelia wiped her damp face with a tissue. 'For me?'

Lucia looked up from the notes she was writing. 'You look like you've just run a marathon. Has Rico taken your car again?'

Amelia nodded and tossed the tissue in the bin under the desk. 'His is still in the workshop. They won't release it until he pays the bill, but I can't see that happening too soon now he's out of work. I had to use the pushbike.'

'You should have called me. I could have taken a detour to pick you up.'

'And add to your already frantic morning getting the children off to school and your husband off to work? No, the exercise will do me good. I quite enjoyed it actually.'

'I'd offer to run you home but I've already promised the girls I'd take them swimming at the beach after school.' Lucia gave her an apologetic look.

'I'll be fine,' Amelia assured her. 'Anyway, Rico might make it in time to pick me up.' She opened the drawer and took out the neatly wrapped parcel and stared at it for a moment.

'Aren't you going to open it?' Lucia asked.

She turned the package over in her hands and frowned. 'It doesn't say who it's from.'

'Go on, open it. It's addressed to you.'

Amelia undid the slim ribbon before unpicking the tape holding the brightly coloured wrapping in place. The paper fell open to reveal a beautiful summer dress in three bright shades of pink, the skirt soft and voluminous, the fabric exquisite to touch.

'Wow!' Lucia breathed a sigh of wonder. 'Someone has very good taste. If I'm not mistaken, that looks like a Mardi D'Avanzo original.'

Amelia checked the label on the collar of the dress, her heart giving a sudden lurch as she saw the famous Italian designer's name printed there. 'It is…'

Lucia's eyes twinkled. 'So who is your admirer? It's not your birthday for months.'

Amelia carefully rewrapped the dress, scrunching up the little card she'd found inside the wrapping. 'Is Dr Hunter in yet?' she asked.

Lucia leaned forward in her chair, her eyes going wide. 'Did Dr Hunter buy that for you?'

Amelia straightened her spine resolutely. 'Yes, and I am giving it back to him right now.'

Lucia looked confused. 'How come he bought you a dress?'

'I'll tell you later. Where is he?'

'I think he's in the office Dr Morani organised for him. But aren't you being a bit hasty? I mean, that's a designer outfit!'

Amelia gave her a determined look. 'I can buy my own clothes. I am not going to accept his or anyone else's charity.'

She strode down the corridor and gave the office door a couple of hard raps with her knuckles.

'Come in,' Alex called out cheerily.

She opened the door and closed it behind her with a little snap and locked gazes with him where he was sitting behind his desk.

'What is the meaning of this?' she bit out, thrusting the parcel at him.

He got to his feet and smiled. 'Did you like it? I kind of had to guess your size but you're about the same size as my younger sister Megan.'

Amelia slapped the parcel on the top of his desk. 'I cannot accept this from you,' she said, her tone crisp with pride.

'If you don't like the colour I can always change it,' he offered.

'It's got nothing to do with the colour!' she said, only just resisting the urge to stamp her foot at him.

'Then what's the problem?' he asked.

'You had no right to buy me this.'

'On the contrary, I thought I had a perfect right to do so,' he said, his dark eyes running over her lazily before returning to her fiery gaze. 'I was partly responsible for you ruining your dress the other day, so I thought it was the very least I could do to replace it.'

'With this?' She pointed to the parcel on his desk.

He rubbed at his cleanly shaven jaw for a moment, his eyes still holding hers. 'Mmm…now what did I get wrong? It must be the size. I know women absolutely hate it when the men in their lives get their size wrong.'

'You did not get the size wrong and I am not the woman in your life.' This time she did stamp her foot. 'I just cannot accept such an expensive outfit from you or indeed from anyone.'

'I thought the colour would bring out the raven's wing darkness of your hair.'

She glared at him without answering.

'It's meant to be a compliment,' he explained. 'You have the most beautiful, shiny hair. It was the first thing I noticed about you when I saw you perched on the top of my back fence.'

Amelia fought against the compliment's effect on her feminine psyche but it took a huge effort. Her hair was cut short, she did nothing to it but wash it each day. She couldn't remember anyone ever calling it beautiful before, or at least not in a very long time.

'It makes you look like an elf,' he added with a tilt of his mouth.

She gave him a scornful look. 'I thought you said I looked like a pixie?'

He grinned down at her. 'Pixie, fairy, elf—what's the difference?'

She pursed her mouth at him. 'A pixie has funny ears.'

'Show me your ears,' he said.

She stepped backwards. 'I—I beg your pardon?'

He stepped forwards. 'Go on. Prove to me you're a pixie not an elf. I dare you.'

'This is a t-totally ridiculous c-conversation,' she said and backed away even farther, but she came up against the closed door. She had to crane her neck to keep eye contact, her heart skipping as fast as a professional boxer in training.

'W-what are you doing?' she squeaked as his hand reached for her hair.

She shivered all over as his fingers tucked her hair behind one of her ears, his touch so gentle it felt like a caress of a long, soft feather against her sensitive skin. She couldn't get her lungs to inflate properly and all of a sudden she had an almost uncontrollable urge to drop her gaze to the sensual curve of his mouth...

'Well, how about that?' he said as he stepped backwards. 'I was wrong. There's absolutely nothing weird about your ears.'

Amelia was completely lost for words. She opened her mouth a couple of times but nothing came out.

She watched as he walked back over to his desk, his long legs encased in dark trousers that highlighted his lean, athletic build. His light blue shirt was rolled back at the cuffs, revealing his tanned wrists with the sprinkling of dark masculine hair running down his arms to the backs of his fingers. He was wearing a silver watch—she couldn't make out the brand but she assumed it was worth a small fortune.

She stiffened as he picked up the parcel but instead of handing it to her he pulled out the bin from beneath his desk and dropped it into it.

'What are you doing?' she blurted, pushing herself away from the door.

He gave her a guileless look. 'I'm throwing the dress away.'

'B-but...*but why?*'

He gave a loose shoulder shrug. 'You don't want it.'

'But that doesn't mean you have to throw it away! You can give it to someone else...your sister, for instance.'

'I bought it for you, not my sister,' he said. 'And besides, how would you feel if a guy bought a present for another woman and ended up giving it to you?'

'Um...'

He gave her a knowing little smile. 'See? I told you. You wouldn't like it one little bit.'

Amelia's eyes went to the bin and she swallowed. 'I—I could find someone who would really like it...I mean...rather than you throw it away...'

'Oh, would you?' He gave her a grateful smile. 'I'd really appreciate it. It cost an absolute packet—not that I mind, of course, as I can afford it—but my parents always taught me to be responsible with money. What's that old saying? If you look after the pennies the pounds look after themselves?'

Amelia was starting to think Alex Hunter had far too much talent in the way of charm. She could feel her mouth twitching and had to bite her tongue to stop herself from laughing out loud. No man, not even Benito with his silver tongue, had had this effect on her.

He handed her the parcel, his fingers brushing against hers. 'Please try and find it a good home,' he said soberly. 'I was getting very attached to that dress.'

A burst of laughter spilled from her mouth. She tried to cover it with a cough, but she could see he wasn't fooled.

He gave a huge grin and raised his closed fist in the air in a punch of victory. 'I knew I could do it!' he crowed delightedly.

'D-do what?' She tried to restrict her smile but her mouth wouldn't cooperate.

'I wanted to make you smile and I did it. I had my doubts there for a while, but I finally wore you down.'

'You're impossible,' she said and turned to leave, a ridiculous smile still stuck on her face.

'Hey, are we still on for a date some time?' he called out as she got to the door.

She turned around to look at him. 'I can't possibly go on a date with you,' she said, her belly doing a funny little flip-flop as she met his eyes once more.

'Why not?'

She hunted her brain for a valid excuse. 'I…I have nothing to wear.'

His gaze went to the parcel under her arm before returning to hers, a smile tilting up the corners of his mouth. 'You could always wear that, but to tell you the truth, I really liked the one you had on the other day.'

She frowned at him in puzzlement. 'The long black one?'

He shook his head. 'No, the one with the great view.'

Amelia could feel the colour firing in her cheeks and wished she had more poise to deal with his effortless charm and playful banter.

'I have to go…' She reached for the door with clumsy fingers, her heart fluttering like a confined sparrow.

'Here.' He reached past her shoulder and opened the door for her. 'Allow me.'

She breathed in the fragrance of his aftershave, its citrus grace notes making her senses whirl all over again at his closeness. 'Th-thank you.'

He waved her through gallantly. 'It was so nice of you to call round to see me,' he said with another stomach-flipping grin. 'Feel free to drop around any time.'

She shook her head at him and left, but it took most of the morning before she could wipe the smile off her face, and even longer before the mad fluttery sensation in her stomach died down to a soft little pulse....

CHAPTER FOUR

IT WAS a punishing ride home. Amelia gave the hot sun a resentful scowl as she pedalled up the hill, certain it had come out in full force just to make her journey all the more tiresome.

It had been a long day. One of the cardiac patients had taken a turn for the worse and she'd had to deal with distressed relatives who wanted a miracle to happen when a lifetime of bad diet and bad habits had led to the damage in the first place.

She hadn't run into Alex Hunter since she'd gone to his office. She'd heard he was taking the registrars through the procedure in a workshop prior to a case organised for Theatre the following morning.

Somehow she had fielded Lucia's questions when she'd come back to the ward, giving her a cut-down version of what had happened when she'd first met the visiting specialist.

Amelia felt a little guilty that she hadn't yet asked Alex about her father's request to see him. She knew her father would question her as soon as she returned for news of when he would come to visit, but somehow the thought of Alex seeing where she and her family lived embarrassed her. He was clearly very wealthy—how would he react to entering a cottage that hadn't seen a brush of paint in close to twenty years? The furniture was threadbare and mostly unstable, the floorboards rickety and the curtains at the windows let more light in than they kept out. Spiders had taken up residence in every corner in spite of her best efforts to keep them at bay, and the hens that fought over every last crumb in the yard had made what was left of her mother's garden a pock-marked wasteland.

She sighed as she forced the stiff pedals around yet another time, sweat breaking out on her upper lip at the effort.

'Vialli villain!' a youthful voice called out from the grass verge as a rock flew past her ear.

She flinched and wobbled on her bike, but somehow managed to keep it upright. She turned her head to see who had thrown the rock, but whoever it had been had run off.

It wasn't the first time she'd encountered missiles along this section of the road that led to the cottage; over the last few months some of the local youth had taken it upon themselves to regenerate the hostility of the past, more from mischief, she imagined, but it didn't make it any easier to cope with.

She pedalled on, gritting her teeth for the next hill when another rock flew past her head. This time the bike tilted and she lost control, tumbling off to land in the gravel on the side of the road.

It was all she could do not to cry. She got to her feet with an effort and righted her bike, but the fall had punctured the front tyre. She looked around but there was no sign of anyone to help. She was at least ten kilometres from the cottage and it was uphill all the way.

She brushed at her dusty face and plodded on, the parcel containing the dress Alex Hunter had given her strapped to the rack on the back of the bike.

After fifteen minutes or so she heard the sound of a powerful car coming up the hill behind her. She moved to the side of the road, her shoulders hunched as she pushed the bike through the loose gravel, the perspiration stinging as it streamed past her eyes.

'Hey there, little elf.' A familiar voice spoke from the open window of the car as it pulled up alongside her. 'You look like you need a lift.'

Amelia's bottom lip wobbled dangerously as she turned to look at Alex Hunter. 'I—I'm fine, thank you,' she said, somehow summoning up a tattered remnant of pride.

His playful smile disappeared to be replaced by a frown. He killed the engine and got out of the car to take the bike from her. She tussled with him for a moment before finally letting it go, her hands going up to her face to cover the shame of her tears.

'Oh no,' he said softly, and, putting the bike to one side, gathered her up against his broad chest, his deep voice rumbling against her breasts where they were crushed up against him. 'What on earth is the matter?'

'I—I have a p-puncture…and s-someone threw a rock at me,' she sobbed.

She felt him tense against her. 'A rock? What sort of rock?' he asked.

'I don't know… It was probably just a pebble…' She gave a little sniff. 'It happens now and again…'

He held her from him to look down at her, his expression serious. 'What do you mean it happens now and again?'

She brushed at her eyes with the back of her hand. 'It happens a lot. They're just kids making mischief. It's because of my family's history.… It's too hard to explain.'

'The Vialli bandits?'

She looked up at him in surprise. 'You've heard of them?'

He nodded. 'I've been reading up on the history of the island. It's quite a colourful past.'

A shadow came and went in her eyes. 'Yes, well, if only people would leave it in the past where it belongs…'

'So you're a relative of the original Vialli gang?' he asked.

'Yes and no. My father was only on the fringe of the operation. He wasn't directly responsible for anything that happened,' she explained.

'So who was the ringleader?'

'One of my uncles,' she said. 'He was killed during the takeover bid, along with several other relatives. My father has been made the scapegoat for the last thirty-four years. He virtually lives the life of a hermit to keep away from the past.'

'That's tough,' Alex said. 'What about your mother?'

Amelia bent her head to stare at the front of his shirt where her tears had left a damp mark. 'She died when I was eighteen. It broke her heart living up here away from all her family who had turned their backs on her.'

'So what actually happened?'

'It's a long story.'

He gave her an encouraging smile. 'I love long stories.' He led her to the grassy verge away from the dusty gravel. 'Here, sit down and tell me all about it.'

Amelia sat next to him on the cushion of grass so they could face the view as she related the story, hastily covering her scratched and dirty knees with her uniform. She could feel his broad shoulder close to hers and her nostrils flared again to breathe in the alluring scent of his maleness.

She took and a breath and began, 'Well…the Vialli bandits were originally ex-Barbary corsairs.'

'Pirates, huh?'

'Yes, amongst other things. Anyway, they formed a resistance to overturn the monarchy. They kidnapped one of the king's twin grandsons and demanded a ransom. The king refused to pay it.'

Alex frowned. 'Why did he do that?'

'I don't know.' She glanced at him briefly, her teeth capturing her bottom lip for a moment before she released it and turned back to look down at the lush valley below. 'Maybe he didn't want to be seen being manipulated or something.'

'So the kidnappers killed the little prince?'

She hesitated for a fraction of a second. 'Yes…his body

was found after an undercover rescue attempt failed. He had been blown up by a bomb.'

She felt Alex wince. 'Hard to live down that sort of stuff,' he said.

'Yes.'

'So what was left of your family has had to live with that ever since?' he asked.

'Yes. It's been hard…you know…everyone looking at you as if you have murder and insurgence on your mind,' she said with a dejected slump of her shoulders.

'Poor little elf,' he said, turning her head so he could cup her face as he looked into her eyes. 'It sounds to me as if you need to be taken away from all this drama for a while. Are we still on for dinner?'

'D-dinner?' She looked at him with a shadow of uncertainty in her green-flecked hazel eyes.

'Yes, that's why I came up here in the first place. One of the nursing staff said you lived up here in the foothills. I was taking a chance on finding you at a loose end so I could take you out to dinner somewhere.'

'There aren't any restaurants up here.'

'I know, but what about down at Porto di Castellante?' he suggested.

Amelia lowered her gaze, frightened of the temptation he was dangling before her and even more terrified she wouldn't be able to resist it. 'I have to cook my father something….'

'I heard he's not well and not keen on seeing anyone professional,' Alex said. 'I thought if I came up to take you out it might be a way of breaking the ice in case there's anything I can do for him.'

She raised her gaze back to meet his, a look of surprise flickering there momentarily before she looked away again.

'Did I say something wrong?' he asked.

'No…it's just that he asked me to ask you to visit him, but I just didn't get around to it when I…er…saw you earlier today.'

'I can't promise to be of any help but sometimes it helps to get a second opinion.'

'He's got advanced lung cancer,' she said, the bleak resignation evident in her tone. 'A second opinion is not going to save him.'

'That's sad,' he said. 'What about palliative care? Who is overseeing that?'

She let out a defeated sigh. 'He won't accept any treatment.'

'So you are managing him on your own?'

'Not very well, I'm afraid,' she confessed, her eyes drifting to the view once more. 'I have tried my best to get him to be reassessed but he won't budge. He's not in much pain as yet but I dread what is ahead.'

'It's a brute of a disease,' he said with feeling. 'I'll have a chat with him and see if I can change his mind. Besides, we can always organise some self-administered morphine for him to use at home when things start to go downhill.'

'You're a heart specialist,' she said, looking at him again. 'This is not your responsibility.'

'Perhaps not, but how else am I going to get you to agree to come out with me?' he asked with a twinkling smile.

Amelia felt the familiar kick of panic deep in her stomach. She had travelled this road before and it had almost ruined her life. Alex Hunter was here for work and pleasure; there was no promise of permanency. How could there be? She would be a fool to even dare to dream otherwise.

'You're only here for a month,' she reminded him, a tight set to her mouth.

'So?'

'So…that's not long enough to get to know someone properly.'

'Listen, Amelia, I'm an open book. What you see is what

you get. I'm not hiding any dark secrets. I'm not married and nor am I currently involved with anyone and haven't been for quite some time.'

'So that's supposed to reassure me?' she asked with a deepening frown.

He smiled at her. 'Of course.'

Amelia felt herself caving in in spite of her every attempt to counteract it. He was so utterly charming and irresistible. What would it hurt to go on one little date with him? she wondered. The fact that he was only here for a short time made it even less likely for her to be in any danger of losing her head or heart, she reasoned. Besides, this was a chance for her to prove to herself once and for all she had moved on after her experience with Benito. Only a naïve fool would fall into the same trap twice and she was no fool, or at least not any more.

Besides, Lucia and her brother were right—she *did* need to have a bit of a life now and again. All work and no play was a sure-fire recipe for burn-out and then who would look after her father and brothers?

'I don't know...' she began hesitantly, not wanting him to see how tempted she really was.

'Come on, give me a chance. I promise not to step over any boundaries. No sex, well...not on the first date anyway, but after that who knows?' He gave her another teasing grin.

She gave him a school-mistress look. 'You really are incorrigible.'

'I know, but you're so cute I can't resist trying to win your heart.'

'It would take a whole lot more than a sexy smile and a quick wit to win my heart,' she said, trying to purse her lips but failing hopelessly.

'You think I've got a sexy smile?' His eyes glinted as they held hers. 'I have to confess I've had extensive orthodontic work done.' He tapped his two front teeth. 'These are totally fake—porcelain veneers. I had my teeth knocked out during a football match.'

There was nothing she could do to stop her smile. 'You really are unbelievable.'

He tapped her on the end of her nose. 'So are you, elf.' He got up and pulled her to her feet beside him. 'Now, come on— let's get this poor bike in the back of my car and get you home and hosed, and ready for our first date.'

Amelia sat in the front seat of his car as he loaded her bike in the back and mentally prepared herself for the first time he saw the poverty of her home. She could already feel herself cringing in shame. It had been years since she had brought anyone to the cottage. She always arranged to meet the few friends she had kept over the years at their homes, or at a quiet café well away from the main centres of the island.

'It's this turn here on the left,' she directed him after they had gone a few kilometres, a fluttering sense of nerves assailing her the closer they got. 'I'm sorry the road is not in better condition. Your car will be filthy.'

'No problem.' He sent her another one of his high-beam smiles.

She took an unsteady breath and looked forwards once more. 'It's very good of you to come up here like this…but I must warn you it's probably nothing like you're used to.'

Alex concentrated on negotiating the rough driveway that led to a dilapidated cottage in the shelter of the trees. He could sense her embarrassment and wondered how he could put her at ease. He'd seen his share of poverty-stricken homes during his various field trips to less developed countries, and knew how important it was to not jeopardise someone's sense of dignity just because they didn't live in a house that met the western standards he'd grown up with and more or less taken for granted.

'It must be really peaceful living way up here,' he commented as he parked the car underneath one of the trees.

'Yes…it is.'

He came around and opened her door for her, frowning when he saw her scraped knees as she got out of the car. 'You've hurt yourself. Why didn't you tell me? I could have done something earlier.'

'It's nothing…just a scratch.' She brushed her uniform back down over her legs.

'I've got my doctor's bag in the back. I'll dress those grazes for you now.'

'No, please…it's fine…really. I have my own first-aid kit things inside.'

He didn't press the issue; instead he followed as she led the way to the cottage, but he noticed how her brow was furrowed and her shoulders slightly hunched as if she carried a too-heavy weight on her back.

Amelia opened the front door but there was no sign of her father when she entered the cottage. *'Papà?'* she called out.

Alex came up behind her. 'Has he gone out?'

She frowned as she led the way inside. 'He hardly ever goes out.'

She looked around the kitchen where the dishes her father had used that morning were still on the table. Her gaze went to a note propped up against a mug. It was in her father's roughly scrawled handwriting informing her he'd gone somewhere with Silvio and would be back late and not to worry.

'What does it say?' Alex asked.

She folded the note and pocketed it, a shadow of unease in her hazel eyes as they met his. 'My younger brother has taken him somewhere.'

'Is that unusual?'

'No…not really, except Silvio hasn't been home or even in contact for two weeks…' A small frown tugged at her smooth forehead.

'Maybe he's taken your father out for a meal or something.'

She nibbled at her bottom lip for a moment. 'Maybe.'

'Well, look on the bright side,' he said. 'You don't have to cook dinner for him after all.'

'But you came up to see him and now he's not here.'

'I can come some other time,' he said. 'It's no trouble.'

'Maybe something's happened.' Her frown deepened. 'What if he's taken a bad turn?'

'Then your brother will take him to the hospital. Why not call the switchboard and ask if he's been admitted?' he suggested.

A tide of colour washed into her cheeks and Alex mentally kicked himself. Of course she couldn't call the hospital. There was no electricity that he could see or any sign of a telephone. He could only assume she wouldn't have the funds available for a mobile either. He reached for his own mobile. 'I'll give them a quick call myself. What's his first name?' he asked.

'Aldo,' she answered, twisting her hands together.

He made the call and after a brief conversation replaced the phone in his pocket. 'No, he hasn't been admitted.'

She blew out a tiny breath. 'I can't help worrying about him.'

'That's understandable, but at least he's with your brother so you can take the rest of tonight off and kick your heels up with me.'

She gave him an apologetic glance. 'I don't think I should go out tonight. I'm sorry.'

'I'm not taking no for an answer,' he said. 'You deserve some time off. A quick dinner by the seaside will be good for both of us. Besides, I gave you a lift home so you owe me.'

Amelia could tell by the determined look in his eyes that she was going to have a hard time convincing him to leave without her. The thought of spending the evening alone in the cottage wasn't too appealing, but she felt she should at least put up a token resistance. 'I don't know…I have an early start tomorrow.'

'No earlier than mine. Come on, get a wriggle on. We're

wasting valuable time here when we could be sitting watching the sun go down with a glass of wine in our hands.'

She could feel herself weakening. 'I need to freshen up first. Do you mind waiting?'

'I don't mind at all,' he said, and pulled out a chair and sat down. 'I've got a couple of calls to make anyway. I'm expected at the castle tomorrow evening. I guess there's some sort of protocol I'm meant to follow. I don't suppose I can turn up there and slap the old guy on the back and say, "G'day, mate, I'm Alex Hunter." I'd better check with the castle staff on how I'm supposed to address him.'

Amelia fought back a wry smile as she left him busily punching in numbers. She was certain he knew exactly how to address anyone from royalty to the lowliest commoner without turning a single hair. He hadn't given any sign of being put off by the run-down nature of her family home, which made it all the harder for her to keep him at a relatively safe distance. Most men would have turned up their noses and backed out without even bothering to say goodbye. Her ex-lover, Benito, had been appalled by the distance he'd had to travel to pick her up, let alone the condition of the cottage when he'd got there. He had made her feel so ashamed, and in her youth and innocence she had failed to see the warning signs that their relationship was not as it should have been. But perhaps she hadn't wanted to, she thought with a little pang of sadness as she moved towards the cramped bathroom.

After a quick, cold bath because there wasn't time to heat water on the fuel stove, she spent ten minutes agonising over what to wear. Her choices were limited to start with, but she finally narrowed it down to the dress Alex had bought her or a skirt and blouse that had belonged to her mother. However, her mother's outfit was ruled out as soon as she put it on. It had faded over time and did nothing for her, hanging off her slight frame like a sack.

With almost reverent fingers she picked up the dress Alex had bought and slipped it over her head, gently doing up the zipper at the side. She twirled in front of her mottled mirror, amazed at how the beautiful fabric brought out the creamy tone of her skin and the green flecks in her hazel eyes.

She rummaged in her small supply of cosmetics and found a lip-gloss and applied it to her mouth, wondering what the nuns at Saint Gregorio's would say if they could see her now.

Then, giving herself one last twirl, she picked up her only evening purse and went back to where Alex Hunter was waiting for her, a tiny, moth-like fluttery sensation in the middle of her stomach at the thought of being alone with him for the rest of the evening.

CHAPTER FIVE

'I'VE changed my mind,' Alex said, getting up from the chair as she came back to the kitchen. 'You're not an elf or a pixie—you're a princess.'

Amelia knew her cheeks were glowing but there was nothing she could do to disguise it. 'It's a beautiful dress,' she said softly. 'Anyone would look like a princess in it.'

'Do you think you should leave your father a note in case he gets back before you do?' he asked.

She nodded and, quickly scribbling a message on the back of the note her father had left, she propped it up against his mug again.

Alex escorted her out to the car, shooing the hens away from her as they went. 'Make way for Her Royal Highness Princess Amelia,' he said. 'Come on, ladies, be off with you.'

Amelia giggled as the hens scuttled off with ruffled feathers. 'They're not all ladies,' she said, pointing to the proudly strutting rooster amongst them.

'Sorry, mate,' he addressed the rooster. 'I didn't see you there.' He turned back to Amelia and grinned cheekily. 'What a life he must have, all those ladies to himself with no competition.'

Amelia felt her cheeks grow warm as she thought about how many women had flown in and out of his life. His playboy lifestyle afforded him numerous opportunities to flit from one relationship to the other, and with his easy charm and unmistakable sexual potency she began to realise she was in very real danger of joining their number.

Alex tipped up her chin with one hand while he used the other to graze his knuckles over the bright pool of colour on her cheek. 'Do you know you're the first woman I've been able to make blush in years?'

She looked into his dark eyes, her pulse beginning to race as his knuckles caressed her again. Her heart felt as if it were growing in size, her legs as if they had been disconnected from the bones that were supposed to hold them upright.

'I—I'm not used to this sort of thing,' she said, her tongue sneaking out to unconsciously moisten her mouth.

'What sort of thing?'

'Flirting, joking, dating...that sort of thing.'

He looked puzzled for a moment. 'How old are you?'

Her cheeks fired up again. 'Thirty.'

'Then you really have to make up for lost time,' he said, and, stepping away from her, opened the car door. 'I've got a whole six years on you.'

Amelia waited until they were on their way before speaking again. 'I suppose you are very experienced in the ways of the world and find me something of a novelty.' She hadn't really intended to sound quite so priggish but it was too late to take the words back now.

'To tell you the truth I find you delightfully refreshing,' he said, sending her a quick glance, the white slash of his smile devastatingly attractive against the olive tone of his skin.

'But you're laughing at me all the same. I can tell.'

'That chip on your shoulder will ruin that dress by stretching it all out of shape,' he warned her playfully.

'I haven't got a chip on my shoulder.'

Alex flicked another glance her way and skilfully redirected the conversation. 'You have two brothers, right? What do they do for a living?'

She let out a little sigh. 'Rico, my older brother, recently lost his job at one of the vineyards. He hasn't had a lot of luck with steady employment. Silvio, my younger brother, has been even worse. He's been restless most of his life, flitting from one thing to another. He's employed down at the main port but he doesn't really talk about what it is he actually does.'

'I guess that puts an extra strain on you,' he said.

'It does.' She looked down at her hands in her lap. 'I've had to take up some extra work…at the palace.'

She felt his gaze swing her way. 'Doing what?' he asked.

'Nursing the king two nights a week.'

'So what's the old guy like?' he asked.

'His bodyguards don't really encourage conversation with him,' she said. 'Besides, I prefer to play a low profile.'

'Because of your family's history?'

'That and…other things,' she said, tucking a strand of hair behind her ear self-consciously.

'You're not intimidated by all that monarchy stuff, are you?' he asked, swinging another quick glance in her direction.

She met his eyes briefly. 'So you're not a monarchist yourself?'

He gave a little noncommittal shrug. 'It's an ongoing debate in Australia about whether we should become a republic. I haven't really made up my mind. Too busy saving lives I guess.'

'Your work is very demanding,' she said, releasing a tiny breath to counteract the effect of his close proximity. 'It's a wonder you had the time to come over here to help our people.'

'When I received a royal summons I was a bit intrigued, I can tell you,' he said. 'I had heard about the island before but, while it was somewhere on my list of must-see places, I wouldn't have come right now, but my parents were keen for me to do it.' He sent a quick smile her way and added, 'I guess they want to dine out on it a bit. "Have we told you about our son who mixes with Italian royalty?" That sort of thing goes down a treat at a dinner party.'

'But you're not fazed by it all—or, if you are, you're not showing it,' she surmised.

'I'm a doctor, Amelia. My first priority is to heal the sick and if I can do that in a way that helps the underprivileged then I'm more than happy. Don't get me wrong, I come from a wealthy background which has given me some wonderful privileges, but my parents have always encouraged both Megan and I to give something back to the community and not just our neighbourhood one.'

'Your family sounds wonderfully supportive,' Amelia said, thinking sadly of all she had missed out on in hers.

'They are. I am very lucky.'

'How old is your sister?' she asked after a little silence.

'She's twenty-five.'

'That's quite an age gap between you—eleven years,' she observed.

'I know, but it was a long time after my adoption papers were processed before they could adopt another child,' he said.

Amelia swung her gaze to look at him again. 'You're… you're adopted?'

'Yes, and very proud of it.' His dark eyes met hers briefly. 'My adoptive parents are fabulous people. I owe them a great deal. When you think about it, I could have ended up with much worse.'

She waited until he'd brought the car to a stop outside one of the restaurants in Santa Fiera before asking, 'Have you ever thought of tracing your biological parents?'

He met her gaze across the small width of the car. 'Now and again I've thought of it but I haven't done anything about it. I guess my main reason has been to save my adoptive mother the hurt she might feel if I were to go looking for the woman who gave birth to me. It's a sensitive subject. My adoptive mother was unable to have children of her own. She grieved terribly that she couldn't give my father what he most wanted. Of course, the reproductive technology available today would have solved her problems in an instant. But she is the only mother I've ever known, even though I was what was considered in those days a late adoption.'

Amelia felt the small silence begin to tighten the air in her chest. 'How late?' she asked, glancing at him.

'I was two years old.'

A tiny shiver passed over the back of her neck, lifting each and every fine hair. 'So…so you don't recall anything at all of your infancy? I mean, before you were adopted?' she asked.

He answered her question with a question of his own. 'Tell me, Amelia, what's your very first memory?'

She thought about it for a moment. 'I was about three, I think, when my mother made me a fairy dress with wings on the back of it. She told me later how she had made it from the material of her wedding dress and veil. I can't really remember anything before that.'

'That's about average for most people. Neurological studies have shown that the infant brain is not mature enough to store reliable memories until about the age of three.'

'What about in terms of emotional and physical abuse?' she asked. 'Surely if the infancy was traumatic enough there would be some trace of it in the child's later behaviour?'

'Perhaps, but that would not necessarily be because the child actually remembered what had happened, but more of an instinctive feeling in an evolutionary sense that life was unsafe and chaotic during that time.'

Amelia mused over his answer as they walked into the restaurant. They were led to a table near the windows that overlooked the beach of the main tourist area, which had been recently developed on the island, the casino, restaurants and health spa attracting large crowds during the spring and summer months.

The waiter handed them menus and the wine list and left them alone to decide.

'What wine do you recommend?' Alex asked, looking at the list in his hands.

'I'm not much of a wine connoisseur but the Porto Castellante Blanco is known as the signature wine of the island. The Niroli vines have been cultivated since Roman times,' she said, recalling what Rico had told her while he had been working at the vineyard. 'It's said that the Niroli vines produce the queen of white grapes.'

'Let's give it a go, then,' he said, and signalled to the waiter.

Amelia tried to relax as their wine was poured a short time later but she was way out of her comfort zone and felt sure it showed. She glanced at the other couples and parties dining and wished she could appear less gauche, but she had so rarely eaten out and was terrified in case she picked the wrong piece of cutlery.

Alex picked up his glass and raised it in a toast against hers. 'Here's to mending the broken hearts of Niroli.'

She lowered her gaze for a moment, a shadow passing over her features.

'What's wrong?' he asked.

'Nothing.'

'Confession time, little elf.' He reached across the table and tipped up her chin with his finger, his dark eyes meshing with hers. 'If you tell me who broke your heart I'll tell you who broke mine.'

'I can't imagine you having your heart broken,' she said, her gaze slipping away from his to stare into the contents of her glass.

'It happens to the best of us, believe me,' he assured her

as he leaned back. 'My work gets in the way a lot. I guess that's why I've reached this age without settling down.'

'Is that what you want to do some time? Settle down?' she asked, taking a tentative sip of wine.

'I don't know.' A small frown brought his dark brows closer for a fraction of a second. 'I thought I wanted to once but it didn't work out.'

Amelia wondered if she'd been wrong about assuming his heart was unbreakable. He acted like a carefree playboy, but she couldn't help wondering now if it was a cover-up for deeper hurt.

'What about you?' he asked, his expression lightening once more. 'Are you like most other young women living in hope that Prince Charming will come along one day and sweep you off your feet?'

She gave him a twisted smile as she reached for her wine again. 'It's a nice fantasy, but hasn't anyone told you there aren't enough princes to go around?'

He smiled back at her. 'You could always settle for an ordinary bloke. How about me? Want to run away and get married and have my babies?'

Amelia's mouthful of wine burst from her mouth and sprayed across the table to pepper the front of his shirt. She gasped and choked and died a thousand deaths of embarrassment, but all he did was hand her his napkin and chuckle with amusement.

'I think I must have jumped the gun a bit. Maybe I should have kept that for our second date.'

'I can't believe you *said* that…' She glanced around to see if anyone had seen her mortifying moment, but to her relief no one had appeared to, or if they had they were too polite to stare. She brought her gaze back to his. 'You're joking…right?'

He leaned forward again and took one of her hands in the warmth of his, his dark gaze holding hers. 'What if I wasn't?'

She pulled her hand out of his, her mouth tightening with reproach. 'Please don't make fun of me. I might not have the experience of other women my age, but I'm not a complete fool.'

'I had no intention of making fun of you. It kind of slipped out. I didn't even know I was going to say it until the words were out of my mouth—honestly.'

She gave him a hardened little glare. 'I know what you're up to but it won't work with me. You're only here for a month and you're looking for a playmate to pass the time.' She got to her feet and thrust her napkin on the table. 'Go and find someone else to warm your bed. I'm not interested.'

Alex gave the waiter a handful of notes and brushed past the other diners to follow her, finally catching up to her a couple of blocks down the street. 'Amelia, listen to me.'

'Go away.'

'Damn it, will you stop walking so fast and listen to me for a minute?'

She swung around to face him, her chest heaving, her eyes flashing with green and brown sparks of fury. 'You really take the prize for the biggest ego. I thought my first lover was bad, but you surpass him in spades.'

He stood watching her without speaking, a small smile tipping up the edges of his mouth.

'Stop looking at me like that.' She glared at him crossly.

'Like what?'

'You keep smiling at me.'

'You make me want to smile.'

'I don't want you to smile at me.'

'Then you're going to have to stop doing that.'

'Doing what?'

'That little thing you do with your mouth.'

She scowled at him. 'What little thing?'

He took her hands in his and pulled her up against him.

'That pursed-lipped thing. You do it all the time. It drives me crazy. It makes me want to kiss you.'

'That's…that's ridiculous,' she said, staring at his mouth.

'Is it?' He pressed a hand to the small of her back and brought her even closer.

'O-of course it is…. You hardly know me….'

'I know. It's never happened like this before.'

'I don't believe you. You're just saying that to tempt me into allowing you to kiss me.'

'Is it working?'

'Is…is what working?' She was still staring at his mouth, her gaze mesmerised by its sensual contours, made all the more captivating by the gentle curve of his smile.

He lowered his head until his lips were so close to hers they almost grazed them as he spoke. 'I've wanted to kiss you from the first moment I saw you on my back fence.'

Amelia knew if she moved her lips to form a single word the battle to keep him at bay would be lost. She stood, totally transfixed, her body tingling all over at the feel of his pressed so closely, his maleness against her femaleness, his muscular strength against the yielding softness of hers.

But then, almost without her realising she was doing it, her tongue sneaked out to moisten her lips and involuntarily brushed against his bottom lip, sending sparks of electricity right through her.

'You really shouldn't have done that, little elf.' This time his lips did graze hers, his warm wine-flavoured breath mingling with her quickly expelled one.

'I—I didn't mean to do that…' she breathed, her lips buzzing with sensation as they moved against his.

He pressed a soft, barely touching kiss to her mouth. 'Sure you did.'

'No…' She kissed him back, softly, shyly. 'No…no…I didn't….'

He smiled against her lips, making them instantly vibrate with intense longing. 'You're lying to me. You really want to kiss me. I can tell.'

'No…it's you that wants to kiss me.'

He lifted his head a fraction, just enough to meet her gaze, his eyes dark and gleaming with desire. 'You're right. That's exactly what I want to do.'

Amelia watched as his gaze dipped to her mouth, the thick black lashes fanning down over his eyes, his head coming down…

'Wait!' She placed her flattened palm to his chest.

He lifted his head to look down at her. 'What's the matter?'

'We're standing in the middle of the street,' she whispered as some people strolled by.

'Are we?'

'You know we are.'

He looked down at her mouth again. 'I forgot about that.'

She gave a small, embarrassed laugh. 'Just as well I reminded you. We could have made complete fools of ourselves.'

'I guess we'll have to do this some other time, then.'

'I guess.'

He held her gaze for a long moment without speaking.

'I'm sorry about dinner,' she began awkwardly. 'I shouldn't have rushed out of the restaurant like that.'

'We can always go back in and start over,' he suggested. 'I'm sure the waiter won't mind. Besides, I'm starving.'

'So…shall we do it?' she asked after a tiny pause.

'Do what?' he said, looking at her mouth again.

'Go and have dinner.'

'Oh, I thought you were talking about the other thing.'

She wrinkled her nose at him. 'What other thing?'

'This other thing,' he said, and before she could do a thing to prepare herself his mouth came down and set fire to hers.

CHAPTER SIX

AMELIA felt the full-throttle passion of Alex's kiss in every nerve and cell of her body, leaving her starved senses reeling. His tongue was slow and languorous at first, but then as if fuelled by his growing desire it became more demanding, drawing hers into a mutual sexy tango that sent lightning bolts of feeling to her toes and back. She could feel his reaction to her against her stomach, the rapid thickening of his body reminding her of how very powerful human desire was and how easily it could slip out of one's control.

She fought against her own response but her body seemed to have a mind of its own, unleashing a wild and uncontrollable urge to feel more and more of his touch. It made her press closer and closer against his hardness, her breasts swelling as if reaching out to him for his intimate attention, her skin prickling with the need to feel his body move and slide against hers.

She felt the moistening of her feminine core where the pulse of desire was already drumming a primitive beat low and deep inside her, her whole body humming with an escalating need she had never experienced in such an out-of-control way before.

She heard him groan, a deep, guttural, almost primal sound that rumbled against her breasts and fuelled her reaction to him until she forgot they were standing in full view of the public.

One of his hands cupped her cheek to angle her head for deeper access, his other hand in the small of her back to press her even harder against him.

He was incredibly aroused, the length of him surprising her even though she wasn't completely without experience.

The sound of voices and footsteps approaching must have jolted Alex into awareness of where they were as he suddenly pulled away, and, giving her a quick, almost self-conscious grin, ran a hand through his hair in a distracted manner. 'Now *that* is what I call a kiss. Where'd you learn to do that?'

She gave him a flustered look. 'Um...I...'

He smiled and, tucking her arm through his, escorted her back to the restaurant. 'Never mind—I don't think I really want to know. I might start to feel jealous.'

They were soon re-seated at the same table and the waiter refreshed their glasses with the chilled wine. Food orders were taken and fresh crusty bread and a little plate of warmed marinated local olives appeared.

After their main course was set before them Amelia found herself finally beginning to relax, the wine easing a bit more of her tension with every sip she took. Alex had done his best to put her at ease, chatting in his easygoing manner to her about his work and how he hoped to train the cardiac team at the Free Hospital, but, even so, every now and again her mind kept drifting back to that explosive kiss. She could still taste him in her mouth and her lips felt swollen and overly sensitive each time she sipped her wine. She could even feel the hard, warm presence of his legs beneath the table; once or twice as he shifted in his chair they brushed against hers, unleashing a shock wave of awareness through her lower body.

Alex reached across to refill her wineglass, his dark eyes meeting hers. 'How is your meal?'

'It's wonderful,' she said, sending him a shy smile. 'I haven't been out to dinner for years.'

His eyebrows lifted. 'How many years?'

She ran a fingertip around the rim of her glass, her eyes watching the movement of her finger rather than meet the dark probe of his gaze. 'Eleven.'

He whistled through his teeth. 'That must have been one hell of a bad meal you had way back then.'

She felt a reluctant smile tug at her mouth as she lifted her eyes to his. 'It was. I got my heart broken for dessert.'

'Not a good way to end a meal or a relationship.'

'No.'

Their gazes locked for a moment and then, as if in unison, slowly lowered to each other's mouths, the air suddenly charged with erotic possibilities.

Alex was the first to break the spell. 'So what happened?' he asked, reaching for his wine.

'I was too young and inexperienced to see the signs. I had not long lost my mother and was feeling a bit rudderless. A handsome man visiting the island paid me a lot of attention and I stupidly fell for it,' she said, trying not to let her gaze drift back to the warm temptation of his.

'A handsome married man, I suppose,' he commented.

'Yes, very much so.' She let out a tiny sigh. 'He had two little children back in Milan. Their photographs fell out of his wallet when he dropped it. I picked it up and of course he had all the usual excuses—my wife doesn't understand me, we no longer have a physical relationship, blah, blah, blah.'

His dark gaze softened with concern. 'How did you cope?'

She brushed her hair back with a soft movement of her hand, her cheeks going a delicate shade of pink. 'I got myself to a nunnery.'

He gave her an incredulous look. 'You're kidding, right?'

'No.' She toyed with the rim of her glass with her fingertip again, her expression clouding briefly.

'Were you going to take vows?'

'I was seriously considering it.'

'What changed your mind?'

She gave him a wry smile. 'The vow of chastity wasn't really hard for me, but the vow of silence was.'

He laughed. 'Yeah, I can see how that might have been a problem for you.'

'It was. I had a tendency to answer back, which didn't go down very well.'

'So you left and took up nursing?' he said.

'Yes, I wanted to do something with my life, something for other people instead of hiding away in a convent.'

'Not all nuns hide away in convents,' he pointed out. 'I've worked with several who were teaching or nursing in some of the developing countries I'd visited.'

'I know, but I missed my father and brothers after three years. I decided I could do more good on Niroli by working at the Free Hospital as well as one or two community shifts.'

'You weren't tempted to take your skills to the private hospital where the pay would be better?' he asked.

'No, never. I think it's terribly unfair that the well-to-do have top-quality health care while the poorer members of our community have to do with second best.'

'It's a real problem in most developed countries,' he said. 'Those who can afford private health cover often need it less than those who can't.'

'So that's part of the reason you are here, isn't it?' she asked. 'Apart from the royal summons, of course.'

'Yes, I thought it would be a good opportunity to train the cardiac team while I was here on sabbatical. Vincenzo Morani in particular is keen to learn the technique.'

'You're employed at a teaching hospital in Sydney?' she said, this time unable to keep her gaze from tracking back to the warm intensity of his.

'Yeah, I get the fancy title of Associate Professor, which

basically means I have to do a whole lot of paperwork for the university as well as juggle tutorials in amongst my regular clinical work. Some days I don't even have time to think. My folks are always at me to slow down, but it's hard to get a good balance of work and play.'

'I know. It's hard when your skills are needed so much.'

'Like you, right?' he guessed.

She lowered her gaze self-consciously. 'I don't have the demands on me that you do.'

'I don't know about that,' he said. 'From what I hear you don't get to play too often either.'

'No, not much, I guess.'

'Are you planning to spend the rest of your life on Niroli?' he asked after a tiny, almost imperceptible pause.

'I'm not sure…' She picked up her glass and stared at its contents. 'I would like to travel, perhaps see a bit of the world, but I have responsibilities here for now.'

'Your father and brothers?'

'Yes…it might be different when my father…passes, but for now I have no immediate plans to leave.'

A small silence settled in the space between them. Amelia was hunting her brain for something to say to break it, when a man suddenly approached their table to stare at Alex, his face almost white with shock. 'Antonio?'

Alex turned his head. 'Sorry, I think you've got the wrong guy.'

'I am sorry…' The man backed away. 'You look like someone I once knew.'

Alex gave him a friendly smile. 'It happens all the time,' he said. 'I guess I have one of those boring generic faces.'

Amelia saw the up and down movement of the other man's throat, his pallor still sickly white. He apologised once more and returned to his table where the two other people sharing a meal with him had their gazes still trained on Alex. Their heads came together as the man resumed his seat, their voices low but extremely agitated if the gesticulations of their hands were any indication.

'Sorry about that.' Alex smiled at her. 'That's the third time that's happened to me this week. One guy even asked if he could take a photo of me. Kind of freaky, huh?'

Amelia stared at him, her heart feeling like a pendulum that had been knocked out of its steady rhythm. 'It's happened before?' She leaned forward in her chair, her voice lowering. 'Here? On…on the island?'

'Yeah, but I guess it's because I look like a native,' he said with a rueful grin. 'I mean, it's not like I can hide it in spite of my Aussie accent. So far I've been mistaken for an Antonio and a Marco. I think there was one other name but I can't remember what it was. Perhaps I look like an Italian movie star—what do you reckon?'

Her heart gave another hard ram against her sternum.

'So…' she paused for a moment to moisten her suddenly bone-dry lips '…you are of Italian heritage?'

'It's on my birth certificate. I was born in Agrigento in Sicily.'

'Sicily?'

'Yes. That's why I thought I'd take up this offer to visit Niroli, being so close and all.'

Amelia stared at the table for a moment as her heart gradually went back to normal.

He had been born in Sicily.

It was on his birth certificate.

He couldn't possibly be…

'I haven't gone there yet but I thought I might,' he said into the silence.

She looked up at him blankly. 'Where?'

'Agrigento.'

'Why?'

'I just thought I'd have a look around. I haven't told my

parents of my plans, but I kind of figured it wouldn't hurt to have a wander around the churchyards, see if I recognise any names.'

'Do you know your original Italian name?'

'Yes. It's a bit of a mouthful—Santocanale.'

'It's…nice… Very Sicilian…'

'It's not bad, I suppose, but of course it went once I was formally adopted. However, I absolutely refused to go by my Italian first name. I changed it as soon as I went to school,' he said with a wry twist to his mouth.

'What is your first name?'

'Alessandro,' he said, sending another shock wave through her chest. 'Mind you, it's kind of different now—most Australians have no trouble with pronouncing unusual names, but thirty-odd years ago I would have been asking to be singled out and bullied for having such an Italian-sounding name. I've been Alex ever since.'

Alex—*Alessandro*…

Amelia's mind was racing along with her heart. People had stopped him in the street, telling him he looked like someone called Antonio…

Antonio Fierezza, the king's son who had been killed two years ago in a yachting accident.

And Marco…

Her heart gave another sudden sickening lurch.

Marco Fierezza, the twin grandson of the king, Antonio's son, the man who had recently given up his right to the Niroli throne to marry the woman he loved more than the kingdom.

The *non*-identical male twin…

'Is something wrong?' Alex leaned forward. 'You've gone a little pale.'

'I'm fine…it's just a bit hot in here…'

'Want to go for a walk along the shore to cool off?' he suggested, offering her a hand as he stood up.

Amelia placed her hand in his, her stomach feeling hollow

and uneasy as he led her past the table of diners who were still watching him with wide, fearful eyes.

The cooler air outside helped to clear the clutter of her mind.

It was impossible, she reassured herself as they made their way down to the gently lapping shore.

It was just a coincidence as Signora Gravano had said the other day. Alex looked as if he had been born and bred on the island, but so too did many other Italians who visited from the mainland. The olive skin and dark eyes were so common-place it was understandable people would mistake him for someone else.

A coincidence.

That was all it was.

It couldn't possibly be anything else....

'Feeling better now?' Alex asked as a salty sea breeze licked at their faces a short time later.

'Much better.' She tried a smile but it wasn't entirely successful.

'I guess I should take you home and let you get a good night's sleep,' he said, looking down at her, his expression still soft with concern.

'I guess so.'

'Can we do this again?' His deep velvet voice was a brush-like caress against her face.

She ran her tongue across her lips and lowered her eyes. 'You don't have much time here.'

He nudged up her chin with his finger. 'For you I will make the time.'

Amelia looked into his eyes, her chest filling with unex-pected emotion. She didn't want to fall in love, certainly not with a man who was only here for a month. How could she bear it when he left if she let her guard down in such a way? But something about Alex Hunter was totally captivating. Not just his sense of humour but also his sincerity. He laughed at life but he also treated it with a great deal of respect. She couldn't help admiring that quality in him. There was a solid depth to his character that no amount of playful banter could hide. His consideration of his adoptive parents' feelings showed his ability to put others' needs before his own, so too did his commitment to the Free Hospital, offering his services free of charge.

It would be all too easy to fall in love with him but where would that leave her in the end?

'Alex…can I ask you a question?' She looked up at him, her hazel gaze troubled.

'Sure.'

'You said that you weren't really interested in finding out who your biological parents were…but what if *they* came looking for you?'

He compressed his lips for a moment as he gave it some thought. 'I don't know…I hadn't thought of it from that angle. I'd always assumed since I was given away at the age of two that my parent—or parents as the case may be—had no further interest in me. How could they? If they had developed a loving relationship with me over that time why would they have had me adopted out?'

It was a salient point, she had to admit. It would be hard enough relinquishing a newborn infant, let alone one you had reared to the age of two, watching all those tiny milestones on the way past. The first smile, the first steps, the first words. How could anyone do it without a very good reason?

'Were you adopted from Sicily or Australia?' she asked.

'Australia,' he said. 'I guess my biological parent or parents had migrated there.'

'What about your sister?' she asked. 'Has she traced her biological parents?'

'Megan was adopted by my parents when she was twelve,'

he said in a sober tone. 'Her biological parents were abusive. I don't think she would ever consider seeing either of them again.'

'How tragic. It must be very hard for her.'

'My parents have done the very best they can to help her overcome her past, but some things are not so easily resolved.'

'I can see why you are so hesitant to go looking for your own birth parents. Like you said, you never know what you might find.'

'Exactly,' he said. 'There are some things in life that are best left well alone.'

She fell into step beside him as they made their way back to his car. Alex Hunter was right, she thought as they drove back towards the turn-off to the foothills.

Some things were better left well alone…

CHAPTER SEVEN

THE cottage was in total darkness when Alex drove up the pot-holed driveway. He glanced at the little figure sitting so silently beside him, wondering if she was going to baulk at going out with him again. He had enjoyed the evening much more than he'd expected to. He knew he had limited time on the island, but it didn't mean he couldn't have a little dalliance without strings. Certainly Amelia Vialli was nothing like any other woman he had ever dated, and after his most recent break-up that was exactly what he needed right now. It had nothing to do with Amelia's lack of experience of the world, although he would be lying to himself if he didn't admit to how quaint and refreshing he found it. So many women he knew were way too polished and worldly, and Sarah, his ex-girlfriend, had been no exception. It was such a change to be in the company of a young woman who didn't hide behind layers of make-up and cloying perfume and flirtatious, manipulative wiles. Amelia had a feisty spirit underneath that quiet humility and he loved that she showed it without reserve. And she was passionate, much more so than he could ever have imagined. One kiss had shown him what was simmering under the surface, no doubt hidden for all this time for fear of being hurt again.

'Would you like me to wait with you until your father and brothers return?' he offered as he brought the car to a standstill.

'No, I'll be fine. They could be ages and you have to operate tomorrow,' she said. 'Thank you for a lovely evening. The meal was wonderful.'

He came around to help her out of the car, the moonlight highlighting the perfect oval of her small pixie face. 'But we didn't even have dessert.' He gave her a twinkling look. 'That's my favourite part of the meal.'

He heard the soft intake of her breath. 'Maybe some other time…'

He smiled as he pressed a soft kiss to the corner of her mouth. 'I'll hold you to that.'

He walked her to the door, waiting for her to light a candle before he left. The soft, flickering light gave her an almost ethereal look as she turned to face him.

'I suppose you're wondering why we don't have electricity connected,' she said, a tiny glimmer of pride showing in her hazel eyes.

'I hadn't noticed,' he lied.

He felt his stomach tighten with anger at how she and her family had been treated. 'It's not right you have to live like this, Amelia. There must be something that can be done. I could speak to someone about it for you.'

She lifted her chin as she held the door open for him. 'We come from completely different worlds, Alex. Don't go looking for a bridge between them. There isn't one.'

'That's crazy and you know it. We are just two ordinary people who are interested in each other. Why not explore that interest and see where it takes us?'

'It will take you back to Australia and leave me here.'

He frowned at her. 'You don't know that.'

'It won't work, Alex. I know it won't.'

'So you're suddenly an expert on intimate relationships after one bad experience in eleven years?' He hadn't meant to sound so angry, but the determination in her manner and tone had got under his normally unflappable skin. 'Come on, Amelia. Give this a chance. We struck sparks off each other from the word go. I haven't felt like that before. I know this could work for now.'

'Do they have a playboy manual that all you men consult to give you the best pick-up lines to use?' she asked with a little curl of her lip. 'So far this evening on at least two occasions you've used the very same lines my ex-lover used to get me to sleep with him.'

Now he *was* really angry. 'Amelia, don't cast me in the same mould as that idiot. I don't see why we can't just see what happens.'

'You want a relationship with an outcast peasant?' she asked with an arch of one brow.

'You are *not* a peasant. I don't see you as anything other than a beautiful young woman who is throwing her life away.'

'So you fancy yourself as Prince Charming intent on rescuing Cinderella from her life of drudgery, do you?' she asked with biting sarcasm.

'I'm no prince,' he said tightly. 'I'm just a regular guy who is very attracted to a woman for the first time in I don't know how long.'

She rolled her eyes. 'That is *such* a line.'

He clenched his fists, trying to get control. 'Look, I can't help it if some things I say have been said before in another context. That's not my problem—that's yours. All I know is I have a short time here and I don't want to waste any of it on arguing when we could be developing a connection instead.'

She gave him a smile touched with sadness. 'You're wasting your time with me, Alex. Go and find yourself someone who is able to move with grace and ease in your world. I would only embarrass you. After all, isn't that really why you bought me this dress? So you could take me out in public without cringing?'

He raked a hand through his hair in frustration. 'I give up. All right, you win. I'll leave you alone. I get the message loud and clear. Sorry it's taken me so long. I must have dating dyslexia or something. You can live your little nun's life hidden up here in the woods—see if I care. I have better things to do with my time than try and get you to change your mind.' He moved through the open door to the moonlight outside. 'I guess I'll see you some time on the ward.'

She didn't answer.

But in a way that was in itself an answer, Alex thought as he drove back down the road, bumping over the pot-holes without a thought to his hire car's suspension.

Amelia Vialli had given him the brush-off and he'd damn well better get over it.

When she came out into the kitchen the next morning Amelia found her father sitting at the table, his pain-glazed eyes briefly meeting hers.

'I do not want anything to eat,' he said as she reached for the utensils to prepare his breakfast.

'But, *Papà*, you have to have something,' she insisted.

He sent her an embittered glance. 'What need does a dying man have for food?'

'*Papà*—' she began.

'Do not patronise me, Amelia.' He gave a hacking cough and continued, 'I know I am dying. As far as I am concerned the sooner it happens, the better.'

'You can't mean that!'

'I do,' he said with a grim look. 'Especially now.'

She frowned at his tone. 'Why…especially now?'

He shifted his eyes from hers and she saw his throat tighten, along with his hands, which were in white-knuckled knots on the table in front of him.

'*Papà?*'

He raised his head to look at her. 'A long time ago…before you and Rico and Silvio were born I did a very bad thing.'

Amelia felt something thick and immovable settle in the middle of her chest, robbing her of the air she needed to breathe. 'W-what sort of bad thing?' she asked, her voice coming out as a cracked whisper.

His eyes were filled with shame as they held hers. 'I was responsible for the kidnap of Prince Alessandro Fierezza.'

She stared at him, her insides shuddering, her heart racing and her palms damp with the dew of dread.

'I am sorry, Amelia,' he went on brokenly. 'I know it is a terrible shock but I was young and got caught up in the rebellion.'

'But you said you were never part of it! You've always told us you were not involved in any way!'

He coughed so hard and for so long, she became seriously frightened. *'Papà?'* She stepped towards him. 'Are you all right?'

He waved his hand as he used the other to bring an old rag to his mouth to spit out the bloody mucus. His gaze returned to hers. 'I started out on the fringe and was never too heavily involved—always kept in the dark. But gradually, over time, I was given more and more responsibility, especially as the movement to kidnap the prince gathered momentum.'

'Y-you…you mean you…*killed* him?'

He shook his head and sighed. 'No, I did not kill him. Do you really believe me capable of such a thing, your own father?'

Amelia swallowed and reached for his age-ridden hand. 'No, *Papà*, but, w-what did you do with him?'

His eyes glistened with moisture, something she had never seen in them before, not even after her mother had died.

'I organised for him to be shipped away,' he said. 'I had some connections, a couple who were prepared to take the child.'

'Take him where?'

'To somewhere he could not be easily traced.'

'But what about the other child?' she asked after a throbbing silence that seemed to be keeping erratic time with her heart. 'The child who is now buried at the palace?'

'King Giorgio had activated an undercover operation to get his grandson back but it backfired. The parents of the child were part of the resistance group and when the explosions happened during the rescue operation they were all killed. Because they had no other relatives it was easy for me to pass the boy off as the prince. No one questioned it. I saw the chance to get out of the contract that had been handed to me.'

'The contract?'

'To kill the prince if the ransom bid failed.'

Amelia stiffened at her father's harsh words. 'But you couldn't go through with it?'

'No.' He gave a ragged sigh. 'He was a little boy of two, barely speaking, crying for his *mamma* and brother all the time. It nearly broke my heart. I just couldn't do it.'

Tears burned at the back of Amelia's eyes. 'Oh, *Papà.*'

'I had to rely on the silence of other people to ship the boy out of danger. It cost me everything. That is why we have lived in poverty ever since. But it was the only thing I could do, Amelia. I suddenly found myself in over my head with the rebellion. Your mother had just found out she was pregnant. I could not extricate myself without losing my life or hers if it became known I had not carried out the plan to kill the prince.'

'Have you heard anything of what happened to him?' she asked.

'There are rumours…' he paused, his throat moving up and down again '…rumours that he is alive and currently on the island.'

Amelia stared at him in growing alarm.

'Of course, no one has verified it but it should not be hard to do so,' he said. 'One look will be enough for me to know if he is the prince.'

'One look?' She frowned at him in bafflement. 'But, *Papà*, a tiny child of two will be hard to recognise thirty-four years later, surely?'

His pain-filled eyes came back to hers. 'Prince Alessandro has a birthmark, a strawberry one. I saw it when I was looking after him. It is very distinctive. It is shaped like the island of Niroli.'

'A birthmark…' she breathed. 'Where?'

'It is on his right forearm, on the underside near the elbow. You would not see it unless he turned his arm right over.'

Amelia let out her breath in a jagged stream, her thoughts clanging together in her head like discordant cathedral bells. She mentally backtracked, going over each time she had been with Alex Hunter, trying to recall whether he had been wearing shirt sleeves or whether they had been rolled up….

'The new doctor,' her father said into the heavy silence. 'I want to see him. But it must be in private. Up here. Can you arrange it?'

'Why him, *Papà*?'

'I want to make sure.'

She swallowed again. 'Y-you think Dr Hunter is the prince?'

'I do not know but I must make certain before I die.'

The stark reality of the situation was fast dawning on Amelia and it terrified her. If news got out of her father's role in the kidnap of the prince he would be hauled before the courts and charged. His last few weeks of life would be spent in prison, not with his family. Their name would again be vilified in every way imaginable; her brothers would never find work again on the island and her life would be even more difficult than it currently was.

And if it was true that Alex Hunter was indeed Prince Alessandro, what would that information do to him? How would he cope with the news that he was not a simple commoner but a member of the richest royal family in Europe? And not only a member, with his twin brother's recent decision—now the rightful heir to the throne…

Her father jolted her out of her tortured reverie. 'I want you to know that I am prepared to be punished for what I did, Amelia. I have always been prepared, but I did not come forward at the time for your mother's sake. I kept everything from her. I had to. She was expecting a child, your brother Rico. I did not want her to see me as a man capable of such a crime. It was even worse after your brothers and you were born. Having my own children made me realise the enormity of what I had done. I could tell no one and the fight to keep those who knew silent became all the more desperate. It has cost me dearly.'

'It has cost the prince his birthright!' she said, unable to contain her despair and shame at what he had done. 'No matter if the Australian doctor is the prince or not, whoever the prince is now has been robbed of everything that is rightly his. He has never known his real parents, never lived on the island, and never spoken the language and a thousand other things that can never be replaced or put right by a last-minute deathbed confession!'

'I know, but I must put right what I can,' he said. 'I must see this man who has the whole island talking of his likeness to Antonio Fierezza.'

'And Prince Marco,' she put in heavily.

'Is that true?' he asked, his throat moving up and down again. 'You have seen Prince Marco up at the palace, have you not? Does he look anything like the doctor?'

She frowned as she thought about it. There was a similarity; they were both dark of hair and eyes, although she seemed to recall Marco's were not as coal-black as Alex's, and he seemed a bit taller, not much, maybe only an inch if that.

'I don't know…maybe a little bit,' she said.

'So you will do this for me? Bring the doctor to me as soon as you can arrange it?'

'He was here last night,' she informed him.

He coughed out the word. *'Here?'*

She nodded. 'He came across me on the road. and gave me a lift and somehow talked me into having dinner with him. I decided to go because you and Silvio were out. Where is Silvio, by the way?'

'He has been working on a boat that goes between here and Sicily. He heard the rumours and took me down to the port to talk to some people who had seen the doctor and become suspicious.'

'Papà…you do realise if Alex Hunter is the child you spirited away that there will be consequences, not just for you, but for Rico and Silvio and me?'

'Yes…' His thin chest deflated on a ragged breath. 'I have thought long and hard about it. For some years now, in spite of my efforts to distance myself from the organisation, my name has been brought up whenever the Vialli bandits are mentioned. Every finger is now pointing to me. I cannot allow you or your brothers to live any longer under the shame of a murder that never took place.'

'The kidnap of a small child is almost as bad.'

'I did the best I could do under the circumstances,' he said. 'I did not kill him. I had every chance but I did not do it. I would like to tell that to him…to ask for forgiveness. Then I can die in peace.'

She let out another sigh. 'There can be no peace, *Papà*, can't you see that? Not now, not if what you've said is true.'

'What would you have me do?' he asked. 'If he is the prince, he has the right to know.'

'But what if he's not?'

Her father looked at her, the sadness of his life shining in his eyes. 'Just bring him to me, Amelia. Bring the Australian doctor to me so I can find out once and for all.'

CHAPTER EIGHT

'AREN'T you heading up to Theatre to watch the procedure?' Lucia asked when Amelia came on the ward the next morning.

'I thought I would give it a miss,' she answered, putting her bag in the bottom drawer of the filing cabinet in the nurses' station and turning the key.

She had spent a sleepless night thinking about her father's confession, her mind unable to grasp the enormity of what he had done. The thought of trying to remain professionally calm watching Alex Hunter perform a highly technical procedure while suspecting what she did was unthinkable.

'But Dr Morani organised cover for you down here on the ward,' Lucia said. 'He wants you in particular to see how Dr Hunter performs the off-pump procedure.'

'I'm sure I'll hear all about it.'

'Hearing is one thing, seeing is another,' Lucia said. 'If I were you I'd go. There's not much happening here. I might even get time for a cup of coffee if Signor Ruggio in bed eight behaves himself.'

Amelia forced a little smile to her lips at the mention of their elderly patient. 'He's such a sweet old man and never complains.'

'He's a cheeky old flirt, that's what he is. But you're

right—he's a sweet man.' Lucia gave her a probing look. 'Is something wrong? You look worried. Is it your father again?'

'Yes…' At least that wasn't a lie, Amelia thought. 'But it's nothing I can't deal with.'

'Well, if there's anything I can do just let me know,' Lucia offered. 'Oh, here's the nurse who's covering for you.'

'They're waiting for you in Theatre,' the fill-in nurse said.

Amelia tried to disguise her panic but Lucia wasn't fooled. She gave her a little grin. 'You're not going to go all squeamish now, are you?'

'Of course not,' Amelia said with already sagging confidence. 'I've been to Theatre enough times to know it's not always a pretty sight.'

'Just as well the visiting surgeon is so easy on the eye,' Lucia said. 'If you can't bear looking at the patient, look at him instead.'

I will be looking at him, Amelia wanted to say. *Very closely*.

Amelia made her way to the change room and changed into Theatre gear. The operating staff were busily preparing when she arrived in the cardiac theatre.

The patient, a man in his early fifties with a long family history of heart disease, had already been anaesthetised. He wasn't attached to the bypass pump although it was available and primed if an emergency situation developed.

'Stand in here near the anaesthetic machine, Sister,' directed the anaesthetist. 'I can stay out of your way so you can get a good look at the procedure.'

As she moved into position Alex Hunter emerged from the scrub room, arms in the air ready for the scout nurse to assist with gowning. It was a perfect opportunity for Amelia to see his uncovered arms, but just as she moved to gain a better look the instrument nurse moved in front of her with a tray and blocked her view.

Alex turned around once he was gowned and gloved and met her eyes. 'How nice you could join us, Sister Vialli. I take it you had no other pressing engagements?'

So he was still annoyed with her for rejecting him, Amelia mused as she lifted her chin. 'I am here, as you see,' she said.

He held her defiant look for a moment before turning to the anaesthetist. 'Carlo, you can start the heparin now, one milligram per kilo heparin, and we'll monitor the clotting profile every half-hour as we go through in the protocol.'

'Right,' Carlo said, beginning the IV heparin infusion.

Amelia watched from the head of the operating table as the patient was prepped and draped by Alex together with the cardiac registrar and the scrub nurse.

Alex made a midline incision over the sternum, and, using the powered bone saw, completed a median sternotomy, his deep, calm voice taking the theatre staff through each step. As Alex and the registrar opened the chest, Dr Morani harvested the left long-saphenous vein in the patient's left leg to be used for the bypass.

Alex then took the team step by step through the moving-heart bypass procedure, taking special care to show how the vessel stabiliser was used to reduce movement of the vessels to be sutured during the movement of the heart.

'As you can see, Dr Morani, the vessel stabiliser must be adjusted so as not to leave too much coronary artery exposed, otherwise movement is not damped enough, and getting a good quality anastomosis becomes a real struggle,' Alex explained.

'Yes, that appears the hardest bit to get right,' the surgeon agreed. 'That's much clearer now—even I could do the anastomosis now that you've set it up.'

'I'm sure you could do as good a job as me, Doctor, but I'd like to do the first anastomosis to show you a couple of tricks to damp down movements between the instruments and the heart.' He flicked a glance from above his surgical mask in the direction of Amelia. 'What do you think of the procedure so far, Sister Vialli?'

'You are obviously well practised in working with the heart,' she answered.

'You have to have an intuitive feel for the heart in this type of surgery,' he said, then, addressing the senior cardiac surgeon beside him, added, 'Now it's your turn, Dr Morani. We'll set up the vessel dampening clamps for the LAD and you can do the second anastomosis.'

Under Alex's guidance, the fellow surgeon sutured the freed-up internal mammary artery to the LAD distal to its stenosis. Finally, using the Doppler flow meter, Alex was happy that blood flow into the bypassed coronaries was satisfactory and left the senior surgeon and the registrar to routinely close the chest.

As Alex stripped off his gloves and gown he turned from the laundry bin to see Amelia staring at him, and folded his arms across his chest, his dark eyes narrowing and hardening as they met hers. 'Are you by any chance waiting to speak to me, Sister?'

'No…no, I was just leaving.'

'Don't let me keep you. I'm sure you have plenty of things to do on the ward.'

She wanted to stare him down, but in the end she had to push her pride to one side. 'Actually I would like to speak to you if I may.'

'I'll have to check my diary to see if I can squeeze you in.'

'I would appreciate it…thank you.'

'Dr Hunter, there's a phone call on line one for you,' one of the scout nurses informed him. 'It's a young woman. She wouldn't give me her name.'

Amelia saw the flicker of something in his dark eyes before he turned away to address the nurse. 'Can you put it through to the office next door?' he asked.

By the time he turned back to Amelia she had a cynical set to her mouth. 'It hasn't taken you long to find a replacement, has it?' she said in an undertone.

'Last time I checked I was a free man,' he returned coolly. 'Now, if you'll excuse me I'd better take that call.'

Amelia watched as he shouldered open the theatre change-room door, his arms now stiffly by his sides...

'There's a message for you, Amelia,' Lucia informed her as soon as she returned from her afternoon tea break later that day. 'Signora Gravano wants you to call on her this afternoon after your shift finishes, as if you haven't got enough to do.'

'It's all right,' Amelia said, wondering if the old woman had had another fall and reopened her leg wound. 'She's lonely with her daughter living abroad. I'll go straight there after I finish.'

Once her shift was over Amelia left a message for Rico at the front desk in case he arrived to pick her up before she got back, and made her way to the old lady's house.

There was no sign of movement at Alex's cottage although it appeared as if he or someone had done some preliminary work in the garden. The brambles had been trimmed back and the sweet smell of newly cut grass filled her nostrils on the way past.

Signora Gravano didn't really need her leg redressing but seemed in want of a chat, so Amelia sat with her for a while, all the time trying not to glance at the clock on the wall. Rico wasn't the most patient of young men and she knew if she didn't come out on time he would leave without her. There was a bus that took her as far as the turn-off to the cottage, but that still meant a walk of at least five kilometres.

'I have heard some disturbing rumours I think you should be informed of if you haven't already heard them,' Signora Gravano said just as Amelia finally made a move to leave.

'Oh?' she said, wondering why the old woman had waited

until now to state the real reason for her request to see her. 'What rumours are they?'

'People are saying that Prince Alessandro is not dead after all,' Signora Gravano informed her.

Amelia hoped her face wasn't showing the panic and dread she was feeling. 'That seems rather far-fetched,' she said. 'I mean, the child's grave is at the palace for anyone to see.'

'I know, but there could be another explanation for that—some other child put in his place, for instance.'

'I suppose that's a possibility, but you know what these rumours are like. They come and go and are best ignored,' Amelia said.

'I have heard the king's medical advisors noticed a startling similarity to Antonio Fierezza when they were researching the new technique Dr Hunter is pioneering. Dr Hunter's photograph was in the medical journal they had researched and they began to wonder if he was in some way related to the family.'

Amelia sat back down, not because she wanted to but because her legs were threatening to give way. 'Is that why he received a royal summons?' she asked.

'It makes sense, does it not?' the old woman said. 'The king does need heart surgery, of course, but this was a way of bringing Dr Hunter to Niroli to see if the likeness was something that needed further investigation by the royal officials.'

'It is said we all have a double somewhere in the world,' Amelia said, trying to put some rationality in place. 'It's just one of those things.'

'Perhaps, but if what they suspect is true, there will be hell to pay.'

Amelia moistened her dry-as-dust mouth. 'You mean for whomever is responsible?'

'I would not like to be that person,' Signora Gravano said, her black eyes suddenly very direct. 'They have been responsible for a terrible crime for which they have never been charged.'

Amelia forced her shoulders to relax. 'It is surely a better outcome than the original verdict of murder…I mean, if the prince is in fact still alive…somewhere…'

'Yes, indeed, but how will the prince feel once he finds out his true identity? His biological parents are dead. He will never have the chance to meet them in person. And what of Prince Marco, who for all this time has grieved the loss of his twin?'

'I am sure the prince can't even remember his twin brother,' Amelia said, recalling her conversation with Alex. 'He was far too young.'

The old woman grunted. 'He has lived with his parents' grief, which would have no doubt affected him and his sisters.'

'Is Alex Hunter aware of any of this…er…speculation?'

'I am not sure. He is going to the palace this evening to meet the king. Perhaps the subject will be raised then,' Signora Gravano said.

'Someone should prepare him…' Amelia got to her feet, testing her legs, which still felt watery. 'It would be unfair to surprise him with this information without some sort of lead up.'

Signora Gravano smiled sagely. 'That is why I asked you to come, Amelia. You will understand much better than the palace staff about the sensitive nature of this. Dr Hunter should be home by now. Why not go around and talk to him now before he leaves for his meeting with the king?'

Amelia ignored the short cut and made her way past Alex's hire car to his front door, her hand visibly shaking as she lifted it to the brass knocker.

There was no answer.

She frowned as she looked back at the car parked in the shade. He must be somewhere about. He had finished at the hospital at least two hours ago.

'Are you looking for me?' Alex asked from the other side of the front step.

She swung around to face him, her throat closing up at the sight of him dressed in running shorts and T-shirt, the perspiration from his workout plastering the material to his toned body. 'Er…yes…' she said. 'I was hoping to catch you before you left for the palace.'

One of his dark brows rose in an arc above his right eye. 'Why?'

She shifted from foot to foot. 'I wanted to speak to you—privately.'

Alex held her anxious gaze for a lengthy moment. She looked tired and he felt a little ashamed of his attitude earlier. He blew out a breath and motioned for her to go inside. 'Come on, I've got something I need to say to you too.'

He waited until she was seated and with a cold drink in front of her before he took the chair opposite, giving his face a quick rub with a hand towel. 'So who's going to go first?' he asked.

'I don't mind.' She chewed her bottom lip momentarily and added, 'You can if you like.'

'Right,' he said as he pushed the towel to one side. 'I have an apology to make. I was an idiot last night. Simple as that. No wonder you gave me the heave-o.' He sent his fingers through the damp thickness of his hair, a small frown beetling his brows. 'I don't know why I came on so strong,' he continued. 'I know you're not going to believe this, but it's really not my style at all.' He gave her a sheepish look and added, 'I guess it's been too long between relationships or something.'

She twisted her mouth wryly. 'I bet it wasn't as long as eleven years.'

'No.' He laughed lightly. 'More like eleven months, but long enough to make me a bit trigger-happy.'

'It's all right. I understand.'

'I wish you did.'

'I do,' she insisted.

'Believe me, you don't.'

'How do you know what I feel?' she asked.

He smiled at her then. 'Yep, that vow of silence would never have worked.'

She started to purse her mouth but thought better of it. 'I didn't come here to argue with you,' she said.

'Where do you usually go?'

'Must you make a joke of everything?' she asked in frustration. 'I'm trying to be serious here.'

'So am I, Amelia.' He reached for the towel once more. 'Now what did you come all this way to tell me?'

Amelia stared at his right arm as he lifted it to his face to wipe the moisture from his brow, her breath coming to a stumbling halt in her chest.

There was absolutely no sign of a birthmark.

CHAPTER NINE

ALEX put the towel back down and caught her staring at him. 'Is something wrong?'

'No…no, nothing.' Amelia lowered her gaze and focussed on the table separating them. She'd checked his left arm while he'd changed hands to dry off, but it too was clear of any distinctive birthmarks.

'What did you come here to tell me?' he asked into the suddenly crackling silence.

'It was nothing important.' She got to her feet and pushed in the chair. 'I should get going. The last bus leaves at six-thirty.'

'Wait.' He came around to her side and stalled her with a hand on her arm. 'Listen, I know this is going to sound really dumb, but would you consider doing me a favour tonight?'

Amelia met his dark gaze, her heart and stomach still both feeling as if they had just performed a complicated gymnastics routine. 'W-what is it?'

His hand fell away from her arm, his expression turning awkward again. 'To tell you the truth I'm a bit nervous about going to the palace tonight. I know it's a lot to ask, but, since you go there all the time, would you consider coming with me tonight sort of as moral support?'

She stared at him for a beat or two, wondering if he was

genuine or whether this was another ploy to get her to go out with him. 'I don't go there *all* the time,' she corrected him.

'But at least you've met the king and the staff and are more or less familiar with the layout of the place.'

'If you think I believe for even one second that you are intimidated in any way by royalty, you must think me even more gullible than I thought,' she said. 'Besides, the royal aides will escort you in and escort you out. Don't worry—you won't get lost and end up in a dungeon with chains around your ankles.'

'What if I strike up a deal with you?' he said with a little glint in his eyes. 'If you come with me to the palace I will give you a ride home and visit your father, free of charge. Will he be home tonight?'

Five minutes ago Amelia would not have bought in to his offer, but now, with his arm showing no sign of the birthmark that would have sent her father to prison, she knew she would have to accept. Without that sign there was nothing to connect her father to the disappearance of the prince all those years ago. She wanted her father to see it for himself, to put his fears to rest. Besides, her last glance at her watch had told her the bus would have long gone. A taxi fare was out of the question even if she could convince a driver to take his car up the somewhat perilous section of road.

'All right,' she said. 'It's a deal. But I will have to stay in the background. I'm still wearing my uniform.'

'That's OK.' He smiled a victor's smile. 'I'm only going to be there for ten minutes or so according to the invitation I received. I'll just grab a quick shower. Make yourself at home.'

Amelia let out her breath once he had gone to the bathroom and wondered if she should still warn him of the suspicions or leave it for him to deal with if and when they were raised during his visit. No doubt the king would be looking closely for the mark that would establish his lost grandson's identity.

How he would do so she couldn't even hazard a guess. But she reasoned that if, like her, the king saw the clear skin on Alex Hunter's arm he might not even raise the topic at all, simply treating the visit as the royal summons as which it was originally portrayed. The rumours would hopefully die down and she would then be able to nurse her father to his final rest without the threat of exposure.

Alex came out a few minutes later looking refreshed and smelling of his aftershave, a heady combination of lemons and spice that reminded Amelia of the sun-drenched citrus orchards on the island.

She felt grubby and uncomfortable in her uniform, especially now he was dressed in a dark suit and tie, the crisp whiteness of his shirt highlighting the healthy colour of his skin and the darkness of his eyes. He had shaved, which she assumed he would have to do twice a day to keep that chiselled jaw smooth. Her skin gave a little all-over shiver as she thought about how his mouth had felt on hers, and the gentle but imminently sexy abrasion of his skin as it had moved over the creamy softness of her face.

She watched as he straightened his tie, the movement of his neck indicating it probably wasn't his preferred choice of dress.

'Is my tie tucked in at the back?' he asked, turning around for her to inspect it.

She had to stand on tiptoe to tuck a thin strip of his tie under the collar, her fingers skating over his skin as if they had a mind of their own. 'There…that's it,' she said a little breathlessly.

He turned back around before she could step away, his eyes locking with hers. Amelia felt the air between them begin to tighten as if an invisible force were drawing her inexorably closer to him. She could even feel the sway of her body towards him, her chest brushing against his as his hands came out to hold her steady.

His eyes grew darker as his head came closer, the warmth of his mint-flavoured breath caressing her up-tilted face. She felt her eyelids dropping as his mouth came down, the first brush of his lips on hers setting her alight like a match to a meticulously laid fire. The combustion was instantaneous and enthralling; there was nothing she could do to hold back her response. It consumed her totally, the sensations rushing through her like a hot river of flame.

His tongue came searching for hers, drawing it into an intimate tangle of slow but drugging dance-like movements, each intimate thrust mimicking the pulse of his lower body where it was pressed so close to hers. She could feel the imprint of his maleness, the hard evidence of how his body responded to hers. It excited her to think he was still attracted to her, even though she had done her best to spurn him. It showed he wasn't going to go down without a fight, that he would throw everything he could at their developing relationship no matter what the cost.

But any cost would be hers, she hastily reminded herself. As thrilling at this sizzling attraction was, it wasn't going to last beyond a month, not unless he was prepared to take her with him, which seemed an impossible dream. He had a life in Australia, a busy career, a loving family and a chance to change the world with this pioneering breakthrough in cardiac surgery.

What place could she have in such a life? She had been reared in poverty and shame, her life so far spent in the service of others.

And yet what made this attraction all the more irresistible was she was no longer a young naïve girl hardly out of her teens. She was a fully grown woman now, with needs and desires that could no longer be ignored. She had thrown herself into hard work to distract herself from the emptiness of her existence, but now it seemed as if that lonely existence was crying out for more. She wanted to feel like an attractive woman again. She wanted to be swept up in the magic of emotion and desire.

She wanted Alex Hunter even if she could only have him temporarily....

Alex pulled back reluctantly, his breathing still choppy. 'Whoa there, princess,' he said. 'I'm drifting out of my depth here.'

'I'm sorry.'

'Hey,' he said, cupping her face so she couldn't escape his gaze. 'Don't be embarrassed. It's a good thing. In fact it's a rare thing. I don't usually lose my head in these types of situations.'

'I'm sure you're just saying that.'

'I wish I was, truly.' His expression was surprisingly sincere.

'I don't know what to say....' She lowered her gaze, her tongue running over her lips, tasting him, savouring him.

'Don't say anything,' he said. 'Let's just take it one step at a time.'

She raised her eyes back to his. 'I'm frightened, Alex. I don't want to let things get out of control.'

He let out a sigh and hugged her close. 'I know you're frightened, but you don't need to be. I want you and I intend to have you. Surely you know that by now?'

She leaned back to look up at him, her stomach quivering at the determined promise of his statement. 'Is that why you've been so persistent?'

'Have I been persistent?'

She gave him a mock-reproving look, desperately trying to maintain a level head when all she wanted to do was throw herself back into his arms. 'You know you have,' she said. 'You just won't take no for an answer.'

'Well, can you blame me? As soon as I met you I felt something drop into place, as if a piece of a puzzle had been missing all this time and now I'd suddenly found it.'

She narrowed her eyes at him. 'So who was the woman who phoned you today?'

'It was my sister, Megan. She's backpacking around Europe and wanted to say hi.'

It was impossible to disguise her tiny sigh of relief. 'She's lucky to have a brother like you,' she said.

'That's what I keep telling her, but do you think she will listen?' His smile lit up his eyes.

'I like you, Alex Hunter,' she said softly. 'I really like you.'

'That's a start, I guess,' he said, his dark eyes twinkling. 'Any chance of an upgrade on that?'

She met his smile with one of her own. 'Perhaps. I'll have to think about it.'

'Well, in the meantime I'll try and be patient,' he said and brought his mouth back down to hers.

This time his kiss was even more demanding, the searing thrust of his tongue taking her breath away as his hands skimmed her curves. Her breasts leapt at his touch, even though the fabric of her uniform still covered them. She could feel herself being swept away on the tide of spiralling need that flowed between them. She could feel it in his body, the energy and strength that pulsed there. She could taste it in his kiss, the heat and fire that burned against her mouth as she returned his kiss with fevered urgency. She could feel it in her own body, the ache and throb of unmet needs that refused to be denied any longer.

'This is crazy,' Alex said, suddenly pulling away. 'My timing as usual is way off. I have to be at the palace in ten minutes. That's not nearly long enough to pleasure you in the way I want to.'

Amelia felt her stomach hollow at his words. 'We can do this some other time,' she said, surprising herself more than him. 'That's if you still want to....'

He pressed a quick, hard kiss to her mouth. 'I want to. I'll be thinking of nothing else the whole time I'm with the king.'

She wrinkled her nose at him. 'I'm sure he would be very shocked to hear that.'

He smiled down at her. 'I don't care if he is. What's an old man with a medieval castle got to do with me? I'd much rather be with you.'

Amelia decided then to tell him of the rumours. What harm could it do for him to know? At least then he would be able to meet the king's questions levelly now there was no doubt he was not the prince.

'Alex…there's something you should know before you meet the king… Something important.'

Alex frowned at her grave tone. 'What?'

She took a steadying breath. 'You're probably going to think this is ridiculous in the extreme, but there have been rumours circulating on the island ever since you arrived that you are in some way related to the king.'

'Related?' His frown deepened.

'You remember the kidnap and murder of the king's grandson we discussed the other day?'

He gave a brief nod without responding.

'Well,' she said, 'there's been a recent disclosure that the infant prince was not in fact murdered as first thought, but spirited away to be brought up by someone else.'

'Someone else where?' he asked.

'I don't know all the details, just that the prince—according to my sources—was well and truly alive the last time…this person saw him.'

'So what's all this got to do with me?' he asked, his brow still furrowed.

'At the restaurant last night you were mistaken for someone else. You said it had happened ever since you arrived on the island. I thought you should know that the king as well as others has seen a likeness in your features to his dead son,

Antonio, and his surviving grandson, Marco. They've been wondering if you are in fact the prince.'

His breath came out in a whooshing rush. 'Amelia, this island is teeming with male look-alikes. There's hardly a man here who doesn't have black hair and brown eyes.'

'I know… I just thought I should tell you, that's all. It seemed a little far-fetched to me when I first heard, but then when you said you were adopted and that your Italian name was Alessandro I started to wonder about it myself.'

Alex gave a chuckle of incredulous laughter. 'Far-fetched? It's bloody ridiculous! Me? A prince? Don't make me laugh.'

Amelia started to smile. 'I guess it does sound a bit crazy, doesn't it?'

'Just wait till my sister hears about this.' He grinned. 'It's not every day one gets mistaken for royalty. A mate of mine once got mistaken for a famous actor. He even had to sign autographs as the fans just wouldn't believe he wasn't the real deal, but I think this is going one better than that.'

'I hope you didn't mind me telling you,' she said. 'I just thought it would be better to know about it in case they ask you any personal questions at the palace tonight.'

He dropped a quick kiss to the soft bow of her mouth. 'You did the right thing telling me. To tell you the truth I was starting to get a little spooked by all the weird looks I was getting. Now I can rest easy.'

So can I, Amelia thought as they made their way out to his car. *Thank goodness he was plain old Alex Hunter and not the missing prince.…*

The fourteenth-century castle was situated on a rocky promontory overlooking the main port of Niroli, the hills behind covered with scented orange groves.

Amelia looked up at it standing so majestically over all it surveyed. The palace had its own private beach and boat houses and the views over the wide horizons were breathtaking. As settings went it was surely one of the most spectacular in the region if not the entire world.

'Quite some beach house,' Alex remarked from beside her.

She smiled and took a step backwards as the royal officials approached. 'I'll wait for you over there,' she said, pointing to a sun-drenched terrace where a bougainvillea vine was trailing over the balustrade in a scarlet arras.

Alex gave her a wink and made his way towards the castle entrance flanked on either side by the uniformed officials.

Amelia turned to look at the sea sparkling in the distance, the tang of salt reaching her from below.

She turned about twenty minutes later as she heard the sound of footsteps and watched as Alex walked towards her, a hint of a smile reflected in his dark eyes as they met hers.

'How was it?' she asked once they were back in his car.

'As house calls go it was certainly unusual,' he said. 'I met with the king and discussed his treatment options. I spoke to him of the risks involved with a patient his age and how I would be prepared to do it at the private hospital as a one-off in a couple of days.'

'Did he mention anything to you about the rumours?'

'No and I didn't bring the topic up. I thought someone was going to at one stage. I was getting some pretty intense scrutiny from the staff as they served drinks, but apart from a few questions about my background things were pretty relaxed.'

'Did you meet any of the royal family? Prince Marco or Prince Luca or the princesses?'

'I did, actually,' he said. 'If you hadn't told me what you had, I would have thought it a bit unusual since I was ostensibly there to see the king on a health matter, but I guess they too wanted to check on any likeness. They were very polite and seemed interested in the procedure I'm pioneering, but they didn't stay long.'

'Could you see any likeness to yourself?' she asked.

'Not so much with Prince Marco or Prince Luca, although of course there are similarities, but I did happen to see a portrait of Antonio and his wife Francesca on one of the walls as I walked past.'

Amelia glanced at him. 'And?'

His eyes met hers briefly, a small frown bringing his brows together as he returned to the task of driving. 'I know this is going to sound a bit strange, but I felt like I'd seen them before. Crazy, huh?'

'Perhaps you've seen a photograph of them in the press,' she suggested. 'The news of their yachting accident hit the headlines all over the world.'

'Yeah, that's probably what it was,' he said, sending her a quick smile.

Amelia settled back in her seat, but the next time she chanced a glance at him his smile had disappeared....

CHAPTER TEN

'How about we have a quick dinner at my place before I visit your father?' Alex suggested a short time later.

'I don't want to put you to any trouble…'

'I'm not quite a celebrity chef or anything, but I can whip up a mean omelette and salad. My mother always told me women are super impressed by a man who can cook.'

'I'm super impressed by a man who can clean up *after* he cooks,' Amelia said with a wry smile. 'My father and brothers are absolutely hopeless.'

'You have it tough up there, don't you?' he asked as he led her into the cottage. 'But you have no need to be ashamed. Home is home, Amelia.'

She lowered her eyes. 'I'm sorry I was so rude to you last night. I'm just not used to people seeing where I live.'

'I've seen some wonderful mansions in my time, and, let me tell you, some miserable souls living in them,' he said. 'Some of the happiest and most well-adjusted people I've met have lived in virtual squalor. Where you live is not important, it's who you are as a person.'

She smiled up at him. 'So while you were up at the palace did you think about how it would be to live like a prince?'

'Yeah, I did a bit, but do you know something? I think it would get on my nerves after a while. All those eyes watching your every move and obsequious staff rushing to pull out your chair for you, or wipe a crumb off your lap. *Sheesh!* I bet you couldn't even go the bathroom without someone peering through the keyhole to see if you really are human after all.'

Amelia laughed. 'I'm sure it's not that bad!'

He grinned as he pulled her towards him. 'What do you say, little elf? Shall we have our main course now or go straight to dessert?'

She gazed up at him with shining eyes. 'What did you have in mind for dessert?'

His mouth came down towards hers, his warm breath caressing the surface of her lips. 'How about strawberry kisses?'

'Is there such a dessert?' she asked breathlessly.

He pressed his mouth against hers for a moment before running his tongue over his lips as if to taste her. 'Yep, there definitely is,' he said, 'and I can't get enough of it.'

Amelia totally melted as his mouth moved over hers, his sensual tongue pushing between her lips to find her own. Each sweeping, sexy movement set her on fire; her skin tingled and shivered with the warm glide of his hands as they moved to shape her form. She felt his hands cup the light weight of her breasts and her stomach hollowed as he began to undo the top buttons of her uniform, one by one, leaving a trail of scorching kisses as he went. Her bra slipped to the floor along with her uniform, leaving her at the mercy of his hungry dark gaze.

'You're so beautiful.' He almost growled the words, so deep and low was his voice as he pulled the tie from his throat and tossed it to the floor.

Her hands helped him with his shirt, her fingers skating over the buttons until it too was at their feet along with her uniform. He stepped out of his trousers and she felt the full thrust of his body against her, the heat of his arousal burning into the soft skin of her stomach.

'Am I going too fast for you?' he said next to her ear where he was nibbling her until her skin started to lift all over.

'Not fast enough,' she breathed and, kicking off her shoes, pushed herself closer.

'It's been a long time for both of us,' he said as he kissed the upper side of one breast. 'I want to pace myself but you're making it hard for me.'

'I can't help it,' she said, and started kissing his throat, hot, sucking little kisses that made him groan with need. 'I want you.'

He picked her up and carried her to his bedroom, his weight coming down on top of her as he joined her, his long legs anchoring her to the bed. He kissed his way down her stomach but she wouldn't let him go below her belly button. She brought his head back up and wriggled until he was pushing against her soft folds.

He wrenched his mouth off hers long enough to gasp something about a condom and she waited impatiently as he reached across her to find one. She heard him rummaging about in the drawer with little success.

'Damn!'

'Here.' She pushed him aside. 'Let me have a girl look.'

'A girl look?'

She smiled coyly as she found a little foil packet and held it up. 'See?'

'I swear you must have planted that in there.'

'I did not! You just weren't looking.'

He ripped the packet open with his teeth and handed her the condom. 'Why don't you put it on in case I can't find what I'm looking for?'

She bit her lip in sudden shyness. 'No...you do it... I might not do it properly.'

He lifted her chin so she met his eyes. 'That's what I like about you, little elf. You're so adorably shy.'

A small frown wrinkled her brow. 'I can't help it.'

He kissed the little crease on her forehead. 'I've never made love to a woman like you before.'

Her brow wrinkled even more. 'Like me?'

He smiled and, taking her hand, placed it on the rigidity of his erection. 'Amelia, do you see what you are doing to me?'

'Oh…'

'You're not disappointed?'

'Why would I be disappointed?' she asked.

'If the rumours were true about me, you could be seconds away from sleeping with a prince. Isn't that every girl's dream?'

Amelia looked at his mouth, the sexy curve of his smile sending sparks of sensation right to the core of her being. 'Just how many seconds are we talking about here?' she asked.

He smiled and pushed her back down, taking her breath away with his first deep thrust, and covered her mouth with his.

The silky slide of his thick body in hers was almost too much for her sensation-starved body to cope with. She felt every nerve jump to attention, every single cell and pore screaming for more and more of his touch. He drove deeper and deeper, obviously trying to pace himself, but she was too greedy for more and lifted her hips to bring him closer. She felt him brush against the pearl of her desire but the tingling sensation didn't last long enough to bring her the release she craved. He shifted position, driving forward with increasing urgency until she was almost screaming with the intimate slippery abrasion of his body rubbing so closely against hers. She arched her back and suddenly everything fell into place. He was where she most wanted him, the deeper, longer strokes of his aroused length taking her to lift-off so that her senses finally soared into oblivion.

She was vaguely aware of his own release, the deep throb of his heart against her naked breasts as he pumped himself into her, his body collapsing like a wind-depleted sail as soon as it was over.

Amelia gently stroked the length of his back, amazed at how she had responded to him but even more amazed at how he had responded to her.

Alex lifted himself up on one elbow to look at her. 'I hope this doesn't sound like a line from that playboy manual you referred to the other night, but that was the most amazing experience I've had in years.'

Amelia ran her hand up and down his forearm in a tickling caress. 'It does sound a bit like something on about page twenty-three, but I agree, it was amazing. Certainly nothing like I've ever experienced before.'

He let out a deep, contented sigh as she moved her fingers farther along his arm. 'That feels nice. You have such soft hands.'

Amelia watched the pathway of her fingers as they went towards his elbow, her brow furrowing when she came to some tiny white, almost undetectable scars on the underside of his arm. 'What did you do to yourself here?' she asked.

He looked down at where she was pointing. 'Oh, that. That was years ago. I had some laser work done.'

'Laser work?' She sat up and stared at him. 'Laser work for what?'

'I had a birthmark.'

She stared at him in shock. '*A birthmark*?' she gasped.

He gave her a world-weary look. 'And here I was thinking you were going to be different. That's why I had it removed in the first place.'

'Y-you had it removed?' she croaked.

'My ex-girlfriend Sarah hated it,' he said with a curl of his lip. 'So did a couple of other girlfriends in the past. Quite frankly I couldn't see what the fuss was all about. It was only small and no one could see it unless I had my arm in a certain position.'

'*You had a birthmark?*' Amelia was aware she was still gaping at him but there was nothing she could do to stop it. '*A strawberry birthmark?*'

'Don't worry, Amelia, it's not catching.'

'But...but you don't understand...'

He got off the bed and roughly disposed of the condom. 'Oh, I understand all right. I've been dealing with this for years. What is it with women these days? A birthmark isn't contagious. It's not as if any children I sire will inherit it or anything.'

'Alex—'

'Don't start, Amelia.' He rounded on her. 'I had enough of this from Sarah.'

Amelia knew she was still staring at him but she couldn't seem to get her voice to work.

'Ever heard of a copper bromide machine?' he asked. 'Or perhaps the newer V-beam machine used in laser and sclerotherapy clinics?'

Her eyes widened, her heart starting to hammer in her chest. 'You mean for the...the removal of lesions?'

'Lesions, pigmentation, spider veins, sun damage, broken capillaries and birthmarks can all be removed, without trace in some instances, with laser-beam therapy.' He sounded as if he were reading it from a brochure.

The silence that fell was so heavy she felt it like a crushing weight against her chest. She could hardly breathe for the pressure, her lungs feeling as if they were full of lead instead of oxygen.

'S-so...' she moistened her parched lips '...so what you're saying is you...you had a birthmark and...and h-had it removed?'

He nodded again. 'I wouldn't have bothered except a mate of mine set up a cosmetic surgery practice with a sclerotherapy clinic attached. Strawberry birthmarks are harder to remove if they're not attended to while the person is young. The birthmark develops nodules over time which have to be surgically removed, hence the tiny scars.'

The silence was thrumming in Amelia's ears. Her head

eemed to be full of it, making it difficult for her to think, let
lone speak.

'Alex…I don't know how to tell you this but the prince who
was kidnapped thirty-four years ago had a birthmark. A very
distinctive birthmark.'

He looked at her without speaking, but she could see the
way his throat tightened, the muscles contracting as if he
were trying to swallow something too big to go down.

'Y-you know what this means…don't you?' she finally
managed to ask as a sinking feeling settled in the middle of
her stomach.

'I'm not sure it means anything,' he said in an offhand
manner. 'Lots of people have birthmarks.'

'But don't you see how it all makes sense?' she asked. 'You
were adopted—a late adoption at two years of age, the exact
age of the prince when he was supposedly murdered. You even
had the same Christian name. People have remarked on your
resemblance to Antonio and Marco Fierezza from the moment
you stepped on the island. Don't you see it all adds up?'

'My birth certificate documents—'

'Birth certificates can be forged!' she interrupted him, her
eyes wide with anguish. 'Especially when lots of money
changes hands.'

'You seem to know an awful lot about all this,' he observed
with a slight narrowing of his eyes. 'You said someone told
you the prince wasn't murdered. Was that person by any
chance your father?'

Amelia felt the trickle of ice-cold dread make its way down
her spine. She had desperately wanted to protect her family
from the fallout from all of this, but how could she now? Alex
had a right to know the truth. He had been denied all of his
other rights since the age of two when he had been snatched
from his parents. How could she stand by now and not tell him
everything she knew?

'Yes,' she said on the back end of a wobbly sigh. 'H[
knows he's dying. My brother told him of the rumours dow[
at the port. My father wants to see you.'

Alex blew out a breath and ran a hand through his hair a[
he began to pace the room. 'This is totally surreal. I can'[
believe any of this.'

'I know it must be hard for you to grasp…but it's real, Alex[
It has to be. It all adds up.' Tears burned in her eyes as sh[
realised that what she was about to say would permanentl[
sever any chance of a relationship between them. Their tw[
worlds were now even farther apart and could never be bridge[

'You aren't simply Dr Alex Hunter, the visiting surgeo[
from Australia.' She took a scalding breath and continued[
'You are His Royal Highness Prince Alessandro Fierezza c[
Niroli, the next in line to the throne.'

CHAPTER ELEVEN

No,' ALEX said, stopping his pacing for a moment to face Amelia. 'No way. That's not going to happen. *No way.*'

'You can't escape it, Alex. That's why the king asked to see you. He must have suspected who you were but without proof couldn't tell you.'

'It will totally devastate my parents,' he said, beginning to pace once again, even more agitatedly this time. 'They will think they are in some way responsible for this.'

'How can they be held responsible?' she asked.

He turned around to face her again. 'My adoption was legal. I can't imagine for a moment that my parents would have settled for anything less than that. Sure, they wanted a child, but not someone else's, or at least not without that other person's permission.'

'The adoption probably was legal, or at least on the surface,' he said. 'My father said he'd had to pay dearly for it. It totally ruined him. That's why we've lived with so little for so long.'

'Nice to know there's been some sort of rough justice in all of this,' Alex said before he could restrain himself.

He saw the sudden slump of her slim shoulders and gave himself a mental kick. It was totally wrong that she'd had to suffer for her father's actions so long ago. She had nothing to do with this.

Or had she?

The suspicion crept towards him like a lurking shadow
stealthily consuming the sunlight of his belief in her inno
cence. What if she had known all along? Was that why sh
had agreed to go out with him, her little act of initial reluc
tance a ploy to keep him interested?

He looked down and saw tears sparkling in her eyes. 'Yo
have every right to say that,' she said. 'My father took yo
away from everything that was rightfully yours.'

'Yeah, well, at least he didn't kill me,' he said, still trying t
make up his mind about her. 'I guess I should be grateful for that.

'He couldn't do it,' she said. 'He was given the order to d
so but he just couldn't do it.'

'So he shipped me away, one imagines to Sicily, and go
some papers doctored in order to send me to Australia.'

'I haven't asked him how he did it but I'm sure he will tel
you. I don't expect you to forgive him…it would be hard fo
anyone to forgive such an action, but it's a thousand time
worse for you have lost so much.'

Alex felt the see-saw of doubt tipping back the other way
making it hard for him to believe her capable of such complicity

'I don't see it quite like that,' he said after a little pause
'Or at least I haven't as yet. I have a wonderful family. I hav
wanted for nothing my whole childhood and adult life.'

She gave him an agonised look. 'Your biological parent
were killed two years ago in a yachting accident. They went t
their graves not knowing the truth about your existence. You ca
never meet them or talk to them now, even if you wanted to.'

He frowned as he took it all in. 'I hadn't thought about that

'There's more,' she went on. 'You have siblings. Your twi
brother for one thing and two sisters. Can you imagine hov
thrilled they will be to know you are alive?'

He shook his head as if he still couldn't quite make sens
of all she'd told him. 'This is going to take some getting use

o. What's my kid sister going to say when she finds out her brother is a prince?'

'She will love you just the same. So will your adoptive parents. It doesn't change anything in that regard.'

He gave her an incredulous look. 'It changes everything, can't you see that? Damn it, Amelia, what the hell am I going to do? I have a life and a career back in Sydney. I don't belong here. I don't even speak Italian!'

'Language is not an issue—almost everyone speaks English now anyway. This is your rightful heritage, Alex. You can't ignore your right to the throne.

'The king is your grandfather,' she continued. 'It will bring him much joy to finally meet you, having believed for so long that his reluctance to pay the ransom for your return led to your death.'

Alex came back to her and took her hands in his, hoping his gut feeling was right in all this. 'How like you to think of the other innocents in all of this,' he said, watching her closely. 'Is that something the nuns taught you?'

'They taught me that forgiveness is not always clear-cut but it's essential to let go of the things you cannot change,' she said softly. 'It's sometimes the only thing you can do.'

'I can't change who I am.'

'No one wants you to.'

'You don't know that,' he said. 'I bet as soon as the palace officials hear about this there will be members of the press running about shoving cameras under my nose, people following me no doubt trying to kiss my feet or whatever it is that people do with royalty. I'll go crazy within days and then they *will* have to find a dungeon for me with a strait-jacket as well as ankle chains.'

'It might not be anything like that. I would assume for the sake of everyone's privacy that they will keep this quiet for a while. They'll want to make absolutely sure of everything

before it is announced publicly. They will probably organise
a DNA test to establish your identity once and for all.'

'You already said the island was rife with rumours,' he
pointed out. 'How much worse will it be trying to do what I
came here to do with everyone gawking at me as if I'm some
sort of freak?'

Amelia let out a ragged sigh. 'I know this is hard… You'll
get used to it in time.'

'And what about us?' he asked, his eyes coming back to
pin hers.

She gave him a look of immeasurable sadness. 'There can
be no "us" now. Surely you can see that?'

Alex let a little silence count the seconds as doubt and
belief each jostled for position in his head.

'I can see no reason why I shouldn't live my life the way I
want to,' he said. 'If I want to be involved with you or anybody
then surely that's up to me, not someone else to decide.'

'My father is responsible for what happened,' she said. 'It
would be unthinkable for you to be involved with me now. The
palace will outlaw it as soon as they find out.'

'No one's going to tell me what I can and cannot do. Come
on, Amelia, surely you're not going to fall for that rubbish?
This is about you and me. We've got something going, a good
thing. Don't let this other stuff get in the way.'

'It will always get in the way, Alex. This is not something
you can brush to one side as if it's nothing. This is your birthright, your heritage. You were born to this.'

'But I didn't grow up with any of this! How can I change
my life now? I want to be a normal person. Damn it! I am a
normal person. I make my own meals, I drive my own car, and
I even do my own tax income forms. I would have a hard time
accepting a knighthood let alone a royal throne.'

'You have to accept it!' she cried. 'You have to.'

'I'm not accepting anything until I know what exactly

happened to me when I was two. This could all be a mistake. There's no guarantee that any of this is true,' he said. 'We're going to visit your father and I'm not taking no for an answer.'

He reached for his keys and held open the door. 'Come on, let's get this over with.'

He didn't speak again until they were driving along the foothills to Amelia's cottage. 'I know you think I should come forward, Amelia, but don't forget I have to perform heart surgery on the king in a matter of days. I think it's better all round to continue to view him as a patient like any other, despite the fact that he may be my grandfather.'

Amelia could appreciate his point of view. It would make the surgery a lot more stressful if Alex was in some way emotionally involved with the patient. Surgeons were usually discouraged from operating on close relatives in case their clinical judgement was affected.

'Besides,' Alex continued, 'I want to investigate this myself before anyone else jumps to conclusions that may not be accurate. If it turns out to be true, then I'll have to cross that bridge when I come to it.'

'But how will you investigate it?'

'Firstly I want to talk to your father and get his angle on what happened, and then I'll get someone to run a check on my birth certificate and adoption details, which will no doubt take a week or two.'

'Will you tell your parents and sister?'

'Not at this stage,' he said, shifting the gears. 'For now this is between us and your father—no one else.'

Amelia sank back in her seat, her thoughts flying off in all directions.

'I mean it, Amelia,' he said, flicking a quick glance her way. 'I'm only here for a short time. I want this time we have together to be about us, not some myth about me being a long-lost prince.'

'But you are the prince,' she said softly. 'I just know you are.'

'Maybe, but princes can still be attracted to beautiful women, can't they?' he said.

She felt her heart give a painful contraction. 'Yes, they can, but it would be unwise to do so with a woman from a background such as mine.'

'I have no problem with your background,' he said. 'In fact I think it's one of the most enchanting things about you.'

She frowned at him. 'But my father is solely responsible for what happened to you! How can you even think of a relationship with me?'

One of his hands left the steering wheel to capture one of hers. She held her breath as he brought her hand up to his mouth, her stomach turning inside out when he placed his lips to her fingers in a soft-as-air kiss. 'That's why,' he said, and keeping her hand in his, brought it to rest on the top of his thigh.

Amelia thought her father's cottage looked even tawdrier in the fading light of the evening as Alex parked his car under the trees a little while later. There was an unmistakable irony in its stark contrast from the castle they had visited a few hours earlier. It seemed to drive home all the more forcefully the inherent differences between their backgrounds. Even without the spectre of his royal status, Alex's childhood had still been leagues away from hers. She had never known the comfort of a well-tended home and reliable income to provide the standard of living he more or less had taken for granted. She felt sure he had never come home from school or university to a sink full of unwashed dishes, and dust like carpet on the floor.

She felt the shame rush through her as soon as Alex came up behind her when she opened the front door, imagining how he too would be making his own comparisons.

Her father looked up from his slumped position at the table.

is bleary-eyed gaze widening when it encountered the tall
figure carrying a doctor's bag who had followed Amelia inside.

'*Papà*, this is Dr Alex Hunter,' she said in a subdued tone.

Alex saw the older man's struggle to get to his feet and
gently laid a hand on his shoulder. 'No, please don't get up.'
He offered his hand. 'How do you do, Signor Vialli?'

Amelia could see the mortal fear on her father's already
too-pale face. He choked back a hacking cough and gave
Alex's outstretched hand a feeble shake, mumbling something
inaudible in return.

'Your daughter tells me you've not been well,' Alex said,
pulling out a chair and sitting beside him.

'I'm dying,' Aldo Vialli said. 'It's what I deserve.'

'There's no need to suffer unnecessarily,' Alex said. 'There
are things we can do to help you through the difficult stages.'

'*Papà*, I've talked to Alex about what happened,' Amelia said.

Her father's eyes glazed with pain as another bout of
coughing took over his emaciated form. She saw the sympathetic wince Alex tried to disguise, and she felt as if her heart
had swelled to twice its size.

'Do you feel up to answering some questions for him?'
he asked.

Her father looked at her. 'The birthmark?' he croaked.

Amelia nodded gravely. 'He had one but had it removed.
It was as you described.'

Tears began to shine in Aldo Vialli's eyes as he faced Alex.
'I was supposed to kill you.... I could not do it....'

'Thank you,' Alex said with gracious sincerity.

Her father blinked back the tears. 'I never intended to get
so involved, not in that way. I had to think of an alternative....
It was never my intention to bring such suffering on you or
your family. But what is done is done, and cannot be undone.'

'I understand,' Alex said, wondering if he really did. He
was feeling more than a little shell-shocked as he faced the

man supposedly responsible for the bizarre circumstances
that had led to his adoption. None of it seemed real. It was
the stuff of Hollywood thrillers, not normal life. How could
it be true? Sure, he'd been adopted at the age of two, but that
didn't mean he was the king's grandson. There could be thou-
sands of men his age who could just as easily fit the bill.

'You are so like your father,' Aldo choked out. 'It is my
fault that you have not had the chance to meet him in person.'

'Nothing's been established as yet,' Alex said. 'There are
legal channels that need to be investigated first. I know it all
seems to fit, but what if I'm not who you think I am?'

'There is no doubt in my mind,' Aldo said. 'You had the birthmark that, if nothing else, brands you as Alessandro Fierezza.'

'Look, to make things a little clearer in my head I'd like to
know a few more details, if you feel up to telling me?' Alex said.

'Of…course,' Aldo said in between another hacking cough.
'I will tell you…'

Amelia sat in silence as her father relayed the events of
thirty-four years ago, the picture he painted so painful to hear
she had trouble keeping her emotions at bay.

It was clear to Amelia after his confession that her father
was exhausted. His skin had taken on a clammy sheen and his
eyes had flickered once too often with increasing pain. His
breathing was laboured and when he turned to spit some
mucus into his old rag her stomach clenched at the sight of
how bright the blood was.

'*Papà*, would you like Alex to look at you now?' she asked.
'He might be able to do something to ease your suffering.'

After another bout of gut-wrenching coughs, Alex ex-
changed a glance with Amelia before he bent to his bag on
the floor and retrieved his stethoscope.

'Amelia, help take off your father's shirt so I can examine
his chest,' he directed.

Once the shirt was removed Alex looked at the degree of

chest expansion as Aldo took in a few breaths and then percussed the chest and listened with his stethoscope.

'You have a very large pleural effusion on the right side of your chest, Signor Vialli. That is making it hard for you to breathe, and may be precipitating a lot of the coughing. I may be able to at least temporarily relieve some of your symptoms by draining off the fluid with a needle,' he said.

'I am not going to go to the hospital. I will die here in my house, not in some institution, where everyone will know who I am, what I have done,' Aldo said.

'Signor Vialli—' Alex's voice deepened with professional authority '—performing a pleural drainage here would be too risky. For one thing there's the risk of infection, and secondly there's the possibility of me pricking the lung and causing a pneumothorax —puncturing the lung, I mean. If that were to happen, you could be worse off. We could go to the hospital now and do it without anyone but the night staff knowing about it. The procedure is relatively simple and will give you a few weeks' relief.'

'Papà, surely it's worth letting Alex try to help you,' Amelia pleaded.

Aldo let out a broken sigh. 'Very well…I will have the procedure done…but I do not want to stay in hospital.'

'That shouldn't be necessary if all goes well,' Alex said and helped the ill man from the chair, taking most of his weight on his arm.

Amelia sent him a grateful glance as they made their way out to Alex's car, her father's coughing increasing with every shuffling step he took.

The drive down to the Free Hospital was mostly silent. Alex tried once or twice to make conversation with Signor Vialli, but it was obvious both breathing and talking caused him too much discomfort.

Their arrival at the hospital was met with some slight

surprise on the part of the night staff nurse on duty, but once Alex explained what he intended to do she organised the equipment for him and led him to one of the treatment bays and drew the curtains around them.

Amelia helped her father into a sitting position on the bed at Alex's direction and supported his leaning-forward position by holding his shoulders.

Alex pulled on a pair of sterile gloves after washing and drying his hands, and, using the swabs from the disposable dressing tray, cleaned an area on the right side of Aldo's chest, his ribs clearly obvious because of marked weight loss.

'I'm going to put in some local anaesthetic so it doesn't hurt too much,' Alex explained.

He injected ten milligrams of one per cent xylocaine with adrenaline into the area for the pleural tap. Then, taking a fourteen gauge IV canula, to the end of which he attached a three-way tap and a twenty-mil syringe, Alex punctured the right pleural space just lateral to the tip of the right scapula, and aspirated 20ml of blood-stained pleural fluid. He then withdrew the IV needle, leaving the plastic canula in the pleural cavity, and aspirated the pleural effusion 20ml at a time, discarding each aspirate by using the three-way tap, into the stainless steel container the nurse had provided.

'You may feel like coughing as the fluid comes out, Signor Vialli. Try to suppress coughing as much as possible, just do little coughs if you have to, and try to keep as still as possible while I remove the fluid,' Alex said.

For Amelia, it seemed as though the fluid would never end; so far Alex had removed two litres of blood-stained effusion. But at about three litres, the pleural cavity was drained, and Alex removed the needle, taping a dressing over the puncture site.

'How does that feel? Can you breathe any easier?' Alex asked.

Aldo took a deep breath, and let it out slowly. This time there was no hacking cough.

'This is much better, Dr Hunter. I can breathe freely again. How long will this last?' Aldo asked.

'I can't really say,' Alex said. 'The fluid may come back very quickly, and you'll be thirsty and have to drink. Or it may accumulate very slowly, maybe over a few weeks. When much of the fluid comes back, I can drain it off again.'

'Do you think there will be any problems from the tap, Alex, infection or a pneumothorax?' Amelia asked, moving just out of her father's hearing.

Alex moved back to listen to Aldo's chest again with his stethoscope. 'The air entry is much better, and there isn't clinical evidence of a pneumothorax. I'll give him some sample packs of amoxicillin. He should start those now, and we'll get some more from the pharmacy tomorrow.'

'Thank you, Dr Hunter,' Aldo said as Amelia helped him to his feet once more.

'No problem.' Alex smiled. 'Let's get you home and into bed.'

Once her father was settled back at the cottage Amelia walked out with Alex to his car to see him off.

'Your father should really be in hospital,' he said as he drew her closer. 'He's in a bad way and it's only going to get worse.'

'I know.' She let out a tiny sigh and looked up at him. 'Thank you for what you did for him tonight.'

'I didn't do much.'

'You did more than you realise,' she said. 'Apart from relieving the pressure in his chest, you listened to his reasons for doing what he did without judgement and yet you of all people should be angry. He took your childhood away and exchanged it for another.'

'Maybe, but who's to say the one I got in exchange wasn't as good? I don't have a single bad memory of my childhood, that's more than what most people can say these days. It might have been a completely different story living a royal life. Who knows? I might have become horrendously overindulged and totally obnoxious.'

She smiled at his self-effacing humour. 'I can't imagine you ever being any such thing.'

He lifted her hand to his face and pressed a soft kiss to her palm, his eyes still locked to hers. 'You didn't like me the first time you met me, though, did you?'

'I didn't know you the first time I met you.'

'And you do now?' he asked after a protracted silence.

'I know you're a very special person....'

He narrowed his eyes at her playfully. 'If you mention the *P* word again I won't be answerable to the consequences. As far as I'm concerned I'm still Alex Hunter. Even if someone hands me a pedigree several centuries long I will still always feel like Alex Hunter, no one else.'

'But you'll have to face it soon,' she said with a troubled frown.

'Not yet.' He pulled her closer, his hands settling on her hips. 'Let's just be two ordinary people for a little while longer.'

'But the king should be told.'

'He will be told, but not right now. He's not well, for a start, and the shock of it could trigger a heart attack. I'd like to see him come through the procedure first. And anyway, I still have work to do at the Free Hospital. Can you imagine what would happen to that if I suddenly put my hand up for the throne? I came here to be a cardiac surgeon, not a prince. Once my work is completed I will have to face the issues surrounding my parentage, but until that time I'd rather just be me.'

She gave him a shadowed smile. 'I have spent most of my life wishing I was someone else. When I was a little girl I used to dream of being rescued out of poverty. I would imagine someone coming up here and informing me I had been mistakenly swapped at birth and that I no longer had to play with dolls made out of paper and sticks but real ones, ones that looked like the princess I felt I was really meant to be.'

His eyes were very dark as they held hers. 'I know what's happened might seem like a fairy tale to others, but let me tell you it's not. I guess I'm trying to keep my head by looking at this from a clinical distance. Although I met the king and some of my supposed siblings earlier this evening they felt like strangers to me. They still feel like strangers.'

'You have the same blood running in your veins.'

'Genetics is only a fraction of the equation,' he said. 'The nurture of a child is far more of an indicator than DNA profiles. I can't explain it any other way but I *feel* like the son of Clara and Giles Hunter. I always have, even though I've always been aware of being adopted.'

'I'm sure your adoptive parents will want you to do what's right for you. They will not be thinking of themselves but of what is best for you.'

He gave her a crooked smile. 'Like you, huh?'

She held his gaze, even though her heart felt as if it were being squeezed. 'What I want doesn't come into it at all.'

He frowned at her tone. 'What is it you want, Amelia?'

She looked up into his face, her eyes shining with moisture. 'I want you to be who you are called to be. It's your life and only you can make that choice.'

'For now this is my choice.' His voice was gravel rough and deep as his mouth came down towards hers. 'To be with you.'

But for how long? Amelia thought sadly as she lost herself in his kiss. It was too easy to forget about tomorrow when the heat and fire of the moment blazed so blindingly today.

Alex lifted his mouth from hers a few breathless minutes later. 'Have dinner with me tomorrow night,' he said. 'Bring some casual clothes and bathers with you to work so you can change at my house. We'll go on a sunset picnic to one of the beaches away from all the crowds. I don't want people staring at us.'

'I'm not sure…' She hesitated. 'My father—'

'Will want you to spend time with me,' he assured her. 'After all, he owes me, right? If I want to take his daughter out, then what can he say?'

'Good point,' she said with a smile.

He grazed his knuckles over her cheek. 'You see what dastardly means I have to resort to in order to get you to come out with me? I've never had to work quite so hard before. You are doing serious and very likely irreversible damage to my fragile male ego.'

'I don't think your ego has ever been in any sort of danger.'

He gave her a quick grin. 'No, you're right. Not while you keep looking at me with those big hazel eyes of yours.' He dropped a swift kiss to the end of her nose. 'Till tomorrow, little elf.'

'Till tomorrow,' she echoed softly as she watched the fiery red glare of his tail-lights disappear into the darkness of the night.

CHAPTER TWELVE

AMELIA couldn't wait for her shift to be over the next day. She checked her watch for the tenth time in as many minutes, scoring yet another speculative look from Lucia.

'You seem very impatient to be out of here,' the nurse observed. 'Could it be that you have something special planned for this evening?'

'No...no, nothing special.'

Lucia smiled knowingly. 'I don't think Dr Hunter would like to hear you describe your date with him as "nothing special".'

Amelia stared at her. 'He *told* you about that?'

'Not in as many words,' Lucia said. 'I just put two and two together. I saw the way he looked at you every time he was on the ward today. I met him in the canteen and asked him how he was enjoying the island and whether he'd been to any of the beaches. He said he was taking a friend this evening for a sunset picnic.'

'So you immediately thought that friend was me?'

Lucia's smile widened. 'It was a good guess, I thought, and, judging by the colour of your cheeks—spot on.'

Amelia considered denying it just for the sake of it, but she knew Lucia well enough to know she wouldn't be fooled.

'You went to the palace with him last night, didn't you?' Lucia said.

'How *do* you find out all this stuff?'

Lucia grinned. 'I have connections.'

'Well, tell your connections to mind their own business,' Amelia said. 'I don't want the whole island talking about one casual date.'

'Two if you count the other night, which, young lady, I am quite peeved that you didn't tell me about.' She leaned closer and added, 'Did he kiss you?'

Amelia frowned. 'I'm not going to answer that.'

'No, you don't need to as your face just did it for you,' Lucia said with another cheeky grin.

Amelia sent her a reproving glance. 'Don't go ordering the invitations and caterers. He's only on the island for a month.'

'So who's counting the days?'

'I'm just being realistic,' Amelia said. 'Besides, he comes from a totally different world. We have hardly anything in common.'

'He's a man—you're a woman. That's all that matters,' Lucia said. 'You of all people deserve to have a little fling. Who cares how long it lasts?'

I care, Amelia thought as she reached for her bag. *I care too much.*

Alex watched as she came towards him in the hospital car park, her small bag in one hand and a worried frown disturbing the elfin perfection of her face.

He eased himself away from the car and took her bag, smiling down at her. 'Hi.'

She looked up at him with a nervous smile. 'Hi.'

'Are you OK?'

She moistened her mouth. 'Yes.'

'Hey—' he pushed up her chin '—I'm just Alex tonight. Got that?'

She gave him a rueful look. 'Yes, and I'm a princess,' she said.

He laughed. 'Yeah, that's right. You are.'

'Alex…'

'Stop worrying about it,' he said as he helped her into the car. 'I've got it all under control.'

She waited until he was behind the driver's wheel before speaking. 'Have you found out anything yet?'

He started the engine and backed out of the space, swinging a quick glance her way as he drove out of the hospital grounds. 'I have someone working on it as we speak. But just for tonight let's forget all about it, OK?'

'If that's what you'd prefer.'

He sent her a warm smile that momentarily suppressed the dark shadows she'd seen in his eyes. 'It's what I prefer,' he said.

Amelia sat in silence as he drove the short distance to his cottage, her senses on high alert. She could smell the sexy musk of his body intermingled with the lingering fragrance of his citrus aftershave, and her skin began to prickle all over at the thought of feeling his kiss, his touch and his intimate caresses.

How would it feel to have his arms around her, his skin on her skin, his body within hers again?

She knew their relationship was being conducted on borrowed time, but the sense of urgency only heightened her attraction to him and she wondered if he felt it too.

She sneaked a look at him as he drove, his long-fingered hands steady on the wheel, his face showing nothing of the inner turmoil he surely must be going through.

Alex caught her looking at him. 'I hope you're not having second thoughts.'

'About what?'

'About us.'

She looked down at her hands. 'This is temporary, Alex. You and I both know that.'

'You're putting up obstacles that don't need to be there.'

'But they *are* there,' she insisted. 'Pretending they're not isn't going to make them go away.'

His jaw tightened. 'I don't want to talk about it tonight, remember? Tonight we're just a man and a woman who are attracted to each other.'

'I'm not denying that, but I think we both should be realistic.'

'You're being fatalistic, not realistic,' he said.

'I'm trying to protect myself from hurt.'

He let out a deep sigh and reached for her hand, bringing it up to his mouth to press a soft kiss to her fingertips. 'I don't want to hurt you, Amelia.'

'You won't be able to avoid it.'

He met her troubled gaze. 'I will do everything in my power to avoid it. Trust me.'

Could she risk her heart another time? She had spent the last eleven years regretting the one and only time she had let her guard slip.

'Trust me?' he said again.

She gave him a tremulous smile. 'I know I'm going to regret this, but I do trust you.'

'Good girl,' he said. 'Now we're getting somewhere.'

Amelia used the bathroom to change out of her uniform while Alex organised the picnic and within a few minutes they were on their way to a beach at the far end of Santa Fiera where the sandy shore was less frequented by tourists.

'How about a swim first?' Alex suggested once he'd laid a blanket on the sand and anchored it with the picnic basket.

'You go. I'll sit here and watch for a while,' Amelia said.

Alex could sense her self-consciousness. In spite of the evening's warmth she was dressed in a shapeless cotton shift that looked at least three sizes too big. He could also see the thick straps of the dark one-piece bathing costume she was wearing, its unflattering lines suggesting she hadn't been to the beach in a very long time.

He wondered if he'd done the right thing in bringing her here, but he'd figured that at least on a picnic she hadn't had to worry about dressing up. Besides, he wanted time with her away from other people and their increasingly speculative stares.

He still couldn't get his head around the circumstances surrounding his infancy. At first he had hoped it was all a mistake but the investigations he'd set in motion so far had led him to suspect the opposite. The legal people he'd engaged to work on it had already come across one or two discrepancies in the paperwork regarding his adoption and had hinted that there could be even more. He couldn't bear the thought of informing his parents of what he'd discovered. He knew it would hurt them immeasurably to find they had inadvertently adopted a child who had had parents who had loved him and desperately longed for his return.

Alex felt as if he was in limbo; he couldn't go back and neither could he go forward until he knew for sure what was expected of him. But for the time being he had a responsibility to get the king through his surgery; that was a main priority—everything else would have to wait.

He had even shelved his earlier concerns about Amelia's family connections, unable to accept her as anything other than a young woman who was learning how to live again after a bitter let-down, not unlike his own. He had found it hard to become involved with anyone since his break-up with Sarah and instead had thrown himself into work as a distraction. The hurt he had felt about her affair with another man had niggled at him for so long and yet when he was with Amelia he completely forgot about it.

He let out a small sigh as he walked down towards the ocean. The water was refreshing after the heat of the day and he struck out vigorously, hoping to exercise some of his tension away.

* * *

Amelia sat on the sand hugging her bent knees, watching as Alex swam further than most people could walk. He was a picture of health and vitality, his tanned, muscular body carving through the water like a streamlined torpedo.

She couldn't help a little sigh of envy. She had never learned to swim with any proficiency. Her family circumstances had ruled out swimming lessons during her childhood and as she'd grown older she'd become too embarrassed to admit to her inability.

Her mother's bathing costume felt scratchy and uncomfortable and she longed to remove it. This end of the beach was deserted, but the thought of sitting next to Alex with nothing on but her thin shift was too disturbing.

She saw him make his way towards her, his strong legs slicing through the shallows, the crystal droplets of salt-water making his whole body glisten in the evening sunlight.

'Come on in,' he said, offering her a hand.

'No…I'm fine here.'

'Come on, Amelia. It's not the least bit cold.'

'Please…I'd rather not.' She hugged her knees even tighter.

He frowned as he joined her on the sand. 'What's the problem?'

'Nothing.'

He grazed her cheek with the back of his fingers. 'Look at me, Amelia.'

She met his dark gaze and suddenly found herself confessing, 'I…I can't swim.'

His eyes softened like melted chocolate. 'That's nothing to be ashamed of. It can take a long time to learn to swim properly.'

She chewed at her lip. 'I've never had lessons.'

'Well, then, now's a perfect time to start. I can teach you. It's like riding a bike—once you learn, you learn for life.'

He got to his feet and hauled her upright before she could protest. 'Take off your dress and let's go in to our knees.'

Amelia self-consciously wriggled out of her cotton dress and followed him to the water's edge, stepping into the water tentatively, her toes looking for stability in the shifting sand. After a moment or two she felt more secure and went in a little farther, this time up to her thighs as she held tightly to Alex's hand.

'That's great. Now let's go to your waist,' he said.

She took a deep breath and walked in a little farther, wincing as the water swirled around her middle and almost made her lose her balance.

'Easy does it,' he said, holding her waist with his hands from behind.

Amelia could feel his body behind her like a strong wall of muscle, his legs braced against the frothing surf. It was the most erotic sensation having his hard body so close to hers. She could even feel the beginnings of his arousal, the gradual thickening of his body, a heady reminder of all that set them apart as man and woman. Her breasts felt tight and heavy, her legs felt insecure and weak and her heart began to race.

They were totally alone on the beach.

They were practically skin on skin.

All she had to do was turn around and his mouth would find hers....

She turned around and met his glittering gaze, her throat locking up at the desire she could see reflected there. He brought her closer so there was no room, not even for water to separate them.

His head came down, his mouth capturing hers in a searing kiss that swept her away on a rushing tide of rapture. It felt so good to be crushed against him, his tongue swooping and meeting hers, his body pressing urgently against her.

She felt his hands leave her hips to explore the curves of her breasts, his thumbs rolling over each tight nipple until she was mindless with sensation. Without taking his mouth off hers, he pushed the straps of her bathing costume aside to access her naked breasts with the warmth of his palms. The feel of his hands caressing her stole her breath and made her legs wobble beneath her.

The pulse of the ocean around them only added to the swirl of sensual feelings swamping her; no part of her was unaffected by his touch. With her bathers practically around her waist she knew she should be calling some sort of halt to this onslaught of sensuality, but there was nothing she could do to pull away.

His mouth left hers and began to kiss its way down the side of her neck on a slow but steady passage towards her aching, swollen breasts. She could feel her skin tightening all over in tiny goose-bumps at the erotic press of his lips as they made their way down…down…

'Oh…' She let out a hoarse gasp as his hot mouth closed over her engorged nipple, the rasp of his tongue turning her insides to liquid. She clutched at his head to hold herself upright, her breath coming in stunted little bursts as he suckled on each of her breasts in turn.

He brought his mouth back to hers and her loose bathers slipped even farther so that she could feel his erection on the bare skin of her quivering stomach. It was shockingly intimate, but she couldn't stop herself from reaching down and tracing his rigid contours with the tips of her fingers, tentatively at first and then with increasing boldness as his throaty groans filled her mouth.

His kiss became more urgent, the mastery of his tongue leaving her in no doubt of his expertise as a lover. She could almost feel him inside her again as she stood there in the rocking ocean with him, his body burning into hers with unmistakable purpose. She had never felt anything like the passion filling her; it consumed her totally, leaving no room for common sense.

Alex tore his mouth off hers and looked down at her with assion-glazed eyes, his chest rising and falling as he strug-led to regain control. 'I guess I'm not the world's best wimming teacher, huh?'

She gave him a shy smile and covered her naked breasts /ith her hands. 'I don't know about that—I certainly felt like was floating there for a while.'

He smiled. 'Me too, especially when you did that little ning with your fingers.'

She felt her colour rise and bit her bottom lip in embarrass-ent. 'I don't know what came over me.'

'Hey, do you hear me complaining?' He removed her hands rom her breasts, running his dark gaze over her hungrily.

'Alex…'

'Mmm?' He pressed a burning kiss to the top of her right reast, so close to her aching nipple she could barely think.

She squirmed and tried again. 'My…er…bathers are lipping.'

She felt his smile on the side of her other breast. 'Want a and to take them off?' he asked.

She clutched at his head again, her voice totally reathless as his tongue rasped over her puckered nipple. N-no…no…someone might see us.'

He lifted his head and glanced around them. 'There's no ne around for miles. Come on, if you take yours off, I'll ke off mine.'

She stared at him in alarm. 'You're surely not serious?'

He gave her a stomach-flipping smile. 'As your very own ersonal swimming coach I insist you get a feel for the water. Believe me, it makes the world of difference. Besides, that ostume of yours is like a diving weight belt. You'd sink to ne bottom in two strokes.'

Amelia hesitated for a moment. What harm would it do? he wondered. Wasn't it about time she learned to put the past

aside and enjoy life for once? Lucia was right: Alex was a man
and she was a woman. This was the twenty-first century;
women were entitled to have temporary lovers. It didn't mean
they were promiscuous or bad people. It was natural to feel
desire; it was even healthy.

She took an unsteady breath and pushed the bathers down
with her hands and stepped out of them. She felt Alex's gaze
sweeping over her and her heart kicked in response to the
almost palpable desire she could feel coming off him.

'Now it's your turn,' she said huskily.

His gaze locked down on hers challengingly. 'You do it.'

She swallowed and squeaked, 'Me?'

He nodded.

She moistened her mouth and reached blindly with
unsteady hands for the waist of his black bathers, her fingers
curling into the fabric for purchase as she pulled them down
past his lean hips. She felt him spring against her nakedness,
the length and strength of him sending shock waves of delight
between her legs. She could feel her womb pulsing with need,
her whole body coming alive with escalating desire.

The wild sea air crawled with tension as he brought his
hands to her hips, gently pulling her against him, his hardened
length slipping between her legs in an erotically teasing
embrace that sent her senses into uncontrollable mayhem.

She raised herself on tiptoe to accommodate him, her
breath rushing out of her when he probed her intimately. She
felt the separation of her tender flesh as he surged forwards,
his deep, rumbling groan of pleasure as he filled her drowning
out the breathless gasp of her own.

His movements quickened, carrying her with him on a
roller coaster of feeling as her sensitive nerves responded
with increasing fervour to each of his determined thrusts. She
felt her body tingling as it steadily climbed towards the
summit of release, the inner muscles clamping on his thick

ess made slippery with the dew of her desire. His mouth rushed hers once more, his hot breath filling her as he lunged again and again until she was hovering in the alance—the pleasure she craved was close, but not quite lose enough. She whimpered against his lips, unable to xpress her need, but in the end she didn't need to; he felt it or himself. She quivered against his searching fingers, the ngorged pearl of her womanhood responding with a heady ush, triggering a volley of panting cries from her throat as he waves of delight crashed in and over her. Her body rocked nd shuddered against his until she felt him, too, tumble into he abyss of pleasure with deep, pumping thrusts that nudged er womb and made her skin prickle all over with sensation.

Alex gradually eased himself away, his hands still holding er to counteract the swell of the ocean. 'I guess you're not oing to believe me when I tell you I didn't really intend for hat to happen,' he said with a wry grimace, 'or at least not vithout protection.'

Her eyes clouded and her cheeks went a delicate shade of pink s she bent down to retrieve her bathers. 'It was just as much my ault as yours,' she said as she wriggled back into them.

'It was no one's fault,' he said, holding on to her arm to teady her. 'I guess sooner or later I knew it was going to be ike this.'

She looked up at him. 'Y-you did?'

'Sure I did. It's called chemistry.' He smiled at her as he ook her hand and led her to the picnic blanket on the sand.

Amelia curled up beside him with a sigh of contentment, is arms holding her loosely as they watched the waves rolling o the shore. She pressed a kiss to his neck, the salt of his skin nd the sea making her lips tingle.

'You must be getting hungry,' Alex said, dropping a swift, ard kiss to her mouth.

'What makes you say that?' she asked with a twinkling smile.

'You're starting to gnaw on me.'

'You don't like the feel of my mouth on you?'

He pushed her back down and covered her with his body, a teasing smile playing at the corners of his mouth. 'Do you hear me complaining?'

'I guess not,' she breathed as his lips claimed hers in a searing kiss.

CHAPTER THIRTEEN

THE first stars were in the sky when Amelia surfaced from the sensual haven of Alex's arms.

'Are you cold?' he asked as he handed her a glass of wine.

'No, I'm fine.' She toyed with the glass for a moment before looking up at him. 'Alex…this thing between us…this chemistry you spoke of…don't you mean lust?'

'Lust sounds a bit shallow and transient to me,' he said.

'But this *is* transient…'

'That subject is off limits, remember? This is for now, Amelia. We'll take it one day at a time and enjoy what happens.'

'It's so easy for men to cast aside the practicalities,' she said. 'Sex is just sex for men—it's much more emotionally complicated for women.'

'That's a sweeping generalisation that does a lot of men a disservice,' he said. 'I know you've had a bad case of lover let-down, but not all men are after a one-night stand or brief fling. I haven't had a one-night stand in my life and my shortest relationship lasted two years. It broke up about this time last year.'

'Were you in love with her?' she asked.

His eyes moved away from hers as he picked up his glass again. 'Yes, I loved her in my own way. I guess if I was honest with myself there had always been something missing in our relationship, but I chose to ignore it until it was too late. She'd been having an affair with a guy behind my back.' His brows came together slightly. 'She's married to him now and expecting his baby.'

Amelia wondered if that was why he had charged headlong into his relationship with her, out of a sense of loss. It made sense in a way, the holiday romance to dull the pain of rejection, especially since the woman he had loved had moved on with her life without him. She couldn't help wondering if his easygoing attitude covered much deeper hurt.

'I don't suppose a good convent girl like you would happen to be on the pill?' he asked after a moment or two of silence.

She almost choked on her mouthful of wine. 'I…um…I…'

His mouth tilted. 'That appears to be a straight-out no.'

She gnawed her bottom lip as she thought of their unprotected coupling. 'I didn't think…'

'Don't worry,' he said. 'I haven't got anything other than rampant fertility to threaten you with.'

Her eyes flew to his, her mouth dropping open. 'Isn't that bad enough?'

He gave a casual shrug and reached for his wine. 'Contrary to what people think, a woman is only fertile for about two days of every monthly cycle.'

She looked at him closely, trying to read his expression. 'Today could be one of the days,' she pointed out. 'What then?'

He held her gaze for several pulsing seconds. 'Would it be a problem for you?' he asked.

She gaped at him. 'Of course it would be a problem for me!'

'You're thirty years old,' he said. 'Aren't you hearing any ticking yet?'

She frowned at him. 'I suppose by that you're referring to my biological clock?'

'Every woman's got one even if she says she hasn't.' He turned to look out to sea and added, 'My ex-girlfriend always trenuously denied it because she sensed I wasn't ready for ids, but within no time after replacing me she was waving a lue dipstick in the air.'

Amelia felt her jaw tightening. 'I suppose that's why ou've singled me out? Who better to knock up than a naïve eft-on-the-shelf thirty-year-old woman whom you no doubt ssumed would be far too grateful to notice the insincerity of our stupid proposal.' She tossed the contents of her glass to ne sand and got to her feet and glared down at him furiously. How dare you toy with me in such a way?'

He stood up and frowned back at her. 'I was doing no uch thing.'

Her eyes flashed at him. 'I don't believe you.'

'That's your choice,' he said in a hardened tone.

'I can see why your girlfriend left you,' she said. 'No woman vants to have a child with a man who refuses to grow up.'

'And I suppose you've got maturity down to an art form, ave you?' he retorted with a touch of spite. 'You've spent the ast eleven years running away from life. Don't tell me I aven't grown up when you've hidden away from everything nat's adult.'

'I suppose it's adult to pretend things you don't feel to chieve your ends, is it?' she shot back.

His eyes blazed with growing anger. 'I haven't pretended nything. I've made my motives more than clear.'

She gave a mocking laugh. 'Oh, yes, indeed you have. From ne first moment I met you your motives were blatantly obvious.'

'Would you care to explain that comment?'

She sent him a paint-stripping look. 'You don't need me o spell it out. Besides, you've already achieved your goal, aven't you? The little seduction routine worked, didn't it? I ell for it as you intended me to.'

'I don't deny I wanted to make love with you, and if you're onest with yourself you'll admit the same. You wanted me too, Amelia, so don't do that outraged little virginal routine with me. It just won't work.'

She stamped her foot on the sand. 'Take me home this instant.'

His lip curled insolently. 'I will when I'm good and ready.'

She let out a furious breath and, scooping up her things off the sand, turned for the twinkling lights of Santa Fiera in the distance.

'I would advise against walking all that way in the dark,' Alex called out after her.

'I'll take a chance on it,' she flung back at him.

He let out a frustrated sigh and followed her, his long legs swiftly closing the distance. He snagged one of her arms and turned her round to face him, deftly dodging her hand as it swung up for his face. 'Oh, no, you don't,' he warned as he captured her hand on its second attempt.

'If you don't let me go I'll scream,' she threatened, her chest heaving with rage.

'If you scream I'll kiss you until you shut up.'

Her eyes narrowed into slits. 'If you kiss me I'll bite you!'

He suddenly laughed and tugged her closer. 'I can hardly wait,' he said and covered her mouth with his.

Amelia opened her teeth to bite him but his tongue slipped through and found hers, taking her breath away as well as her urge to fight. She felt herself go weak in his arms, her legs softening until she was only remaining upright because he was holding her so tightly. Her head spun with every bold flick of his tongue against hers, the movement so deliciously evocative of what they had experienced earlier she could feel her lower body turning to liquid all over again. She leaned into him unashamedly, her pelvis on fire where his body pressed against her.

He lifted his mouth from hers and looked down at her with a teasing glint in his eyes. 'Are you still angry with me?'

She pursed her mouth at him. 'Furious.'

'Do you still want me to take you home straight away or an I tempt you back into sharing a picnic fit for a prince?'

Her mouth opened but she closed it again.

'I guess that wasn't such a great choice of words,' he cceded wryly.

Her shoulders gave a little slump. 'It was a mistake for me o come with you tonight.'

'I shouldn't have mentioned the *P* word.'

'What about the other *P* word?' she asked. 'What if I did ecome pregnant?'

'As long as you were happy, I'd be happy,' he said. 'We ould get married straight away and live snappily ever after.'

She rolled her eyes at him. 'Very funny.'

'We'd be a great couple. I can see it now—every single ght would end up in bed.'

'Only because you don't fight fair.'

'Look who's talking.' He slung a casual arm around her houlders and led her back towards the picnic blanket. 'You ere the one threatening to bite me and you tried to throw me right hook.'

'You made me angry.'

'I like it when you're angry,' he said. 'You turn me on.'

She glanced up at him. 'Did your ex-girlfriend ever make ou angry?'

He met her eyes briefly before turning away to open the icnic basket. 'That's another *P* word I'd like to stay away om tonight—past lovers.'

'You're not over her, are you?' she said as he handed her plate.

His eyes came back to hers. 'I would be a shallow sort of loke if I could walk away after two years without some egrets. But I am over her. I hardly even think of her now.'

Amelia felt something heavy begin to weigh her chest own. 'What do you regret?'

He shifted his lips from side to side as if thinking about i
'I don't know… Maybe I should have been more spontane
ous. I worked too hard and forgot how to have fun. I woke u
three weeks after Sarah left me for another man and realise
I had to loosen up, you know, laugh at life a bit more.'

'So you suddenly found yourself a sense of humour?'

'No, not really. I guess I've always been a happy-go-luck
sort of guy, but years of study and long hours and being re
sponsible for patients' lives took its toll. I was heading toward
a total burn-out and Sarah giving me the boot was the wake
up call I needed.'

'Do you ever see her?'

'What would be the point? It's over. She has a new life an
I don't belong in it.'

'She's going to kick herself when she finds out sh
knocked back a prince,' she said without thinking.

His expression clouded as he rummaged for cutlery an
napkins. 'As far as I see it, it's a title, not a description of wh
I am as a person.'

'I know, but people will still have certain expectations.'

'I have to live up to my own expectations, not those c
other people.'

'This is really hard for you, isn't it?' she asked after a tar
little silence.

He met her gaze, his small smile slightly skewed. 'Hov
would you feel to suddenly find out you weren't who yo
thought you were?'

'You're still Alex Hunter.'

'But for how long?' he asked.

Amelia sighed as she reached for his hand and gave it
little squeeze. 'It's still a secret,' she tried to reassure him. 'N
one needs to know a thing until you feel ready to tell ther
who you are.'

His dark eyes became shadowed. 'I'd just like anothe

veek or two,' he said. 'That will be enough time to get the
ing through the surgery and my work commitments at the
'ree Hospital seen to. After that I guess it will have to be dealt
vith in some way or another, but I can't help feeling it's
oing to be hard on your father.'

'I know. My father wants the truth to be told, but I don't
hink he realises yet the implications for him. He'll be charged
nd no doubt sent to prison.'

He began to stroke her cheek with his fingers. 'You realise
e hasn't got much time left, don't you?'

She nodded silently.

'At least this way you get the chance to say goodbye,' he
aid, dropping his hand and looking out to sea again. 'So
nany people don't.'

Amelia looked at him, wondering if he was thinking of his
iological parents. It was hard to tell from his expression, but
he couldn't help feeling he was trying to come to terms with
is new-found identity instead of pushing the reality of it
way as he had insisted on doing earlier.

'Alex…can I ask you something?'

He turned back to look at her. 'Of course.'

'I want to know what your intentions are in regards to me.'

'I thought I'd made it pretty clear a few minutes ago exactly
vhat my intentions are.'

She bit her lip momentarily. 'I can't help feeling you're
loing the whole rebound thing.'

A shutter came down over his face as he turned to look out
t the ocean. 'I'm over that part of my life,' he said. 'I told
ou—I don't even think of her any more.'

Amelia wondered if that was true. She had noticed a
ension in him every time his ex-partner was mentioned, as if
he pain was still festering deep inside him. He had said she'd
eft him for another man, which would no doubt have hurt him
leeply, in spite of his laid-back personality. No man liked to

be betrayed in such a way. But it still plagued Amelia to think
he had only become involved with her to expunge the pain of
his past relationship. She could hardly hope to measure up to
a woman who moved in the sort of circles Alex did. She'd had
nothing to offer him before and now even less so.

'She was crazy to let you go,' she said softly, trailing her
fingers down the length of his arm closest her.

'Because of my royal connections?' he asked, turning to
face her with a teasing smile, his earlier tension gone.

'You're not supposed to say the *P* word, remember?'

He laughed and pressed her down onto the sand and kissed
her soundly before lifting his head to look down at her. 'How
about this for another *P* word. Want to come back to my
house and play?'

She ran her fingertip over his bottom lip. 'What did you
have in mind?'

He drew her finger into his mouth and sucked on it hard,
his dark eyes sending her a message that set off a riot of sensation deep and low inside her. 'Do I really need to answer
that?' he asked.

'No,' she said as she raised her mouth to meet his. 'You don't.'

A short time later, Alex led her inside his cottage and directed
her towards the bathroom. 'You can have the first shower. I
have a couple of e-mails to send. I promised my parents I'd
keep in close contact with my sister. She's backpacking her
way around Europe.'

She gave him a grateful look. 'Thanks. I feel as if I've got
sand in places I didn't even know I had places.'

He gave her a sexy smile. 'But don't take too long or I
might come in and join you.'

Amelia deliberately took her time to see if he was as good
as his promise. She used the fragrant shampoo and conditioner
in the shower stall and the shower gel that made her skin silky

smooth. She closed her eyes and lifted her face to the shower head, delighting in the luxury of hot water that she hadn't had to heat herself.

Her eyes sprang open when the shower stall door opened and Alex stepped in, his naked body brushing up against hers.

'Any hot water left?' he asked.

She stared at the droplets of water running down his face to his mouth. 'Yes.'

'Want to soap my back for me?'

'Um...all right...'

He turned around and, taking a breath, she ran her hands over his muscled back with the shower gel, her fingers lingering over his taut buttocks.

'How about the front?' he asked.

She swallowed. 'The front?'

He turned around, a twinkle appearing in his dark gaze as it meshed with hers. 'The front.'

She took a handful of shower gel and placed it on his chest, keeping her eyes well away from what was probing insistently against the softness of her belly.

'Lower,' he said, his eyes burning into hers.

She swallowed again, her stomach tripping over itself. 'L-lower?'

'Much lower.'

Her soapy hands went down, pausing over his belly button, her fingertip exploring the tight, hairy cave before her hand went a little farther...

His groan as her fingers brushed against him gave her courage and she did it again, more confident this time, shaping him with increasing boldness.

'Look at me,' he commanded roughly.

'I am looking at you,' she said.

'No,' he said. 'Look at what you're doing to me.'

Another tiny swallow and she looked. He was turgid with

need, a need she could feel building in her own body. Her breasts were tight, her legs watery and her stomach quivering with anticipation.

'Now it's my turn,' he said and spun her around.

She sucked in a ragged breath as he soaped her back in long, sensual strokes, his fingers dipping in between her legs in a tantalising not-quite-where-she-wanted-it-most caress.

He stood so close she could feel the hard probe of his body against her, the satin strength of him reminding her of how her gently upward-slanted body was perfectly designed to accept him.

'Turn around,' he said, his voice sounding deep and uneven.

Amelia slowly turned around, her body brushing against the entire length of his.

Hot liquid fire was blazing in his eyes as they met hers. His hands went to the smooth swell of her breasts, his thumb finding each tight nipple until she could hardly think for the pleasure his touch evoked. He bent his head and suckled on her, his tongue sending arrows of heat to the tender, dark, moist recess of her body that was already pulsing with a drumbeat-like need.

His mouth left her breast to capture her mouth in a drugging kiss that left her feeling as liquid as the water spilling around them. The back of the shower stall supported her, for her legs would not, the pressure of his body against hers the only thing keeping her from sliding to the floor.

Alex lifted his mouth from hers, his eyes sending her a message that was as timeless as it was overwhelmingly tempting.

She drew in a scalding breath and ran her hands over him, less shyly this time, her fingers taking him on a journey of sensuality that surprised her even as it drew the harsh guttural groans from the depths of his throat.

'No,' he groaned, stilling the increasingly rapid movement of her hand. 'I can't take any more.'

She wriggled her fingers in his hand but he refused to let her have access to him, instead holding her hand above her head against the back of the shower as he fed hungrily off her mouth.

She felt herself sagging into him, her body thrumming with a need so consuming she pushed herself against him, her body searching for the heated trajectory of his.

She heard him groan as he surged forward, sheathing himself completely, the liquid silk of her body grabbing at him possessively.

Her head rolled back as he drove forward again, her eyes tightly shut as the sky-rocketing sensations flooded her being. It was wild and wanton, urgent and frantic, leaving no room for thoughts, just feelings. She could feel the delicious pressure building, every nerve in her body climbing higher and higher for the release it craved.

He increased his pace at the same time as he reached between her legs, his long fingers touching her where she needed it most. It triggered the response her body ached for, sending a riot of exploding sensations right throughout her, leaving her weightless and trembling in his tight embrace, the echo of her panting cries filling her ears.

She opened her passion-slaked eyes to see his face contort with pleasure as he surged forward again, once, twice, three times, his whole body shuddering against her with the force of his explosive release. He sagged against her, his head burrowed into her neck, his erratic breathing moving his chest in and out against hers.

Amelia held him close, the water cascading around them mingling with the essence of maleness that had burst from his body and branded her as his in the most intimate way possible.

Alex gave her an apologetic grimace as he eased himself out of her hold. 'I told myself I was going to resist you until we got to the bedroom so I could use a condom. I'm not normally so irresponsible, but I just can't seem to help myself around you.'

'I'm sure it will be all right,' she said. 'My period is due any day now.'

'That's not the point,' he said as he turned off the water. 'Cycles can go out of whack and you could find yourself in a situation you hadn't planned for. I won't let it happen again, I promise.'

He reached for a towel and began drying her, each brush of his hands through the towel making her skin cry out for the touch of his bare flesh on hers.

They were both still wet when they landed on the bed in a tangle of limbs, but it only added to the sensations coursing through Amelia as she fell back amongst the pillows with his weight on top of her.

His kiss was hot and demanding, his obvious impatience the biggest compliment she had ever received. It made her feel womanly, powerful and irresistible.

His mouth was on her breasts, then on her stomach, his tongue anointing the tiny dish of her belly button before going lower. Her breath came to a screeching halt when his warm breath fanned over her sensitive feminine folds, her limbs tightening in both apprehension and anticipation. When he parted her tenderly with his tongue, her whole body shivered with reaction, the overly sensitive nerves fizzing with the electric current of his intimate touch. Her response was too hard to hold back; it came in wave after wave of escalating ecstasy until her mind was empty of everything but the exquisite feelings he triggered in her.

Her breathing was still erratic as he reached across her for a condom, deftly placing it on himself before he moved between her thighs with unmistakable urgency. She felt her body grip him, the silken sheath slippery with her fragrant response to him.

She felt him check himself, as if he was trying to hold back his pace, but she wouldn't allow it, her body wanted him hot, hard, heavy and full speed ahead. She arched her back to bring herself closer to him, her hips undulating with the pleasure of his strong movements, each deep thrust sending a shock wave of feeling through her entire body.

Suddenly she was there again, at that impossibly high altitude of pleasure where thoughts were lost in the moment of utterly fulfilling release. Her whole body shivered with it, every nerve and muscle reacting to the flood of sensation that flowed over her and through her like a tide of warm, bubbly water.

Even as her tension left her body, Amelia felt his tension building as each deep thrust brought him closer to the edge. She felt it in his iron-like hold, she felt it in the hot moistness of his mouth as it fed hungrily off hers, and she felt it in the bunched muscles of his buttocks where her hands were holding on to him like an anchor.

He gave one harsh groan into her mouth as he fell forward, the sudden expulsion of his life force rendering him momentarily powerless. He relaxed under her stroking hands, his chest rising and falling against hers, his sweat-slicked body still intimately joined to hers.

Amelia didn't want to move. Her body felt languorous with the aftermath of his lovemaking, all her limbs feeling weightless, as if the bones had been taken out and marshmallow put in their place.

Alex propped himself up on one elbow and pressed a soft kiss to her mouth. 'I bet you didn't learn any of that in that convent of yours, huh?'

She smiled and stretched like a well-fed cat. 'No, I certainly didn't.'

He brushed a strand of her hair away from her cheek. 'You totally rock me, Amelia, do you know that?'

She lowered her gaze a fraction. 'We're not in love with each other.... I know you'll think it terribly old-fashioned of me, but to me it seems a little wrong to be sharing this level of intimacy when we're not committed emotionally.'

'I don't see anything wrong with exploring the attraction we both feel,' he said.

'But how long will it last without stronger feelings to support it?'

'You never know—you might fall in love with me,' he said with a glinting smile.

'I'm not too sold on rapid emotional responses,' she said with a small, almost undetectable downturn of her mouth. 'They can't really be counted on as the real thing.'

'Ah, such cynicism in one so young,' he lamented playfully.

'I'm not being cynical, I'm being realistic. Flash-in-the-pan emotions are exactly that—one flash and they're gone. It happened that way with my ex-lover. I felt sure I was in love with him, I would have staked my life on it, but in the end those feelings died.'

'Plenty of people develop strong and lasting feelings in a short space of time. My parents are living proof of love at first sight.'

Her face clouded with sadness. 'My mother fell in love with my father and it destroyed her life....'

Alex was still thinking about how to respond when his mobile phone began to ring from the bedside table. He reached across Amelia to pick it up.

'Dr Hunter?' an urgent male voice spoke. 'My name is Rico Vialli. I'm looking for my sister, Amelia. Is she with you?'

'Yes, she is. Do you want to—'

'Oh, thank God...' The man's voice broke over the words. 'I thought she was dead too....'

Alex sat up, his hand tightening on the phone as his gaze flicked to Amelia's puzzled one. 'What's wrong?' he asked. 'Has something happened?'

He heard Amelia's brother take an unsteady breath and it seemed an eternity before he spoke, his voice coming out like a hoarse croak as he finally announced, 'Our father died earlier this evening.'

'I'm so very sorry—' Alex began but Rico cut him off.

'You don't understand, Dr Hunter,' he said hollowly. 'My father did not die of lung cancer after all. He was burned to death in the cottage. And I don't think it was an accident.'

CHAPTER FOURTEEN

'WHAT'S wrong?' Amelia got to her feet unsteadily as Alex put the phone down after he finished the call.

He met her worried gaze. 'I'm sorry, Amelia, but I have some terrible news for you.'

'My father's dead?'

Alex wished he could find a way to soften the blow. He sat her down and took her hands in his, gently stroking them as he told her what Rico had told him.

'*Murdered?*' She gaped at him in horror.

'It appears that way according to what your brother just said. The cottage was completely gutted.'

She pulled out of his hold and got to her feet, reaching for something to cover herself with. 'I can't believe it...' she said as she struggled back into her clothes. 'I was only talking to him this morning.... *Oh, Papà!*' She put her head in her hands.

Alex threw on his bathrobe and came to her and held her close. 'Rico said the police are interviewing the nearest neighbours to see if they heard or saw anything. He borrowed one of their phones to call me. He was worried you might have been in the cottage when it burned down.'

She eased herself away to look up at him. 'Is there nothing left? Nothing at all?'

He shook his head grimly.

She sagged against him. 'I don't know what to do....'

'You can stay with me,' he said. 'The police will no doubt want to speak with you at some point, but there's no need to go up there right away. The forensics team will need to do their investigations.'

'W-where is my father's body?'

'I'm not sure,' he said. 'But I would advise against seeing him.'

'He's my father. I want to say goodbye.'

'I know you do, but do you really want your last memory of him to be tainted by what you'll see if you go there this minute?'

Amelia knew he was right; she'd seen enough burn victims to know how hard it was to cope with seeing their often disfiguring wounds. It was distressing enough dealing with strangers as patients, let alone a full-blood relative.

'Has Silvio been contacted?' she asked.

'Yes, Rico said he was on his way,' Alex said. 'He has taken charge of everything.'

'Is he all right?'

'He's pretty shaken up but then who wouldn't be?'

She moved out of his hold and rubbed at her upper arms in agitation. 'My father was dying—everyone knew that. Who would want to hurry his death in such a way?'

Alex had been thinking the very same thing and so far hadn't come up with any answers. 'I'm not sure. Maybe someone wanted him to keep quiet about his role in my kidnap. When you think about it, he's really the only one who could verify who I am.'

She turned to look at him, her eyes wide with alarm. 'Do you think someone else knows who you are—apart from my brothers and me, I mean?'

He frowned as he thought about it. 'I don't know...possibly.'

'My father is not the only person who could verify your

identity,' she said. 'What about the couple who took you to Australia to be adopted?'

His brows met over his eyes. 'You think they could have something to do with this?'

'My father said it cost him everything to keep things quiet. I can only assume he meant the couple he paid to take you away.'

Alex rubbed at his jaw for a moment, the rasp of his hand against his unshaven skin almost too loud in the silence of the room. 'It would seem feasible they wouldn't want their role in it exposed,' he said. 'If they got wind of your father wanting to confess to his part in it they might have wanted to shut him up in case they were hauled before the courts.'

'The whole island has been talking about you ever since you arrived,' she reminded him. 'News often travels between the ports of Mont Avellana and Sicily. Perhaps the couple heard of it and became worried.'

'The one thing I know is you are best kept out of it, Amelia,' he said with a worried frown. 'Your brothers, too, need to keep their heads down until the police find out who is responsible.'

Amelia felt her stomach drop. 'You think we could be in some sort of danger?'

He gave her a sombre look. 'You're a Vialli. You've told me yourself how you've been a target for taunts. Who knows what people will be incited to do?'

She bit her lip in agitation. 'Maybe you should tell the king who you are right away.'

'I don't really think that's necessary just yet. I think we should stick with the plan to get his surgery over and done with, and once he's on the mend I might come forward.'

'What do you mean you *might* come forward? You *have* to come forward!'

'I came to this island as a commoner and I can just as easily leave as one,' he said.

She frowned at him incredulously. 'You mean not tell anyone?'

He gave an indifferent shrug. 'It would save a lot of heartache for my family if I leave things as they are. They're going to find it very hard to deal with the circumstances surrounding my adoption. My mother will blame herself, so will my father, not to mention my little sister, who has enough issues of her own to deal with.'

'But what about your other family, your biological brother and sisters?' she asked. 'Aren't they entitled to meet you after all these years of suffering? Don't they have the right to get to know you and welcome you into the family you were born into?'

His jaw tightened a fraction. 'I can't be Alessandro Fierezza.'

'You *are* Alessandro Fierezza whether you like it or not.'

He blew out a heavy sigh. 'What did I do to make my life so complicated?'

She moved towards him and grasped him by the hand. 'I know this is hard for you. It's hard for me too. I have to live with the guilt of my father's role in the destruction of your life. Don't make it worse by turning your back on your heritage.'

He gave her a lopsided smile. 'Those nuns did a really good job on you, didn't they?'

'What do you mean?'

He flicked her cheek with one finger in a gentle caress. 'You positively ooze with guilt.'

'I can't help it… I feel as if this is all my fault.'

'You're not responsible, Amelia. You didn't do anything wrong.'

'Other people won't see it that way.'

'I'm not interested in what other people think.'

Amelia sighed as Alex held her close, her thoughts tumbling around her head erratically.

Her father was dead.

It didn't seem real even though she had been preparing herself for this moment for months.

Alex spoke into her hair, his warm breath lifting the soft strands closest to her face. 'Your father wouldn't have suffered, Amelia. You have to comfort yourself with that. He would have died of smoke inhalation, especially with his lungs under-functioning the way they were. Rico said there was no sign of him trying to escape. He was found in bed.'

She suppressed a shudder and looked up at him. 'I should have been there. If I hadn't been out with you I would have heard something and perhaps been able to save him.'

'You are not to blame yourself,' Alex insisted. 'You had a perfect right to go out. Besides, if your father hadn't wanted you to go he would have said so, don't you think?'

'Yes…I guess you're right.' She gave a little sigh as she recalled her conversation with her father that morning before Rico had driven her to work. Her father had seemed pleased to hear she was spending time with the Australian doctor. He had even smiled as she'd bent down to kiss his sallow cheek and told her to have a good time.

She moved out of Alex's embrace to pace the room, her stomach churning as she thought about the future. The very few possessions she owned were lying in ashes in the remains of the cottage along with the body of her father.

'I don't know what to do…' She savaged her bottom lip again. 'This seems so…so…unreal. I feel like I'm on the outside of myself looking in. It's like it's happening to someone else, not me. How can I have lost my father in such a way? I mean, he was dying of cancer.… Every morning for the last month I've walked past his room and leaned against the door to check if he was still breathing. Now he's dead, murdered…'

'Listen, Amelia,' Alex said, taking her by the arms and holding her still in front of him. 'The police will take charge of this. You will be safe with me. I'll organise for you to have some clothes and essentials brought here. No doubt Rico and Silvio will have friends they can bunk down with.'

Her frown deepened as she looked up at him. 'But the police will surely ask a lot of questions. They'll want to know about possible motives and so on. How can we tell them of our suspicions without revealing your identity? Besides, Rico might have already mentioned something about you....'

Alex's expression clouded for a moment. 'It will take a few days for them to conduct their enquiries. Let's hope that's long enough for me to do the king's surgery. After that, if the news comes out about who I am, then so be it.'

There was the sound of a car pulling up outside and Amelia's eyes widened as they met his. 'Is that the police?' she asked in a whisper.

Alex looked through the gap in the curtains and nodded. He quickly dressed and answered the door and showed the two officers into the room where Amelia was standing, her hands in tight knots in front of her trembling body.

Alex stood to one side as the officers asked a series of questions, which Amelia answered as carefully as she could. Every now and again her worried gaze would flick to his, but if the police thought there was anything suspicious in it they didn't let on, although Alex couldn't help noticing the way the more senior officer watched Amelia with an intensity that was rather unsettling. But after he took copious notes and asked a few more questions about her father's affairs, he reiterated his earlier condolences and left soon after with the junior officer close behind.

Alex closed the door on their exit, his eyes meeting Amelia's across the room. 'I think our secret is safe for the time being but I suspect it won't be long before they put two and two together.'

'I know....' She hugged her arms close to her body. 'I felt like a criminal the whole time they were talking to me. I

always do around the police… It's because of my name.' She
eased herself away to look up at him. 'I need to see Rico and
Silvio just to make sure they're all right. Would you mind if
I borrowed your car?'

'Don't be silly,' he said, searching for his keys. 'I'll drive
you myself. Do you think they'll still be up there?'

She gave him a weary look as she followed him out to his
car. 'They'll be there.'

The thin curl of smoke rising eerily in the night air sent an
icy chill down Amelia's spine as Alex drove up the uneven
driveway. She stared at the remains of her family home,
unable to get her head around the fact that there was nothing
left. Not a single photo or article of clothing. There was
nothing but the grotesquely charred skeleton of the cottage
and silver ashes and the lingering smell of acrid smoke.

Once the last police vehicle drove away Rico and Silvio
came over to where she and Alex were standing, their faces
white with shock and their bodies visibly shaking as they
each in turn enveloped her in a short, somewhat awkward hug.

Rico held out his hand to Alex. 'My father told me who
you are,' he said with obvious embarrassment. 'I don't know
what to say.…'

Alex shook his hand. 'Your father did what he thought was
best at the time. It could have been much worse.'

Rico seemed at a loss for words and looked to his younger
brother for help. Silvio shifted uncomfortably and, with a slight
hesitation, offered his hand as well. 'I can see the likeness even
though it's dark up here,' he said. 'I was the one who first alerted
my father to the rumours about you. Does the king know?'

Alex shook his head and explained his reasons for keeping
his identity quiet until the king was out of danger.

'Did either of you mention anything to the police about the
rumours?' Amelia put in.

'No,' Silvio said. 'I don't even think the police are going to treat this as a murder investigation.'

She stared at him in shock. 'But why not?'

He gave a cynical shrug. 'One less Vialli on the island,' he said. 'There are plenty of people who have always suspected *Papà* was involved with the bandits. They'll be celebrating his death, not grieving it.'

'Has *Papà*…been taken away?' she asked.

'He was taken away a short time ago,' Rico said, swallowing convulsively as he glanced back at the remains of the cottage.

Amelia felt her insides cave in at what her older brother must have come upon when he'd returned to the cottage that evening.

'I was worried you were in there with him,' he said, and took a cigarette from Silvio with a distinct tremble of his hand.

She watched as Silvio flicked his lighter to ignite his brother's cigarette, the sudden flare of light illuminating the shocked pallor of his and Rico's faces, but for once she decided against lecturing them both on the dangers of smoking.

'Have the police found out anything?' she asked instead.

Silvio lit his own cigarette and took a deep drag before answering. 'Apparently no one in the neighbourhood heard or saw anything, or if they did they're not saying. But Rico's right—no doubt the police will make some token enquiries, but this is one case they won't be in a hurry to solve.'

Amelia felt her body begin to shake with reaction. The night was warm, but she began to shiver uncontrollably until Alex drew her close.

'I've arranged for your sister to stay with me for the time being,' he informed Rico and Silvio. 'Do you both have somewhere to stay?'

'Yes,' Silvio answered. 'I have some friends down at the port who will put us both up. I've been staying with them for the last couple of weeks.'

'I'm not planning on staying around once my father's

funeral is over,' Rico stated. 'I want to get away and start a new life without the past getting in the way.'

'Me too,' Silvio said. 'I have work lined up on Mont Avellana. You should think about leaving too, Amelia. Once the news breaks about Dr Hunter's identity it could get really unpleasant for you. Don't forget that whoever is responsible for *Papà*'s death was probably hoping you were in the cottage with him as you have been most nights.'

Amelia swallowed the lump of fear clogging her throat. 'I'm not going to run away,' she said with a determined lift of her chin. 'I have work to do here.'

'I'll keep an eye on her,' Alex assured them. 'She'll be safe with me.'

Physically maybe, but not emotionally, Amelia ruminated sadly as they left a short time later. She sat silently in the car beside Alex as he drove away from the ghostly remains of her family home, her grief over her father taking a second place to the sense of loss she felt at the thought of never being able to tell Alex how much she loved him. Once the news broke of his true identity their relationship would have to end.

Their two worlds had briefly collided but could never stay connected, not unless he was prepared to walk away from everything that was rightfully his, from everything her father had taken away from him thirty-four years ago....

CHAPTER FIFTEEN

ONCE they were back at his cottage, Alex handed Amelia a small tumbler of brandy, his expression still full of concern. 'How are you holding up? This must be such a terrible shock for you.'

She took the brandy and cupped it in her hands. 'It is.... I feel sort of numb.'

'That's understandable. Even when a death is expected it's still a shock when it finally happens, but in this instance it's much harder to deal with, given the circumstances.'

Amelia took a tiny sip of the fiery liquid. 'I know this sounds a bit strange, but I can't help feeling relieved he didn't suffer in the end. Dying from a terminal illness can be so...so awful for the patient as well as the relatives.'

Alex took one of her hands in his and began to stroke it soothingly. 'I know what you mean. I've seen too many people die from lung cancer to be under any illusions of how difficult it is in the last stages.'

Amelia looked at their joined hands before raising her gaze to meet his. 'Alex...it's very kind of you to offer to have me stay here with you, but I feel uncomfortable about what people will say, especially once the news breaks about your identity.'

'They can say what they like,' he said. 'They don't have to know our private arrangements. For all they know you could be sleeping in the spare room just like any other house guest.'

'Maybe I should do that.' She chanced a quick glance at him. 'Sleep in the spare room, I mean.'

He gave her a studied look. 'Is that what you'd prefer?'

She forced herself to hold his unwavering gaze. 'I'm not cut out for this…er…arrangement, as you call it.'

'You want to end our relationship?' he asked.

'I've known from the first that I'm being used to fill in the time,' she said.

His frown brought his dark brows together. 'You think that's what this is about?'

'Isn't it?'

'Of course it isn't. Look, I admit I've fast-tracked our relationship a bit, but that doesn't mean I'm not genuinely attracted to you.'

'But for how long?'

'How can anyone answer that?' he asked. 'I spent two years of my life with a woman I thought was in love with me but she apparently changed her feelings overnight. I'm sorry, Amelia, but I don't feel like making myself that vulnerable again. If you're not happy with our relationship as it stands, then feel free to walk away.'

Amelia inwardly cringed at his words. How could their relationship be genuine when he had no intention of it continuing? He was content to flirt and have fun, but it wasn't for ever. She had been a silly fool to even think for a moment that things could be any different.

'So what you want from me is a no-strings-and-no-emotions-involved temporary sexual relationship?' she asked.

'I hate to drag you kicking and screaming out of the Dark Ages, but being in love with a sexual partner is no longer a prerequisite,' he said. 'People nowadays can have very satisfactory relationships without the complications of feelings that rarely last the distance anyway.'

'So I'm a sex buddy—isn't that what it's called these days?'

'This is not the time for this discussion. You've just lost your father in terrible circumstances. Your whole world is crumbling around you. You need time to get your head around all this and quite frankly so do I.'

Amelia watched as he moved across the room, his back turned towards her. He was right, she thought. This wasn't just about her; it was about him as well. In some ways he had received an even bigger shock than she had. His whole life had changed and he was still trying to negotiate his way through it. She had at least been well prepared for the news of her father's death, and even though it had happened, as Alex had described, under terrible circumstances, at least she was still who she had always been—Amelia Vialli. Alex, on the other hand, had suddenly found himself caught between two worlds: that of his life back in Australia as Dr Alex Hunter surrounded by his loving adoptive family, and his new one here on Niroli, as Prince Alessandro Fierezza with a role set before him that was as daunting as it was inescapable.

But even so it was painful to accept that what they had experienced together was coming to its inevitable end. It had to. She was part of the family that had taken his heritage away from him.

'You're right,' she said, releasing a little sigh. 'This is hard for both of us.'

He turned to look at her. 'It's going to get harder, Amelia. I have to make some decisions in the next few days that less than one per cent of the population ever has to make. Whatever I decide is going to hurt someone somewhere and I'll have to live with that for the rest of my life.'

She swallowed at the anguish she could see written in stark lines on his face. She knew she too was going to be one of the people most likely to be hurt by whatever decision he made. 'I wish I could help you,' she said.

He gave her a twisted smile. 'No one can help me. I have

to do this alone. But right now you are the one who needs support. The next few days are going to be tough on you.'

'I'll be fine,' she said, knowing it was a lie. Inside she felt shell-shocked and vulnerable in a way she hadn't felt since her mother had died. She ached to feel secure, but it was as if her whole world were tipping out of control. Alex was offering her his support, but she knew it could only be temporary. He'd made it perfectly clear his emotions were not involved, which she could only assume meant he only saw their relationship as a brief interlude before he made his final decision about his future. The most painful part was recognising that, no matter what he decided, there was no place for her in either choice he made.

The day of the funeral was one of the most miserable days of Amelia's life. For a start it rained constantly, which meant the very few people who were considering attending decided against doing so at the last minute. Even Alex was unable to offer his support when a difficult case went overtime in Theatre.

Her brothers stood stiffly beside her during the brief service, their faces largely impassive, but inside she knew they were feeling the loss as keenly as she was.

Alex showed up just as they were leaving the cemetery and respectfully stood to one side as she said goodbye to her brothers, who were leaving the island the following day.

She joined him a few moments later, her face looking pinched and white, but even so she managed a small smile for him when he took her arm.

'Are you all right?' he asked.

She nodded and let out a little sigh and looked back at the grave that marked her father's final resting place. 'He lived such a hard life, but I can't help feeling he's finally at peace.' She turned back to look at him. 'How did your case go?'

'It was touch and go there for a while, but we managed to pull a miracle out of the hat. Sorry I couldn't make it in time.'

'It's all right,' she said as she let down her umbrella now he rain had ceased. 'You of all people wouldn't be expected o pay your last respects.'

He let a small silence fill the space between them before e announced, 'I'm doing the surgery on the king first thing omorrow.'

Her throat moved up and down as she held his gaze. 'Are ou nervous?'

'Why should I be?' he asked. 'As far as I'm concerned he's ust like any other patient.'

'But he's not just any other patient. He's—'

Alex placed the pad of his index finger against her lips to ilence her. 'As far as I'm concerned he's just an old man in eed of bypass surgery.'

Amelia felt her lips tingling at his touch, brief as it was. he felt as if she couldn't get enough of his touch even though he had spent every night since her father's death in Alex's rms. She knew their relationship was on borrowed time; the ense of urgency she felt had taken their intimacy to increas-ngly erotic levels until her whole body felt as if it would ever be the same. She longed to tell him she loved him but new it would not achieve anything except further pain for er in the end.

'I have to get back to the hospital,' Alex said with a quick lance at his watch. 'Are you working at the palace tonight?'

She nodded. 'But don't worry, I can make my own way here. Rico has left me the car.'

'I guess I'll see you at the hospital tomorrow afternoon.'

'Yes,' she said, forcing her lips into a tight smile. 'Good uck in the morning. I hope it goes well.'

His expression clouded for a brief moment. 'Yeah... hanks. I hope it does too.'

She watched him walk back towards his car, his long trides taking him farther and farther away. She could feel the

words to call him back tightening her throat, but they couldn'
get past the knot of emotion lodged there.

'I'm so sorry about your father,' Lucia said the following af
ternoon when Amelia came on the ward. 'Are you all right?

'I'm fine,' Amelia said as she put her bag away. 'It was :
horrible shock, but I'm coming to terms with it…more or less.

'Have the police found out what happened?'

'The case is now closed,' she said with a despondent sigh
'I was speaking to them before I came on duty. They're puttin;
it down to an accident, apparently suggesting my father fel
asleep while he was smoking in bed.'

Lucia grimaced in empathy. 'That's exactly what happenec
to my grandmother. She'd been told a thousand times not t(
smoke in bed, but she wouldn't listen. Fortunately she woke
up before things got out of control, but the very next week sh
was back at it, much to my mother's disgust.'

Amelia met Lucia's gaze. 'My father gave up smoking a:
soon as he found out he had cancer.'

Lucia's eyes went wide. 'What are you saying?'

'I don't know. He could have fallen asleep with a candle
burning, but I can't help feeling uneasy about it all.'

'You mean you think it wasn't an accident? That he was…
she swallowed over the word '…murdered?'

'I don't know. The police don't think so, but there are certainly
people on the island who would have liked to see him dead.'

'Has this got something to do with Alex Hunter?' Lucia asked

Amelia tried to disguise her startled look. 'What make:
you say that?'

'I don't know. It's just when my mother came over to hel;
me with the girls she told me how everyone is talking abou
Alex Hunter's amazing likeness to the Fierezzas and how
people are speculating on whether the prince was actually
killed all those years ago. I suppose you've heard the

rumours? They think Alex Hunter is Prince Alessandro.' Lucia gave a little chuckle of disbelief. 'It's totally crazy, don't you think? If you ask me, I think it shows just how old and desperate the king has become in looking for an heir to take his place.'

'Yes…it's certainly crazy…'

Lucia gave her a probing look. '*You're* not starting to believe all that nonsense, are you?'

Amelia avoided the other woman's eyes as she tidied some papers on the desk. 'If the palace officials think Alex Hunter is the prince, then surely they will conduct their own investigations to prove it either way.'

'Have you heard how the king's surgery went?' Lucia asked, glancing at the clock on the wall. 'It should be over by now.'

'No, not yet, but no news is good news, I suppose.'

'Were you on at the palace last night? How did the king seem?'

'He didn't sleep very well,' Amelia answered. 'But I guess that was to be expected. It's a big operation for an elderly man.'

She didn't tell her friend about the general air of excitement she'd been able to feel the whole time she had been there. The castle staff had bustled about in an atmosphere of high expectation, which she felt sure had nothing to do with the king's surgery. She wondered how they had come to know of Alex's identity. Had her father spoken to someone before he had died or had the palace staff activated their own investigation?

As she'd left the palace that morning she had wandered past the tiny grave of the child who had been buried in place of the prince, but there had been no fresh flowers in the brass vase, which had seemed to her to be rather remiss. It was as if the little child was to be of no significance now the real prince had been located.

'Poor little baby,' she'd murmured softly as she'd bent down to empty the sour water from the vase and replace the faded blooms with some sweet-smelling roses that had been growing nearby.

Lucia broke through her thoughts. 'At least the king is in the very best of hands,' she said, and then added with a teasing smile, 'and, speaking of those very clever hands, have they been anywhere near you lately? I heard you're sharing his cottage. Could it be you're sharing his bed as well?'

Amelia could feel her face heating, but forced herself to meet the other woman's gaze. 'Alex Hunter isn't going to be here for much longer. I would be a fool to get involved with him in anything other than a temporary way.'

Lucia's eyes twinkled as she leaned closer conspiratorially. 'But you're tempted, aren't you? Go on, admit it. He's totally irresistible. If I wasn't married with two kids and in desperate need of a tummy tuck, I'd make a play for him myself.'

Amelia was relieved when a patient pressed the buzzer by his bedside for attention. She gave Lucia a weak smile and headed off down the corridor, but she felt her friend's speculative gaze following her all the way.

Amelia had not long finished attending to the patient who had summoned her when she caught sight of Alex coming down the corridor to the cardiac unit with Dr Morani by his side.

'Ah, Amelia,' the doctor greeted her cheerily. 'We've just returned from the private hospital. We have wonderful news. The king has come through the surgery very well. He is expected to make a full recovery. Alex did a brilliant job.'

'Congratulations,' she addressed Alex, not surprised at how tired he looked. 'It must be a relief to have it over with.'

He let out a barely audible sigh. 'It is.'

'Dr Hunter?' The cardiac unit ward clerk came towards them with a harried look on her face. 'There are some royal officials waiting to speak to you in your office. They refused to make an appointment and insisted on waiting.'

Alex met Amelia's eyes briefly before turning back to the ward clerk. 'It's all right. I'll see them now. I can do a round later.' He looked at Dr Morani and asked, 'You don't mind if Sister Vialli comes with me, do you, Vincenzo?'

'Of course not,' Dr Morani replied. 'Things are pretty quiet on the ward.'

Amelia blinked at Alex once the others had moved on. 'Me?'

'Yes, you,' Alex said, leading her by the elbow towards his office.

'Do you think this is about you know what?' she asked in a worried undertone.

His expression was grim as he glanced down at her. 'It looks like it,' he said. 'Just before I scrubbed for his operation the king grasped my arm before being anaesthetised. He looked at my birthmark scars for a moment and then looked me in the eye and called me Alessandro with tears in his eyes. I had a hard time keeping my head throughout the procedure, especially as the theatre staff were giving me speculative looks all the time.'

'But you did it, Alex,' she said softly. 'The operation was a success.'

He didn't answer, but opened his office door and indicated for her to go in before him, but Amelia could tell he was struggling to deal with the situation now it was coming to a head.

Four men in suits stood as they came into the room, their expressions speaking for them as their collective gaze went to Alex.

Amelia stood silently as the leader stepped forward and informed Alex of the investigations that had been conducted over his identity, including the details of his adoption. They had even gone so far as to apply for a warrant to examine his medical records, which clearly documented the removal of a strawberry birthmark several years ago. They had also gone to the extraordinary lengths of conducting a DNA test on the glass he had sipped from on the first night he had gone to the palace.

'So there's absolutely no doubt?' Alex asked once the man finished.

The official shook his head. 'No doubt at all. You are His Royal Highness Prince Alessandro Fierezza. Your family will want to spend time with you as soon as the king is out of hospital and a press release has already been prepared to be released immediately.'

Alex visibly stiffened. 'I'd like this kept out of the press for as long as possible. I would like some time to prepare my adoptive family of this news. It will come as a dreadful shock to them.'

'We will do what we can, but I can make no promises,' the official said. 'The king gave instructions that as soon as your identity was verified a press statement would be released.'

Amelia saw Alex's throat move up and down and her heart tightened painfully at what he must be going through.

'We have made arrangements for you to move into the royal household immediately,' the official said.

'No.' Alex held up his hand. 'I need some time to get used to this. I'd prefer my own private space for the time being.'

'But King Giorgio will be concerned for your safety,' the official insisted. 'And you will need to be briefed on your royal duties.'

'I don't care,' Alex said implacably. 'I still have work to do and I don't see any reason to change my living arrangements.'

'Your work will have to end,' the official said. 'The king will not allow you to maintain your profession. It is against royal protocol. The ruler of Niroli must devote his life to the kingdom. Therefore maintaining a profession is out of the question.'

Alex's jaw tightened, but he didn't answer, Amelia assumed because he didn't trust himself to remain polite. She could see the tension move from his jaw to encompass his whole body; even his spine was rigid with it and his expression dark as a stormy cloud.

'There is one other rather sensitive subject we wish to bring up with you.' The leading official spoke into the stiff silence. 'But perhaps it would be best if the young lady was not present when we discuss it.'

Amelia felt her face begin to flame, but as she made a move to leave Alex's strong fingers captured her wrist and brought her back to his side. 'No,' he said. 'I would prefer for her to stay.'

'Very well.' The official looked distinctly uncomfortable. 'It has come to the king's attention that you are currently...er...involved in a relationship with Miss Vialli. Is that correct?'

'I don't see that it's anyone's business but my own,' Alex responded coolly.

'It is everybody's business when the woman you have chosen to be involved with is the daughter of the man who kidnapped you when you were an infant. The people of Niroli will not accept her, not even as your mistress.'

'Amelia had nothing to do with her father's activities,' Alex pointed out. 'I don't see why she should be discriminated against for something she had nothing whatsoever to do with.'

'Are you saying that your current relationship with Miss Vialli is likely to become more permanent?'

Amelia held her breath as she waited for Alex to respond to the official's blunt question. The silence stretched and stretched like a thin wire that at any moment could snap and flick back with a stinging blow.

'My relationship with Miss Vialli is not something I am prepared to discuss right now,' Alex finally said. 'Now if you'll excuse me, I have patients to see.'

'We will be in contact with you tomorrow,' one of the other officials informed him. 'There are legal matters to see to and you will need to be advised on official protocol and your schedule of duties. Also, your siblings will want to speak with you.'

'Thank you for your time,' the leading official said. 'We realise this is a very difficult situation for you and the king will not want you to suffer any undue stress.'

'Thanks, I really appreciate it,' Alex said, with no attempt to tone down his sarcasm.

One of the men turned to face Amelia just as they were leaving. 'The king has advised me to terminate your contract at the palace. He will no longer need your services as a nurse,' he informed her officiously before turning with the others to leave.

Amelia waited until the door had closed on their exit before she brought her gaze to meet Alex's. 'You really didn't have to spare my feelings, Alex,' she said with a distinct chill in her tone. 'You could have told them straight out that our relationship wasn't permanent.'

He frowned darkly. 'I'm not prepared to be told how to live my life, certainly not at my age.'

'But it's true what they said. I won't be accepted as your mistress. They don't even want me to take care of the king any more.' She took an unsteady breath and continued, hoping he wouldn't be able to see through her emotionally detached act. 'I think it's time to say goodbye, Alex. It's not as if we have any lasting feelings for each other. It was nice while it lasted and I really appreciate what you did for me in stepping into the breach after my father died. But I think it's time we ended this relationship. It's not what I want and, if you're honest with yourself, it's not what you want either.'

His mouth was white-tipped as he looked down at her. 'You seem to have made up your mind about this. Is there any point in me trying to convince you otherwise?'

'What would be the point?' she asked. 'You have responsibilities to face now that people know who you are. Like my brothers, I no longer want to live my life in the shadow of what my father did. If I remain involved with you, even temporarily, it will cause further shame and hurt for me and I just can't face

t.' She stepped towards him and offered him her hand.
Goodbye, Alex.'

He took her hand and held it for longer than necessary.
Where will you stay?' he asked, his fingers intertwining with
ers.

She hoped he couldn't see the glimmer of tears in her eyes
s she raised her gaze to his. 'Signora Gravano is planning to
isit her daughter. I will probably house-sit for her until I
ecide what to do.'

He gave her a ghost of a smile. 'If ever you need to take the
hort cut I'll make sure that bramble is under control.'

She smiled at his attempt at his old humour. 'I won't be
aking any short cuts any more. I think I might too move on
nce I get a bit of money behind me.'

His eyes were dark and serious as they held hers. 'If you
eed anything I'd be happy to help. Money or whatever, you
nly have to ask.'

Amelia adopted a flippant tone for the sake of her pride.
I guess I could always get a personal reference from you.
Now that would look good on my CV. I'd be able to get any
ob I wanted.'

A small frown began to wrinkle his brow. 'The press will
o doubt start hounding you. Can I trust you to keep our
revious relationship out of the newspapers?'

It hurt her that he even had to ask, but she did her best not
o show it. 'What happened between us was a little fling that
as no relevance to anyone but us.' She gave him a fabricated
mile and hoped it would pass for the real thing. 'I bet you
von't even remember what my name was in a year's time,
Alex—or should I call you Prince Alessandro?'

His eyes fell away from hers as he released her hand. 'Right
t this moment, little elf, I don't know who the hell I am.'

'You'll always be Alex Hunter to me,' she said softly, but
he wasn't sure if he'd even heard her. He had moved to stand

in front of the window, his eyes looking out to the distance, his back turned towards hers, his shoulders looking as if the weight of the whole new world he was about to face were pressing down on them.

CHAPTER SIXTEEN

'OF COURSE you can stay with me,' Signora Gravano said as she ushered Amelia inside her cottage. 'So it's true then? Dr Hunter is actually the prince?'

'Yes, it's true,' Amelia said, letting her small bag drop to the floor with a sad little thud. 'He is the prince.'

'The poor man.' Signora Gravano sighed. 'Think of what he must be going through.'

'I know,' she said with a sigh. 'I can't help thinking about his adoptive family as well. This sort of thing affects everyone.'

'I know it must be hard for you too, Amelia, but you surely can't have been thinking there was a future in your relationship with him, especially once you knew who he really was?'

Amelia sank to the nearest chair and put her head in her hands. 'I know...but a girl can always dream, can't she?'

The old woman stroked the black silk of Amelia's hair. 'I feel sorry for both of you. You have both been caught between two very different worlds. He has responsibilities he must face now that he has discovered his birth origins.'

'I just wish I could have had more time with him.'

'He is a member of a royal family, my dear. You have to accept that.'

Amelia lifted her reddened eyes to the old woman's. 'I now...it's just hard to fall in love with someone and then they suddenly turn into someone else…someone unreachable… unattainable…'

'You poor child—so you have truly fallen in love with him?'
She nodded miserably. 'I just couldn't help it.'

'What about his feelings?'

'He's not in love with me,' she said miserably. 'He just wanted a quick fling and, fool that I am, I agreed to it.'

'How has he coped with the news of his past? It must have come as a complete shock to find he is a prince.'

Amelia thought about it for a moment. 'He's definitely changed. When I first met him he was so funny…so light-hearted and easygoing. I really liked that about him. But since he found out about his past he's become…I don't know…sort of different…serious, and he hardly smiles any more.'

'It is a highly unusual set of circumstances,' the old woman pointed out. 'Most people who go in search of their birth parents worry they might uncover some sort of abuse or criminal behaviour in their family of origin. Instead, Dr Hunter has found out he is heir to a throne, not to mention the details of his kidnap as an infant.'

'Which my father was responsible for,' Amelia reminded her unnecessarily.

'Yes, that makes it all the more difficult, but if he had genuine feelings for you he would not let something like that stand in his way.'

Amelia let out a heavy sigh. She had been thinking the very same thing. If Alex Hunter wanted her in his life on a permanent basis wouldn't he have said so by now?

'He doesn't have genuine feelings for me. Right from the start I've known he's been here for a good time, not a long time. Even now that he's found out who he really is doesn't change that. If he decides to stay and take up the throne there would be no way he would be able to have me as his partner. The king has already dismissed me as his nurse and Alex stood there and said nothing in my defence as the officials delivered the news. But even if he did choose to return to his life in Australia and took me with him, how could his adoptive parents ever accept me given my background and my father's role in his kidnap?'

Signora Gravano gave her a sympathetic look. 'It seems you are not unlike your dear mother after all, Amelia. You fell in love with the wrong man at the wrong time.'

Amelia felt the weighty truth of her elderly friend's words like a burdensome yoke around her neck. Her mother's dreams of a happy, settled life with the man she loved so desperately had been totally shattered by circumstances beyond her control. And now Amelia's life was heading along the same pathway to destruction, there seemed no way of avoiding similar heartbreak. She loved a man whom she could not have, a man who did not want her, and—even if he did—would have to give up everything in order to have her.

Amelia was glad her part-time shifts at the community health centre kept her away from the Free Hospital for the next couple of days. The thought of running into Alex in the hospital corridors or on the ward was far too upsetting. She still couldn't quite believe she had managed to convince him she was no longer interested in him. She had secretly hoped he would have put up more of a fight, but he had taken her rejection with barely a flinch of male pride.

She had heard that the king was now back at the palace, having made an excellent recovery from his surgery and, as expected, the press had gone wild with the news of Alex Hunter's true identity. For the most part she had tried to ignore the news reports and papers, but it was impossible to escape the sense of excitement filling the island at the news of the prince's return to his rightful home.

Late one afternoon Amelia ran into Lucia as she was doing a last-minute errand for an elderly patient.

'Amelia, I'm so glad I caught you. There's been a journalist hanging out at the hospital for days desperate to speak to you.'

'They want to speak to *me*?' Amelia blinked at her friend in shock.

'Of course they want to speak to you,' Lucia answered. 'It's exactly what the big-name magazines are looking for, the interview with the prince's recent love interest. You could make an absolute fortune out of it.'

Amelia's heart began to thud in alarm. 'You didn't tell them anything, did you?'

Lucia looked a little shamefaced. 'Well…er…not much.'

Amelia gave her a penetrating look. 'How much?'

Lucia bit her lip. 'I'm sorry…but the journalist was so persistent and since you don't have a phone…I sort of told them what I knew.'

Amelia closed her eyes as she pinched the bridge of her nose in distress. 'Oh, Lucia, how could you?'

'I'm sorry. I just thought since it was all over between you now you wouldn't mind. It's not like you're seeing him any more. He's up at the palace being briefed on what's expected of him now he's finished his work at the hospital.'

So that was why she hadn't seen any sign of him at the cottage, Amelia thought as she chewed the rough end of one nail.

'I'm sure it won't do much harm for people to know you and Prince Alessandro were an item,' Lucia said. 'The journalist was intrigued with the whole Vialli bandit thing. It gave it that whole star-crossed lovers angle.'

'I'll have to see Alex and explain it wasn't me,' Amelia said, beginning to gnaw at her bottom lip instead of her nail.

'Why shouldn't you cash in on this, Amelia?' Lucia asked. 'It's not as if this won't happen again. Any woman he looks at in the future will be instant newspaper fodder. You might

well get something out of it while you can. The way I see
, he used you. He had his little fling, but as soon as he found
ut who he really was he let you go.'

Amelia didn't bother telling Lucia it was her who had been
he one to put an end to their relationship. 'Has the article been
printed yet?' she asked.

'It came out this morning,' Lucia said, and, rummaging in
er bag, handed her a glossy magazine. 'It's on page three.'

Amelia opened the magazine and grimaced as she saw a
photo of Alex and her sitting at the restaurant in Santa Fiera on
heir first date. 'How on earth did they get this photo?' she asked.

'Someone must have taken it in the restaurant and sold it
o the magazine,' Lucia suggested.

Amelia quickly read through the article and closed the
magazine with trembling fingers. 'Oh, Lucia, it makes me sound
ike a social-climbing tart using him to make myself a fortune.'

'Yes…well, the journalist did stretch the truth a bit, I
hought,' Lucia said with another sheepish look as she took
he magazine back and stuffed it in her bag.

Amelia let out her breath in a ragged stream. 'He asked me
ot to speak to anyone about our relationship. I'll have to see
im and apologise.'

'I don't like your chances,' Lucia said. 'He's a prince now,
emember? You can't just turn up and see him or even make
n appointment. Any contact you have has to be approved by
he palace officials.'

Amelia knew she wasn't going to be welcome at the palace,
ut she had to see Alex again regardless. She made her way
here as soon as she could, but, as she had more or less
xpected, the guards refused her entry. She pleaded with them,
ut they remained coldly resolute until Alex appeared from
round a corner.

'It's all right, gentlemen,' he said. 'Miss Vialli will not be
ere for long.'

Amelia felt the bite of Alex's fingers as he practically dragged her into one of the side doors of the ancient palace by one arm. 'Just the person I want to see,' he said, closing the door behind them.

She tried to pull out of his hold but his fingers tightened. 'I should have known you weren't to be trusted,' he ground out. 'How much did they pay you for that interview?'

'I didn't give an interview—' she began, but he cut her off.

'You probably knew all along who I was. No doubt your family put you up to this. You're a Vialli, after all. Treachery is in your blood. You saw a chance to make a fortune out of this and you went for it the first chance you could.'

'No…that's not true, Alex—'

'Don't insult me by lying to me now you've achieved what you set out to achieve,' he lambasted her. 'You lied to me from the start. No doubt that little convent story was part of the whole attempt to lure me in. But you're no innocent. You're a scheming little traitor like the rest of your family. I feel disgusted with myself for falling for it. You were simply waiting until you could get what you wanted out of it.'

'No—' Her one-word denial came out strangled, but he carried on as if she hadn't spoken.

'I even fancied myself in love with you for a time, but that was all part of your plan, wasn't it?' he asked coldly. 'To get me to the point where I had to choose between you and the throne. I can't have both and you knew it. What a victory that would have been for your republican family. The kidnapped heir was finally returned, but he was as good as useless as he wanted the very thing that would take away his right to the kingdom.'

'No,' she began again, her stomach churning in despair. 'You don't understand…'

His eyes blazed like black diamonds as they hit on hers. 'You've wasted your efforts, Amelia. I don't want you or the

hrone,' he said. 'I've made up my mind. I'm going back to
Australia to continue my work. I've already told the king.'

Amelia moistened her dry mouth as she struggled to take
in what he'd said.

He dragged a hand through his hair and continued,
'They're not happy, of course, but I have to do what is right
for me. My real family is the one who reared me and loved
me for the last thirty-four years. I had nothing to do with what
happened in the past. It was a quirk of fate, and I don't see
why I should give up years of intensive training to take on a
role I have no desire for. I might be a prince by birthright, but
that's not who I am now.'

She stared at him speechlessly, her emotions in complete
turmoil. He was turning down his right to the throne, but for
all the wrong reasons. It had nothing to do with her. She
would never have stood in his way, even though it would have
cost her everything.

'Aren't you going to say anything in your defence?' he
asked. 'Haven't you got some carefully prepared speech to
convince me of your innocence? That's what I would expect
from someone like you.'

Amelia met his glittering gaze. 'I can't change your mind,
Alex. You've come to the decisions you'd made on the basis
of what you believe to be true and no doubt anything I say
will not change your views. I didn't know you were a prince.
In fact I didn't even know who you were the first time I met
you. You could have been a peasant just like me rather than
the esteemed surgeon you are, but I loved your quirky sense
of humour and the way you laughed at life.'

Alex watched as she brushed a tear from the corner of her
eye, but he didn't reach out to her.

'I feel sad that you no longer have that ability,' she went
on in a soft, regretful tone. 'You've changed since you've
found out about your birth origins. I liked the old Alex

much more than the new one, but I guess that's what life has dished up to you. You are not one person now, but two and, as you said, you've had to decide which one you will be from now on. I admire your decision to be Alex Hunter the cardiac surgeon, for I think he is the real you, not the Prince of Niroli.'

Alex swallowed, trying to get control of his emotions. Could he have got it wrong about her? The palace officials had hinted at her younger brother's involvement in a second-wave rebellion against the monarchy, warning him of the danger of trusting anyone from within the Vialli family.

'I'm sorry about the article you saw,' Amelia said into the silence. 'I know you won't believe me but I had nothing whatsoever to do with it. I have been working at the community health centre for the last two days. I haven't been in contact with any journalists, but unfortunately one of my colleagues at the Free Hospital took it upon herself to speak for me to a journalist. I am sorry you have been hurt by that disclosure. She meant no harm, so please don't hold it against her.'

Alex watched in silence as she moved past him to leave. He didn't stop her even though he wanted to. The door closed behind her and he was left with the faint scent of her presence, like a ghost coming back to haunt him.

The pastel fingertips of dawn were streaking the sky when Amelia returned to the palace the following morning on a completely different mission. She had determined she would pay her respects to the innocent little boy whom nobody seemed to be considering now the real prince had been found. She had gathered some wildflowers, the early-morning dew still clinging to their delicate petals like crystal tears.

Fortunately one of the guards on duty recognised her from the previous day and allowed her through. She thanked him and moved like a shadow towards the family graveyard only o come up short when she saw a tall figure standing there ooking down at the tiny headstone.

Alex looked up at the sound of her footfall, his expression looking pale, as if he hadn't slept well. His lips moved n the semblance of a rueful smile. 'I thought for a moment ou were a ghost.'

She gave him a wry look. 'I would have thought that should ave been my line.'

His forehead creased into a frown as he turned back to ook at the tiny grave in front of him. 'It's weird looking down t this little grave thinking it could have been me.'

She came to stand next to him, bending down after a noment to carefully arrange the flowers she had brought.

Alex shifted his gaze to the two larger graves with his biological parents' names written above the family motto, an ching poignancy filling his chest that they would for ever emain strangers to him.

'I thought I should do this one last time, but I wonder if nyone will tend to this little boy's grave now,' Amelia said as he straightened and dusted off her hands. 'Maybe they'll dig t up and remove it. After all, he's not the real prince, just a ttle peasant boy of no significance.'

'Amelia…'

She turned to face him, her spine stiff with what little pride he had left. 'As soon as I have some money I will reimburse ou for the items you bought for me after my father's death. t may take a little longer than expected since, as you know, our grandfather no longer requires my services, but I will nake sure I get it to you as soon as possible.'

He drew his brows together in a heavy frown. 'He shouldn't ave fired you like that,' he said. 'The least he could have done vas to tell you to your face instead of sending his officials to lo it for him.'

'I didn't hear you offer a word of protest at the time,' she pointed out a little tightly. 'But then perhaps you'd already decided I wasn't to be trusted and was best removed from your life.'

He looked back at the graves once more, his shoulder hunched as he shoved his hands in the pockets of his trousers. 'I shouldn't have accused you of going to the press without checking the facts first.'

'Oh, so someone verified my story, did they? What a pity you didn't believe me in the first place.'

'I don't blame you for being angry with me,' he said bringing his gaze back to hers. 'I wasn't thinking when I said those things to you last night. I was looking for a scapegoat. Unfortunately my parents had heard the news before I could speak to them personally. It totally devastated them and I'm afraid I took it out on you.'

Amelia's expression softened in concern. 'Are they all right?' she asked. 'What about your sister? Has she heard?'

He gave her a glimmer of a sad smile. 'Not that I know. I've sent her an e-mail, one of many, but she hasn't answered yet. My parents are slowly getting used to the fact of my heritage, but it will take a while for it to sink in.'

'What about you?' she asked, her heart aching all over again for him. 'How are you coping?'

His eyes met hers. 'I feel caught between two very different worlds. The king...' he paused and added with a rueful twist '...I mean, my grandfather, desperately wants me to take up the throne, as do my other relatives I've met, apart from Luca, who seems to be the only one with any real sense of what I'm going through.'

'But you've decided not to take up the throne.'

'I can't turn my back on years of training, Amelia,' he said. 'My adoptive parents sacrificed a lot to get me where I am. Not only that, the patients I've served all these years really mean something to me. If I walk away from the research I've been doing and this new procedure I can't be sure someone else will take up where I left off. I feel I owe it to everyone to carry on the work I'm doing.'

'It's a tough decision,' she said. 'But surely your family will understand…your biological one, I mean.'

He let out a long-winded sigh. 'I'm starting up a fund for the Free Hospital. I thought it was one way I could keep my ties on Niroli without seeming to walk away without some sort of recognition of who I am…or who I was, I suppose I should say.'

'That's a wonderful gesture…. I'm sure much good will come out of it.'

There was a tiny silence broken only by the chirruping of birds in the shrubs nearby.

'Amelia—'

'Alex…I mean, Alessandro…'

He grimaced. 'Please don't call me that.'

'Your Highness?'

'That's even worse,' he said. 'Just call me Alex.'

'Alex, then.' She held out her hand to him. 'I hope you have a good journey home. It was…nice to meet you.'

Alex took her hand in his. 'Amelia…there's something I need to ask you…'

She swallowed at the dark intensity of his eyes as they held hers. 'Yes?'

'When did you know I was the prince?'

Tears burned in the backs of her eyes, but she blinked them back determinedly. She had to let him go, she knew it, but it hurt far more than she could ever have imagined. There was no place for her in his life, not here on Niroli and certainly not in Australia where his family was still trying to get over the shock of his past.

'Answer me, Amelia.' He tightened his hold as she tried to pull away. 'I need to know.'

Her bottom lip started to quiver, but somehow she got it under control as she held his unwavering gaze.

'Did you know who I was before you slept with me that first time?' he asked.

'What difference does it make?'

'Did you sleep with me because I was Alex Hunter or Prince Alessandro?'

'Don't make this any harder for me, Alex,' she begged.

His hold tightened even further. 'Answer me.'

She looked up at him with eyes full of anguish. 'I slept with you because I fell in love with you. I swore I wouldn't be so foolish to fall in love with anyone again, let alone a man who could offer me nothing in return. But I couldn't seem to help myself. I'm sorry....' She brushed at her eyes with the back of her hand. 'I know this is the last thing you need to hear right now.... I won't cause you any trouble. I'm leaving the island so you won't have to see me again.'

'But what if I want to see you again?' he asked. 'What if I told you I was a complete idiot to allow you to walk away from me without telling you how I feel, how I felt from the first moment I saw you, but that I hadn't realised it until the prospect of never seeing you again began to hit home?'

She blinked at him through her tears, her heart leaping in hope. 'Y-you want to see me...some time?'

He smiled one of his lazy smiles. 'I was thinking more along the lines of *all* the time. What do you say, little elf? I know I've asked you this before, but it can't hurt to run it by you one more time. Do you want to run away with me and have my babies?'

Amelia's mouth dropped open. 'I can't believe you said that.'

He grinned down at her. 'That's what you said the last time. I was hoping you might actually believe me this time around. I want you to be my wife. I want you by my side for the rest of my life.'

'You mean…' she swallowed convulsively, her eyes wide and her voice scratchy '…you mean you're not joking?'

He shook his head. 'And to put your mind at ease it didn't just slip out either. I just wanted to make sure you were promising to marry the right guy.'

She looked up at him in growing wonder. 'How do I know if you're the right guy?' she asked as a little smile began to tip up the edges of her mouth.

'Which one of us do you want to marry?' he asked, 'Alex Hunter or His Royal Highness Prince Alessandro Fierezza?'

'I want to marry whichever one loves me the most.'

He kissed the tip of her nose and said, 'Then you've got yourself one hell of a bargain, because we both love you to distraction. Now how's that for a package deal? Are you going to take it or leave it?'

She smiled at him in pure joy and lifted her mouth to meet his. 'I'll take it,' she said.

TURN THE PAGE TO DISCOVER MORE ABOUT

THE

Royal

HOUSE OF NIROLI

THE RULES OF THE
ROYAL HOUSE OF NIROLI

Rule 1: The ruler of Niroli must be a moral leader for the people and is bound to keep order in the Royal House. Any act which brings the monarchy into disrepute through immoral conduct or criminal activity will rule a contender out of the succession to the throne.

Rule 2: No member of the Royal House may be joined in marriage without previous consent and approval of the ruler. Any marriage concluded against this rule implies exclusion from the house, deprivation of honours and privileges.

Rule 3: No marriage is permitted if the interests of Niroli become compromised through the union.

Rule 4: It is not permitted for the ruler of Niroli to marry a person who has previously been divorced.

Rule 5: The ruler forbids marriage between members of the Royal House who are blood relations.

Rule 6: The ruler directs the education of all the members of the Royal House, even when the general care of the education of children belongs to their parents.

Rule 7: Without the approval or consent of the ruler, no member of the Royal House can make debts over the possibility of payment.

Rule 8: No member of the Royal House can accept inheritance nor any donation without the consent and approval of the ruler.

Rule 9: The ruler of Niroli must dedicate their life to the Kingdom. Therefore they are not permitted to have a profession.

Rule 10: Members of the Royal House must reside in Niroli or in a country allowed by the ruler. The ruler can give permission for Royal House members to live elsewhere, but the ruler must reside in Niroli.

THE ORIGINS OF THE RULES OF THE ROYAL HOUSE OF NIROLI

The Rules of Niroli have dictated the lives—and loves—of the Fierezza family for centuries. In a recent speech the ageing King heralded them as the backbone of the monarchy, provoking speculation that, as unrest begins to bubble away under the surface of the Nirolian people, the Royal House is pulling its traditions even closer. The Rules may be deemed old-fashioned, and even out of touch, but to this day they have never failed the turbulent Fierezza family! As a whole, the Rules are designed to provide unity and continuity for the island of Niroli. They ensure that the Royal Family conducts itself with dignity—to set an example for its subjects—and keep all the Fierezza firmly under the control of the monarch.

The Rules

Rule 1: The ruler must be a moral leader. Any act which brings the Royal House into disrepute will rule a contender out of the succession to the throne.

Origin: King Alvaro II, who ruled for forty years in the sixteenth century, was a pious and devoted ruler. He added this rule, claiming that he believed that a King of Niroli could have no greater calling than to ensure that he provided a moral compass for the Royal Family and his subjects.

Rule 2: No member of the Royal House may be joined in marriage without consent of the ruler. Any such union concluded results in exclusion and deprivation of honours and privileges.

Rule 3: No marriage is permitted if the interests of Niroli become compromised through the union.

Origin: Both rule 2 and rule 3 come from the time that the Fierezza dynasty was first formed, when it was considered essential that the King maintained control over his family and who they married, so that any union would strengthen the illustrious House of Niroli.

Rule 4: It is not permitted for the ruler of Niroli to marry a person who has previously been divorced.

Origin: Another ruler, King Benedicio, who was concerned with the morals of the Royal House considered that it was vital that anybody marrying into it had a spotless reputation. Following Prince Francesco's attempt to marry a divorced European countess with a dubious past in 1793, King Benedicio deemed it necessary to add this rule.

Rule 5: Marriage between members of the Royal House who are blood relations is forbidden.

Origin: Many royal houses have suffered from inbreeding, as cousins, and even nieces and uncles, have married each other across the years. King Dominico I declared in 1752 that to keep the Fierezza bloodline strong and healthy, this practice would not be tolerated in the Royal House.

Rule 6: The ruler directs the education of all members of the Royal House, even when the general care of the children belongs to their parents.

Origin: In common with most of the ruling houses of Europe, it has always been considered vital that all members of the Fierezza dynasty are brought up with an education which prepares them for their role in the Royal House of Niroli.

Rule 7: Without the approval or consent of the ruler, no member of the Royal House can make debts over the possibility of payment.

Origin: A relatively recent addition to the rules, this was added in 1950, when Ricardo Fierezza, an inveterate gambler, found himself in huge financial difficulties after he banked on certain deals coming to fruition that subsequently failed. In order to avoid any more scandals of this nature, the Royal House decided that a rule governing the Fierezzas' financial conduct was in order.

Rule 8: No member of the Royal House can accept inheritance nor any donation without the consent and approval of the ruler.

Origin: In the early years of the Fierezzas' rule over Niroli, King Pietro faced a possible usurpation of his throne from his younger brother, Prince Guiseppe, following the latter's acceptance of a huge sum of money from the King of Aragon, Alfonso V. Alfonso wished to gain control of the increasingly wealthy island, already famed for its trading ports, and was prepared to pay Guiseppe to raise an army and buy the support of any dissident nobles. After his defeat, in 1427, Guiseppe was exiled and King Pietro added this rule to ensure that there could be no repeat of this kind of rebellion ever again.

Rule 9: The ruler of Niroli must dedicate their life to the Kingdom. Therefore they are not permitted to have a profession.

Origin: Another rule that is a relatively new addition. As the administrative machine has grown, the kings of Niroli have found themselves less burdened with the machinations of state. In 1897, King Adriano, a scholarly and shy ruler, consulted over the possibility that he would take up a teaching post. It was decided that the ruler of Niroli must be absolutely dedicated to the island and that involvement in other professions was undesirable and detrimental to the long-term survival of the monarchy.

*Rule 10: Members of the Royal House must reside in Niroli or in a country approved by the ruler. However, the ruler **must** reside in Niroli.*

Origin: As the Fierezzas' lifestyles became increasingly jet-set, this rule was added as a pre-emptive measure to ensure that the ruler of Niroli would always be able to control the whereabouts of his family. In addition, it was felt that it should be enshrined that the monarch, as part of his dedication to Niroli, must live on the island to provide a focus and a symbol of unity.

A BRIEF HISTORY OF NIROLI

Niroli has a colourful and fascinating history filled with ancient rivalries, rebellions and the fight for the ultimate prize —the crown of Niroli.

The Fierezza family has ruled since the Middle Ages and is one of the richest royal families in the world, having founded its fortune on ancient trading routes, thanks to Niroli's prime position to the south of Sicily. Thanks to these links, it has traditionally been seen as the 'Gateway to the East'.

Since the establishment of the Fierezza dynasty, Niroli has thrived as an important European port, situated on major trading routes for spice, wine and perfume. However, while Niroli has prospered, it has a turbulent history right up to the modern day, and after a civil war in 1972 Niroli lost control of the neighbouring island Mont Avellana, which has become a republic. In addition to this, a group of bandits, known as the Viallis, who are ex-Barbary corsairs, formed a resistance against the monarchy. The height of their rebellious activity was in the 1970s and a few remaining Viallis still live in the foothills of the Niroli mountain range.

NIROLI – A TOURIST'S GUIDE

The Island of Niroli

With all it has to offer, who would not be tempted by a holiday on the beautiful island of Niroli? The climate is very agreeable, particularly to the south of the island. There are beautiful sandy beaches, especially around the new development area on the south coast which has been built to attract tourists. In this area you will find luxurious five-star hotels, casinos, restaurants, bars, etc., perfect for a relaxing and sophisticated holiday.

Things to See

The island also has a rich and varied history—don't miss the chance to explore its wonderful Roman ruins. In the north east of the island, there is a Roman amphitheatre where concerts are still performed today, particularly during the festivals celebrating the grape- and olive-picking seasons. There are also many fine castles to explore. Visitors must see the stunning main town of Niroli. If you enter the port by boat it is particularly impressive, as you see the town sprawling up the hillside in front of you, with the historic old town to your left and the palace just in view. Do wander round the old town and soak up the atmosphere, as well as stopping at the numerous charming shops and exclusive boutiques.

Things to Do

For those who are into more active pursuits, there are plenty of opportunities for diving and swimming, then afterwards relax in the wonderful spa and beauty treatment area on the east coast. To the west of the island you can walk and climb in the mountains and take in the stunning views across the Mediterranean. The central part of the island is devoted mainly to agriculture, with the vineyards extending to the rolling foothills of the mountains. There are also olive groves, orchards and livestock and Niroli is deservedly famous for its fine olive oil and wonderful wines.

NIROLI – ISLAND PRODUCE

Niroli is a sun-drenched and idyllic Mediterranean isle. Thanks to the now-extinct
volcanoes, Nirolians enjoy lush and fertile
conditions in which to grow a wonderful
range of produce, famed the world over,
and Niroli is surrounded by an abundant
and generous sea which provides wonderful local fare.

Oranges

Niroli is famous for its orange groves of
Cattina, which produce a particularly
sweet-flavoured fruit. **Oil of Niroli** is ex-
tracted from the orange skins. Niroli has
a floral, citrussy, sweet and exotic scent,
which is used to make perfume, aroma-
therapy oil and health and beauty products; it has special healing, rejuvenating,
soothing and restorative properties which
make it especially popular for relaxation
and anti-ageing treatments and scar reduc-
tion therapy at the Santa Fiera Spa, which
has an international reputation for the
excellence of its products.

Olives

Green olive trees flourish on the rocky
limestone soil in the fertile Cattina Valley.

The fruit is prized by cooks and the island exports olives whole, pitted, stuffed and marinated.

Niroli Virgin Olive and Orange Oil is a delicacy; infused with the zest of local oranges, it is particularly delicious when drizzled over fish, seafood, chicken, asparagus or pasta, and you can sample all of these dishes in Niroli's excellent array of restaurants.

Grapes

The Niroli vines produce the queen of white grapes. Cultivated since Roman times on the slopes of the Cattina Valley, and ripened by summer sun and storms, these grapes are harvested to make **Porto Castellante Bianco**, a dry white wine with a crisp, citrussy bouquet, which makes an especially good accompaniment to fish dishes.

Marine life

The seas around the island of Niroli are fertile fishing grounds, filled with bass, bream, tuna, red snapper, squid, shrimp and scallops. The fishing fleet goes out daily to catch the local sea's fine bounty. Natives and tourists alike savour these catches and the island's speciality dish of **Rainbow Mullet**, which is marinated in Niroli Virgin Olive and Orange Oil, then lightly grilled.

The Santa Fiera Spa also makes excellent use of an abundance of marine algae in its skin and beauty treatments.

Volcanic Mud

The volcanoes on Niroli are now extinct, but the area around them is still a rich source of volcanic mud, which is a mixture of rainwater and volcanic ash formed at the time of eruption.

The Santa Fiera Spa specialises in volcanic mud baths and masks as health and beauty treatments, which are reported to rejuvenate and revitalise the skin, drawing women from across the globe keen to take advantage of its miraculous properties!

MORE ABOUT
PENNY JORDAN

PENNY JORDAN

has been writing for more than twenty-five years and has an outstanding record: over one hundred and sixty-five novels published, including the phenomenally successful *A Perfect Family, To Love, Honour & Betray, The Perfect Sinner* and *Power Play* which hit *The Sunday Times* and *New York Times* bestseller lists. She says she hopes to go on writing until she has passed the two hundred mark and maybe even the two hundred and fifty mark.

Although Penny was born in Preston, Lancashire, and spent her childhood there, she moved to Cheshire as a teenager and has continued to live there. Following the death of her husband, she moved to the small traditional Cheshire market town on which she based her Crighton books.

She lives with a large hairy German shepherd dog—Sheba—and an equally hairy Birman cat—Posh, both of whom assist her with her writing. Posh sits on the newspapers and magazines that Penny reads to provide her with ideas she can adapt for her fictional books, and Sheba demands the long walks which help Penny to free up the mental creative process.

Penny is a member and supporter of both the Romantic Novelists' Association and the Romance Writers of America—two organisations dedicated to providing support for both published and yet-to-be published authors.

PENNY JORDAN
QUESTIONS & ANSWERS

Did you enjoy the experience of writing about Niroli?

I found the experience challenging and fascinating, it was a real learning curve for me—a new area to explore as a writer.

Would you like to visit Niroli?

To be honest, I feel as though I already have visited the island—I can even smell its warm scented air whilst I'm writing about it.

Which of the 'Rules of Niroli' would you least like to abide by?

All of them—I hate rules!

How did you find writing as part of a continuity?

Like I said, I hate rules and I found it very challenging! One always wants to give the reader the best possible read and I found my imagination got tangled up in the complexities of writing for a continuity. Having said that, I also felt it was good for me as a writer to meet the challenge it represented.

When you are writing, what is your typical day?

I start work at around 9.30am and normally spend the morning reviewing and editing the previous day's writing. I then write in the afternoon and the evening. Writing is my life and absorbs seventy-five per cent of my waking hours.

Where do you get your inspiration for

the characters that you write?

I let the plot lines inspire me and work from there, trying to build up a character or characters who will logically fit into the emotional conflict I want to create. For me no character ever exists simply in the here and now of the story—I have to know their whole emotional makeup and the events in the lives that have shaped them from childhood.

What, in your opinion, makes a great 'Modern' hero?

For me a hero has to be compelling both sexually and emotionally, he has to be proud and strong and even perhaps a little arrogant, but he also—vitally important to me—has to have some vulnerability. He has to have a human side which allows us to sympathise with him and to see that here in this man there is something genuinely loveable. He also has at some point to show a willingness to understand that his love for the heroine is such that he must overcome whatever inbuilt mindsets he has that are coming between them. Like this writer, he has to grow in awareness and self-knowledge so that he can be worthy of his heroine's love for him.

Tell us about the project you're working on at the moment.

I'm sorry, but I am rather superstitious about discussing my future writing in detail! But I do hope to go on creating truly memorable heroes and stories for the readers for many years to come!

MORE ABOUT
MELANIE MILBURNE

MELANIE MILBURNE

says: "One of the greatest joys of being a writer is the process of falling in love with the characters and then watching as they fall in love with each other. I am an absolutely hopeless romantic. I fell in love with my husband on our second date and we even had a secret engagement, so you see it must have been destined for me to be a Mills & Boon® author! The other great joy of being a romance writer is hearing from readers. You can hear all about the other things I do when I'm not writing, and even drop me a line, at: www.melaniemilburne. com.au "

MELANIE MILBURNE
QUESTIONS & ANSWERS

Did you enjoy writing about Niroli?

I absolutely loved writing this story and felt very fortunate to have been given Alex and Amelia as characters to work with. They seemed to come to life as soon as I typed the first sentence. That's always a great feeling!

Would you like to visit Niroli?

I really would. All those wonderful beaches, that glorious sunshine and the food and wine, not to mention all those gorgeous Fierezza men!

Which of the Rules of Niroli would you least like to abide by?

I think it would have to be the same as my hero Alex had to face—the sacrifice of his career in order to take the throne. He just couldn't do it and nor could I. I love my job too much.

How did you find writing as part of a continuity?

I must admit when first approached to do this story I felt apprehensive. I am so used to making up my own characters and plots, so being handed characters' names and attributes and a synopsis and family bible was a bit daunting. However, the characters became my own as soon as I started typing that first sentence. I still smile when I think of how Alex and Amelia met.

When you are writing, what is your typical day?

Typical day?!!! But I am a woman and a wife and a mother *and* a writer. There is no such thing as a typical day! But that's what I love most about being a full-time writer. I like the flexibility of choosing my hours, although having said that I still have a structure in place. I exercise in the mornings, walk, gym or swim and do household jobs and then the afternoons are mine to write. I spend six to eight hours in my office each day, with of course numerous trips downstairs to the kitchen for cups of tea and biscuits, hence the exercise routine!

Where do you find the inspiration that shapes your characters?

I get a lot of inspiration from reading books. I particularly enjoy biographies and social commentaries, although magazines and the daily newspaper are also great sources. But I would have to say that life itself gives me the most inspiration. It's amazing how often I've got an idea from talking to someone I've just met or sat next to at a dinner party. Something in their life story or personality triggers an idea and I start staring into space thinking…what if?

What in your opinion makes a great hero?

The qualities I look for in a hero are strength of character, leadership, loyalty, and a sense of humour. Oh, and a gorgeous body and a great smile also helps!

Tell us about the project you are working on at the moment.

I have just finished a Presents/Modern™ and I am now about to start a Medical™. I already have the characters talking to me half the night, so I can see this is going to be one of those books that more or less writes itself. Ben Blackwood is a dedicated and hard-working neurosurgeon in a busy public hospital. His new registrar happens to be the daughter of the Professor of Surgery who almost ruined Ben's career when he was training. I can already feel the tension between them!

THE OFFICIAL FIEREZZA FAMILY TREE

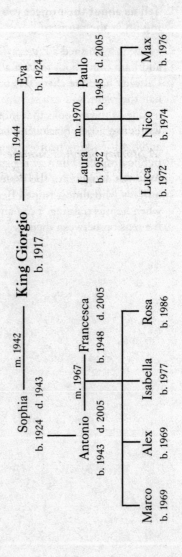

Sophia m. 1942 King Giorgio m. 1944 Eva
b. 1924 d. 1943   b. 1917   b. 1924

Antonio m. 1967 Francesca
b. 1943 d. 2005   b. 1948 d. 2005

Laura m. 1970 Paulo
b. 1952   b. 1945 d. 2005

Marco   Alex   Isabella   Rosa
b. 1969   b. 1969   b. 1977   b. 1986

Luca   Nico   Max
b. 1972   b. 1974   b. 1976

Turn the page for an exciting glimpse of

Bought by the Billionaire Prince
by
Carol Marinelli

the first story in the addictive next volume in
the Royal House of Niroli collection

The Royal House of Niroli:
Billion Dollar Bargains

Available in February 2011
from Mills & Boon

CHAPTER ONE

Is HE good-looking?'

Meg felt her teeth literally grind together as her travel companion, Jasmine, repeated the question for the hundredth time. Here they were docking in Niroli, which was undoubtedly the most beautiful island Meg had seen on her travels to date, and all Jasmine wanted to talk about was potential men.

Coming from Australia, where everything was comparatively new, Meg was in awe of the past that drenched each place she had visited on her travels through Europe, reeling at the ancient architecture and glorious tales of times gone by and, for Meg, Niroli had it all! To the South of Sicily, the island of Niroli, according to the travel guide Meg had devoured on the boat trip, was steeped in history, its colourful past filled with rivalries and wars dating back centuries and still playing out today. They'd just passed the tiny island of Mont Avellana, which, as recently as two decades ago, had been ruled by Niroli, and now they were coming into Niroli's main port. Meg stared in wonder as they approached—sandy beaches rapidly giving way to a lush hillside, which was like a fabulous tapestry, with thick forests, and edged by vineyards that laced neatly around the sprawling town. But a grand castle set on a rocky promontory was for Meg the main focal point, standing tall and proud, looking out towards the ocean, as if somehow guarding it all.

'That's the palace,' Meg pointed out to Jasmine excitedly, checking with the map to get her bearings, 'and over to the right there's a Roman amphitheatre….'

'There's a casino,' Jasmine said, peering over Meg's shoulder, 'oh, and a luxury spa!'

'We can't afford luxury.' Meg smiled. 'We're backpacking!'

'Then we'll just have to find someone who can!' Jasmine countered, her mind flicking back to the inevitable. 'So what sort of doctor is he?'

'Who?' Meg asked, then let out a pained sigh as Jasmine's momentary interest in her surrounds rapidly waned. 'Alex is a surgeon,' Meg admitted, then wished she hadn't, noting Jasmine's eyes literally light up at the prospect of dating a rich surgeon—well, she could dream on. Alex was the least money-minded of persons and would see through Jasmine in a flash.

If only she had, Meg inwardly sighed. At first when Jasmine had befriended her, Meg had been only too glad of the company, only lately the very qualities that Meg had admired had started to repel. Jasmine's impetuous nature, her carefree attitude and her obsession with men were starting to irritate and Meg was actually looking forward to cooling off the friendship a touch—ready now to complete her journey alone.

Backpacking through Europe had seemed the most unlikely of adventures for Meg to embark on. Routine was the key in Meg's life—routine was what saw her through. Routine was the only way she could control her life and the emotions that had overwhelmed her as she'd struggled to come to terms with her difficult childhood.

But now here she was, twenty-five years of age and ready to start living; ready to let go of a difficult past and truly embrace a world that had at times been so very cruel. Backpacking through Europe was the final self-imposed step in her recovery. Casual work, casual clothes and casual meals had at first been a huge enigma for Meg, but gradually she was starting to relax—that knot of tension that had been present for as long as she could remember was slowly unravelling and, as she stepped off the boat and took a deep cleansing breath, closed her blue eyes and turned her face up to the warm sun Meg knew there and then that she had been so right to embark on this journey—could hardly wait to tell her brother just how far she'd come.

'Where is he?' Jasmine's hopeful face scanned the crowd for a first glimpse of a suitable good-looking surgeon. 'Does he look like you?'

'Not in the least.' Meg laughed but didn't elaborate. Alex Hunter was as dark as Meg Donovan was blond, his eyes black where Meg's were blue. They looked nothing alike and with good reason—both were adopted, Alex when he was a toddler, Meg when she was twelve years old. But despite their differences, despite not sharing one shred of DNA, they were as close as any blood brother and sister.

'Does he know what boat you're coming on?'

'I told him ages ago.' Meg frowned. 'Well, I emailed him with the details.'

'And he got it?' Jasmine checked.

'Yes, I'm sure he got it,' Meg answered, but a trickle of unease slid down her spine. 'He *should* be here.'

'Well, it doesn't look like he is,' Jasmine pointed out as the crowd started to disperse. 'Maybe he's stuck at the hospital.'

'Maybe,' Meg answered, but she wasn't convinced. It

was *most* unlike Alex to just not turn up; if he couldn't make it himself then he'd have sent someone. 'Though I haven't checked my emails for ages. Maybe he's been trying to get hold of me.'

'So what do we do now?' Jasmine asked, her eyes scanning the notice boards. 'They said at the youth hostel there were usually loads of signs advertising for seasonal workers, but there doesn't seem to be any—not that I fancy fruit-picking!'

'It sounds fun. And you *do* need the work,' Meg pointed out. Jasmine wasn't just down to her last Euro, she was dipping into Meg's carefully planned budget and, frankly, Meg was tired of hearing Jasmine say she'd pay her back as soon as she got some work.

'Well, I think fruit-picking sounds awful.' Jasmine pouted, but soon cheered up, cheekily ripping down a notice and then pocketing it. 'This is more me. They're looking for casual staff at the casino and there's discounted accommodation—ooh, look, there's even a courtesy bus.'

'I think that's for the clientele,' Meg said as some holiday makers who certainly weren't backpackers were escorted into the luxury vehicle.

'So?' Jasmine shrugged and pulled on her backpack as she called to the bus driver to wait for her—Meg couldn't help but smile; Jasmine was like a cat who always landed on her feet. 'Come on, Meg.'

'I don't think so.' Meg shook her head. 'A casino is the *last* place I want to be. All that noise and bustle…'

'All those rich men!' Jasmine giggled and even Meg managed a laugh. 'Come on, Meg, hold off on your search for inner peace for a few days and come and have some fun at the casino. We can share a room.'

'It's really not me.' Raking a hand through her blond hair, Meg felt the salt and grease and almost relented—given Alex wasn't here, that long soak in a bath she'd been looking forward to wasn't going to eventuate and accommodation at the casino, even if it was budget accommodation, was surely going to be better than some of the hostels she'd stayed in.

'I think I'll head over to the hospital.' Meg checked out her map. 'It isn't very far. Maybe he *is* just caught up at work. You'd better go or you're going to miss that courtesy bus.'

'Well, if it doesn't work out with your brother, you know where I am.'

'Thanks.' Meg grinned, watching as her friend climbed in the bus and waved her off, wishing, *wishing* she could, even for a little while, be as happy and as carefree as Jasmine—could relax just a little bit, could have just a fraction of her confidence. The universe itself seemed to provide Jasmine with her assured nature.

Meg watched until the tiny bus disappeared from view, filled with something she couldn't define—a hunger, a need almost for familiarity, to be able to let down her guard a touch, to be with someone who knew how hard this was for her, someone who knew that this so-called trip of a lifetime, this carefree existence, was in fact an agonising journey for her.

Where the hell was Alex?

The last e-mail he'd sent, he'd confirmed her date and time of arrival, had told her he couldn't wait to catch up, had huge news to share. Surely if his plans had changed he'd have contacted her?

But how?

Meg closed her eyes against a temporary moment of panic. She hadn't been near a computer for the last couple of weeks—happy the next leg of her tour had been arranged,

she'd decided to cut loose for a while—and look where i
had got her!

The taxi rank had long since closed, so, consulting he
map, Meg set out on foot towards the Free Hospital wher
Alex had told her he was working. The midday su
combined with her heavy backpack made the relativel
short distance seem to take for ever. How she'd have love
to have lingered and wandered through the pretty shop
but a backpack and a pressing lack of accommodation fo
the night didn't allow for such luxuries, so instead Me
stopped at one of the pavement cafés and ordered a quic
coffee. Watching intrigued as the town seemingly prepare
for something—shopkeepers were draping their store
with huge vines, hilarity ensuing as a few vocal local
strung banners and lights across the street, calling to eac
other in their colourful language as children watched o
gleefully.

'Is there going to be a party?' Meg asked one of waite
whose English was better than most.

'A bigger party than you have ever seen!' Filling her cu
he elaborated, 'The Niroli Feast starts tomorrow—we part
for the next few days and celebrate the treasures the ric
soil gives us.'

'Here?' Meg checked, gesturing to the street they wer
in, but the waiter just laughed.

'The whole island celebrates—you *must* stay for it,' h
insisted as only the Italians could. 'I ask you—why woul
anyone not want to stay a while in this wonderful place?'

Why indeed?

Boosted from her shot of coffee, Meg made her way mor
briskly to the hospital, hoping against hope that Alex woul
be there and trying to fathom what she'd do if he wasn't.

* * *

Dr Alex Hunter!' Meg tried to keep her voice even, trying not to show her frustration as she said her brother's name for perhaps the tenth time. On perhaps the eleventh, the receptionist nodded her immaculately groomed head.

'*Sì*, Alessandro Fierezza!' Eagerly, again she nodded, tapping details into her computer. 'He no here, I have no contact for him. Try *palazzo!*'

Help!

Meg grabbed her long hair into a tight fist and let out an exasperated breath as the receptionist called on a colleague, who spoke even less English, listening to their vibrant discussion peppered with the names Alex and Alessandro and wondering what on earth she should do.

'Your brother marry.'

'But my brother is not married, he's not even engaged!' Meg gave a helpless laugh, then shook her head as in broken English the two women attempted to explain the impossible.

'*Matrimonio,*' the receptionist said firmly, nodding as Meg frowned. 'Your brother, Alessandro—'

'Alex,' Meg corrected, then slumped in defeat as the receptionist forced her to admit the truth—even if they had got the names mixed up, the simple fact was if Alex was in Tiroli then he'd have met her at the port; her careful plans for the next couple of weeks flying out of the window courtesy of three little words—

'Your brother gone.'

CHAPTER TWO

JASMINE HAD BEEN RIGHT—there *was* work at the casino.

Lots of it!

Working her way through mountain after mountain o
white china plates, Meg tried to block out the noise of a bus
kitchen—the chefs screaming at each other like proud cat
fighting over territory, waiters collecting elaborate dishes
swooshing out of the swing doors only to return moment
later, laden with half-eaten dishes to add to the pile Meg ha
been allocated. Not that Meg minded hard work, she'd bee
more than prepared for the back-breaking work of frui
picking, but being shut up in a kitchen, her face red from th
heat, her blond hair dark with sweat, was a million mile
from what she'd envisaged from her time in Niroli.

Almost as soon as she'd found Jasmine and filled in a
application form, Meg had been given a list of shifts. Si
till ten o'clock each evening, paid in cash at the end of eac
of shift, which meant Meg had the whole day for explorin
Niroli, and it paid well, *much* better than fruit-picking
which meant, Meg realised, if she was careful and perhap
worked a couple of extra shifts she could treat herself to
day at that luxury spa.

With renewed enthusiasm Meg tackled the mountain o

plates—the last hour of her shift made so much easier by fantasising about being smeared in the famous Niroli volcanic mud she'd read about and being thoroughly pampered and spoiled for a day!

'Faster now!' Antoinette, her colleague for the night who was rinsing and stacking the plates that Meg was washing, egged her on in her broken English, but kindly. 'We need empty sink for next staff. Or else they…' She didn't finish what she was saying—in fact a ream of sentences and orders around the kitchen remained forever incomplete, broken off midword for a reason Meg couldn't yet fathom—the swing doors opened and an immediate hush descended on the busy kitchen as a group of dark suits entered.

'Ah—sir!' The head chef jumped to nervous attention as he approached the foreboding-looking men that had entered, yet he addressed only the leader.

And even if he hadn't uttered a single word, even if she had no idea who he was, Meg knew that he was very much in charge. His jet hair was a head above the rest of them, but it wasn't just his height that set him apart—there was an authoritative air about him that would hush any room, an intimidating and overwhelming presence that had everyone in the kitchen, Meg included, on heightened alert.

'Who is he?' Meg whispered to Antoinette as slowly he toured the kitchen, talking with the staff as he did so. There was a slightly depraved look to him, a dangerous glint in those black eyes as he worked the room.

'That,' Antoinette said, in broken English, 'is the boss, Luca Fierezza. He owns the casino. A prince.'

THE *Royal*
HOUSE OF NIROLI

*The richest royal family in the world—united by blood
and passion, torn apart by deceit and desire*

The Royal House of Niroli: Scandalous Seductions
Penny Jordan & Melanie Milburne
Available 17th December 2010

The Royal House of Niroli: Billion Dollar Bargains
Carol Marinelli & Natasha Oakley
Available 21st January 2011

The Royal House of Niroli: Innocent Mistresses
Susan Stephens & Robyn Donald
Available 18th February 2011

The Royal House of Niroli: Secret Heirs
Raye Morgan & Penny Jordan
Available 18th March 2011

Collect all four!

& RIVA™

Live life to the full - give in to temptation

Four new sparkling and sassy romances every month!

Be the first to read this fabulous
new series from 1st December 2010
at **millsandboon.co.uk**
In shops from 1st January 2011

Tell us what you think!
Facebook.com/romancehq
Twitter.com/millsandboonuk

on't miss out!

ailable at WHSmith, Tesco, ASDA, Eason
d all good bookshops
vw.millsandboon.co.uk

0211/24/MB328

ULTIMATE ALPHA MALES:
Strong, sexy…and intent on seduction!

Mediterranean Tycoons
4th February 2011

Hot-Shot Heroes
4th March 2011

Powerful Protectors
1st April 2011

Passionate Playboys
6th May 2011

Collect all four!
www.millsandboon.co.uk

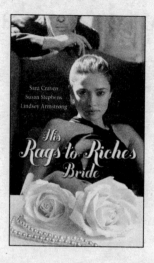

What happens when good dates go bad?

Three easy ways to keep your love life clean and simple:

1. Don't get your friends to fix you up.
2. Don't go on a blind date.
3. Don't try your hand at internet dating.

Because sometimes Cupid gets it really wrong

Three girls, three dates, three more reasons to dislike Valentine's Day!

Available 21st January 2011

www.millsandboon.co.uk

THE *Balfour* LEGACY

ℰIGHT SISTERS, ℰIGHT SCANDALS

VOLUME 1 – JUNE 2010
Mia's Scandal
by Michelle Reid

VOLUME 2 – JULY 2010
Kat's Pride
by Sharon Kendrick

VOLUME 3 – AUGUST 2010
Emily's Innocence
by India Grey

VOLUME 4 – SEPTEMBER 2010
Sophie's Seduction
by Kim Lawrence

8 VOLUMES IN ALL TO COLLECT!

THE *Balfour* LEGACY

*E*IGHT SISTERS, *E*IGHT SCANDALS

VOLUME 5 – OCTOBER 2010
Zoe's Lesson
by Kate Hewitt

VOLUME 6 – NOVEMBER 2010
Annie's Secret
by Carole Mortimer

VOLUME 7 – DECEMBER 2010
Bella's Disgrace
by Sarah Morgan

VOLUME 8 – JANUARY 2011
Olivia's Awakening
by Margaret Way

8 VOLUMES IN ALL TO COLLECT!

Meet Nora Robert's
The MacGregors family

1st October 2010

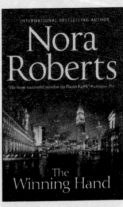

3rd December 2010

7th January 2011

4th February 2011